P9-DNQ-960

INCREDIBLE PRAISE FOR *THE REGULATORS* AND *DESPERATION*

"King has created two of his most substantial characters. *Desperation* and *The Regulators* mark a return for Stephen King to his old stomping grounds: supernatural horror and multicharacter plots that entertain with a vengeance. Both of these novels, which provide entertainment with a moral, are sure to keep you turning pages well past midnight." —*Denver Post*

"A fascinating exercise in storytelling, one that makes us rethink the very idea of narrative. . . . In the interplay between these novels, King reveals his process in a startling, intimate way, inviting us to consider a range of possibilities, and giving us unprecedented access to the play of his mind."
—*New York Newsday*

"Our best novelist of horror and our most serious anatomist of "horror" since Edgar Allan Poe. A tour de force . . . King is having great fun . . . vastly entertaining. He is a quintessentially American writer." —*Atlanta Journal Constitution*

"[*Desperation* is] astonishing. . . . The terror is relentless."
—*Publishers Weekly*

"[*Desperation* is] prime terrifying King." —*Cosmopolitan*

"The pace never flags, the horror never abates. Stephen King, by any name, bowls us over again." —*St. Petersburg Times*

"A performance of considerable technical skill . . . the most formidable bad guy King has produced since Randall Flag in *The Stand*." —*Philadelphia Inquirer*

More praise . . .

"A gory, gut-wrenching exercise in fear and paranoia. *Desperation* is a fast-paced, in-your-face, heart-pounding, horror-thon that builds to an exciting conclusion." —*Detroit Free Press*

"A literary diptych that reflects upon faith, friendship and courage in these times of random violence and changing values. [*Desperation* is] a claustrophobic nightmare of horror and madness." —*Dallas Morning News*

"Heaps and heaps of sure-fire thrills." —*Time*

"A big, serious, scary novel . . . King is at the top of his game." —*Entertainment Weekly*

"No one is as deft with the carnage, or has as much fun with it. . . . King is the Winslow Homer of blood." —*The New Yorker*

"Deeply satisfying . . . [*Desperation* is] his most compelling, artful tale since *Misery*. Deeply spiritual and surprisingly moving." —*Hartford Courant*

"*The Regulators* blends the occult with social commentary for a suburban tale of terror." —*Anniston Star*

"[*The Regulators* is a] devilishly entertaining yarn of occult mayhem married to mordant social commentary. Call him Bachman or call him King, the bard of Bangor is going to hit the charts hard and vast with this white-knuckler knockout." —*Publishers Weekly* (starred review)

"The action is fierce and Bachman's imagination proves boundless." —*Library Journal*

More praise . . .

"[*Desperation*'s] plot is tight, the action is well orchestrated, and King's running theme of redemption packs a mighty wallop."

—*Library Journal*

"*The Regulators* is a rip-roaring fable that exposes suburbia's id and brings all that escapism out in the open where there is *no* escape."

—*Time Out New York*

"Vintage King, USDA prime . . . a first-rate job of what he does best—spinning out exuberant entertainment with a nourishing layer of thoughtful, serious content beneath."

—*Locus*

"A double dose of ghostly horror. *Desperation* is pure King, a rollicking good tale skillfully told of repugnance and godliness doing high-screech battle. A full-blown morality tale, deliciously developed . . . a spiritual odyssey bringing together skeptic and believer."

—*San Francisco Chronicle*

"Promise you, surgeries will be delayed and pizzas delivered late because readers won't be able to quit."

—*New York Daily News*

"Each novel stands alone. You can read either by itself or both in any order. Both are tales of flat-out supernatural horror, narrated in the garrulous, folksy voice King has honed to a precision instrument. *Desperation* builds to a climax reminiscent of *The Stand*. Separately, each is a compelling tale of supernatural horror; together they constitute a *tour de force*. . . . His 'constant readers' will relish their visits to Wentworth and Desperation as much as the long trek down *The Green Mile*."

—*Washington Post Book World*

"Knockout classic horror: King's most carefully crafted, well-groomed pages ever."

—*Kirkus Reviews*

Also by Richard Bachman

Rage
The Long Walk
Roadwork
The Running Man
Thinner

As Stephen King

NOVELS

Carrie
'Salem's Lot
The Shining
The Stand
The Dead Zone
Firestarter
Cujo
The Dark Tower: The Gunslinger
Christine
Pet Sematary
Cycle of the Werewolf
The Talisman (with Peter Straub)
It
Eyes of the Dragon
Misery
The Tommyknockers
The Dark Tower II: The Drawing of the Three
The Dark Tower III: The Waste Lands
The Dark Half
Needful Things
Gerald's Game
Dolores Claiborne
Insomnia
Rose Madder
The Green Mile
Desperation

COLLECTIONS

Night Shift
Different Seasons
Skeleton Crew
Four Past Midnight
Nightmares and Dreamscapes

NONFICTION

Danse Macabre

SCREENPLAYS

Creepshow
Cat's Eye
Silver Bullet
Maximum Overdrive
Pet Sematary
Golden Years
Sleepwalkers
The Stand
The Shining

THE REGULATORS

RICHARD BACHMAN

SIGNET
Published by the Penguin Group
Penguin Books USA Inc., 375 Hudson Street, New York, New York 10014, U.S.A.
Penguin Books Ltd, 27 Wrights Lane, London W8 5TZ, England
Penguin Books Australia Ltd, Ringwood, Victoria, Australia
Penguin Books Canada Ltd, 10 Alcorn Avenue, Toronto, Ontario, Canada M4V 3B2
Penguin Books (N.Z.) Ltd, 182–190 Wairau Road, Auckland 10, New Zealand

Penguin Books Ltd, Registered Offices:
Harmondsworth, Middlesex, England

First published by Signet, an imprint of Dutton Signet,
a division of Penguin Books USA Inc.
Previously appeared in a Dutton edition.

First Signet Printing, September, 1997
10 9 8 7 6 5 4 3 2 1

Computer illustrations by Jaye Zimet; Map by Virginia Norey

ACKNOWLEDGMENTS
"Leaving on a Jet Plane," Words and Music by John Denver. Copyright © 1967 (Renewed) 1995, Cherry Lane Music Publishing Company, Inc. (ASCAP). International Copyright Secured. All Rights Reserved. Reprinted by Permission of Cherry Lane Music Company.

 REGISTERED TRADEMARK—MARCA REGISTRADA

Printed in the United States of America

PUBLISHER'S NOTE
This is a work of fiction. Names, characters, places, and incidents either are the product of the author's imagination or are used fictitiously, and any resemblance to actual persons, living or dead, events, or locales is entirely coincidental.

Thinking of Jim Thompson and Sam Peckinpah:
legendary shadows.

EDITOR'S NOTE

Before his death from cancer in late 1985, Richard Bachman published five novels. In 1994, while preparing to move to a new house, the author's widow found a cardboard carton filled with manuscripts in the cellar. These novels and stories were in varying degrees of completion. The least finished were longhand scribbles in the steno notebooks Bachman used for original composition. The most finished was a typescript of the novel which follows. It was in a manuscript box secured with rubber bands, as if Bachman had been on the verge of sending it to his publisher when his final remission ended.

The former Mrs. Bachman brought it to me for evaluation, and I found it at least up to the standards of his earlier work. I have made a few small changes, mostly updating certain references (substituting Ethan Hawke for Rob Lowe in the first chapter, for instance), but have otherwise left it pretty much as I found it. This work is now offered (with the approval of the author's widow) as the capstone to a peculiar but not uninteresting career.

My thanks to Claudia Eschelman (the former Claudia Bachman), Bachman scholar Douglas Winter, Elaine Koster at New American Library, and to Carolyn Stromberg, who edited the earliest Bachman novels and validated this one.

The former Mrs. Bachman says that, to the best of her knowledge, Bachman never travelled to Ohio, "although he might have flown over it once or twice." She also has no idea when this novel was written, although she suspects it must have been late at night. Richard Bachman suffered from chronic insomnia.

—Charles Verrill
New York City

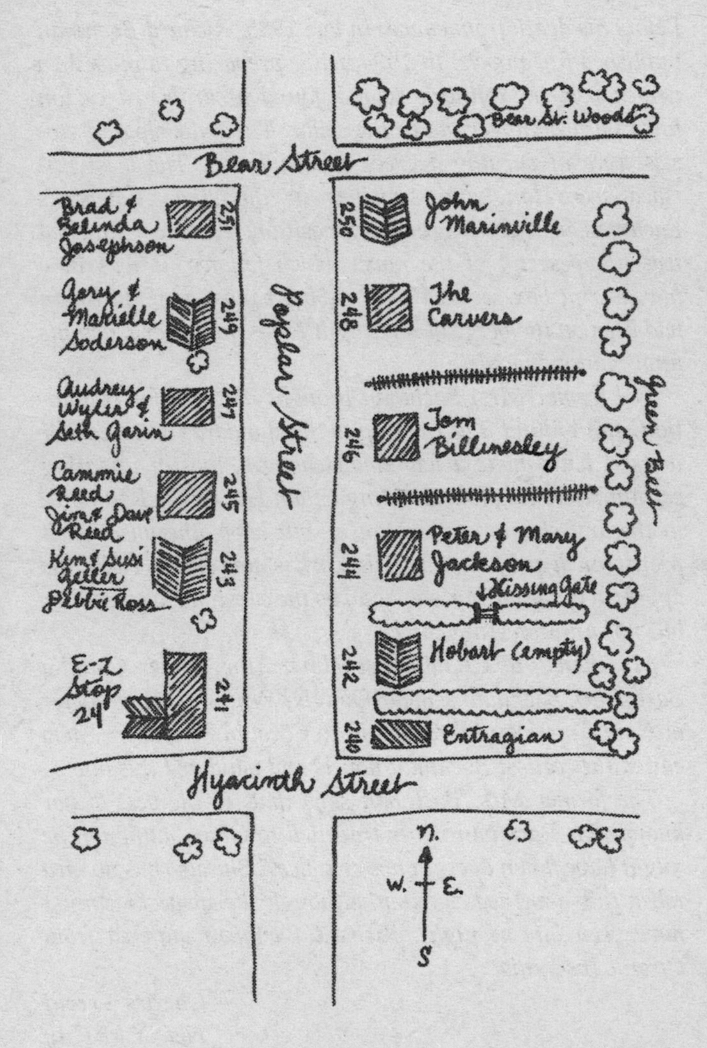

Bear St. Woods
Bear Street
Brad & Belinda Josephson
251
Gary & Marielle Soderson
249
Audrey Wyler & Seth Garin
247
Cammie Reed
Jim & Dave Reed
245
Kim & Susi Geller
Debbie Ross
243
E-Z Stop 24
241
Poplar Street
250
John Marinville
248
The Carvers
246
Tom Billingsley
244
Peter & Mary Jackson
Kissing Gate
242
Hobart (empty)
240
Entragian
Green Belt
Hyacinth Street
N.
W.
E.
S

"Mister, we deal in lead."

—Steve McQueen
The Magnificent Seven

Postcard from William Garin to his sister, Audrey Wyler:

July 24, 1984

Dear Aud,

Well we are in Carson City (Nev.) tonite and expect to hit San Jose tomorrow. I know you were "dubious!" about us driving, but it was the right decision. WE HAVE HAD AN AMAZING BREAKTHRU WITH SETN! More later—I'll phone you from San Jose—all I can say now is God Bless Nevada! Junie sends her luv. ☺ ☺

Bill

CARSON CITY PM

LOVE

Ms. Audrey Wyler
247 Poplar Street
Wentworth, Ohio 43292

CHAPTER 1

Poplar Street/3:45 P.M./July 15, 1996

Summer's here.

Not *just* summer, either, not this year, but the apotheosis of summer, the avatar of summer, high green perfect central Ohio summer dead-smash in the middle of July, white sun glaring out of that fabled faded Levi's sky, the sound of kids hollering back and forth through the Bear Street Woods at the top of the hill, the *tink!* of Little League bats from the ballfield on the other side of the woods, the sound of power-mowers, the sound of muscle-cars out on Highway 19, the sound of Rollerblades on the cement sidewalks and smooth macadam of Poplar Street, the sound of radios—Cleveland Indians baseball (the rare day game) competing with Tina Turner belting out "Nutbush City Limits," the one that goes "Twenty-five is the speed limit, motorcycles not allowed in it"—and surrounding everything like an auditory edging of lace, the soothing, silky hiss of lawn sprinklers.

Summer in Wentworth, Ohio, oh boy, can you dig it. Summer here on Poplar Street, which runs straight through the middle of that fabled faded American dream with the smell of hotdogs in the air and a few burst paper remains of Fourth of July firecrackers still lying here and there in the gutters. It's been a hot July, a perfect good old by God blue-ribbon *jeezer* of a July, no doubt about it, but if you want to know the truth, it's also been a *dry* July, with no water but the occasional flipped spray of a hose to stir those last shreds of Chinese paper from where they lie. That may change today; there's an occasional rumble of thunder from the west, and those watching The Weather Channel (there's plenty of cable TV on Poplar Street, you bet) know that thunderstorms are expected later on. Maybe even a tornado, although that's unlikely.

Meantime, though, it's all watermelon and Kool-Aid and foul tips off the end of the bat; it's all the summer you ever wanted and more here in the center of the United States of America, life as good as you ever dreamed it could be, with Chevrolets parked in driveways and steaks in refrigerator meat-drawers waiting to be slapped on the barbecue in the backyard come evening (and will there be apple pie to follow? what do you think?). This is the land of green lawns and carefully tended flowerbeds; this is the Kingdom of Ohio where the kids wear their hats turned around backward and their strappy tank-tops hang down over their baggy shorts and their great big galooty sneakers all seem to bear the Nike swoosh.

On the block of Poplar which runs between Bear Street at the top of the hill and Hyacinth at the bottom, there are eleven houses and one store. The store, which stands on the corner of Poplar and Hyacinth, is the ever-popular, all-American convenience mart, where you can get your cigarettes, your Blatz or Rolling Rock, your penny candy (although these days most of it costs a dime), your BBQ supplies (paper plates plastic forks taco chips ice cream ketchup mustard relish), your Popsicles, and your wide variety of Snapple, made from the best stuff on earth. You can even get a copy of *Penthouse* at the E-Z Stop 24 if you want one, but you have to ask the clerk; in the Kingdom of Ohio, they mostly keep the skin magazines under the counter. And hey, that's perfectly all right. The important thing is that you should know where to get one if you need one.

The clerk today is new, less than a week on the job, and right now, at 3:45 in the afternoon, she's waiting on a little boy and girl. The girl looks to be about eleven and is already on her way to being a beauty. The boy, clearly her little brother, is maybe six and is (in the new clerk's opinion, at least) already on his way to being a first-class boogersnot.

"I want *two* candybars!" Brother Boogersnot exclaims.

"There's only money enough for one, if we each have a soda," Pretty Sis tells him with what the clerk thinks is admirable patience. If this were *her* little brother, she would be very tempted to kick his ass so high up he could get a job playing the Hunchback of Notre Dame in the school play.

"Mom gave you five bucks this morning, I saw it," the boogersnot says. "Where's the rest of it, Marrrrr-grit?"

"Don't call me that, I hate that," the girl says. She has long honey-blond hair which the clerk thinks is absolutely gorgeous. The new clerk's own hair is short and kinky, dyed orange on the right and green on the left. She has a pretty good idea she wouldn't have gotten this job without washing the dye out of it if the manager hadn't been absolutely strapped for someone to work eleven-to-seven—her good luck, his bad. He *had* extracted a promise from her that she'd wear a kerchief or a baseball cap over the dye-job, but promises were made to be broken. Now, she sees, Pretty Sister is looking at her hair with some fascination.

"Margrit-Margrit-Margrit!" the little brother crows with the cheerfully energetic viciousness which only little brothers can muster.

"My name's really Ellen," the girl says, speaking with the air of one imparting a great confidence. "Margaret's my middle name. He calls me that because he knows I hate it."

"Nice to meet you, Ellen," the clerk says, and begins toting up the girl's purchases.

"Nice to meet you, *Marrrrr-grit*!" the boogersnot brother mimics, screwing his face into an expression so strenuously awful that it is funny. His nose is wrinkled, his eyes crossed. "Nice to meet you, Margrit the Maggot!"

Ignoring him, Ellen says: "I love your hair."

"Thanks," the new clerk says, smiling. "It's not as nice as yours, but it'll do. That's a dollar forty-six."

The girl takes a little plastic change-purse from the pocket of her jeans. It's the kind you squeeze open. Inside are two crumpled dollar bills and a few pennies.

"Ask Margrit the Maggot where the other three bucks went!" the boogersnot trumpets. He's a regular little public address system. "She used it to buy a magazine with *Eeeeeeethan Hawwwwwke* on the cover!"

Ellen goes on ignoring him, although her cheeks are starting to get a little red. As she hands over the two dollars she says, "I haven't seen you before, have I?"

"Probably not—I just started in here last Wednesday. They wanted somebody who'd work eleven to seven and stay over a few hours if the night guy turns up late."

"Well, it's very nice to meet you. I'm Ellie Carver. And this is my little brother, Ralph."

Ralph Carver sticks out his tongue and makes a sound like a wasp caught in a mayonnaise jar. What a polite little animal it is, the young woman with the tu-tone hair thinks.

"I'm Cynthia Smith," she says, extending her hand over the counter to the girl. "Always a Cynthia and never a Cindy. Can you remember that?"

The girl nods, smiling. "And I'm always an Ellie, never a Margaret."

"Margrit the Maggot!" Ralph cries in crazed six-year-old triumph. He raises his hands in the air and bumps his hips from side to side in the pure poison joy of living. *"Margrit the Maggot loves Eeeeethan Hawwwwwke!"*

Ellen gives Cynthia a look much older than her years, an expression of world-weary resignation that says *You see what I have to put up with.* Cynthia, who had a little brother herself and knows *exactly* what pretty Ellie has to put up with, wants to crack up but manages to keep a straight face. And that's good. This girl's a prisoner of her time and her age, the same as anyone else, which means that all of this is perfectly serious to her. Ellie hands her brother a can of Pepsi. "We'll split the candybar outside," she says.

"You're gonna pull me in Buster," Ralph says as they start toward the door, walking into the brilliant oblong of sun that falls through the window like fire. "Gonna pull me in Buster *all the way back home.*"

"Like hell I am," Ellie says, but as she opens the door, Brother Boogersnot turns and gives Cynthia a smug look which says *Wait and see who wins this one. You just wait and see.* Then they go out.

Summer yes, but not *just* summer; we are talking July 15th, the very *rooftree* of summer, in an Ohio town where most kids go to Vacation Bible School and participate in the Summer Reading Program at the Public Library, and where one kid has just *got* to have a little red wagon which he has named (for reasons only he will ever know) Buster. Eleven houses and one convenience store simmering in that bright bald midwestern July glare, ninety degrees in the shade, ninety-six in the sun, hot enough that the air shimmers above the pavement as if over an open incinerator.

The block runs north–south, odd-numbered houses on the Los Angeles side of the street, even-numbered ones on the New York side. At the top, on the western corner of Poplar and Bear Street, is 251 Poplar. Brad Josephson is out front, using the hose to water the flowerbeds beside the front path. He is forty-six, with gorgeous chocolate skin and a long, sloping gut. Ellie Carver thinks he looks like Bill Cosby . . . a *little* bit, anyway. Brad and Belinda Josephson are the only black people on the block, and the block is damned proud to have them. They look just the way people in suburban Ohio like their black people to look, and it makes things just right to see them out and about. They're nice folks. Everyone likes the Josephsons.

Cary Ripton, who delivers the Wentworth *Shopper* on Monday afternoons, comes pedaling around the corner and tosses Brad a rolled-up paper. Brad catches it deftly with the hand that isn't holding the hose. Never even moves. Just up with the hand and whoomp, there it is.

"Good one, Mr. Josephson!" Cary calls, and pedals on down the hill with his canvas sack of papers bouncing on his hip. He is wearing an oversized Orlando Magic jersey with Shaq's number, 32, on it.

"Yep, I ain't lost it yet," Brad says, and tucks the nozzle of the hose under his arm so he can open the weekly handout and see what's on the front page. It'll be the same old crap, of course—yard sales and community puffery—but he wants to get a look, anyway. Just human nature, he supposes. Across the street, at 250, Johnny Marinville is sitting on his front step, playing his guitar and singing along. One of the world's dumber folk-songs, but Marinville plays well, and although no one will ever mistake him for Marvin Gaye (or Perry Como, for that matter), he can carry a tune and stay in key. Brad has always found this slightly offensive; a man who's good at one thing should be content with that and let the rest of it go, Brad feels.

Cary Ripton, fourteen, crewcut, plays backup shortstop for the Wentworth American Legion team (the Hawks, currently 14–4 with two games left to play), tosses the next *Shopper* onto the porch of 249, the Soderson place. The Josephsons are the Poplar Street Black Couple; the Sodersons, Gary and Marielle, are the Poplar Street Bohemians. On the scales of public opinion, the Sodersons pretty much balance each other. Gary is, by and large, a help-out kind of guy, and liked by his neighbors in spite of the fact that he's at least half-lit nearly all of the time. Marielle, however . . . well, as Pie Carver has been known to say, "There's a word for women like Marielle; it rhymes with the one for how you kick a football."

Cary's throw is a perfect bank shot, bouncing the *Shopper* off the Soderson front door and landing it spang on the Soderson welcome mat, but no one comes out to get it; Marielle is inside taking a shower (her second of the day; she hates it when the weather gets sticky like this), and Gary is out back, absent-mindedly fueling the backyard barbecue, eventually loading it with enough briquets to flash-fry a water buffalo. He is wearing an apron with the words YOU *MAY* KISS THE COOK on the front. It's too early to start the steaks, but it's never too early to get ready. There is an umbrella-shaded picnic table in the middle of the Soderson backyard, and standing on it is Gary's portable bar: a bottle of olives, a bottle of gin, and a bottle of vermouth. The bottle of vermouth has not been opened. A double martini stands in front of it. Gary finishes overloading the barbecue, goes to the table, and swallows what's left in the glass. He is very partial to martinis, and tends to be in the bag by four o'clock or so on most days when he doesn't have to teach. Today is no exception.

"All right," Gary says, "next case." He then proceeds to make another Soderson Martini. He does this by (a) filling his martini glass to the three-quarters point with Bombay gin; (b) popping in an Amati olive; (c) tipping the rim of the glass against the unopened bottle of vermouth for good luck.

He tastes; closes his eyes; tastes again. His eyes, already quite red, open. He smiles. "Yes, ladies and gentlemen!" he tells his simmering backyard. "We have a winner!"

Faintly, over all the other sounds of summer—kids, mowers, muscle-cars, sprinklers, singing bugs in the baked grass of his backyard—Gary can hear the writer's guitar, a sweet and easy sound. He picks out the tune almost at once and dances around the circle of shade thrown by the umbrella with his glass in his hand, singing along: *"So kiss me and smile for me . . . Tell me that you'll wait for me . . . Hold me like you'll never let me go . . ."*

A good tune, one he remembers from before the Reed twins two houses down were even thought of, let alone born. For just a moment he is struck by the reality of time's passage, how stark it is, and unappealable. It passes the ear with a sound like iron. He takes another big sip of his martini and wonders what to do now that the barbecue is ready for liftoff. Along with the other sounds he can hear the shower upstairs, and he thinks of Marielle naked in there—the bitch of the western world, but she's kept her body in good shape. He thinks of her soaping her breasts, maybe caressing her nipples with the tips of her fingers in a circular motion, making them hard. Of course she's doing nothing of the damned kind, but it's the sort of image that just won't go away unless you do something to pop it. He decides to be a twentieth-century version of St. George; he will fuck the dragon instead of slaying it. He puts his martini glass down on the picnic table and starts for the house.

Oh gosh, it's summertime, summertime, sum-sum-summertime, and on Poplar Street the living is easy.

Cary Ripton checks his rearview mirror for traffic, sees none, and swerves easterly across the street to the Carver house. He hasn't bothered with Mr. Marinville because, at the start of the summer, Mr. Marinville gave him five dollars not to deliver the *Shopper*. "Please, Cary," he said, his eyes solemn and earnest. "I can't read about another supermarket opening or drugstore jamboree. It'll kill me if I do." Cary doesn't understand

Mr. Marinville in the slightest, but he is a nice enough man, and five bucks is five bucks.

Mrs. Carver opens the front door of 248 Poplar and waves as Cary easy-tosses her the *Shopper*. She grabs for it, misses completely, and laughs. Cary laughs with her. She doesn't have Brad Josephson's hands, or reflexes, but she's pretty and a hell of a good sport. Her husband is beside the house, wearing his bathing suit and flipflops, washing the car. He catches a glimpse of Cary out of the corner of his eye, turns, points a finger. Cary points one right back, and they pretend to shoot each other. This is Mr. Carver's crippled but game effort to be cool, and Cary respects that. David Carver works for the post office, and Cary figures he must be on vacation this week. The boy makes a vow to himself: if he has to settle for a regular nine-to-five job when he grows up (he knows that, like diabetes and kidney failure, this does happen to some people), he will *never* spend his vacation at home, washing his car in the driveway.

I'm not going to have a car, anyway, he thinks. Going to have a motorcycle. No Japanese bike, either. Big damn old Harley-Davidson like the one Mr. Marinville keeps in his garage. American steel.

He checks the rearview again and catches sight of something bright red up on Bear Street beyond the Josephson place—a van, it looks like, parked just beyond the southwestern corner of the intersection—and then swoops his Schwinn back across the street again, this time to 247, the Wyler place.

Of the occupied houses on the street (242, the old

Hobart place, is vacant), the Wyler place is the only one which even approaches seedy—it's a small ranch-style home that could use a fresh coat of paint, and a fresh coat of seal on the driveway. There's a sprinkler twirling on the lawn, but the grass is still showing the effects of the hot, dry weather in a way the other lawns on the street (*including* the lawn of the vacant Hobart house, actually) are not. There are yellow patches, small right now but spreading.

She doesn't know that water isn't enough, Cary thinks, reaching into his canvas bag for another rolled-up *Shopper*. Her husband might've, but—

He suddenly realizes that Mrs. Wyler (he guesses that widows are still called Mrs.) is standing inside the screen door, and something about seeing her there, hardly more than a silhouette, startles him badly. He wobbles on his bike for a moment, and when he throws the rolled-up paper his usually accurate aim is way off. The *Shopper* lands atop one of the shrubs flanking the front steps. He hates doing that, *hates* it, it's like some stupid comedy show where the paperboy is always throwing the *Daily Bugle* onto the roof or into the rosebushes—har-har, paperboys with bad aim, wotta scream—and on a different day (or at a different house) he might have gone back to rectify the error . . . maybe even put the paper in the lady's hand himself with a smile and a nod and a have a nice day. Not today, though. There's something here he doesn't like. Something about the way she's standing inside the screen door, shoulders slumped and hands dangling, like a kid's toy with the batteries pulled. And that's maybe not all that's out of kilter, either. He can't see her well enough to be sure, but he thinks maybe Mrs. Wyler is naked from the waist up, that she's standing there in her front hall wearing nothing but a pair of shorts. Standing there and staring at him.

If so, it's not sexy. It's creepy.

The kid that stays with her, her nephew, *that* little weasel's creepy, too. Seth Garland or Garin or something like that. He never talks, not even if you talk to him—hey, how you doin, you like it around here, you think the Indians'll make it to the Series again—just looks at you with his mud-colored eyes. Looks at you the way Cary feels Mrs. Wyler, who is usually nice, is looking at him now. Like step into my parlor said the spider to the fly, like that. Her husband died last year (right around the time the Hobarts had that trouble and moved away, now that he thinks of it), and people say it wasn't an accident. People say that Herb Wyler, who collected stamps and had once given Cary an old air rifle, committed suicide.

Gooseflesh—somehow twice as scary on a day as hot as this one—ripples up his back and he banks back across the street after another cursory look into the rearview mirror. The red van is still up there near the corner of Bear and Poplar (some spiffy rig, the boy thinks), and this time there is a vehicle coming down the street, as well, a blue Acura Cary recognizes at once. It's Mr. Jackson, the block's other teacher. Not high school in his case, however; Mr.

Jackson is actually *Professor* Jackson, or maybe it's just Assistant Professor Jackson. He teaches at Ohio State, go you Buckeyes. The Jacksons live at 244, one up from the old Hobart place. It's the nicest house on the block, a roomy Cape Cod with a high hedge on the downhill side and a high cedar stake fence on the uphill side, between them and the old veterinarian's place.

"Yo, Cary!" Peter Jackson says, pulling up beside him. He's wearing faded jeans and a tee-shirt with a big yellow smile-face on it. HAVE A NICE DAY! Mr. Smiley-Smile is saying. "How's it going, bad boy?"

"Great, Mr. Jackson," Cary says, smiling. He thinks of adding *Except that I think Mrs. Wyler's standing in her door back there with her shirt off* and then doesn't. "Everything's super-cool."

"Are you starting any games yet?"

"Only two so far, but that's okay. I got a couple of innings last night, and I'll probably get a couple more tonight. It's really all I hoped for. But it's Frankie Albertini's last year in Legion, you know." He holds out a rolled copy of the *Shopper.*

"That's right," Peter says, taking it. "And next year it's Monsieur Cary Ripton's turn to howl at shortstop."

The boy laughs, tickled at the idea of standing out there at short in his Legion uniform and howling like a werewolf. "You teaching summer school again this year?"

"Yep. Two classes. Historical Plays of Shakespeare, plus James Dickey and the New Southern Gothic. Either sound interesting to you?"

"I think I'll pass."

Peter nods seriously. "Pass and you'll never have to go to summer school, bad boy." He taps the smile-face on his shirt. "They loosen up on the teacher dress-code a little come June, but summer school's still a drag. Same as it ever was." He drops the rolled-up *Shopper* onto the seat and pulls the Acura's transmission lever down into Drive. "Don't give yourself a heatstroke pedaling around the neighborhood with those papers."

"Nah. I think it's gonna rain later, anyway. I keep hearing thunder off and on."

"That's what they say on the—*watch out!*"

A large furry shape bullets by, chasing a red disc. Cary leans his bike over toward Mr. Jackson's car and is just feathered by Hannibal's tail as the German shepherd chases after the Frisbee.

"*He's* the one you ought to warn about heatstroke," Cary says.

"Maybe you're right," Peter says, and drives slowly on.

Cary watches Hannibal snatch the Frisbee off the sidewalk on the far side of the street and turn with it in his mouth. He has a jaunty bandanna tied around his neck and appears to be wearing a big old doggy grin.

"Bring it back, Hannibal!" Jim Reed calls, and his twin brother, Dave, joins in: "Come on, Hannibal! Don't be a dork! Fetch! Bring!"

Hannibal stands in front of 246, across from the Wyler house, with the Frisbee in his mouth and his tail waving back and forth slowly. His grin appears to widen.

The Reed twins live at 245, a house down from Mrs. Wyler. They are standing at the edge of their lawn (one dark, one light, both tall and handsome in cut-off tee-shirts and identical Eddie Bauer shorts), staring across the street at Hannibal. Behind them are a couple of girls. One is Susi Geller from next door. Pretty but not, you know, *kabam*. The other, a redhead with long cheerleader legs, is a different story. Her picture could be next to *kabam* in the dictionary. Cary doesn't know her, but he would *like* to know her, her hopes and dreams and plans and fantasies. Especially the fantasies. Not in *this* life, he thinks. That's mature pussy. She's seventeen if she's a day.

"Aw, *sugar*!" Jim Reed says, then turns to his dark-haired sib. "*You* go get it this time."

"No way, it'll be all spitty," Dave Reed says. "*Hannibal, be a good dog and bring that back here!*"

Hannibal stands on the sidewalk in front of Doc's house, still grinning. Nyah-nyah, he says without having to say anything; it's all in the grin and the regally serene sweep of the tail. Nyah-nyah, you've got girls and Eddie Bauer shorts, but I got your Frisbee and I'm leaking canine spit all over it, and in my opinion that makes me the Grand Wazoo.

Cary reaches into his pocket and pulls out a bag of sunflower seeds—if you have to ride the bench, he has discovered, sunflower seeds help to pass the time. He has become quite adept at cracking them with his teeth and chewing the tasty centers even as he spits the hulls onto the cracked cement of the dugout floor with the machine-gun speed of a major leaguer.

"I gotcha covered," he calls back to the Reed twins, hoping the sweet little redhead will be impressed by his animal-taming prowess, knowing this is a dream so foolish only a kid between his freshman and sophomore years in high school could possibly entertain it, but she looks so wonderful in those cuffed white shorts she's wearing, oh great gosh a'mighty, and when did a little fantasy ever hurt a kid?

He drops the bag of sunflower seeds down to dog level and crackles the cellophane. Hannibal comes at once, still with the red Frisbee caught in the center of his grin. Cary pours a few seeds into his palm. "Good, Hannibal," he says. "These're *good.* Sunflower seeds, loved by dogs all over the world. Try em. You'll buy em."

Hannibal studies the seeds a moment longer, nostrils quivering delicately, then drops the Frisbee onto Poplar Street and vacuums them out of Cary's palm. Quick as a flash, the boy bends, grabs the Frisbee (it is sorta spitty around the edges), and scales it back at Jim Reed. It's a perfect, floating toss, one Jim is able to grab without moving a single step. And, oh God, oh Jesus, the redhead is *applauding* him, bouncing up and down next to Susi Geller, her boobs (small but delectable) kind of jiggling inside the halter she's wearing. Oh thank you Lord, thank you so much, we now have enough jackoff material in our memory banks to last at least a week.

Grinning, unaware that he will die both a virgin and

a backup shortstop, Cary throws a *Shopper* onto the stoop of Tom Billingsley's house (he can hear Doc's mower yowling out back), and swoops across the street again toward the Reed house. Dave tosses the Frisbee to Susi Geller and then takes the *Shopper* when Cary flips it to him.

"Thanks for getting the Frisbee back," Dave says.

"No problem." He nods toward the redhead. "Who's she?"

Dave laughs, not unkindly. "Never mind, little man. Don't even bother to ask."

Cary thinks of chasing it a little, then decides it would probably be better to quit while he's ahead—he got the Frisbee, after all, and she applauded him, and the sight of her bouncing around in that little halter would have gotten an overcooked noodle hard. Surely that is enough for a summer afternoon as hot as this one.

Above and behind them, at the top of the hill, the red van begins to move, creeping slowly up on the corner.

"You coming to the game tonight?" Cary asks Dave Reed. "We got the Columbus Rebels. Should be good."

"You gonna play?"

"I should get a couple of innings in the field and at least one ay-bee."

"Probably not, then," Dave says, and yodels a laugh which makes Cary wince. The Reed twins look like young gods in their cut-off tees, he thinks, but when they open their mouths they bear a suspicious resemblance to the Hager Twins of *Hee Haw*.

Cary glances down toward the house on the corner

of Poplar and Hyacinth, across from the store. The last house on the left, as in the horror movie of the same name. There is no car in the driveway, but that means nothing; it could be in the garage.

"He home?" he asks Dave, lifting his chin at 240.

"Dunno," Jim says, coming over. "But you hardly ever do, do you? That's what makes him so weird. Half the time he leaves his damn car in the garage and cuts through the woods to Hyacinth. Probably takes the bus to wherever it is he goes."

"You scared of him?" Dave asks Cary. He's not exactly taunting, but it's close.

"Shit, no," Cary says, cool, looking at the redhead, wondering about how it would feel to have a package like her in his arms, all sleek and springy, maybe slipping him a little tongue as she snuggled up to his boner. Not in *this* life, Bub, he thinks again.

He tosses the redhead a wave, is outwardly noncommittal and inwardly overjoyed when she returns it, then sails diagonally down the street toward 240 Poplar. He'll deliver the *Shopper* onto the porch with his usual hard flip, and then—if the crazy ex-cop doesn't come charging out the front door, foaming at the mouth and glaring at him with stoned PCP eyes, maybe waving his service pistol or a machete or something—Cary will go across to the E-Z Stop for a soda to celebrate another successful negotiation of his route: Anderson Avenue to Columbus Broad, Columbus Broad to Bear Street, Bear Street to Poplar Street. Then home to change into his uniform and off to the baseball wars.

First, however, there is 240 Poplar to get behind him, home of the ex-cop who reputedly lost his job for beating a couple of innocent North Side kids to death because he thought they raped a little girl. Cary has no idea if there's any truth to the story—he has never seen anything about it in the papers, certainly—but he has seen the ex-cop's eyes, and there is something in them that he's never seen in another pair of eyes, a vacancy that makes you want to look away just as soon as you can without appearing uncool.

At the top of the hill, the red van—if that's what it is, it's so gaudy and customized it's hard to tell—turns onto Poplar. It begins to pick up speed. The sound of its engine is a cadenced, silky whisper. And what, pray tell, is that chrome gadget on the roof?

Johnny Marinville stops playing his guitar to watch the van slide past. He can't see inside because the windows are polarized, but the thing on the roof looks like a chrome-plated radar dish, goddamned if it doesn't. Has the CIA landed on Poplar Street? Across from him, Johnny sees Brad Josephson standing on his lawn, still holding his hose in one hand and his *Shopper* in the other. Brad is also gaping after the slow-moving van (*is* it a van, though? *is* it?), his expression a mixture of wonder and perplexity.

Arrows of sun glint off the bright red paint and the chrome below the dark windows, arrows so bright they make Johnny wince.

Next door to Johnny, David Carver is still washing his car. He's enthusiastic, you have to give him that;

he's got that Chevy of his buried in soapsuds all the way to the wiper-blades.

The red van rolls past him, humming and glinting.

On the other side of the street, the Reed twins and their gal pals stop their front-lawn Frisbee game to look at the slow-rolling van. The kids make a rectangle; in the center of it sits Hannibal, panting happily and awaiting his next chance to snatch the Frisbee.

Things are happening fast now, although no one on Poplar Street realizes it yet.

In the distance, thunder rumbles.

Cary Ripton barely notices the van in his rearview mirror, or the bright yellow Ryder truck which turns left from Hyacinth onto Poplar, pulling onto the tarmac of the E-Z Stop, where the Carver kids are still standing by Buster the red wagon and squabbling over whether Ralph will be pulled up the hill by his sister or not. Ralph has agreed to walk *and* keep silent about the magazine with Ethan Hawke on the cover, but only if his dear sister Margrit the Maggot gives him *all* of the candybar instead of just half.

The kids break off their argument, noticing the white steam hissing out of the Ryder truck's grille like dragon's breath, but Cary Ripton pays zero attention to the Ryder truck's problems. His attention is focused on one thing and one thing only: delivering the crazy ex-copper's *Shopper* and then getting away unscathed. The ex-copper's name is Collier Entragian, and he is the only person on the block with a NO TRESPASSING sign on his lawn. It's small, it's discreet, but it's there.

If he killed a couple of kids, how come he's not in jail? Cary wonders, and not for the first time. He decides he doesn't care. The ex-cop's continued freedom isn't his business on this sultry afternoon; *survival* is his business.

With all this on his mind, it's no wonder Cary doesn't notice the Ryder truck with the steam pouring out of the grille, or the two kids who have momentarily ceased their complicated negotiations concerning the magazine, the 3 Musketeers bar, and the red wagon, or the van coming down the hill. He is concentrating on not becoming a psycho cop's next victim, and this is ironic, since his fate is actually approaching from behind him.

One of the van's side windows begins to slide down.

A shotgun barrel pokes out. It is an odd color, not quite silver, not quite gray. The twin muzzles look like the symbol for infinity colored black.

Somewhere beyond the blazing sky, afternoon thunder rumbles again.

From the Columbus Dispatch, *July 31st, 1994:*

MEMBERS OF TOLEDO FAMILY SLAIN IN SAN JOSE

Four Killed in Suspected Gang Drive-by; Six-Year-Old Survives

SAN JOSE, Calif., July 30 (AP) —A family vacation to northern California ended in tragedy yesterday when four members of a Toledo family were slain in a hail of gunfire, victims of what San Jose police speculate may have been misdirected gang violence. Killed in the drive-by shooting were William Garin, 42, June Garin, 40, and two of their three children: John Garin, 12, and Mary Lou Garin, 10. The Garins were visiting Joseph and Roxanne Calabrese, friends from college. The Calabreses were in the backyard at the time of the shooting and were not injured. Also uninjured was six-year-old Seth Garin, who was playing in the backyard sandbox. According to Joseph Calabrese, the Garins and their older children were playing croquet on the front lawn when they were gunned down.

"I can't believe the society we're living in, that such things can happen," a shaken Calabrese said. "This is a good neighborhood. We've never had anything like this happen here before."

Witnesses reported seeing a red van in the vicinity shortly before the shooting. One man claimed it might have been equipped with high-tech monitoring equipment. "It had what looked like a radar dish on the roof," he said. "If the punks don't ditch it, it should be easy to find."

Police have not found the mystery-van yet, however, and no arrests have been made. When asked about the weapons used in the attack, Lieutenant Robert Alvarez would only say that ballistics had not yet been able to make a definite determination, and that the issue is still under investigation.

CHAPTER 2

1

Steve Ames saw the shooting because of the two kids arguing beside the red wagon in front of the store. The girl looked seriously pissed at the little boy, and for one second Steve was sure she was going to give him a shove . . . which might send him sprawling across the wagon and in front of the truck. Running over a brat in a Bart Simpson shirt in central Ohio would certainly be the perfect end to this totally fucked-up day.

As he stopped well short of them—better safe than sorry—he saw their attention had been diverted from whatever they were fighting about to the steam pouring out of his radiator. Beyond them, in the street, was a red van, maybe the brightest red van Steve had ever seen in his life. The paintjob wasn't what attracted his eye, however. What did was the shiny chrome doodad on the van's roof. It looked like some sort of futuristic radar dish. It was swinging back and forth in a short, repeating arc, too, the way that radar dishes did.

There was a kid riding a bike on the far side of the street. The van slid over toward him, as if the driver (or someone inside) wanted to talk to him. The kid had no idea it was there; he had just taken a rolled-up newspaper from the sack hanging down on one hip and was cocking his arm back to throw it.

Steve turned off the Ryder truck's ignition without thinking about what he was doing. He no longer heard the steady hissing sound from the radiator, no longer saw the kids standing by the red wagon, no longer thought about what he was going to say when he called the 800 number the Ryder people gave you in case of engine trouble. Once or twice in his life he'd had little precognitive flashes—hunches, psychic nudges—but he was now gripped not by a flash but a kind of cramp: a certainty that something was going to happen. Not the kind of thing that made you raise a cheer, either.

He didn't see the double barrel poking out of the van's side window, he was placed wrong for that, but he heard the *kabam!* of the shotgun and knew it immediately for what it was. He had grown up in Texas, and had never mistaken gunfire for thunder.

The kid flew off the seat of his bike, shoulders twisted, legs bent, hat flying off his head. The back of his tee-shirt was shredded, and Steve could see more than he wanted to—red blood and black, torn flesh.

The kid's throwing-hand had been cocked to his ear, and the folded paper tumbled behind him, into the dry gutter, as the kid hit the lawn of the small house on the corner in a boneless, graceless forward roll.

The van stopped in the middle of the street just short of the Poplar-Hyacinth intersection, engine idling.

Steve Ames sat behind the wheel of his rented truck, mouth open, as a small window set into the van's right rear side slid down, like the power window of a Cadillac or a Lincoln.

I didn't know they could do that, he thought, and then: What kind of van *is* that, anyway?

He became aware that someone had come out of the store—a girl in the sort of blue smock top that checkout people usually wore. She had one hand up to her forehead, shielding her eyes from the sun. He could see the young woman, but the paperboy's body was temporarily gone, blocked by the van. He became aware that a double-barrelled shotgun was now poking out of the window which had just slid down.

And, last but not least, he became aware of the two children standing by their red wagon—out in the open, totally exposed—and looking in the direction from which the first shots had come.

2

Hannibal the German shepherd saw one thing and one thing only: the rolled-up newspaper which fell from Cary Ripton's hand as the shotgun blast pushed him off his bicycle seat and out of his life. Hannibal charged, barking happily.

"Hannibal, no!" Jim Reed shouted. He had no idea what was going on (he hadn't grown up in Texas, and he *had* mistaken the first twin shotgun blast for thunder, not because it *sounded* like thunder but because he was unable to recognize it for what it really was, not in the context of a summer afternoon on Poplar Street), but he didn't like it. Without thinking about what he was doing—or why—he scaled the Frisbee down the sidewalk toward the store, hoping to catch Hannibal's eye and divert him from his current course. The ploy didn't work. Hannibal ignored the Frisbee and kept on going, arrowing for the fallen copy of the *Shopper,* which he could just see in front of the idling red van.

3

Cynthia Smith also knew the sound of a shotgun when she heard one—her minister father had shot skeet every Saturday when she was a little girl, and had frequently taken her along on these expeditions.

This time, however, no one had yelled *Pull.*

She put down the paperback she had been reading, came around the counter, and hurried out onto the top step of the store. The glare hit her and she raised a hand to shade her eyes against it.

She saw the van idling in the middle of the street,

saw the shotgun slide out of the back, saw it center on the Carver children. They looked puzzled but not, as yet, frightened.

My God, she thought. My God, he means to shoot the kids.

For a moment she was frozen in place. Her brain told her legs to move but nothing happened.

Go! Go! GO! she screamed at herself, and that broke the ice sheathing her nerves. She lurched forward on legs that felt like stilts, almost falling down the three cement steps, and grabbed at the kids. The twin bores of the shotgun looked huge, gaping, and she saw she was too late. That first frozen moment had been fatal. All she had managed to do was to make sure that when the guy in the back of the van pulled the shotgun's triggers, he would kill one twenty-year-old roadbunny as well as two innocent little kids.

4

David Carver dropped his sponge into the bucket of soapy water beside the right front tire of his Caprice and strolled down his driveway toward the street to see what was happening. Next door, one house up the hill on his right, Johnny Marinville was doing the same thing. He had hold of his guitar by the neck. On the other side, Brad Josephson was also walking down his lawn to the street, his hose spouting into the grass behind him. He was still holding his copy of the *Shopper* in one hand.

"Was that a backfire?" Johnny asked. He didn't think it had been. Back in his pre–Kitty-Cat days, when he had still considered himself "a serious writer" (a phrase with all the pungency of "a really good whore," to his way of thinking), Johnny had done a hellish research tour in Vietnam, and he thought the sound he had just heard was more like the kind of backfires he had heard during the Tet offensive. Jungle backfires. The kind that killed people.

David shook his head, then turned his hands up to indicate he didn't really know. Behind him, the screen door of the cream-and-green ranch-house banged shut and there were running bare feet on the walk. It was Pie, wearing jeans and a blouse that had been buttoned wrong. Her hair clung to her head in a damp helmet. She still smelled of the shower.

"Was that a backfire? God, Dave, it sounded like a—"

"Like a gunshot," Johnny said, then added reluctantly: "I'm pretty sure it was."

Kirsten Carver—Kirstie to her friends and Pie to her husband, for reasons probably only a husband could know—looked down the hill. An expression of horror was slipping into her face, seeming somehow to widen not just her eyes but all of her features. David followed her gaze. He saw the idling van, and he saw the shotgun barrel sticking out of the right rear window.

"Ellie! Ralph!" Pie screamed. It was a piercing cry, penetrating, and behind the Soderson house, Gary paused, listening, his martini glass halfway to his lips. *"Oh God, Ellie and Ralph!"*

Pie began to sprint down the hill toward the van.

"Kirsten, no, don't do that!" Brad Josephson yelled. He began to run after her, cutting into the street even as she did the same, angling to meet her in the middle, perhaps head her off between the Jacksons' and the Gellers'. He ran with surprising fleetness for such a big man, but saw after only a dozen running steps that he wasn't going to catch her.

David Carver also began to run after his wife, his gut bouncing up and down above his ridiculously tiny bathing suit, his flipflops smacking the sidewalk and making a noise like cap-pistols. His shadow ran after him in the street, long and thinner than Postal Service employee David Carver had ever been in his adult life.

5

I'm dead, Cynthia thought, dropping to one knee behind and between the kids, reaching to encircle their shoulders with her arms, meaning to pull them back against her. For all the good that would do. I'm dead, I'm dead, I'm totally dead. And still she couldn't take her eyes off the twin bores of the shotgun, holes so black, so like pitiless eyes.

The passenger door of the yellow truck popped open and she saw a lanky man in bluejeans and some sort of rock tee-shirt, a guy with graying shoulder-length hair and a craggy face.

"Get em in here, lady!" he yelled. "Now, *now*!"

She pushed the children toward the truck, knowing

it was too late. And then, while she was still trying to ready herself for the rip of the shot or the pellets (as if you *could* get ready for such a gross invasion), the gun poking from the rear of the van swivelled away from them, swivelled forward, along the red flank of the van. It went off, the report rolling across the hot day like a bowling ball speeding down a stone gutter. Cynthia saw fire lick from the end of the barrel. The Reeds' dog, which had been starting his final approach on the dropped newspaper, was thrown violently to the right, the grace slapped out of him as it had been slapped out of Cary Ripton.

"Hannibal!" Jim and Dave shrieked in unison. The sound made Cynthia think of the Doublemint Twins.

She shoved the Carver kids toward the open door of the truck so hard that Brother Boogersnot fell down. He started to bellow at once. The girl—always an Ellie, never a Margaret, Cynthia remembered—looked back with an expression of heartbreaking bewilderment. Then the man with the long hair had her by the arm and was hauling her up into the cab. "On the floor, kid, on the floor!" he shouted at her, then leaned out to grab the yowling boy. The Ryder truck's horn let out a brief blat; the driver had hooked one sneakered foot through the wheel to keep from sliding out headfirst. Cynthia batted the red wagon aside, grabbed the boogersnot by the back of his shorts, and lifted him into the truck-driver's arms. Down the street, approaching, she could hear a man and a woman yelling the kids' names. Dad and Mom, she assumed, and apt to be shot down in the street like the dog and the paperboy if they didn't look out.

"Get up here!" the driver bawled at her. Cynthia needed no second invitation; she scrambled into the overcrowded cab of the truck.

6

Gary Soderson came striding purposefully (although not quite steadily) around the side of his house with his martini glass in one hand. There had been a second loud bang, and he found himself wondering if maybe the Gellers' gas grill had exploded. He saw Marinville, who had gotten rich in the eighties writing children's books about an unlikely character named Pat the Kitty-Cat, standing in the middle of the street, shading his eyes and looking down the hill.

"What be happenin, my brother?" Gary asked, joining him.

"I think someone in that van down there just killed Cary Ripton and then shot the Reeds' dog," Johnny Marinville said in a strange, flat voice.

"*What?* Why would anyone do that?"

"I have no idea."

Gary saw a couple—the Carvers, he was almost positive—running down the street toward the store, closely pursued by a galumphing African-American gent that had to be the one the only Brad Josephson.

Marinville turned to face him. "This is bad shit. I'm

calling the cops. In the meantime, I advise you to get off the street. *Now.*"

Marinville hurried up the walk to his house. Gary ignored his advice and stayed where he was, glass in hand, looking at the van idling in the middle of the street down there by the Entragian place, suddenly wishing (and for him this was an exceedingly odd wish) that he wasn't quite so drunk.

7

The door of the bungalow at 240 Poplar banged open and Collie Entragian came charging out exactly as Cary Ripton had always feared he someday would: with a gun in his hand. Otherwise, however, he looked pretty much all right—no foam on the lips, no bloodshot, buggy eyes. He was a tall man, six-four at least, starting to show a little softness in the belly but as broad and muscular through the shoulders as a football linebacker. He wore khaki pants and no shirt. There was shaving cream on the left side of his face, and a hand-towel over his shoulder. The gun in his hand was a .38, and might very well have been the service pistol Cary had often imagined while delivering the *Shopper* to the house on the corner.

Collie looked at the boy lying facedown and dead on his lawn, his clothes already damp from the lawn sprinkler (and the papers that had spilled out of his carrysack turning a soggy gray), and then at the van. He raised the pistol, clamping his left hand over his right wrist. Just as he did, the van began to roll. He almost fired anyway, then didn't. He had to be careful. There were people in Columbus, some of them very powerful, who would be delighted to hear that Collier Entragian had discharged a weapon on a suburban Wentworth street . . . a weapon he had been required by law to turn in, actually.

That's no excuse and you know it, he thought, turning as the van rolled, pivoting with it. Fire your weapon! Fire your goddam weapon!

But he didn't, and as the van turned left onto Hyacinth, he saw there was no license plate on the back . . . and what about the silver gadget on the roof? What in God's name had *that* been?

On the other side of the street, Mr. and Mrs. Carver were sprinting into the parking lot of the E-Z Stop. Josephson was behind them. The black man glanced to the left and saw the red van was gone—it had just disappeared behind the trees which screened the part of Hyacinth Street which ran east of Poplar—and then bent over, hands on knees, gasping for breath.

Collie walked across the street, tucking the barrel of the .38 into the back of his pants, and put his hand on Josephson's shoulder. "You okay, man?"

Brad looked up at him and smiled painfully. His face was running with sweat. "Maybe," he said.

Collie walked over to the yellow rental truck, noting the red wagon nearby. There were a couple of unopened sodas lying inside it. A 3 Musketeers candybar lay beside one of the rear wheels. Someone had stepped on it and squashed it.

Screams from behind him. He turned and saw the Reed twins, their faces very pale beneath their summer tans, looking past their dog to the boy crumpled on his lawn. The twin with the blond hair—Jim, he thought—began to cry. The other one took a step backward, grimaced, then bent forward and vomited onto his own bare feet.

Crying loudly, Mrs. Carver lifted her son back out of the truck. The boy, also bawling at maximum volume, threw his arms around her neck and clung like a limpet.

"Hush," the woman in the jeans and the misbuttoned shirt said. "Hush, lovey, it's over. The bad man's gone."

David Carver took his daughter from the arms of the man lying awkwardly over the seat and enfolded her.

"*Dad-dy,* you're getting me all soapy!" the girl protested.

Carver kissed her brow between the eyes. "Never mind," he said. "Are you all right, Ellie?"

"Yes," she said. "What happened?"

She tried to look toward the street, and her father shielded her eyes.

Collie went to the woman and the little boy. "Is he okay, Mrs. Carver?"

She looked at him, not seeming to recognize him, and then turned her attention back to the squalling kid again, caressing his hair with one hand, seeming to devour him with her eyes. "Yes, I think so," she said. "*Are* you okay, Ralphie? Are you?"

The kid drew in a deep, hitching breath and bellowed: *"Margrit's spozed to pull me up the hill! That was the deal!"*

The little snot sounded okay to Collie. He turned back toward the crime-scene, noted the dog lying in a spreading pool of blood, noted that the blond Reed twin was tentatively approaching the body of the unfortunate paperboy.

"Stay away!" Collie called sharply across the street.

Jim Reed turned toward him. "But what if he's still alive?"

"What if he is? Have you got any healing fairy-dust to sprinkle on him? No? Then stand back!"

The boy stepped toward his brother, then winced. "Oh man, Davey, look at your *feet*," he said, then turned aside and threw up himself.

Collie Entragian suddenly felt tumbled back into the job he thought he had left behind for good the previous October, when he had been bounced from the Columbus Police Department after a positive drug test. Cocaine and heroin. A good trick, since he had never taken either drug in his life.

First priority: protect the citizenry. Second priority: aid the wounded. Third priority: secure the crime-scene. Fourth priority . . .

Well, he'd worry about the fourth priority after he'd taken care of one, two, and three.

The store's new day-clerk—a skinny girl with double-colored hair that made Collie's eyes hurt—slid out of the truck and straightened her blue smock, which was badly askew. The truck's driver followed her. "You a cop?" he asked Collie.

"Yes." Easier than trying to explain. The Carvers would know different, of course, but they were occupied with their kids, and Brad Josephson was still behind him, bent over and trying to catch his breath. "You folks get in the store. All of you. Brad? Boys?" He raised his voice a little on the last word, so that the Reed twins would know he meant them.

"No, I'd better get on back home," Brad said. He straightened up, glanced across the street at Cary's body, then looked back at Collie. His expression was apologetic but determined. At least he was getting his breath back; for a minute or two there, Collie had been reviewing what he remembered of his CPR classes. "Belinda's up there, and . . ."

"Yes, but it'd be better for you to come on in the store, Mr. Josephson, at least for the time being. In case the van comes back."

"Why would it?" David Carver asked. He was still holding his little girl in his arms and staring at Collie over the top of her head.

Collie shrugged. "I don't know. I don't know why it was here in the first place. Better to be safe. Get inside, folks."

"Do you have any authority here?" Brad asked. His voice, although not exactly challenging, suggested that he knew Collie didn't. Collie folded his arms over his bare chest. The depression which had surrounded him since he'd been busted off the force had begun to lift a little in the last few weeks, but now he could feel it threatening again. After a moment he shook his head. No. No authority. Not these days.

"Then I am going to my wife. No offense to you, sir."

Collie had to smile a little at the careful dignity of the man's tone. You don't diss me and I don't diss you, it said. "None taken."

The twins looked at each other uncertainly, then at Collie.

He saw what they wanted and sighed. "All right. But go with Mr. Josephson. And when you get home, you and your friends go inside. Okay?"

The blond boy nodded.

"Jim—you *are* Jim, right?"

The blond boy nodded, wiping self-consciously at his red eyes.

"Is your mom home? Or your dad?"

"Mom," he said. "Dad's still at work."

"Okay, boys. Go on. Hurry up. You too, Brad."

"I'll do the best I can," Brad said, "but I think I have pretty well fulfilled my hurrying quota for the day."

The three of them started up the hill, along the west side of the street, where the odd-numbered houses were.

"I'd like to take our kids home, too, Mr. Entragian," Kirsten Carver said.

He sighed, nodded. Sure, what the hell, take them anywhere. Take them to Alaska. He wanted a cigarette, but they were back in the house. He had managed to quit for almost ten years before the bastards downtown had first shown him the door and then run him through it. He had picked up the habit again with a speed that was spooky. And now he wanted to smoke because he was nervous. Not just cranked up because of the dead kid on his lawn, which would have been understandable, but *nervous.* Nervous like-a de *vitch,* his mother would have said. And why?

Because there are too many people on this street, he told himself, that's why.

Oh, really? And what exactly does *that* mean?

He didn't know.

What's wrong with you? Too long out of work? Getting squirrely? Is *that* what's buggin you, booby?

No. The silver thing on the roof of the van. That's what's buggin me, booby.

Oh? Really?

Well, maybe not really . . . but it would do for a start. Or an excuse. In the end a hunch was a hunch, and either you believed in your hunches and played them or you didn't. He himself had always believed, and apparently a minor matter like getting fired hadn't changed the power they held over him.

David Carver set his daughter down on her feet and took his blatting son from his wife. "I'll pull you in the wagon," he told the boy. "All the way up to the house. How's that?"

"Margrit the Maggot loves Ethan Hawke," his son confided.

"Does she? Well, maybe so, but you shouldn't call her that," David said. He spoke in the absent tones of a man who will forgive his child—*one* of his children, anyway—just about anything. And his wife was looking at the kid with the eyes of one who regards a saint, or a boy prophet. Only Collie Entragian saw the look of dull hurt in the girl's eyes as her revered brother was plumped down into the wagon. Collie had other things to think of, lots of them, but that look was just too big and too sad to miss. Yow.

He looked from Ellie Carver to the girl with the crazed hair and the aging hippie-type from the rental truck. "Do you suppose I could at least get you to step inside until the police come?" he asked.

"Hey," the girl said, "sure." She was looking at him warily. "You're a cop, right?"

The Carvers were drawing away, Ralph sitting cross-legged in his wagon, but they might still be close enough to overhear anything he said . . . and besides, what was he going to do? Lie? You start down that road, he told himself, and maybe you can wind up on Freak Street, an ex-cop with a collection of badges in your basement, like Elvis, and a couple of extras pinned inside your wallet for good measure. Call yourself a private detective, although you never quite get around to applying for the license. Ten or fifteen years from now you'll still be talking the talk and at least trying to walk the walk, like a woman in her thirties who wears miniskirts and goes braless in an effort to convince people (most of whom don't give a shit anyway) that her cheerleading days aren't behind her.

"Used to be," he said. The clerk nodded. The guy with the long hair was looking at him curiously but not disrespectfully. "You did a good job with the kids," he added, looking at her but speaking to both of them.

Cynthia considered this, then shook her head. "It was the dog," she said, and began walking toward the store. Collie and the aging hippie followed her. "The guy in the van—the one with the shotgun—he meant to throw some fire at the kids." She turned to the long-hair. "Did you see that? Do you agree?"

He nodded. "There wasn't a thing either of us could do to stop him, either." He spoke in an accent too twangy to be deep southern. Texas, Collie thought. Texas or Oklahoma. "Then the dog distracted him—isn't that what happened?—and he shot it, instead."

"That's it," Cynthia said. "If it *hadn't* distracted the guy . . . well . . . I think we'd be as dead as him now." She lifted her chin in the direction of Cary Ripton, still dead and dampening on Collie's lawn. Then she led them into the E-Z Stop.

From Movies on TV*, edited by Stephen H. Scheuer, Bantam Books:*

(Dir.: Wi...
tures, 105 mins, b&w.)

The Regulators (1958) ** John Payne, Ty Hardin, Karen Steele, Rory Calhoun. Below-average Western melodrama of vigilantes on the rampage; includes some scenes and effects which are surprisingly gruesome for a late-fifties oat opera. Colorado mining town is terrorized by vigilantes (led by Calhoun) who first appear to be supernatural beings but turn out to be post–Civil War baddies of the Capt. Quantrill stripe. Payne is heroic but wooden; Steele makes the most of her low-cut dancehall costumes. (Dir.: Billy Rancourt, American-International Pictures, 81 mins, b&w.)

Rehearsal for M...

CHAPTER 3

1
Poplar Street/3:58 P.M./July 15, 1996

Moments after Collie, Cynthia, and the longhair from the Ryder truck go inside the store, a van pulls up on the southwestern corner of Poplar and Hyacinth, across from the E-Z Stop. It's a flaked metallic blue with dark polarized windows. There's no chrome gadget on its roof, but its sides are flared and scooped in a futuristic way that makes it look more like a scout-vehicle in a science-fiction movie than a van. The tires are entirely treadless, as smooth and blank as the surface of a freshly washed blackboard. Deep within the darkness behind the tinted windows, dim colored lights flash rhythmically, like telltales on a control panel.

Thunder rumbles, closer and sharper now. The summer brightness begins to fade from the sky; clouds, purple-black and threatening, are piling in from the west. They reach for the July sun and put it out. The temperature begins to sink at once.

The blue van hums quietly. Up the block, at the top of the hill, another van—this one the bright yellow of a fake banana—pulls up at the southeast corner of Bear Street and Poplar. It stops there, also humming quietly.

The first really sharp crack of thunder comes, and a bright shutter-flash of lightning follows. It shines in Hannibal's glazing right eye for a moment, making it glow like a spirit-lamp.

2

Gary Soderson was still standing in the street when his wife joined him. "What the hell are you doing?" she asked. "You look like you're in a trance, or something."

"You didn't hear it?"

"Hear what?" she asked irritably. "I was in the shower, what'm I gonna hear in there?" Gary had been married to the lady for nine years and knew that, in Marielle, irritation was a dominant trait. "The Reed kids with their Frisbee, I heard them. Their damn dog barking. Thunder. What else'm I gonna hear? The Norman Dickersnackle Choir?"

He pointed down the street, first toward the dog (she wouldn't have Hannibal to complain about anymore, at least), then toward the twisted shape on the lawn of 240. "I don't know for sure, but I *think* someone just shot the kid who delivers the *Shopper*."

She peered in the direction of his finger, squinting, shading her eyes even though the sun had now disappeared (to Gary it felt as if the temperature had already dropped at least ten degrees). Brad Josephson was trudging up the sidewalk toward them. Peter Jackson was out in front of his house, looking curiously down the hill. So was Tom Billingsley, the vet most people called Old Doc. The Carver family was crossing the street from the store side to the side their house was on, the girl walking next to her mother and holding her hand. Dave Carver (looking to Gary like a boiled lobster in the bathing suit he was wearing—a soap-crusted boiled lobster, at that) was pulling his son in a little red wagon. The boy, who was sitting cross-legged and staring around with the imperious disdain of a pasha, had always struck Gary as about a 9.5 on the old Shithead-Meter.

"Hey, Dave!" Peter Jackson called. "What's going on?"

Before Carver could reply, Marielle struck Gary's shoulder with the heel of her hand, hard enough to slop the last of his martini out of his glass and onto his tatty old Converse sneakers. Maybe just as well. He might even do his liver a favor and take the night off.

"Are you deaf, Gary, or just stupid?" the light of his life inquired.

"Likely both," he responded, thinking that if he ever decided to sober up for good, he would probably have to divorce Marielle first. Or at least slit her vocal cords. "What did you say?"

"I asked you why in God's name anyone would shoot the *paper*boy?"

"Maybe it was someone didn't get his double coupons last week," Gary said. Thunder cracked—still west of them, but nearing. It seemed to run through the gathering clouds like a harpoon.

3

Johnny Marinville, who had once won the National Book Award for a novel of sexual obsession called *Delight* and who now wrote children's books about a feline private detective named Pat the Kitty-Cat, stood looking down at his living-room telephone and feeling afraid. Something was going on here. He was trying not to be paranoid about it, but yeah, something was going on here.

"Maybe," he said in a low voice.

Yeah, okay. *Maybe.* But the phone—

He had come in, propped his guitar in the corner, and punched 911. There had been an uncommonly long pause, so long he had been about to break the connection (*what* connection, ha-ha?) and try again when what might have been a child's voice came on the line. The sound of that voice, both lilting and empty, had surprised Johnny and frightened him badly—he hadn't even tried to kid himself that his fright was only a startle reflex.

"Little bitty baby Smitty," the voice had lilted. "I

seen you bite your mommy's titty. Don't you fret and don't you pout, don't you spit that titty out."

There had been a click followed by the hum of an open line. Frowning, Johnny had redialled. Again the long pause, then a click, then a sound Johnny thought he recognized: a mouth-breather. The sound of a kid with a cold, maybe. Not that it mattered. What mattered was that the phone-lines had gotten crossed somewhere in the neighborhood, and now instead of getting through to the cops—

"Who's there?" he had asked sharply.

No answer. Just the mouth-breathing. And was that sound *familiar*? That was pretty ridiculous, wasn't it? How in God's name could the sound of breathing on the telephone be familiar? It couldn't, of course, but all the same—

"Whoever you are, get the hell off the line," Johnny said. "I have to call the police."

The breath caught, stopped. Johnny was reaching to break the connection again when the voice returned. Mocking this time. He was sure it was. "Little bitty baby Smitty, stuck his prick in Mommy's slitty. Don't you fret and don't you pout, she won't make you take it out." Then, in a voice that was flat and somehow terrible: "Don't you call here no more, you old fool. *Tak!*"

Another click as the line went dead, but this time there was no open-line hum. This time there was just stillness.

Johnny hit the phone's cutoff switch, stuttering lightly with the top of a finger. Nothing happened.

The line remained blank. Thunder boomed, still to the west but closing in, making him jump.

He dropped the phone into the cradle and went into the kitchen, noting how rapidly the light was fading out of the sky and reminding himself to close the upstairs windows if it started to rain . . . *when* it started to rain, judging from the way things looked now.

Out here the phone was on the wall by the kitchen table, where all he had to do was rock back in his chair and snag it if he happened to be eating a meal when it rang. Not that there were many calls; his ex-wife sometimes, that was all. His people in New York knew enough to leave their money-machine alone.

He unracked the phone, listened, and got a second helping of silence. No dial-tone, no staticky crackle when lightning flashed blue in the kitchen window, no wah-wah-wah signalling that the line was out of service. Just nothing. He tried 911 anyway, and there weren't even any tone-beeps in his ear as he pushed the keypads. He hung the telephone up and looked at it in the darkening kitchen. "Little bitty baby Smitty," he murmured, and suddenly shivered in a way that would have been taken for theatrical if he hadn't been alone: a big backward-and-forward snapping of the shoulders. An ugly little jingle, and one he'd never heard before.

Never mind the jingle, he thought. What about the *voice*? You've heard *that* before . . . haven't you?

"No," he said out loud. "At least . . . I don't know."

Right. But the breathing . . .

"Fuck a duck, you don't recognize a person's

breathing," he told the empty kitchen. "Not unless your granddad's got emphysema."

He left the kitchen, heading for the front door. All at once he wanted to see what was going on out there in the street.

4

"What happened down there?" Peter Jackson asked David when the Carver family reached the east sidewalk. He bent his head toward David and lowered his voice so the kids wouldn't hear. "Is that a body down there?"

"Yes," David said in a similarly low voice. "Cary Ripton's his name, I think." He glanced at his wife for confirmation and Kirsten nodded. "The boy who delivers the *Shopper* on Monday afternoons. Guy in a van. A drive-by."

"Someone shot *Cary*?" That was impossible. Impossible that someone he had just been talking to should have been shot. But Carver was nodding his head. "Holy shit!"

David nodded. "Holy shit about covers it, I guess."

"Hurry up, Daddy-doo," Ralphie commanded from his place in the wagon.

David glanced back at him, gave the boy a smile, then looked at Peter again. This time he spoke in a voice so low it was really a whisper. "The kids were down at the store, buying sodas. I don't know for sure, but I've got an idea the guy almost took a shot at them, too. Then the Reeds' dog came by. The man with the gun shot it, instead."

"Jesus!" Peter said. The idea that someone had shot Hannibal—genial, Frisbee-chasing Hannibal with his jaunty neck-scarf—made it impossible not to accept. He didn't know why that should be, but it was. "I mean Jesus *Christ*!"

David nodded. "Although if there was a little more Jesus in the world, there might be a lot less stuff like this. You know?"

Peter thought of the millions up through history who had been slaughtered in the name of Jesus, then pushed the thought away and nodded. He didn't think this was quite the time for a theological argument with his neighbor.

"I want to get them inside, Dave," Kirsten murmured. "Off the street, 'kay?"

David nodded, started up the hill again past Peter, then stopped and looked back. "Where's Mary?"

"Work," Peter said. "She left a note to say she was probably going to swing by the Crossroads Mall on her way home. She should be here any time, though—Mondays are her short days, she's off at two. Why?"

"I'd make sure she comes right inside, that's all. The guy's probably long gone and hard to find, but you never know, do you? And a guy who'd shoot a *paperboy*—"

Peter was nodding. Overhead, thunder boomed loudly. Ellie cringed against her mother's leg, but in the wagon, Ralphie laughed.

Kirsten tugged David's arm. "Come on. And *don't*

stop to talk to Doc." She lifted her chin toward Billingsley, who was standing in the dry gutter with his hands in his pockets and peering down the street. Squinting as he was, his eyes were reduced to a pair of bright blue gleams, like exotic fish caught in nets of flesh.

David started pulling the wagon again. "How you doin', Ralphie?" Peter asked as the wagon rolled past him. He noted the word BUSTER was written on the wagon's side in fading white paint. Ralphie stuck his tongue out and made the wasp-in-the-jar sound again, blowing so hard that his cheeks bulged out like Dizzy Gillespie's.

"Hey, that's charming," Peter said. "That'll get you girls later in life. Trust me."

"Bugger-doody!" the little scamp in the wagon cried, and made a rather mature jacking-off gesture at Peter with one hand.

"That'll be enough of that, big guy," David said indulgently, without turning around. His buttocks worked back and forth in the too-small bathing suit. To Peter they looked like biscuits on pistons.

"What happened?" Tom asked in his gruff voice as the wagon passed by.

Peter tuned out Carver's reply (David, mindful of his wife's concern, kept moving as he filled in the Doc) and looked up toward the corner for any sign of his wife's Lumina. He saw no moving vehicles at all, only a parked van just this side of the Abelsons' house on Bear Street. It was painted a yellow so bright it all but screamed. He supposed that part of its brightness derived from the way the light was fading as the clouds advanced, but still, looking at it made his eyes ache. Must be kids, he thought. No one else would *want* something that color. It hardly looked like a real vehicle at all, more like something out of a *Star Trek* movie, or—

An idea suddenly hit him. Not a very good one.

"Dave?"

Carver looked back, his sunburned belly hanging over the front of his bathing suit, scales of soap from his car-washing operation drying on it.

"What was he driving, the guy who shot Cary?"

"A red van."

"That's right," Ralphie chipped in. "Red like Tracker Arrow."

Peter hardly heard this. He was stuck on the word *van,* feeling his own stomach tighten up like something attached to a crank.

"The reddest red van you ever saw," Kirsten added. "I saw it, too. I was looking out the window and I saw it go by. David, will you *come on*?"

"Sure," he said, and began pulling the wagon again. When David turned away, Peter (his momentary disquiet passing) suddenly stuck his tongue out at Ralphie, who just happened to be looking at him. Ralphie looked comically surprised.

Old Doc strolled down to Peter, hands still in his pockets. Thunder rolled. They looked up and saw dark shelves of clouds overspreading Poplar Street's portion of the sky. Lightning stabbed forks at downtown Columbus.

"Going to rain a bitch," the veterinarian said. His hair was thin, white, baby-fine. "I hope they'll get the boy's body decently covered before it comes." He paused, took one hand out of his pocket, and passed it slowly over his brow, as if to soothe away the beginnings of a headache. "Terrible thing. He was a fine lad. Played ball."

"I know." Peter thought of the way Cary had laughed when he, Peter, had told him that next year it would be his turn to howl at shortstop, and felt a sudden pain in his stomach, the organ (not the heart, as the poets had always claimed) most attuned to humankind's tender emotions. Suddenly it was all perfectly real to him. Cary Ripton wasn't going to be the Wentworth Hawks' starting shortstop next summer; Cary Ripton wasn't going to swing in through the back door tonight, asking what was for supper. Cary Ripton had flown off to Never-Never Land, leaving his shadow behind. He was one of the Lost Boys now.

Thunder bammed again, the sound so close and splintery this time that Peter jumped. "Look," he said to Tom. "I've got a big sheet of plastic in my garage. The size of a car-cover, almost. If I got it, would you come down the street and help me cover him with it?"

"Officer Entragian might not like that," the old man said.

"Screw Officer Entragian, he's no more a cop than I am," Peter said. "They fired his ass last year for graft."

"The other police, though, when they come—"

"I don't care about them, either," Peter said. He wasn't crying, exactly, but his voice had thickened and was no longer quite steady. "He was a nice kid, a really *lovely* kid, and some drugrunner shot him off his bike like an Indian off his pony in a John Ford movie. It's going to rain and he'll get soaked. I'd like to tell his mother I did what I could. So do you want to help me or not?"

"Well, since you put it like that," Tom said. He clapped Peter on the shoulder. "Come on, Teach, let's do it."

"Good man."

5

Kim Geller slept through the whole thing. She was still sleeping on the coverlet of her bed when Susi and Debbie Ross—the redhead with whom Cary Ripton had been so taken—came rushing into her bedroom and shook her awake. She sat up, muzzy and feeling almost hungover (sleeping on dog-hot days like this one was almost always a mistake, but sometimes you just couldn't help it), trying to follow what the girls were saying and losing the thread of it almost at once. They seemed to be telling her that someone had been shot, shot on *Poplar Street*, and that was of course fantastic.

Still, when they got her over to the window, it seemed undeniable that *something* had happened. The Reed twins and Cammie, their mother, were standing at the end of their driveway. The Lush and the Bitch, known as the Sodersons in politer circles, were standing right in the middle of the street up by the end of the block . . . although now Marielle was tugging Gary in the direction of their house, and he seemed to be going. Beyond them, standing together on the sidewalk, were the Josephsons. And, across the way, she saw Peter Jackson and old man Billingsley coming out of the Jackson garage, carrying a great big piece of blue plastic between them. The wind was starting to rise, and the sheet of plastic was rippling.

Everyone on the street, just about. Everyone that was home, anyhow. It was no good trying to get a look at what they were gawking at from here, either. The side of the house cut off any view down the block to the corner.

Kimberly Geller turned back to the girls, trying hard to clear the cobwebs out of her mind. The girls were dancing from foot to foot as if they had to go to the bathroom; Debbie, she saw, was snapping her hands open and closed. They were both pale and excited, a combination Kim didn't care for very much. But the idea that someone had been *killed* . . . they had to be wrong about that . . . didn't they?

"Now tell me what happened," she said. "No faking."

"Someone killed Cary Ripton, we *told* you!" Susi cried impatiently, as if her mother were the dumbest thing in the world . . . which, at this particular moment, Kim felt herself to be. "Come on, Mom! We can watch the police come!"

"I want to see him again before someone covers him up!" Debbie yelled suddenly. She turned and raced off down the stairs. Susi paused for a moment, looking dubious—looking almost sick, in fact—then turned and followed her friend.

"Come on, Mom!" she called back over her shoulder, and then was thundering down the stairs, this spring's Rose Queen at the high-school prom and every bit as graceful as a water buffalo, making the windows rattle and the overhead light-fixture tingle.

Kim walked slowly across to the bed and slipped her bare feet into her sandals, feeling slow and late and confused.

6

"And you ran all the way down there?" Belinda Josephson asked for the third time. This seemed to be the part of the story she couldn't quite get straight. "Fat as *you* are?"

"Shit, woman, I'm not fat," Brad said. "*Large* is what I am."

"Honey, that's what they'll put on your death certificate, if you do many more of those hundred-yard dashes," Belinda said. " 'The victim died of terminal *largeness*.' " The words were nagging, the tone was not. She rubbed the back of his neck as she spoke, feeling the chilled sweat there.

He pointed down the street. "Look. Pete Jackson and Old Doc."

"What are they doing?"

"Going to cover up the boy, I think," he said, and started in that direction.

She yanked him back at once. "No you don't, my friend. No *sir* no *way*. You've had your trip downstreet for the day."

He gave her what Belinda thought of as his Don't Diss Me Woman look—a pretty good one for a Boston-raised black man whose chief knowledge of ghetto life came from TV—but made no argument. Perhaps he would have if Johnny Marinville hadn't come down his walk just then. More thunder boomed. A steady breeze was blowing now. It felt cold to Belinda—showery-cold. There were purplish thunderheads rolling in overhead, ugly but not scary. What *was* scary—a little, anyway—was the yellow sky off to the southwest. She hoped to God they weren't going to see a tornado funnel between now and dark; that would add the final touch to a day that had gone about as wrong as any day in recent memory.

She supposed that the rain would drive people indoors once it started, but for now just about everybody on the street was out, gawking down the hill at Entragian's house. As she watched, Kim Geller came out of 243, looked around, then walked one house up to join Cammie Reed on the Reeds' front porch. The Reed twins (the stuff of which harmless housewife-fantasies were made, in Belinda Josephson's humble opinion), along with Susie Geller and a dishy redhead Belinda didn't know, were standing on the lawn. Davey Reed was kneeling and appeared to be wiping his feet with his shirt, God knew why—

Of *course* you know why, she told herself. There's a body down there, all right, there really is, and Davey

Reed vomited at the sight of it. Vomited and got some on himself, poor kid.

She saw people in front of every house or *from* every house except the old Hobart place, which was empty, the ex-cop's house, and 247, the third house down on their side of the street. The Wyler place. There was a bad-luck family if there had ever been one. Neither Audrey nor the poor orphan child she was raising (not that a boy like Seth could ever exactly be *raised,* Belinda supposed; that was just the hell of it) were outside. Gone for the day? Maybe, but she was sure she'd seen Audrey as late as noon, lackadaisically setting up her lawn sprinkler. Belinda mulled this over and decided she had the time about right. She remembered thinking that Audrey was letting herself go—both the shell top and the blue shorts she'd been wearing had looked dingy, and why the woman had ever dyed her perfectly nice brunette hair that horrible shade of purplish-red, Belinda would never know. If it was supposed to make her look young, it was a miserable failure. It needed washing, too—had a greasy, clumped-up look.

As a teenager, Belinda had occasionally wished she were white—the white girls always seemed to be having more fun, and to be more relaxed—but now that she was pushing on toward fifty and menopause, she was very glad to be black. White women seemed to need so much more *putting together* as they went on. Maybe their glue was just not naturally strong.

"I tried to call the cops," Johnny Marinville was saying. He stepped out into the street as if he meant to cross over to the Josephsons, then stopped. "My phone . . ." He trailed off, seemingly unsure of how to continue. Belinda found this *extremely* odd. She'd have thought this was one fellow who would keep on rattling even on his own deathbed; God would have to reach down and carry him through the golden door just to shut him up.

"Your phone what?" Brad asked.

Johnny paused yet a moment longer, seeming to sort through a variety of responses, then settled on a brief one. "It's dead. You want to try yours?"

"I can," Brad said, "but I imagine Entragian's already called them from the store. He pretty much took over."

"*Did* he?" Marinville said thoughtfully, and looked down the hill. "Did he indeed?" If he saw the two men with the rippling tarp between them and understood what they were up to, he didn't say. He seemed lost in his own musings.

Movement caught Belinda's eye. She looked up Bear Street and saw an olive-green Lumina approaching the intersection. Mary Jackson's car. It passed the yellow van parked near the corner, then slowed.

Made it back before the rain, good for you, Belinda thought. Although they were far from bosom buddies, she liked Mary Jackson as much as anyone on the street. She was funny and had a strutty, no-bullshit way about her . . . although just lately she seemed preoccupied a lot of the time. It hadn't gone to her looks like it had with Audrey Wyler, though. In fact Mary had just lately seemed to be blooming, like a dry flowerbed after a shower.

7

The pay-phone was by the newspaper rack, which was empty except for one lonely left-over copy of *USA Today*'s weekend edition and a couple of *Shoppers*. Last week's. It gave Collie Entragian a queer, thoughtful feeling to realize that the boy who would have restocked the rack with a supply of the current issue was lying dead on his lawn. And meanwhile, this lousy convenience-store pay-telephone—

He slammed it into its cradle and walked back to the counter, using the towel to wipe the last of the shaving cream from his face. The cutiepie with the tu-tone hair and the aging hippie-type from the Ryder truck were both watching him, and he was acutely aware that he was minus his shirt. He felt more like a cashiered cop than ever.

"Damn pay-phone doesn't work," he told the girl. He saw she was wearing a little name-badge pinned to her smock. "Don't you have an out-of-order sign, Cynthia?"

"Yeah, but it was working fine at one o'clock," she said. "The bakery guy used it to call his girlfriend." She rolled her eyes, then said something which Collie found almost surreal, under the circumstances: "Did you lose your quarter?"

He had, but it didn't much matter, under the circumstances. He looked through the E-Z Stop's door and saw Peter Jackson and the retired vet from up the street, approaching his lawn with a large piece of blue plastic. It was obvious that they meant to cover the body. Collie started toward the door, meaning to tell them to stand the hell clear, that was an evidence-scene they were getting ready to screw around with, and then the thunder rolled again—the loudest blast so far, loud enough to make Cynthia cry out in surprise.

Fuck, he thought. Let them go ahead. It's going to rain, anyhow.

Yes, maybe that would be best. The rain would very likely come before the cops got here (Collie didn't even hear any sirens yet), and that would play hell with any hypothetical forensics. So, better to cover it . . . but he still had a dismaying feeling of events racing out of his control. And even that, he realized, was an illusion: nothing about the situation had ever been in his control to start with. He was, basically, just another citizen of Poplar Street. Not that that didn't have its merits; if he fucked up the procedure, they couldn't very well put it in his jacket, could they?

He opened the door, stepped out, and cupped his hands around his mouth so as to be heard above the rising wind. "Peter! Mr. Jackson!"

Jackson looked over, face set, expecting to be told to quit what he was doing.

"Don't touch the body!" he called. *"Do not touch the body!* Just kind of shake that thing down over him like it was a bedspread! Have you got that?"

"Yes!" Peter called. The vet was also nodding.

"There are some cement blocks in my garage, stacked up by the back wall!" Collie yelled. "The door's unlocked! Get them and use them to weight down the tarp so it won't blow away!" They were both nodding now, and Collie felt a little better.

"We can stretch it to cover his bike, as well!" the old man called. "Should we?"

"Yes!" he called back, then had another idea. "There's a piece of plastic in the garage, too—in the corner. You can use it to cover the dog, if you don't mind carrying some more blocks."

Jackson flashed him a thumb-and-forefinger circle, then the two of them started for the garage, leaving the tarp behind. Collie hoped they would get it spread and anchored before the wind strengthened enough to blow it away. He went back inside to ask Cynthia if there was a store phone—there had to be, of course—and saw she had already put it on the counter for him.

"Thanks."

He picked it up, heard the dial-tone, tapped four numbers, then had to stop and shake his head and laugh at himself.

"What's wrong?" the hippie-type asked.

"Nothing." If he told the guy he'd just dialled the first four numbers of his old squadroom—like a retired horse clipclopping back to the old firebarn—he wouldn't understand. He tapped the cutoff button and dialled 911 instead.

The phone rang once in his ear . . . and it *did* ring, as

if he had called a residence. Collie frowned. What you got when you dialled 911—unless they had changed it since the days when listening to the recordings had been part of his job—was a high toneless *bleep* sound.

Well, they *did* change it, that's all, he thought. Made it a little more user-friendly.

It started to ring again and then was picked up. Only instead of getting the 911 robot, telling him what button to press for what emergency, he got soft, wet, snuffly breathing. What the *hell*—?

"Hello?"

"Trick or treat," a voice responded. A young voice and somehow eerie. Eerie enough to send a scamper of gooseflesh up his back. "Smell my feet, give me something good to eat. If you don't, I don't care, you can smell my underwear." This was followed by a high, adenoidal giggle.

"Who is this?"

"Don't call here no more, partner," the voice said. *"Tak!"*

The click in his ear was deafening, so deafening the girl heard it, too, and screamed. Not the phone, he thought. Thunder. She's screaming at thunder. But the guy with the long hair was breaking for the door like his hair was on fire and his ass was catching, the phone was dead in his hand, as dead as the pay-telephone had been even after he dropped his quarter, and when the sound came again, he recognized it for what it was: not thunder but more gunfire.

Collie ran for the door, too.

8

Mary Jackson had left the accounting firm where she worked part-time not at two but at eleven. She hadn't gone to the Crossroads Mall, though. She had gone to the Columbus Hotel. There she had met a man named Gene Martin, and for the next three hours she had done everything for him a woman could possibly do for a man except cut his toenails. She supposed she would have done that, too, if she had been asked. And now here she was, almost home and looking (at least as far as she could tell from the rearview mirror) pretty much put together . . . but she was going to have to get into the shower fast, before Peter got too good a look at her, maybe. And, she reminded herself, she would need to take a pair of panties out of her top drawer to throw into the hamper along with her skirt and blouse. The pair she had been wearing—what was left of them—were currently residing under the bed in room 203. Gene Martin, a wolf in accountant's clothing if ever there had been one, had ripped them right off her. Ooo you beast, quoth the maiden fair.

The question was, what was she doing? And what was she *going* to do? She had loved Peter for the nine years of their marriage, even more after the miscarriage than before, if that was possible, and she still loved him. That didn't change the fact that she already wanted to be with Gene again, doing things she had never even considered doing with Peter. Guilt was freezing half of her mind, lust was frying the other half, and in between, in a kind of shrinking twilight zone, was the reasonable, good-humored, rational woman she had always considered herself to be. She was having an adulterous affair, and the guy she was having it with was just as damned married as she was; she was on her way home to a good man who suspected nothing (she was sure he didn't, prayed he didn't, of *course* he didn't, how could he) with no underwear on under her skirt, she was still sore from their adventures, she didn't quite know how all this had started or how she could want to continue anything so stupid and sordid, goddam Gene Martin didn't have a brain in his head, except of course it wasn't his *head* she was interested in, she could have cared less about his *head*, and what was she going to do? She didn't know. She only knew one thing for sure, and that was how drug addicts felt, and she would never put them down again in her life. Just say no? Mother, *please*.

She drove with these chaotic thoughts swimming in her mind, the suburban streets passing like landmarks in a dream, hoping only that Peter wouldn't be home when she got there, that he would have maybe gone over to Milly's on the Square for ice cream (or maybe to Santa Fe to visit his mother for a few weeks, that would be great, that would maybe give her a chance to work through this awful fever). She didn't notice the way the afternoon was darkening or the fact that many of the cars that passed her on the 290 were using their headlights; she didn't hear the thunder or see the lightning. Neither did she see the yellow van parked near the corner of Bear and Poplar when she passed it.

What jerked her out of her reverie was seeing Brad and Belinda Josephson out in front of their house. Johnny Marinville was with them. Farther down the block she saw more people: David Carver, wearing a bathing suit that looked almost obscenely tight, standing on his walk, hands planted on his meaty hips . . . the Reed twins . . . Cammie, their mother . . . Susie Geller and a friend on their lawn with Kim Geller standing behind them . . .

A wild thought came to her: they *knew.* All of them *knew.* They were waiting for her, they were going to help Peter hang her from a sour apple tree or perhaps stone her the way the townspeople had stoned the woman in that Shirley Jackson story she'd read back in high school.

Don't be stupid, the part of her that still *belonged* to her said. That part was dismayingly small these days, but it was still there. It's not *all* about you, Mare; no matter what shit you've been rolling in, the world still doesn't revolve just around *you,* so why don't you just lighten up a little? You probably wouldn't be half so paranoid if you weren't riding around with no—

Oh shit. Was that *Peter* down at the end of the block? She couldn't tell for sure, but she thought so. Peter and Old Doc from next door. They seemed to be covering something on the lawn of the house across from the little store.

Thunder bammed this time hard enough to make her jump and gasp. The first drops of rain spattered onto the glass of the windshield, sounding like flecks of metal. She realized she had been sitting here at the corner with the engine idling for . . . well, she didn't know just how long, but for quite awhile. The Josephsons and Johnny Marinville must have thought she'd lost her wits. Except the world really *didn't* revolve just around her; they weren't paying her any attention at all, she saw as she turned the corner. Belinda had given her that one little glance, and now she and the rest of them were looking back down the street again, at whatever her husband and old Billingsley were doing. At whatever they were covering.

Trying to see for herself, groping for the windshield-wiper knob as more raindrops—big ones—began to spatter the glass, she didn't have any idea that the yellow space-age van had followed her onto Poplar Street until it rear-ended her.

From Playthings, The International Merchandising Magazine of the Toy Industry, *January 1994 (Vol. 94, No. 2), p. 96. Excerpted from "Licensing '94: An Overview," by John P. Muller:*

Although the selling year has barely begun, one post-Christmas winner has already been crowned by acclamation. Retail response in the usually torpid late-winter months suggests that even such blockbuster licensing deals as those associated with the Teenage Mutant Ninja Turtles and Mighty Morphin' Power Rangers may pale beside the newest craze, which any parent of a 2–8 year-old (girls as well as boys in this case) could tell you is the *MotoKops 2200* crew and their racy, spacey vans.

NBC's Saturday-morning cartoon epic began manufacturing in all major product categories about three weeks too late to catch the major Christmas wave of buying. John Kleist, senior V.P. at Good Palz, Inc., which licenses the MotoKop products, acknowledges that such a miss (in this case occasioned by labor problems, now solved, in the Palz Toledo plant) is usually the smooch of death, but says the late-selling push for the MotoKops may have actually worked in the company's favor. "Sometimes the market sees you more clearly when you show up for the first time outside of Santa's workshop," Kleist opined with a smile.

Whatever the reason, it seems clear that MotoKops Colonel Henry, Snake Hunter, Bounty, Major Pike, Rooty the Robot, and the tough-but-all-girl Cassandra Styles are going to be *the* hot action figures this summer, along with arch-enemies No Face and Countess Lili Marsh.

Chief delight for Palz marketers and manufacturers is the immediate success of the pricey MotoKop vehicles, the so-called Power Wagons, futuristic vans which come with fold-up wheels and stubby extendable wings. Colonel Henry's yellow Justice Wagon, Snake Hunter's red Tracker Arrow, Rooty's silver Rooty-Toot, and Cassie Syles's Mary Kay-pink Dream Floater are all selling well despite hefty pricetags. Overall best-seller of the eight currently on the market is the dead black Meatwagon, piloted by the sinister No Face. This doesn't surprise veep John Kleist at all. "Kids love the bad guys," he laughs.

Some parental groups have protested what they term "the high violence quotient" of the *MotoKops 2200* toon but according to Kleist, new *MotoKops* episodes (which begin on NBC in March) will emphasize "family values and peaceful solutions," Whatever values end up being conveyed to the MotoKops' fans, one can certainly feel the euphoria in the offices of Good Palz. This tiny company seems to have found itself holding a very large winning ticket. ▲

CHAPTER 4

Poplar Street/4:09 P.M./July 15, 1996

He sees everything.

That has been both his blessing and his curse in all his years—the world still falls on his eye as it falls upon the eye of a child, evenly, unchosen, as impartial as the weight of light.

He sees Mary's Lumina at the corner and knows she is trying to puzzle out what she's seeing—too many people standing in stiff, watching attitudes which don't jibe with a lazy late afternoon in July. When she starts to roll again, he sees the yellow van which is now behind her also starting to roll, hears another vicious crack of thunder, and feels the first cold splashes of rain on his hot forearms. As she starts down the street, he sees the yellow van suddenly speed up and knows what's going to happen, but he still can't believe it.

Watch out, old boy, he thinks. You get too busy watching her and you're apt to get run down like a squirrel in the road.

He steps back, up on the sidewalk in front of the Josephsons' house, head still turned to the left, eyes wide. He sees Mary behind the wheel of her Lumina, but she isn't looking at him—she's looking down the street. Probably recognized her husband, the distance wasn't too far to do that, probably wondering what he's doing, and she isn't seeing Johnny Marinville, isn't seeing the weird yellow van with the polarized glass windows looming behind her, either.

"Mary look out!" he yells. Brad and Belinda, now mounting their front steps, wheel around. At the same moment, the van's high, blunt front end crashes into the rear of the Lumina, splintering the taillights, snapping the bumper and crimping the trunk. He sees Mary's head snap back and then forward, like the head of a flower on a long stalk pushed back and forth by a high wind. The Lumina's tires scream, and there is a loud dry bang as the right front blows out. The car veers left, the flat tire flapping, the hubcap running off the rim and streaking down the street like the Reed kids' Frisbee.

Johnny sees everything, hears everything, feels everything; input floods him and his mind insists on lining up each crazy increment, as if something coherent were happening here, something which could actually be narrated.

The stormy sky is coming apart, starting to release its cold reservoir. He sees spots darkening all over the sidewalk, feels drops hitting the back of his neck in an increasing tempo as Brad Josephson shouts "What the *Christ*!" behind him.

The van is still on the Lumina's ass, bulldozing it, digging into its flimsy New Age back deck; there is a hideous metallic squall and then a *thunk!* as the trunk latch lets go and the lid flies up, disclosing a spare tire, some old newspapers, and an orange styrofoam cooler. The Lumina's front end bounces up over the curb. The car crosses the sidewalk and comes to rest with its bumper against the fence between Billingsley's house and the next one down the hill, Mary's own.

Lightning—it's close, very close—paints the street a momentary lurid violet, thunder follows like a mortar barrage, the wind begins to pick up, hissing in the trees, and the rain starts coming in sheets. Visibility is closing down fast, but there's enough for him to see the yellow van picking up speed, racing away into the rain, and to see the Lumina's driver's-side door open. A leg sticks out and then Mary Jackson emerges, looking as if she has absolutely no idea of where she is.

Brad is gripping his arm now with a very large and very wet hand, he's asking if Johnny saw that, if he saw it, that yellow van *deliberately rammed her*, but Johnny barely hears him. Johnny can now see *another* van, this one with scooped sides and metal-flake blue paint. It comes looming out of the storm like the snout of a prehistoric beast, the rain running in rivers down a steep polarized windshield on which no wipers move. And suddenly he knows what is going to happen.

"Mary!" he screams at the dazed woman staggering away from her car on high heels, but another brazen cannonade of thunder drowns out his cry. She doesn't even look his way. Rain is running down her face like extravagant tears in a South American soap opera.

"MARY, GET DOWN!" screaming so loud this time he thinks his vocal cords may rupture. *"GET UNDER THE CAR!"*

Then the windshield of the blue van goes down. *Slides* down. Yes. That steep windshield slides into the front of the van like the front of a glass elevator, and behind it is darkness, and in the darkness there are ghosts. Ghosts. Yes. Two of them. Surely they *must* be ghosts; they are beings as brightly gray as a fog-shrouded landscape just before the sun burns its way through. The one behind the wheel is wearing a Confederate States of America uniform—Johnny is almost sure of this—but it is not human. Beneath its pinned-back cavalry hat is a bulging forehead, weird almond-shaped eyes, and a mouth that pulses out from its face like a fleshy horn. Its companion, although also a bright and illusory gray, at least looks human. He wears a buckskin trapper's shirt with a bandolier belt across it. His face is stubbled with what might be a week's growth of beard; the bristles look very black against the unnatural silver of his skin. He is standing, this fellow, and in his hands is a heavy double-barrelled shotgun. Trapper John raises it as Johnny watches, leaning out into a teeming, streaming world full of colors he does not in the slightest share, and he is grinning, lips drawing back to reveal a mouthful of tangled teeth which have clearly never known a dentist's ministrations. This dreamlike creature looks like something from a horror movie about inbred cretins living far back in some swamp.

No he doesn't, Johnny thinks. He looks like something from a movie, all right, but not that one.

"MARY!" he screams, and beside him, Brad joins in: *"YO, MARY, LOOK OUT BEHIND YOU!"*

But she never sees. The guy in the buckskin shirt opens up, firing three times, pumping his weapon rapidly after each shot and then reshouldering it. The first round goes wild, as far as Johnny can see. The second erases the Lumina's radio aerial. The third blows off the left side of Mary Jackson's head. She staggers away from her car and toward Old Doc's house nevertheless, blood pouring down her neck and soaking the left side of her blouse, her hair briefly burning in the rain (he sees this, he sees everything), and then for a moment she turns in Johnny's direction and looks at him with her one remaining eye and the lightning flashes, filling that eye with fire; in the last second or two of her life she is empty of everything but electricity, it seems. Then she stumbles out of one of her high heels and falls backward, swandives into the sound of thunder, the brief low flames in her hair going out, her head still smoking like the tip of an indifferently butted cigarette. She sprawls near the ceramic German shepherd on Billingsley's lawn, the one with his name and the number of his house on it, and as her legs relax apart Johnny sees something which is terrible and sad and inexplicable, all at the same time: a dark shadow that can only be one thing. Grotesquely, the punchline of an old joke goes on for a moment in his head like a neon sign: *I don't know about the other two, but the guy in the middle looks like Willie Nelson.* He laughs out loud in the rain. Peter Jackson's accountant wife has just been killed by a ghost, shot from a van piloted by another ghost (this one the ghost of an alien in a Sesech uniform), and the lady has died drawerless. None of this is funny, but he laughs just the same. Maybe to keep himself from screaming. He's afraid that if he starts doing that, he won't be able to stop.

Now the shining creature behind the wheel of the blue van turns toward him and for just a moment Johnny sees it looking at him, marking him with its huge almond eyes, and he has a sense of *having seen this thing before,* insanity, of course, but the feeling is nevertheless very strong. It is only for a moment and then the van is past.

But he saw me, all right, Johnny thinks. That thing in the mask (it *must* have been a mask) saw me, and it marked me, the way you might turn down the corner of a book-page for later reference.

The shotgun goes off twice more, and at first Johnny can't see what this is about, because the blue van is in the way—he thinks he can hear shattering glass over the roar of the storm, but that's all. Then the van is retreating into the teeming, driving rain and he sees David Carver lying dead in his driveway in a litter of glass from the blown-in picture window. There's a huge red puddle in the center of Carver's stomach, it is surrounded by gobbets of torn white flesh that looks like suet, and Johnny reckons that Carver's days as a postal worker—not to mention his days as a suburban car-washer—are over.

The blue van rolls rapidly up to the corner. By the time it gets there and turns right on Bear Street, it looks to Johnny like the mirage it should by all rights have been.

"Christ, lookit him!" Brad screams, and runs into the street.

"Bradley, no!" His wife grabs for him, but she's too late. Down the street, angling toward them, are the Reed twins.

Johnny walks out into the street on numb, unsteady legs. He raises a hand, sees that the fingertips are already white and pruney (he sees it all, yes indeed, and how could a guy in a *Close Encounters* alien mask possibly look *familiar*), and swops his soaked hair out of his eyes. Lightning jags across the sky like a bright crack in a dark mirror; thunder chases it. His feet are squelching in his sneakers, and he can smell damp gunsmoke. It'll be gone in another ten or fifteen seconds, he knows, driven to earth and then washed away by the pounding rain, but for the time being it's still there, as if to keep him from even *trying* to believe it was all just a hallucination . . . what his ex-wife Terry called "a brain-cramp."

And yes, he can see Mary Jackson's pussy, that highly sought-after part of the female anatomy that was known, in those dim old junior high school days, as "the bearded clam." He doesn't want to be thinking this—doesn't want to be seeing what he's seeing, for that matter—but he's not in charge. All the barriers in his mind have fallen, the way they used to when he was writing (it was one of the reasons he had quit writing novels, not the only one, but a biggie), time's passage slowing as perception grows, widening until it's like being in a Sergio Leone movie where people die the way people swim in underwater ballets.

Little bitty baby Smitty, he thought, again hearing the voice from the telephone. *I seen you bite your mommy's titty.* Why should that voice remind him of the man in the bizarre costume and even more bizarre almond-eyed alien mask?

"What in the name of Jesus H. Sodapop Christ happened?" a voice asks from beside him. The others have converged on David Carver, but Gary Soderson has come over here, onto Old Doc's lawn. With his pale face and scrawny body, he looks like a man suffering from mid-stage cholera. "Holy shit, Johnny! I see Paris, I see France, but I don't see her—"

"Shut up, you drunken asshole," Johnny says. He looks to his left and sees the Reed twins and their mother, Kim Geller and her daughter, plus a redhead he doesn't know at all. They are gathered around David Carver's body like ballplayers clustered around an injured teammate. Gary's shrew of a wife is also there, but she's spied Gary and is now drifting in the direction of *chez* Billingsley. Then she stops, fascinated, as the Carvers' door smashes open and Kirstie comes flying out into the pelting rain like the governess in an old gothic novel, shrieking her husband's name as the lightning flashes and the thunder rolls.

Slowly, like a stupid child who has been called upon to recite, Gary says: "*What* did you call me?" He isn't looking at Johnny, though, or even at the crowd on the Carvers' lawn; he is looking at what the dead woman's hiked-up skirt has revealed, storing it up for later reference (and, perhaps, conversation). Johnny suddenly feels an almost irresistible urge to punch the man in the nose.

"Never mind, just keep your mouth shut. I mean it." He looks to his right, down the street, and sees Collie Entragian running this way. He appears to be wearing pink plastic shower-sandals. Behind him is a long-haired guy Johnny has never seen before, and the new girl from the market—Cynthia, her name is.

And behind them, quickly outdistancing old Tom Billingsley and closing in on Cynthia, wild-eyed, comes the street's resident expert on James Dickey and the New Southerns.

"Daddy!" A piercing, desolate little-girl shriek: Ellen Carver.

"Get those kids out of here!" Brad Josephson, hard and commanding, God bless him, but Johnny doesn't even look in that direction. Peter Jackson is coming, and there is something here he probably has even less business seeing than he and Gary Soderson, even though Peter has surely seen it before and they haven't. An English teacher's riddle if ever there was one, he thinks. Another crazy old punchline rockets through his head: *Hey mister, your sign fell down!* He can't even remember the fucking joke it came from. He takes one more look around to make sure no one but Gary is paying attention to Mary, and no one is. This is surely a miracle that won't last long. He bends down, turns Mary's hip—how heavy she is now that she's dead, how Christing *heavy*—and her legs fall together. Water runs down the side of one white thigh like rain on a tombstone. He yanks the hem of her skirt, deliberately turned so his action is blocked to the people coming up the hill. Already he can hear Peter bellowing "Mary? *Mary?*" He will have seen her car, of course, the Lumina with its nose against the stake fence.

"Why—" Gary begins, then stops when Johnny looks up fiercely.

"Say anything and I'll punch your lights out," he says. "I mean it."

Gary looks vague—almost doltish—for a moment, and then his face fills first with a goaty sort of understanding, followed by fake solemnity. He makes a zipping motion across his lips, though, and that's good. In the long run Gary will almost certainly talk, but Johnny Marinville has never been less concerned with the long run in his whole life.

He turns toward the Carver house and sees David Reed carrying the little Carver girl—she is shrieking and kicking her legs in vast scissoring motions—toward the house. Pie Carver on her knees, wailing as Johnny heard the village women wail in Vietnam all those years ago (only it doesn't seem that long ago, with the last scent of gunsmoke still on the air); she has her arms around the dead man's neck and David's head is wagging in a horrible way. Even more horrible is the little boy, Ralphie, standing beside her. Under ordinary circumstances he is a ceaseless, tireless noisebox, a pint-sized pisspot of the purest ray sublime, but now he is a wax dummy, staring down at his dead father with a face which appears to be melting in the rain. No one is taking him away because it's his sister making the noise for a change, but someone should be.

"Jim," Johnny says to the other Reed twin, walking to the back of Mary's car so he can be heard without having to shout. The boy looks up from the dead man and the wailing woman. His face is dazed.

"Take Ralphie inside, Jim. He shouldn't be here."

Jim nods, picks the boy up, and trots up the walk with him. Johnny expects shrieks of protest—even at six, Ralphie Carver knows it is his destiny to run the world someday—but the boy only hangs in the big teenager's arms like a doll, his eyes huge and unblinking. Johnny believes the influence of childhood trauma on the lives of adults has been wildly overrated by a generation that listened to too many Moody Blues records in its formative years, but something like this must be different; it will be a long time, Johnny thinks, before the chief behavioral factor in Ralph Carver's life ceases to be the sight of his father lying dead on the lawn and his mother kneeling beside him in the rain, hands locked beneath his neck, screaming his daddy's name over and over, as if she could wake him up.

He thinks of trying to separate Kirsten from the corpse—it'll have to be done sooner or later—but Collie Entragian arrives at the Billingsley house before he can make his move, with the counter-girl from the E-Z Stop right behind him. The girl has pulled ahead of the long-hair, who is puffing badly. The guy isn't as young as his rock-and-roll hair made him look from a distance. Johnny is perhaps most struck by the Josephsons. They are standing at the foot of the Carver driveway, holding hands, looking somehow like a Spike Lee version of *Hansel and Gretel* in the pouring rain. Marielle Soderson passes behind Johnny and joins her husband on the Billingsley lawn. Johnny decides that if Brad and Belinda Josephson can be Hansel and Gretel in Spike's new G-rated joint, Marielle can play the witch.

It's like the last chapter of an Agatha Christie, he thinks, when Miss Marple or Hercule Poirot explains everything, even how the murderer got out of the locked sleeping-car berth after doing the deed. We're all here except for Frank Geller and Charlie Reed, who are still at work. It's a regular block-party.

Except, he realizes, that's not quite true. Audrey Wyler isn't here, and neither is her nephew. The edge of something glimmers in his mind at that. He has a flash memory—*the sound of a kid with a cold,* he had thought—but before he can do more than start to reach for it, wanting to see if it's connected to anything (it *feels* connected, God knows why), Collie Entragian comes over to Mary's car and grabs his shoulder, hard enough to hurt, with one dripping hand. He's looking past Johnny, at the Carver place.

"What—*two?*—how—*Christ!*"

"Mr. Entragian . . . Collie . . ." He tries to sound reasonable, tries not to grimace. "You're breaking my shoulder."

"Oh. Sorry, man. But—" His eyes go back and forth from the shotgunned woman to the shotgunned man, David Carver with tendrils of blood washing down his white, blubbery sides in tendrils. Entragian can't seem to pick one to settle on, and consequently looks like a guy watching a tennis match.

"Your shirt," Johnny says, thinking what a stupendous nonstarter of a conversational gambit this is. "You forgot to put it on."

"I was shaving," Collie replies, and runs his hands through his short, dripping hair. The gesture expresses—as probably nothing else could—a mind that has progressed beyond confusion to a state of almost total distraction. Johnny finds it strangely endearing. "Mr. Marinville, do you have the slightest clue what's happening here?"

Johnny shakes his head. He only hopes that, whatever it was, it's now over.

Then Peter arrives, sees his wife lying in front of Billingsley's ceramic German shepherd, and howls. The sound brings out fresh goosebumps on Johnny's wet arms. Peter falls on his knees beside his wife just as Pie Carver fell on her knees beside her husband, and oh gosh, does John Edward Marinville have a case of Dem Ole Kozmic Vietnam Blues again or what? All we need, he thinks, is Hendrix on the soundtrack, playing "Purple Haze."

Peter grabs her and Johnny sees Gary watching with a kind of frozen fascination, waiting for Peter to roll her body into his arms. Johnny can read Soderson's thoughts as if they were printed on tickertape and running across his brow: *What's he going to make of it? When he rolls her over and her legs flop apart and he sees what he sees, what's he going to make of it? Or maybe it's no big deal, maybe she always goes around that way.*

"*MARY!*" Peter cries. He doesn't turn her (thank God for small favors) but lifts her upper body, getting her into a sitting position. He screams again—no word this time, no vocal shape at all, just a streamer of amazed grief—as he sees the state of her head, half the face gone, half the hair burned off.

"Peter—" Old Doc begins, and then the sky is split by a long lance of electricity flowing down the rain. Johnny spins around, dazzled but still (oh yes of course you bet) seeing perfectly well. Thunder rips the street before the lightning can even begin to fade, so loud that it feels like hands clapped to the sides of his head. Johnny sees the lightning strike the abandoned Hobart place, which stands between the cop's house and the Jacksons' place. It demolishes the decorative chimney William Hobart added last year before his problems started and he decided to put the house up for sale. The lightning also ignites the shake roof. Before the thunder has finished pummelling them, before Johnny even has a chance to identify the flash-fried smell in his nostrils as ozone, the deserted house is wearing a crown of flames. It burns furiously in the driving rain, like an optical illusion.

"Ho-lee shit," Jim Reed says. He's standing in the Carver doorway with Ralphie still in his arms. Ralphie, Johnny sees, has reverted to thumb-sucking. And Ralphie is the only one (besides Johnny himself, that is) who isn't still looking at the burning house. He is looking up the hill, and now Johnny sees his eyes widen. He takes his thumb out of his mouth, and before he begins to shriek in terror Johnny hears two clear words . . . and again, they seem hauntingly, maddeningly familiar. Like words heard in a dream.

"Dream Floater," the boy says.

And then, as if the words were some sort of magical incantation, his waxy, unnatural limpness departs. He begins to scream in fear, and to twist in young Jim Reed's arms. Jim is caught by surprise and drops the boy, who lands on his ass. That must hurt like a bastard, Johnny thinks, heading in that direction without even thinking about it, but the kid shows no sign of pain; only fear. His bulging eyes are still staring up the street as he begins paddling frantically with his feet, sliding back into the house on his bottom.

Johnny, now standing on the edge of the Carver driveway, turns to look, and sees two more vans swinging around the corner from Bear Street. The one in the lead is candy-pink and so streamlined it looks to Johnny like a giant Good & Plenty with polarized windows. On the roof is a radar dish in the shape of a Valentine heart. Under other circumstances it might look cute, but now it only looks bizarre. Curved aerodynamic shapes protrude on either side of the Good & Plenty van. They look like lateral fins or maybe even stubby wings.

Behind this vehicle, which may or may not be called Dream Floater, comes a long black vehicle with a bulging, dark-tinted windshield and a toadstool-shaped housing, also black, on the roof. This ebony nightmare is chased with zigzag bolts of chrome that look like barely disguised Nazi SS insignia.

The vehicles begin to pick up speed, their engines purring with a humming, cyclic bent.

A large porthole irises open in the left side of the pink vehicle. And on top of the black van, which looks like a hearse trying to transform itself into a locomotive, the side of the toadstool slides back, revealing two figures with shotguns. One is a bearded human being. He, like the alien driving the blue van, appears to be wearing the tags and tatters of a Civil War uniform. The thing beside him is wearing another sort of uniform altogether: black, high-collared, dressed with silver buttons. As with the black-and-chrome van, there's something Nazi-ish about the uniform, but this isn't what catches Johnny's eyes and freezes his vocal cords so he is at first unable to cry a warning.

Above the high collar, there seems to be only darkness. He has no face, Johnny thinks in the second before the creatures in the pink van and the dead black one open fire. He has no face, that thing has no face at all.

It occurs to Johnny Marinville, who sees everything, that he may have died; that this may be hell.

Letter from Audrey Wyler (Wentworth, Ohio) to Janice Conroy (Plainview, New York), dated August 18, 1994:

Dear Janice,

Thanks so much for your call. The note of condolence, too, of course, but you'll never know how good it was to have your voice in my ear last night—like a drink of cool water on a hot day. Or maybe I mean like a sane voice when you're stuck in the booby hatch!

Did any of what I said on the phone make sense to you? I can't remember for sure. I'm off the tranks—"Fuck that shit," as we used to say back in college—but that's only been for the last couple of days, and even with Herb pitching in and helping like mad, a lot of the world has been so much scrambled eggs. Things started being that way when Bill's friend, Joe Calabrese, called and said my brother and his wife and the two older kids had been killed, shotgunned in a drive-by. The man, who I've never met in my life, was crying, hard to understand, and *much* too shaken to be diplomatic. He kept saying he was so ashamed, and I ended up trying to comfort *him*, and all the time I'm thinking, "There's got to be a mistake here, Bill can't be dead, my brother was supposed to be around for as long as I needed him." I still wake up in the night thinking, "Not Bill, it's just a goof-up, it *can't* be Bill." The only thing in my whole life I can remember that felt this crazy was when I was a kid and everybody came down with the flu at the same time.

Herb and I flew out to San Jose to collect Seth, then flew back to Toledo on the same plane as the bodies. They store them in the cargo hold, did you know that? Me neither. Nor wanted to.

The funeral was one of the most horrible experiences of my life—probably the most horrible. Those four coffins—my brother, my sister-in-law, my niece, and my nephew—lined up in a row, first in the church and then at the cemetery, where they sat over the holes on those awful chrome rails. Wanna hear something totally nuts? During the whole graveside service I kept thinking of my honeymoon in Jamaica. They have speed-bumps in the road that they call sleeping policemen. And for some reason that's how I started thinking of the coffins, as sleeping policemen. Well, I told you I've been crazy, didn't I? Ohio's Valium Queen of 1994, that's me.

The service at the church was packed—Bill and June had a lot of friends—and everyone was bawling. Except for poor little Seth, of course, who can't. Or doesn't. Or who knows? He just sat there between me and Herb with two of his toys on his lap—a pink van he calls "Dweem Fwoatah" and the action figure that goes with it, a sexy little redhead named Cassandra Styles. The toys are from a show called *MotoKops 2200*, and the names of the damned MotoKops vans (excuse me, the MotoKops *Power Wagons*, lah-di-dah) are among the few things Seth says which are actually understandable ("Doughnuts buy 'em for me" is another one; also "Seth go potty," which means you're supposed to go in there with him—he's trained but very weird about his bathroom habits).

I hope he didn't understand the service meant the rest of his family is dead, gone from him forever. Herb is sure he *doesn't* know ("The kid doesn't even know where he is," Herb says), but I wonder. That's the hell of autism, isn't it? You always wonder, you never really know, they're broadcasting but God hooked them up with a scrambler-phone and nothing's coming through at the receiving end but gibberish.

Tell you one thing—I've gained a new respect for Herb Wyler in the last couple of weeks. He arranged EVERYTHING, from the planes to the obituaries in both the Columbus *Dispatch* and Toledo *Blade*. And to take Seth in as he has, without a word of complaint—not just an orphan but an *autistic* orphan—well, I mean, is it amazing or is it just me? I vote for amazing. And he seems to really care for the poor kid. Sometimes, when he looks at the boy, a preoccupied expression comes into his face that could even be love. The beginnings of it, anyway.

This is even more remarkable, it seems to me, when you realize how little a child like Seth can give back. Mostly he just sits plonked down out there in the sandbox Herb put in as soon as we got back from Toledo, like a big boy-shaped raisin, wearing only his *MotoKops 2200* Underoos (he has the lunchbox, too), mouthing his nonsense words, playing with his vans and the action figures that go with them, especially the sexy redhead in the blue shorts. These toys trouble me a bit, because—if you're not entirely sure I've lost it, this should convince you—*I'm not sure where they came from, Jan!* Seth sure didn't have any such expensive rig the last time I visited Bill and June in Toledo (I checked in Toys R Us, and the *MotoKops* stuff is VERY pricey), I can tell you that. They aren't the sort of toys Bill and Junie would have approved of, anyhow—their toy-buying ideas ran more to Barney than *Star Wars*, much to their kids' disgust. Poor little Seth can't tell me, that's for sure, and it probably doesn't matter, anyway. I only know the names of the vans and the figures that go with them because I watch the cartoon-show with him on Saturday mornings. The chief bad guy, No Face, is *très* creepy.

He's so strange, Jan (Seth, I mean, not No Face, har-har). I don't know if Herb feels that as much as I do, but I know he feels *some* of it. Sometimes when I look up and catch Seth looking at me (he has eyes of such dark brown that sometimes they actually look black), I get the weirdest chill—like someone's using my spine for a xylophone. And some odd things have happened since Seth came to live with us. Don't laugh, but there've even been a couple of incidents like the poltergeist phenomena they sometimes dramatize on what Herb calls "the psycho reality shows." Glasses flying off shelves, a couple of windows that broke seemingly for no reason, and weird wiggly shapes that sometimes appear in Seth's sandbox at night. They're like strange, surreal sand-paintings. I'll send you some Polaroids next time I write, if I think of it. I wouldn't tell *anybody* this stuff besides you, Jan, believe me. Thank God I know and trust your wonder . . . your curiosity . . . your DISCRETION!

Mostly Seth is no trouble. The most annoying thing about having him around is the way he breathes! He takes in air in these big, sloppy gusts, *always* through his mouth, which is always hung open and halfway down to his chest. It makes him look like the village idiot, which he really is not, regardless of the problems he *does* have. Mr. Marinville from across the street was over the other day with a banana cake he baked (he's quite a sweetie for a guy who once wrote a book about a man having a love-affair with his own daughter . . .

and called the book *Delight*, of all things), and he spent some time with Seth, who was taking a sandbox-break to watch *Bonanza.* Remember that one? TNT shows the reruns every weekday afternoon (they call 'em the Afternoon Ponderosa Party, ain't that cute), and Seth just loves 'em. Wessurn, Wessurn, he says, when they come on. Mr. Marinville, who likes to be called Johnny, watched with us for quite awhile, the three of us eating banana cake and drinking chocolate milk like old pals, and when I apologized for Seth's wet breathing (mostly because it drives *me* nuts, of course), Marinville just laughed and said that Seth couldn't help his adenoids. I'm not even sure what adenoids *are,* but I suppose we'll have to have Seth's looked at. Thank God for the Blue twins—Cross and Shield.

One thing keeps nagging me, and that's why I've enclosed a Xerox of the postcard my brother sent me from Carson City shortly before he died. He says on it that they've had a breakthrough—an *amazing* breakthrough is what he says, actually—with Seth. Capital letters, lots of exclamation points. See for yourself. I was curious, natch, so I asked him about it the next time we talked on the phone. That must have been on July 27th or 28th, and it was the last time I spoke to him. His reaction was very peculiar, very unlike Bill. A long silence, then this weird artificial laugh, "ha-ha-ha!" the way it gets written out but the way real laughter hardly ever sounds, except at boring cocktail parties. I never heard my brother laugh like that in his life. "Well, Aud," he sez, "I might have overreacted a little on that one."

He didn't want to say any more on the subject, but when I pressed him he said that Seth seemed brighter, more *with* them, once they got far enough into Colorado to see the Rockies. "You know how he's always loved Western movies and TV shows," he said, and although I didn't then, I sure do now. Nuts for cowboys and posses and cuttin' 'em off at the pass is young Seth Garin. Bill said Seth probably knew he wasn't in the real Old West because of all the cars and campers, but "the scenery still turned him on." That's how Bill put it.

I might have let it go at that if he hadn't sounded so funny and vague, so really unlike himself. You know your own kin, don't you? Or you think you do. And Bill was always outgoing and bubbly or indrawn and pouty. There wasn't much middle ground. Except during that phone call, it seemed to be *all* middle ground. So I kept after him about it, which I wouldn't have done ordinarily. I said that AN AMAZING BREAKTHROUGH sounded like one specific event. So he said that well, yes, something *had* happened not too far from Ely, which is one of the few good-sized towns north of Las Vegas. Just after they went by a road sign pointing the way to a burg called Desperation (charming names they have out there, I must say, makes you just wild to visit), Seth "kinda freaked out." That's how Bill put it. They were on Route 50, the non-turnpike route, and there was this huge ridge of earth on their left, south of the highway.

Bill thought it was sort of interesting, but no more. Seth, though—when he turned in that direction and saw it, he went nuts. Started waving his arms and gabbling in that private language of his. To me it always sounds like talk on a tape that someone is playing backward.

Bill and June and the two older kids went along with him the way they do—*did*—when he gets excited and starts verbalizing, which is rare but far from unheard-of. You know, kind of like Yeah, Seth, you bet, Seth, it sure *is* wild, Seth—and all the time they're doing it, that embankment is slipping farther and farther behind them. Until finally Seth—get this—speaks up, not in gibberish but in English. He *really talks*, says "Stop, Daddy, go back, Seth want to see mountain, Seth want to see Hoss and Little Joe." Hoss and Little Joe, in case you don't remember, are two of the main characters on *Bonanza*.

Bill said it was more real words than Seth had put together in his whole life, and some time spent around Seth has convinced me of how unusual it would be for him to say so much in clear language at one time. *But* . . . AMAZING BREAKTHROUGH? I don't want to be mean or anything, but it was hardly the Gettysburg Address, was it? I couldn't make it jibe then, and I can't now. On his postcard, Bill sounds so pumped he's just about blowing his stack; on the phone he sounded like a pod-person in *The Invasion of the Body Snatchers*. Plus one other thing. On the card he says "more later," as if he can't wait to spill the whole thing, but once I had him on the phone, I just about have to drag it out of him. Weird!

Bill said what happened made him think of an old joke about a couple who think their son is mute. Then one day, when the kid's six or so, he speaks up at the dinner table. "Please, mother, may I have another ear of corn?" he says. The parents fall all over him and ask why he's never spoken up before. "I never had anything to say," he tells them. Bill told me the joke (I'd heard it before, I think back around the time they burned Joan of Arc at the stake) and then gave out with the phony cocktail-party laugh again, ha-ha-ha. Like that closed the subject for good and all. Only I wasn't ready for it to be closed.

"So did you ask him, Bill?" I asked.

"Ask him what?" he says.

"Why he never spoke before."

"But he *does* talk."

"Not like *this*, though. He doesn't talk like *this*, which is why you sent me the excited postcard, right?" I was getting mad at him by then. I don't know why, but I was. "So did you ask him why he hadn't ever strung fifteen or twenty words of clear English together before?"

"Well, no," he says. "I didn't."

"And did you go back? Did you take him to Desperation so he could look for the Ponderosa Ranch or whatever?"

"We really couldn't do that, Aud," he says after another of those long silences. It was like waiting for a chess computer to catch up with a tough move. I don't like to be talking this way about my brother, who I loved and will miss for the rest of my life, but I want you to understand how really strange that last conversation was. The truth? It was hardly like talking to my brother at all. I wish I could explain why that was, but I can't.

"What do you mean, you *couldn't*?" I ask him.

"Couldn't means couldn't," he says. I think he was a little pissed at me but I didn't mind; he sounded a little more like himself, anyway. "I wanted to be sure of getting to Carson City before dark, which we wouldn't have done if I'd turned around and backtracked to that little town he was so excited about. Everyone kept telling me how treacherous 50 can be after sundown, and I didn't want to put my family into a dangerous situation." Like he'd been crossing the Gobi Desert instead of central Nevada.

And that's all there is. We talked a little more and then he said, "Take it easy, babe" the way he always did, and that's the last I'll ever hear from him . . . in this world, at least. Just take it easy, babe, and then he disappeared down the barrel of some travelling asshole's gun. All of them did, except for Seth. The police haven't even been able to identify the caliber of the guns they used yet, did I tell you that? Life is so *unfinished* compared to books and movies! Like a fucking *salad*.

Still, that last conversation nags me. More than anything I keep coming back to that stupid cocktail-party laugh. Bill—*my* Bill—never laughed like that in his life.

I wasn't the only one that noticed he was a little off the beam, either. His friend Joe, the one they were out there visiting, said the whole *family* seemed off, except for Seth. I had a conversation with him at the undertaker's, while Herb was signing the transferral forms. Joe said he kept wondering if they had a virus, or the flu. "Except for the little one," he said. "He had lots of zip, always out there in the sandbox with his toys."

Okay, I've written enough—way, way too much, probably. But think all of this over, would you? Put those good inventive brains of yours to work, because THIS IS REALLY BUGGIN' ME! Talking to Herb is no good; he calls it displaced grief. I thought about talking to J. Marinville from across the street—he seems both kind and perceptive—but I don't know him well enough. So it has to be you. You see that, don't you?

Love you, J-girl. Miss you. And sometimes, especially lately, I wish that we were young again, with all the dirty cards life can deal you still buried well down in the deck. Remember how it was in college, when we thought we'd live forever and only our stupid periods ever caught us by surprise?

I've got to stop or I'll be crying again.

XXX (and tons more),

Andi

CHAPTER 5

1

Standing bare-chested at the bathroom mirror that afternoon before the world dropped into hell like a bucket on a broken string, Collie Entragian had made three large resolutions. The first was to quit going around unshaven on weekdays. The second was to quit drinking, at least until he got his life back on an even keel—he was doing far too much boozing, enough to make him uneasy, and it had to stop. The third was to stop procrastinating about looking for a job. There were three security firms in the Columbus area, people he knew worked for two of them, and it was time to get cracking. He hadn't *died,* after all; it was time to quit yowling and get on with his life.

Now, as the Hobart house burned merry hell down the street and the two bizarre vans approached, all he cared about was holding on to that life. Mostly it was the black vehicle creeping along behind the pink one that galvanized him, that engaged every instinct to immediately relocate, possibly to Outer Mongolia. He didn't catch more than a rain-blurred glimpse of the figures in the black van's turret, but the van itself was enough. It looked like a hearse in a science-fiction movie, he thought.

"Inside!" he heard himself screaming—some part of him apparently still wanted to be in charge. "Everybody inside *now*!"

At that point he lost track of the people clustered around the late postman and his keening, shrieking wife—Mrs. Geller, Susi, Susi's friend, the Josephsons, Mrs. Reed. Marinville, the writer, was a little closer, but Collie lost track of him, too. His focus shrank to the ones in front of Old Doc's bungalow: Peter Jackson, the Sodersons, the store clerk, the longhair from the Ryder truck, and Old Doc himself, who had retired from veterinary practice the year before with absolutely no clue that something like *this* was waiting for him.

"Go!" Collie screamed into Gary's wet, gaping, half-drunk face. In that moment he wanted to kill the man, just haul off and kill him, set him on fire or something. *"Go in the fucking HOUSE!"* Behind him he could hear Marinville screaming the same thing, although it was presumably the Carvers' house he had in mind.

"What—" Marielle began, stepping to her husband's side; then she looked past Gary and her eyes widened. Her splay-fingered hands rose to the sides of her face, her mouth dropped open and for one mad moment

Collie expected her to drop to her knees and start singing "Mammy" like Al Jolson. She screamed instead. And as if that had been all their attackers had been waiting for, the gunfire began—harsh, compact explosions that no one could have mistaken for thunder.

The hippie guy grabbed Peter Jackson by Peter's right wrist and tried to haul him away from his dead wife. Peter didn't want to let go of her. He was still howling, and seemed completely unaware of what was happening around him. There was a KA-POW, as deafening as dynamite, followed by the sound of shattering glass. A KA-BAM, even louder, followed by a shriek of either fear or pain. Collie's dough was on fear . . . *this* time, at least. A third report, and Billingsley's ceramic German shepherd disappeared from the forelegs up. Old Doc's inner front door stood open behind a screen with a scrolly, ornamental *B* in the middle of it. That dark rectangular hole—an opening which might lead to a cave of safety—looked a thousand miles away.

Collie ran for Peter first, with no thought of bravery so much as crossing his mind; it was just where he went first. Another deafening report, and he was tightening his back and buttocks against a potentially lethal hit even while his mind was informing him that one, at least, *was* thunder. The next one wasn't. It was another whiplash KA-POW, and he felt something slap a groove in the air past his right ear.

First time shot at, he thought. Nine years as a cop before they stuck it to me and broke it off—four beat, four plainclothes, one IA—and never shot at until now.

Another report. One of Billingsley's living-room windows blew in, billowing the white curtains like ghost-arms. Guns going off behind him like artillery now, just *bam-bam-bam-bam,* and he felt another hot load go hustling by, this one to the left of his hand, and a black hole appeared in the siding below the broken window. To Collie the hole looked like a big startled eye. The next one hummed by his hip. He couldn't believe he wasn't dead, just couldn't believe it. He could smell burning cedar shingles and had time to think about October afternoons spent in the backyard with his dad, burning leaves in smouldery aromatic piles.

He had been running for hours, he felt like a goddam ceramic duck in a goddam shooting gallery, and he hadn't even reached Peter Jackson yet, what the fuck was going on here?

It's been five seconds since the shooting started, the colder side of his mind informed him. Maybe only three.

The hippie guy was still yanking Peter's wrist, and now the girl, Cynthia, muckled on above the hippie guy's grip. But Peter was actively resisting them, Collie saw. Peter wanted to stay with his wife, who had chosen a divinely bad time to arrive back home.

Still picking up speed (and he could boogie pretty good when he really wanted to), Collie bent and hooked a hand under the kneeling man's left armpit on the way by. Just call me the mail train, he thought. Peter thrashed backward, trying to stop the three of them from pulling him from his wife. Collie's hand began to slip. Oh fuck, he thought. Fuck us all. Sideways.

There was another shriek from behind him, at the Carvers'. In the corner of his eye he saw the pink van, now past them and speeding up, accelerating down the hill toward Hyacinth Street.

"Mary!" Peter screamed. *"She's hurt!"*

"I got her, Pete, don't worry, I got her!" Old Doc screamed cheerfully, and although he had no one—was, in fact, running past Mary's sprawled body without so much as a glance down at it—Peter nodded, looking relieved. It was the tone, Collie thought. That crazily cheerful tone of voice.

The hippie guy was actually helping now instead of just trying to. He had Peter by the belt, for one thing, and that was working better. "Help out, fella," the hippie guy told Peter. "Just a little."

Peter ignored him. He stared at Collie with huge, glazed eyes. "He's getting her, right? Old Doc. He's helping her."

"That's right!" Collie shouted. He tried for Doc's tone of good cheer—a kind of sprinting bedside manner—and heard only terror. The pink van was gone but the black one was still there, rolling slowly, almost stopped. There were figures—too bright, almost fluorescent—in the turret. "Billingsley—"

Marielle Soderson bashed past him on the left, almost knocking Collie flat in her sprint toward Old Doc's front door. Gary blew by on the right, hitting the store-girl with his shoulder and knocking her to one knee. She cried out in pain, mouth pulling down in a bow-shape as something—probably her ankle—twisted. Gary did not so much as spare her a glance; his eyes were on the prize. The girl was up again in a flash. The pain-grimace was still on her face but she was holding gamely to Peter's arm, still trying to help out. Collie was gaining an appreciation for her, schizo tu-tone hair or not.

Onward sprinted the Sodersons. It had taken them a moment or two to get the general idea, but it had certainly clicked for them now, Collie saw.

There was another report. The longhair shouted in surprise and pain, grabbing at his right leg. Collie saw blood, amazingly bright in the gray gloom of the storm, seeping through his fingers. The girl was staring at him, her mouth open, her eyes wide.

"I'm okay," the hippie said, regaining his balance. "It's just a graze. Go on, go on!"

Peter was finally finding his feet, both literally and metaphorically. "What in the fuck . . . is going on?" he asked Collie. He sounded drugged.

Before Collie could say anything, there was a final shot from the black van and a sound—he would have sworn it—like the whistle of an artillery shell. Marielle Soderson, who had reached the stoop (Gary had already disappeared inside, no gentleman he), screamed and staggered sideways against the door. Her left arm flew bonelessly upward. Blood splashed Doc's aluminum siding; the rain began to wash it down the side of the house in membranes. Collie heard the store-girl scream, and felt a little like screaming himself. The slug had taken Marielle in the shoulder and torn her left arm almost entirely off her body. It flopped back down and dangled precariously from a glistening knot of flesh with a mole on it. It was the mole—a flaw Gary might have lovingly kissed in his younger, less pickled days—that made it somehow real. She stood in the doorway, shrieking, her left arm hanging beside her like a door which has been ripped off two of its three hinges. And behind her, the black van now also accelerated down the hill, the turret sliding closed as it went. It disappeared into the rain and the billowing smoke from the empty Hobart house, where the roof was now sharing its gift of fire with the walls.

2

She had a place to go.

Sometimes that seemed like a blessing, sometimes (because it extended things, kept the hellish game going) like a curse, but either way, it was the only reason she was still *herself,* at least some of the time; the only reason she hadn't been eaten alive from the inside out. The way Herb had been. In the end, though, Herb had been able to find himself one more time. Had been able to hold on to himself long enough to go out to the garage and put a bullet in his brain.

Or so she wanted to believe.

Sometimes, however, she believed otherwise. Sometimes she would think of the endless evenings before the gunshot from the garage and she would see Seth in his chair, the one with the horse-and-rider decals she and Herb had put on when they came to realize just how much the boy loved "Wessurns." Seth just sitting there, ignoring whatever was on TV (unless it was an oat-opera or a space-show, that was), looking at Herb with his horrible mud-brown eyes, the eyes of a creature that has lived its whole life in a swamp. Sitting there in the chair which his aunt and uncle had decorated so lovingly back in the early days, before the nightmare had started. Before they'd *known* it had started, at least. Sitting there and looking at Herb, hardly ever at her, at least not then. Looking at him. *Thinking* at him. Sucking him dry, like a vampire in a horror film. And that was what the thing inside Seth really was, wasn't it? A vampire. And their lives here together on Poplar Street, that was the film. Poplar Street, for God's sake, where there was probably still at least one Carpenters album in every home. Nice neighbors, the kind of folks that drop everything when they hear on the radio that the Red Cross is getting low on O, and none of them knew that Audrey Wyler, the quiet widow who lived between the Sodersons and the Reeds, was now starring in her own Hammer film.

On good days she would think that Herb, whose sense of humor had served as both a shield and a goad to the thing inside of Seth, had held on long enough to escape. On bad ones she knew that was bullshit, that Seth had simply used all of Herb there was to use and had then sent him out to the garage with a self-destruct program flashing away in his head like a neon Schlitz sign in a taproom window.

It *wasn't* Seth, though, not really; not the Seth who had sometimes (in the early days) hugged them and given them brief openmouthed kisses that felt like bursting soap-bubbles. "I 'owboy," he would occasionally say while sitting in the special chair, words rising out of his usual unintelligible babble and making them feel, however fleetingly, that they were getting somewhere: *I'm a cowboy*. That Seth had been sweet; lovable not just in spite of his autism but partly because of it. That Seth had also been a medium, however, like contaminated blood which simultaneously nourishes a virus and transports it.

The virus—the *vampire*—was Tak. A little gift from the Great American Desert. According to Bill, the Garin family had never turned back to Desperation, had never stopped to investigate what was behind the bulwark of earth they had seen from the road, the bulwark that had excited Seth enough for him to briefly transcend his usual gabble and speak in clear English. *We really couldn't do that, Aud,* Bill had said. *I wanted to be sure of getting to Carson City by dark.* But Bill had lied. She knew because of a letter she'd gotten from a man named Allen Symes.

Symes, a geologist-engineer for something called the Deep Earth Mining Corporation, had seen the Garin family on July 24th of 1994, the same day Audrey's brother had sent her the exuberant postcard. Symes had assured her that nothing very interesting had happened, that he had simply taken the Garins to the edge of the open-pit mine (actually going in would have been against MSHA regulations, his letter said) and given them a little history lecture before sending them on their way again. It was a good story, both boring and plausible. Audrey wouldn't have questioned a word of it under ordinary circumstances, but she knew something Mr. Allen Symes of Desperation, Nevada, had not: that Bill had denied stopping at all. Bill said they had simply hurried on their merry way, because he wanted to be sure of getting to Carson City by dark. And if Bill had lied, wasn't it possible—even likely—that Symes had also lied?

Lied about what? Lied about what?

Stop, Daddy, go back, Seth want to see mountain.

Why did you lie to me, Bill?

That was a question she thought she could answer: Bill had lied because Seth had *made* him lie. She thought that Seth had probably been standing right there by the phone during her conversation with Bill, watching the creature it no longer regarded as its father with mud-brown eyes that belonged under a log in some swamp. Bill had been allowed to say only what Tak wanted him to say, like a person who speaks with a gun pointed at his head. He had told his clumsy lies and laughed the unnatural cocktail-party laugh, ha-ha-ha.

The thing in Seth had eventually eaten Herb alive and now it was trying to eat her, but she was apparently different from Herb in one crucial way: *she* had a place to go. She had discovered it perhaps by accident, perhaps with help from Seth—the *real* Seth—and she could only pray that Tak would never discover what she was doing or where she was going. That the monster would never follow her to her sanctuary.

In May of 1982, when she was twenty-one and still Audrey Garin, she and her roommate (who was also her best friend, then and ever), Janice Goodlin, had spent a wonderful weekend—very likely the most perfect weekend of Audrey's life—at Mohonk Mountain House in upstate New York. The trip was a present from Jan's father, who had won some sort of cash award from his company for selling and had been promoted two or three rungs up the corporate ladder in the bargain. If his intention had been to share some of his happiness, he had succeeded splendidly with the two young women.

On the Saturday of that magic weekend they had taken a picnic lunch (packed by the kitchen in a wonderful old-fashioned wicker hamper) and walked for hours, hunting for the perfect spot in which to settle. Usually when you're doing that you don't find it, but they had gotten lucky. It was a beautiful and half-wild upland meadow, rife with buttercups and daisies and wild roses. It hummed with bees; white butterflies danced on the warm air like enchanted confetti which never fell to earth. At one end of this meadow was an eccentric little cupola-shaped thing—Janice said it was called a folly, and they were spotted all over the Mohonk grounds. It was roofed to provide shade and shelter, but open on every side to provide air and view.

The two women had eaten enormously, talked prodigiously, and at three different points laughed so hard that tears ran down their faces. Audrey didn't think she had ever laughed with quite that same heartiness since. She never forgot the long, clear summer light of that afternoon, or the dancing white shreds of the butterflies.

This was the place she returned to when Tak was fully out and fully in command of Seth. This was where she hid, with a Janice who was still Goodlin instead of Conroy, a Janice who was still young. Sometimes she would tell Janice about Seth—how he had come to stay, and how neither she nor Herb had seen or suspected (at least at first) what was inside Seth, a thing that was being very still, watching them and husbanding its strength and waiting for the right time to come out. Sometimes on these occasions she would tell Jan how much she missed Herb and how terrified she was . . . how she felt caught, like a fly in a web or a coyote in a leghold trap.

But that kind of talk felt dangerous, and she tried to stay away from it. Mostly she just replayed the sweet inconsequentialities of that long-ago day when Reagan had still been in his first term and there had been real vinyl records in the record stores. Stuff like whether or not Ray Soames, Jan's current boyfriend, would be a considerate lover (pig-selfish, Jan had reported matter-of-factly three weeks later, just before bidding adieu to Ray's sultry good looks forever), and what sorts of jobs they would have, and how many kids they would have, and who, in their circle of friends, would be the most successful.

Running through it all, large but unspoken—perhaps they hadn't *dared* to speak of it, for fear of ruining it—was their joy in the day, in the unremarkable good health of young women, and their love for one another. It was these things and not her current troubles that Audrey concentrated on when she felt Tak digging into her with its unseen but exquisitely painful teeth, trying to batten on her and feed from her. It was to that day's love and brightness that she fled, and so far it had given her succor and shelter.

So far, she was alive.

More important, so far she was still she.

In the meadow, the confusion and darkness melted away and everything stood *clear:* the splintery gray poles which held up the folly's roof, each casting its thin precise shadow; the table (equally splintered) at which they sat on opposing wooden benches, a table that was deeply carved with initials, mostly those of lovers; the picnic basket, now set aside on the board floor, still open but really finished for the day, the utensils and plastic food-containers neatly packed for the trip back to the hotel. She could see the golden highlights in Jan's hair, and a loose thread on the left shoulder of her blouse. She heard every cry of every bird.

Only one thing was different from the way it had really been. On the table where the picnic hamper had rested until they had repacked it and set it aside, there was a red plastic telephone. Audrey had had one exactly like it at the age of five, using it to hold long and deliriously nonsensical chats with an invisible playmate named Melissa Sweetheart.

On some visits to the folly in the meadow, the word PLAYSKOOL was stamped on the phone's handset. At other times (usually on days that had been particularly horrible, and there were a lot more of those lately), she would see a shorter and much more ominous word stamped there: the name of the vampire.

It was the Tak-phone, and it never rang. At least not yet. Audrey had an idea that if it ever did, it would be because Tak had found her safe and secret place. If it did, she was sure it would be the end of her. She might go on breathing and eating for a little while, as Herb had, but it would be the end of her, nevertheless.

She occasionally tried to make the Tak-phone disappear. It had occurred to her that if she could dispose of it, get rid of the damned thing, she could perhaps escape the creature on the Poplar Street end of her life for good. Yet she couldn't alter the phone's reality, no matter how hard she tried. It *did* disappear sometimes, but never while she was looking at it or thinking about it. She would be looking into Jan's laughing face instead (Jan talking about how she sometimes wanted to leap into Ray Soames's arms and suck his face off, and how sometimes—like when she caught him furtively picking his nose—she wished he would just crawl off into a corner and die), and then she would look back at the table and see that the surface was bare, the little red phone gone. That meant *Tak* was gone, at least for awhile, that he was sleeping (dozing, at least) or had withdrawn. On many of these occasions she came back to find Seth perched on the toilet, looking at her with eyes that were dazed and strange but at least recognizably human. Tak apparently didn't like to be around when its host moved his bowels. It was, in Audrey's view, a strange and almost existential fastidiousness in such a relentlessly cruel creature.

She looked down now and saw the phone was gone.

She stood up, and Jan—that young Jan, still with both breasts intact—stopped her chatter at once and looked at Audrey with sad eyes. "So soon?"

"I'm sorry," Audrey said, although she had no idea if it was soon or late. She'd know when she got back and looked at the clock, but while she was here, the whole concept of clocks seemed ridiculous. The meadow which lay upland of Mohonk in May of 1982 was a no-clock zone, blessedly tickless.

"Maybe someday you'll be able to get rid of that damned phone for good and stay," Jan said.

"Maybe. That would be nice."

But would it? Would it really? She didn't know. And in the meantime, she had a little boy to take care of. And something else: she wasn't quite ready to give up yet, which was what coming to live permanently in May of 1982 would mean. And who knew how she would feel about the upland meadow if she could never leave it? Under those circumstances, her haven might become her hell.

Yet things were changing, and not for the better. For one thing Tak wasn't weakening, as she had perhaps foolishly hoped it would with the passage of time; Tak was, if anything, getting stronger. The TV ran constantly, broadcasting the same tapes and recycled series programs (*Bonanza, The Rifleman* . . . and *MotoKops 2200*, of course) over and over. The people on the shows had all begun to sound like lunatic demagogues to her, cruel voices exhorting a restless mob to some unspeakable action. Something was going to happen, and soon. She was almost sure of it. Tak was planning something . . . if it could be said to plan, or even to think at all. Perhaps *change* was too mild a word. It felt like things were going to turn upside down and inside out, the way they did in an earthquake. And if they did, *when* they did—

"Escape," Jan said, and her eyes flashed. "Stop thinking about it and *do* it, Aud. Open the front door while Seth's sleeping or shitting and run like hell. Get out of the house. Get the fuck away from that thing."

It was the first time Janice had ever presumed to give her advice, and it shocked her. She had no idea at all how to answer. "I'll . . . think about it."

"Better not think long, kiddo—I've got a feeling you're almost out of time."

"I ought to go." She took another flustered glance down at the table to make sure the PlaySkool phone was still gone. It was.

"Yes. All right. Bye, Aud." Jan's voice seemed to come from a great distance now, and she was fading like a ghost. As the color went out of her, she began to look more like the woman who was waiting for her to catch up, a woman with one breast and a narrow, often ungenerous point of view. "Come again soon. We'll talk about *Sergeant Pepper*, maybe."

"All right."

Audrey stepped out of the folly, looking downhill

toward the rock wall with the wild pink roses growing along it, watching the white butterflies pirouette. Thunder rumbled across a hazy blue sky. God was sending a shower in from the Catskills, and no surprise; nothing as perfect as this afternoon could be allowed to last for long. *Nothing gold can stay . . .* which poet had said that? Frost? It didn't matter. Janice Goodlin Conroy had found out it was true as well as poetic. So, in time, had Audrey Garin.

She turned back to look for the stormclouds, but instead of spring thunderheads over the Catskills she saw her own living room, dingy and in need of cleaning, dust under every piece of furniture, every glass surface bleared with fingerprints, cooking grease, spilled soda, or all three. The air smelled of sweat and heat, but mostly it smelled of canned spaghetti and old fried hamburger, which was all her strange boarder seemed to want to eat.

She was back.

She was cold, too. She looked down at herself and saw she was wearing nothing but shorts and a pair of sneakers. Blue shorts, of course, because blue shorts were what Cassandra Styles wore most of the time, and Cassie was Seth's favorite MotoKop. Her hands, wrists, ankles, and calves were all filthy. The plain white sleeveless blouse she had put on that morning (before it took control of her; she had been in and out since then, but mostly Tak had been in charge, running her like his private electric train set) was now tossed indifferently on the couch. Her nipples throbbed.

He's been making me pinch myself again, she

thought as she walked across to the sofa and picked up the blouse. Why? Because Cary Ripton, the kid who delivered the *Shopper*, had seen her without her top on? Yes, maybe. Probably. It was hazy, as always, but she was pretty sure that was it. Tak had been angry . . . the punishment had started . . . and away she had gone, to those fabulous days of old. As soon as he'd gone back into the den to watch his goddam movie again.

The pinching scared her a lot. The pain had been worse on other occasions, not to mention the crappy little humiliations—Tak was an artist when it came to those—but there was a clear sexual aspect to the nipple-pinching. And there was the way she was dressed . . . or undressed. More and more Tak was making her take her clothes off when it was angry with her, or just bored. As if it (or Seth, or both of them) sometimes saw her as its own private gatefold version of the tough but unremittingly wholesome Cassie Styles. Hey, kids, check out the tits on your favorite MotoKop!

She had almost no insight into the relationship between the host and the parasite, and that made her situation even worse. She thought Seth was a lot more interested in buckaroos than in breasts; he was only eight, after all. But how old was the thing inside him? And what did it want? There were possibilities, things far beyond pinching, that she didn't want to consider. Although, not long before Herb died—

No. She wouldn't think about that.

She slipped the blouse on and did up the buttons,

glancing at the clock on the mantel as she did so. Only 4:15; Jan had been right to say *so soon*. But the weather had certainly changed, Catskills or no Catskills. Thunder rolled, lightning flashed, and rain pelted so furiously against the living room's picture window that it looked like smoke.

The TV was playing in the den. The movie, of course. The horrible, hateful movie. They were on their fourth copy of *The Regulators*. Herb had brought the first one home from The Video Clip at the mall about a month before his suicide. And that old film had been, in some way she still didn't understand, the final piece in the puzzle, the final number in the combination. It had freed Tak in some way . . . or *focused* it, the way a magnifying lens can focus light and turn it into fire. But how could Herb have known that would happen? How could either of them have known? At that time they had barely suspected Tak's existence. It had been working on Herb, yes, she knew that now, but it had been doing so almost as silently as a leech that battens on a person below the waterline.

"You want to try me, Sheriff?" Rory Calhoun was gritting.

Murmuring under her breath, unaware she was doing it, Audrey said, "Why don't we just stand down? Think this thing over?"

"Why don't we just stand down?" John Payne said from the TV. Audrey could see light from the screen flickering against the curved arch between the two rooms. "Think this thing over?"

She tiptoed to the arch, tucking the blouse into the

waistband of her blue shorts (one of roughly a dozen pairs, all dark blue with white piping on the side-seams, there was certainly no shortage of blue shorts here at *casa* Wyler), and looked in. Seth was on the couch, naked except for a grimy pair of MotoKops Underoos. The walls, which Herb had panelled himself in first-quality finished pine, had been stippled with spikes Seth had found in Herb's garage workshop. Many of the pine boards were split vertically. Poked onto these badly pounded nails were pictures which Seth had cut from various magazines. They were mostly of cowboys, spacemen, and—of course—MotoKops. Interspersed among them was a scattering of Seth's own drawings, mostly landscapes done with black felt-tip pens. On the coffee table in front of him were glasses scummed with the residue of Hershey's chocolate milk, which was all Seth/Tak would drink, and jostling plates with half-eaten meals on them. All the meals were Seth's favorites: Chef Boyardee spaghetti and hamburger, Chef Boyardee Noodle-O's and hamburger, and tomato soup with big chunks of hamburger rising out of the gelling liquid like baked Pacific atolls where generations of atomic bombs had been tested.

Seth's eyes were open but blank—both he and Tak were gone, all right, maybe recharging the batteries, maybe sleeping open-eyed like a lizard on a hot rock, maybe just digging the goddamned movie in some deep and elemental way Audrey would never be able to comprehend. Or want to. The simple truth was that she didn't give a shit where he—it—was. Maybe she could get a meal in peace; that was enough for her. *The*

Regulators had about twenty minutes left to run in this, its nine-billionth showing at *casa* Wyler, and Audrey thought she could count on at least that long. Time for a sandwich and maybe a few lines in the journal Tak might well kill her for keeping—if Tak ever found out about it, that was.

Escape. Stop thinking about it and do it, Aud.

She stopped halfway back across the living room, the salami and lettuce in the fridge temporarily forgotten. That voice was so clear that for a moment it didn't seem to be coming from her mind at all. For one moment she was convinced that Janice had somehow followed her back from 1982, was actually in the room with her. But when she turned, wide-eyed, there was no one. Only the voices from the TV, Rory Calhoun telling John Payne that the time for talking was done, John Payne saying "Well now, if that's the way you want it." Very soon Karen Steele would run between them, screaming at them to stop it, just stop it. She would be killed by a bullet from Rory Calhoun's gun, one meant for John Payne, and then the final shootout would begin. KA-POW and KA-BAM all the way home.

No one here but her and her dead friends on the TV.

Open the front door and just run like hell.

How many times had she considered it? But there was Seth to think about; he was as much a hostage as she was, and maybe more. Autistic he might be, but he was still a human being. She didn't like to think what Tak might do to him, if it was crossed. And Seth *was* still there, all of him—she knew that. Parasites feed on their hosts but don't kill them . . . unless it's on purpose. Because they're pissed off, maybe.

She had herself to think about, too. Janice could talk about escape, just opening the door and running like hell, but what Janice perhaps didn't understand was that if Tak caught her before she was able to get away, it would almost certainly kill her. And if she *did* get out of the house, how far would she have to go before she was safe? Across the street? To the bottom of the block? Terre Haute? New Hampshire? Micronesia? And even in Micronesia, she didn't think she would be able to hide. Because there was a mental link between them. The little red PlaySkool phone—the Tak-phone—proved that.

Yes, she wanted to get away. Oh yes, so much. But sometimes the devil you knew was better than the devil you didn't.

She started for the kitchen again, then stopped again, this time staring at the big window with its view of the street. She had thought the rain was pelting the glass hard enough to look like smoke, but actually the first fury of the storm was already passing. What she was seeing didn't just *look* like smoke; it *was* smoke.

She hurried to the window, looked down the street, and saw that the Hobart place was burning in the rain, sending big white clouds up into the gray sky. She saw no vehicles or people around it (and the smoke itself obscured her view of the dead boy and dog), so she looked up toward Bear Street. Where were the police cars? The fire engines? She didn't see them, but she saw enough to make her cry out softly through hands—she didn't know how they had gotten there—that were cupped to her mouth.

A car, Mary Jackson's, she was quite sure, was on the grass between the Jackson house and Old Doc's place, its nose almost up against the stake fence between the two properties. The trunk-lid was popped, and the rear end looked trashed. The car wasn't what had made her cry out, though. Beyond it, sprawled on Doc's lawn like a fallen piece of statuary, was a woman's body. Audrey's mind made a brief attempt to persuade her it was something else—a department-store mannequin, perhaps, dumped for some reason on Billingsley's lawn—then gave it up. It was a body, all right. It was Mary Jackson, and she was as dead as . . . well, as dead as Audrey's own late husband.

Tak, she thought. Was it Tak? Has it been out?

You knew it's been getting ready for something, she thought coldly. You *knew* that. You've felt it gathering its forces, always in the sandpile playing with those damned vans or in front of the TV, eating hamburger meals, drinking chocolate milk, and watching, watching, watching. You've felt it, like a thunderstorm building up on a hot afternoon—

Beyond the woman, at the Carvers' house, were two more bodies. David Carver, who had sometimes played poker with Herb and Herb's friends on Thursday nights, lay on his front walk like a beached whale. There was an enormous hole in his stomach above the bathing suit he always wore when he washed the car. And, lying face-down on the Carver stoop, there was a woman in white shorts. Yards of red hair spilled out around her head in a frizzy corona. Rain glistened on her bare back.

But she's not a woman, Audrey thought. She felt cold all over, as if her skin had been briskly rubbed with ice. That's just a girl, probably no more than seventeen. The one who was visiting over at the Reeds' this afternoon. Before I went away to 1982 for a little while. That was Susi Geller's friend.

Audrey glanced down the block, suddenly sure she was imagining the whole thing, and that reality would snap back into place like a released elastic as soon as she saw the Hobart place standing intact. But the Hobart place was still burning, still sending huge white clouds of cedar-fumed smoke into the air, and when she looked back up the street, she still saw bodies. The corpses of her neighbors.

"It's started," she whispered, and from the den behind her, like a horribly prescient curse, Rory Calhoun screamed: *"We're gonna wipe this town off the map!"*

Escape! Jan screamed back, a voice inside her head instead of from the TV, but just as urgent. *You're not just about out of time, not anymore, you are out of it! Escape, Aud! Escape! Run! Escape!*

Okay. She'd let go of her concern for Seth and run. That might come back to haunt her later—if there *was* a later—but for now . . .

She started for the front door and was reaching for the knob when a voice spoke up from behind her. It sounded like the voice of a child, but only because it was coming to her through a child's vocal cords. Otherwise it was toneless, loveless, hideous.

Worst of all, it was not entirely without a sense of humor.

"Hold on, there, ma'am," Tak said, the voice of Seth Garin imitating the voice of John Payne. "Why don't we just stand down, think this thing over?"

She tried to turn the doorknob, meaning to chance it anyway—she had gone too far to turn back now. She would hurl herself out into the pelting rain and just run. Where? Anywhere.

But instead of turning the knob, her hand fell back to her side, swinging like a nearly exhausted pendulum. Then she was turning around, resisting with all her will but turning anyway, to face the thing in the archway leading into the den . . . and she thought, considering what spent most of its time in there, *den* was exactly the right word for what the room had become.

She was back from her safe place.

God help her, she was back from her safe place, and the demon hiding inside her dead brother's autistic little boy had caught her trying to escape.

She felt Tak crawling inside her head, taking control, and although she saw it all and felt it all, she couldn't even scream.

3

Johnny lunged past the sprawled, face-down body of Susi Geller's redheaded friend, his head ringing from a slug which had screamed past his left ear . . . and it really *had* seemed to scream. His heart was running like a rabbit in his chest. He had moved far enough in the direction of the Carvers' house to be caught in a kind of no-man's-land when the two vans opened fire, and knew he was extremely lucky to still be alive. For a moment there he had almost frozen, like an animal caught in a pair of oncoming headlights. Then the slug—something that had felt the size of a cemetery headstone—had gone past his ear and he had streaked for the open door of the Carver house, head down and arms pumping. Life had simplified itself amazingly. He had forgotten about Soderson and his goaty expression of half-drunk complicity, had forgotten his concern that Jackson not realize his freshly expired wife was apparently coming home from the sort of interlude about which country-western songs were written, had forgotten Entragian, Billingsley, all of them. His only thought had been that he was going to die in no-man's-land between the two houses, killed by psychotics who wore masks and weird outfits and shone like ghosts.

Now he was in a dark hall, just happy to realize he hadn't wet his pants, or worse. People were screaming somewhere behind him. Mounted on the wall was a jury of Hummel figures. They had been placed on little platforms . . . and the Carvers had seemed so normal in other respects, he thought. He started to giggle and shoved the heel of one hand against his lips to stifle the sound. This was definitely not a giggling situation. There was a taste on his skin, just the taste of his own sweat, of course, but for a moment it seemed almost to be the taste of pussy, and he leaned forward, sure he was going to vomit. He realized he would almost certainly pass out if he did and that thought helped him to control the urge. He took his hand away from his mouth, and that helped more. He no longer felt much like laughing, either, and that was probably good.

"My *daddy*!" Ellen Carver was howling from behind him. Johnny tried to remember if he had ever—in Vietnam, for instance—heard such piercing, keening grief coming out of such a young throat and couldn't. *"My DADDY!"*

"Hush, honey." It was the new widow—Pie, David had always called her. Still sobbing herself but already trying to comfort. Johnny closed his eyes, trying to get away from it like that, and instead his hideous memory showed him what he had just stepped over—*lunged* over, really. Susi Geller's friend. A little red-headed girl, just like in the *Peanuts* comic strip.

He couldn't leave her out there. She had looked as dead as Mary and poor old Dave, but he had leaped over her like Jack over the candlestick, his ear screaming from the near miss and his balls drawn up and as hard as a couple of cherrystones, not a state in which a man could make a reasonable diagnosis.

He opened his eyes. A Hummel girl wearing a bonnet and holding a shepherd's crook was giving him a dead china come-on. Hey, sailor, want to comb some wool with me? Johnny was leaning against the wall on his forearms. One of the other Hummel figures had fallen off its little platform and lay in shards at his feet. Johnny supposed he had knocked it off himself while he had been struggling not to puke and trying to get that awful punchline—I don't know about the other two, but the guy in the middle looks like Willie Nelson—out of his head.

He looked slowly to his left, hearing the tendons in his neck creak, and saw the Carvers' front door still standing open. The screen was ajar; the redhead's hand, white and still as a starfish cast up on a beach, was caught in it. Outside, the air was gray with rain. It came down with a steady hissing sound, like the world's biggest steam iron. He could smell the grass, like some sweet wet perfume. It was spiced with a tang of cedar smoke. God bless the lightning, he thought. The burning house would bring the police and the fire engines. But for now . . .

The girl. A little redheaded girl, like the one Charlie Brown was so crazy for. Johnny had jumped right over her, gripped by the blind impulse to save his own ass. Understandable in the heat of the moment, but you couldn't leave it that way. Not if you wanted to sleep at night.

He started for the door. Someone grabbed his arm. He turned and saw the intent, fearful face of Dave Reed, the dark-haired twin.

"Don't," Dave said in a conspirator's hoarse whisper. His Adam's apple went up and down in his throat like something in a slot. "Don't, Mr. Marinville, they could still be out there. You could draw fire."

Johnny looked at the hand on his arm, put his own

hand over it, and gently but firmly removed it. Behind Dave he could see Brad Josephson watching him. Brad's arm was around his wife's considerable waist. Belinda appeared to be quivering all over, and there was a lot of her to quiver. Tears were streaming down her cheeks, leaving shiny mocha tracks.

"Brad," Johnny said. "Get everybody who's here into the kitchen. I'm pretty sure that's the farthest room from the street. Sit them on the floor, okay?" He gave the Reed boy a gentle push in that direction. Dave went, but slowly, with no rhythm in his walk. To Johnny he looked like a windup toy with rust in the gears.

"Brad?"

"Okay. Don't you go getting your head blown off, now. There's been enough of that already."

"I won't. I'm attached to it."

"Just make sure it stays attached to you."

Johnny watched Brad, Belinda, and Dave Reed go down the hall toward the others—in the gloom they were just clustered shadows—and then turned back to the screen door. There was a fist-sized hole in the upper panel, he saw, with jags of torn screen curling in from the edges. Something bigger than he wanted to think about (something almost the size of a cemetery headstone, perhaps) had come through there, miraculously missing his clustered neighbors . . . or so he hoped. None of them were screaming with pain, anyhow. But Jesus, what in God's name had the guys in the vans been shooting? What was that big?

He dropped to his knees and crawled toward the

cool, wet air coming through the screen. Toward that good smell of rain and grass. When he was as close as he could get, with his nose almost on the mesh, he looked to the right and then to the left. To the right was good—he could see almost all the way up to the corner, although Bear Street itself was lost in a haze of rain. Nothing there—no vans, no aliens, no loonies dressed like refugees from Stonewall Jackson's army. He saw his own house next door; remembered playing his guitar and indulging all his old folkie fantasies. Ramblin Jack Marinville, always headed over the next horizon-line in those thirsty Eric Andersen boots of his, lookin for them violets of the dawn. He thought of his guitar now with a longing as sharp as it was pointless.

The view to the left wasn't as good; was lousy, in fact. The stake fence and Mary's crashed Lumina blocked any significant sight-line down the hill. Someone—a sniper in Confederate gray, say—could be crouched down there almost anywhere, waiting for the next good target. A slightly used writer with a lot of old coffeehouse fantasies still knocking around in his head would do. Probably no one there, of course—they'd know the cops and the F.D. would be here any minute and would have made themselves scarce—but *probably* just didn't seem good enough under these circumstances. Because none of these circumstances made sense.

"Miss?" he said to the sprawled tangle of red hair on the other side of the screen door. "Hey, miss? Can you hear me?" He swallowed and heard a loud click in his throat. His ear was no longer screaming, but there was a steady hum deep inside it. Johnny had an idea he was going to be living with that for awhile. "If you can't talk, wiggle your fingers."

There was no sound, and the girl's fingers didn't wiggle. She didn't appear to be breathing. He could see rain trickling down her pale redhead's skin between the strap of her halter and the waistband of her shorts, but nothing else seemed to be moving. Only her hair looked alive, lush and vibrant, about two tones darker than orange. Drops of water glistened in it like seed pearls.

Thunder rumbled, less threatening now, moving off. He was reaching for the screen door when there was a much sharper report. To Johnny it sounded like a small-caliber rifle, and he threw himself flat.

"That was just a shingle, I think," a voice whispered from close behind him, and Johnny cried out in surprise. He turned and saw Brad Josephson behind him. Brad was also on his hands and knees. The whites of his eyes were very bright in his dark face.

"What the fuck're you doing here?" Johnny asked.

"White Folks' Fun Patrol," Brad said. "Somebody's got to make sure you guys don't have too much of it—it's bad for your hearts."

"Thought you were going to get the rest of them in the kitchen."

"And there they be," Brad said. "Sitting on the floor in a neat little line. Cammie Reed tried the phone. It's dead, just like yours. Probably the storm."

"Yeah, probably."

Brad looked at the mass of red hair on the Carvers' stoop. "She's dead, too, isn't she?"

"I don't know. I think so, but . . . I'm going to ease the screen door open, try to make sure. Any objections?"

He rather hoped Brad would say hell yes, he had objections, a whole damn *book* of them, but Brad only shook his head.

"You better stay low while I do it," Johnny said. "We're okay on the right, but on the left I can't see past Mary's car."

"I'll be lower than a garter-snake in a stamping press."

"I hope you're never in a writing seminar I teach," Johnny said. "And watch out for that broken china widget—don't cut your hand."

"Go on," Brad said. "If you're going to do it, do it."

Johnny pulled the screen door open. He hesitated, not sure how to proceed, then picked up the girl's cold starfish hand and felt for a pulse. For a moment there was nothing, and then—

"I think she's alive!" he whispered to Brad. His voice was harsh with excitement. "I think I feel a pulse!"

Forgetting that there might still be people with guns lurking out there in the rain, Johnny yanked the screen wide, grabbed a handful of the girl's hair, and lifted her head. Brad was crowded into the doorway with him now; Johnny could hear his excited breathing, could smell mingled sweat and aftershave.

The girl's face came up, except it didn't, not really, because there was no face there. All he could see was a shattered mass of red and a black hole that had been her mouth. Below it was a litter of white that he at first thought was rice. Then he realized it was her teeth, what was left of them. The two men screamed together in perfect soprano harmony, Brad's shooting directly into Johnny's humming ear like a spike. The pain seemed to go all the way into the middle of him.

"What's wrong?" Cammie Reed cried from behind the swinging door that led into the kitchen. "Oh God, what's wrong now?"

"Nothing," the two men said, also together, and then looked at each other. Brad Josephson's face had gone a queer ashy color.

"Just stay back," Johnny called. He wanted it to be louder, but couldn't seem to get any real volume into his voice. "Stay in the kitchen!"

He realized he was still holding the dead girl's hair. It was kinky, like an unravelled Brillo pad—

No, he thought coldly. Not like that. Like what holding a scalp would be like, a human scalp.

He grimaced at that and opened his fingers. The girl's face dropped back onto the concrete stoop with a wet smack that he could have lived without. Beside him, Brad moaned and then pressed the inner part of his forearm against his mouth to stifle the sound.

Johnny pulled his hand back, and as the screen door swung closed, he thought he saw movement across the street, in the Wyler house. A figure moving in the living room, behind the picture window. He couldn't worry about the people over there now, though. He was currently too freaked to worry about anybody, including himself. What he wanted—the only thing in the world he *did* want, it seemed—was to hear the warble of approaching police cars and fire trucks.

All he did hear was thunder, the crackle of the fire at the Hobarts', and the hiss of falling rain.

"Leave—" Brad began, then stopped and made a sound caught somewhere between a retch and a swallow. The spasm passed and he tried again. "Leave her."

Yes. What else, at least for now, was there?

They began to retreat down the hall on their hands and knees. Johnny went backward at first, then swung around, brushing the splinters of the fallen Hummel figure with his moccasins. Brad was already past the doorway to the Carver dining room and most of the way to the kitchen, where his wife, also on her knees, waited for him. Brad's considerable rear end wagged back and forth in a way Johnny might have considered comical under other circumstances.

Something caught his eye and he stopped. There was a small decorative table by the entrance to the dining room where David Carver would never preside over another Thanksgiving turkey or Christmas goose. This table had been loaded down with, gee, what a surprise, a dozen or so Hummel figures. The table wasn't standing flat but leaning back against the wall to the right of the door, like a drunk dozing against a lamppost. One of its legs had been sheared off. The Hummel shepherdesses and milkmaids and farmboys were now mostly on their backs or faces, and there were more china fragments under the table where one or more had fallen off and shattered. Among the painted pieces there was something else, something black. In the gloom, Johnny first took it for the corpse of some huge dead bug. Another crawling pace disabused him of that idea.

He looked back over his shoulder at the fist-sized hole in the upper panel of the screen door. If a slug had made that, one running the last part of a downward trajectory—

He traced the course such a hypothetical slug might have taken and saw that, yes, it could have sheared off the table-leg, knocking the table itself back into that posture of leaning drunken surprise. And then, its force spent, come to rest?

Johnny reached into the litter of china, hoping he wouldn't cut himself (his hand was shaking badly, and concentration would not still it), and picked up the black object.

"What you got?" Brad asked, crawling toward Johnny.

"Brad, you get back here!" Belinda whispered fiercely.

"Hush, now," Brad told her. "What you got there, John?"

"I don't know," he said, and held it up. He supposed he *did* know, actually, had known almost as soon as he had determined that it wasn't the remains of some weird summer beetle. But it was like no fired slug he had ever seen in his life. It wasn't the one that had taken the girl's life, that much seemed certain; it would have been flattened and twisted out of shape.

This thing didn't seem to have so much as a scratch on it, although it had been fired, had gone through a panel of the screen door, and had sheared off the table-leg.

"Let me see," Brad said. His wife had crawled up beside him and was looking over his shoulder.

Johnny dropped it into Brad's pale palm, a black cone about seven inches long from its tip, which looked sharp enough to cut skin, to its circular base. He guessed it was about two inches in diameter at its widest point. It was solid black metal, and completely unmarked, so far as Johnny could see. There were no concentric rings stamped into the base, no sign of a firing point (no bright nick left by the firing pin of the gun which had thrown it, for that matter), no manufacturer's name, no caliber stamp.

Brad looked up. "What in the *hell*?" he asked, sounding as bewildered as Johnny felt.

"Let me see," Belinda said in a low voice. "My father used to take me shooting, and I was his good little helper when he did reloads. Give it over."

Brad passed it to her. She rolled the metal cone between her fingers, then held it up to her eyes. Thunder banged outside, the sharpest peal in the last few minutes, and they all jumped.

"Where'd you find it?" she asked Johnny.

He pointed at the litter of china under the leaning table.

"Yeah?" She looked skeptical. "How come it didn't go into the wall?"

Now that she posed the question, he realized what a good one it was. It had only gone through a screen and a flimsy table-leg; why *hadn't* it gone into the wall, leaving just a hole behind?

"I've never seen anything like this puppy in my life," Belinda said. "Of course, I haven't seen *everything,* far from it, but I can tell you that this didn't come from a pistol or a rifle or a shotgun."

"Shotguns are what they were firing, though," Johnny said. "Double-barrelled shotguns. You're sure this couldn't—"

"I don't even know how it was launched," she said. "There's no firing nipple on the bottom, that's for sure. And it's so *clunky*. Like a kid's idea of what a bullet looks like."

The swing-door between the hall and the kitchen opened, banging against the wall and startling them even more badly than the thunder had done. It was Susi Geller. Her face was horribly white, and to Johnny she looked all of eleven years old. "There's someone screaming next door, at Billingsley's," she said. "It sounds like a woman, but it's hard to tell. It's scaring the kids."

"All right, honey," Belinda said. She sounded perfectly calm, and Johnny admired her for that. "You go on back in the kitchen, now. We'll be along in a second."

"Where's Debbie?" Susi asked. Her view down the hall to the stoop was mercifully blocked by the wide-bodied Josephsons. "Did she go next door? I thought she was right behind me." She paused. "You don't think that's her screaming, do you?"

"No, I'm sure it's not," Johnny said, and was appalled to find himself once more on the edge of crazy laughter. "Go on, now, Suze."

She went back into the kitchen, letting the door close behind her. The three of them looked at one another for a moment with sick conspirators' eyes. None of them said anything. Then Belinda handed the gawky-looking black cone back to Johnny, duck-walked past him to the kitchen door, and pushed it open. Brad followed on his hands and knees. Johnny looked at the slug a moment longer, thinking of what the woman had said, that it was like a kid's idea of a bullet. She was right. He had visited his share of lower-elementary-school classrooms since beginning to chronicle the adventures of Pat the Kitty-Cat, and he had seen a lot of drawings, big grinning mommies and daddies standing under yellow Crayola suns, weird green landscapes festooned with bold brown trees, and this looked like something that had fallen out of one of those pictures, whole and intact, somehow made real.

Little bitty baby Smitty, a voice said way back in his mind, but when he tried to chase after that voice, wanting to ask if it really knew something or was just blowing off its bazoo, it was gone.

Johnny put the slug in his right front pants pocket with his car keys and then followed the Josephsons into the kitchen.

4

Steven Jay Ames, pretty much of a scratched entry in the great American steeplechase, had a motto, and this motto was

NO PROBLEM, MAN.

He had gotten D's in his first semester at MIT—this in spite of SAT scores somewhere in the ionosphere—but, hey,

NO PROBLEM, MAN.

He had transferred from electrical engineering to general engineering, and when his grades still hadn't risen past the magical 2.0 point, he had packed his bags and gone down the road to Boston University, having decided to give up the sterile halls of science for the green fields of English Lit. Coleridge, Keats, Hardy, a little T. S. Eliot. I should have been a pair of ragged claws scuttling across the floors of the universe, here we go round the prickly pear; twentieth-century angst, man. He had done okay at BU for awhile, then had flunked out in his junior year, as much a victim of obsessive bridge-playing as of booze and Panama Red. But

NO PROBLEM, MAN.

He had drifted around Cambridge, hanging out, playing guitar and getting laid. He wasn't much of a guitar-player and did better at getting laid, but

NO PROBLEM, MAN,

really. When Cambridge began to get a tad elderly, he

had simply cased his guitar and ridden his thumb down to New York City.

In the years since, he had scuttled his ragged claws through salesman's jobs, gone around the prickly pear as a disc jockey at a short-lived heavy-metal station in Fishkill, New York, gone around again as a radio-station engineer, a rock-show promoter (six good shows followed by a nightmarish exit from Providence in the middle of the night—he'd left owing some pretty hard guys about $60,000, but

NO REAL PROBLEM, MAN),

as a palmistry guru on the boardwalk in Wildwood, New Jersey, and then as a guitar tech. That felt like home, somehow, and he became a gun for hire in upstate New York and eastern Pennsylvania. He liked tuning and repairing guitars—it was peaceful. Also, he was a lot better at repairing them than he was at playing them. During this period he had also quit smoking dope and playing bridge, which simplified things even further.

Two years before, living in Albany, he had become friends with Deke Ableson, who owned Club Smile, a good roadhouse where you could get a bellyful of blues almost any night you wanted. Steve had first shown up at Smile in his capacity as a freelance guitar tech, then had stepped up when the guy running the board had a minor heart attack. At first that *had* been a problem, maybe the first real one of Steve's adult life, but for some reason he had stuck with it in spite of his fear of fucking up and being lynched by drunk cycle-wolves. Part of it was Deke, who was unlike every club owner Steve had known up until then: he was not a thief, a lecher, or a fellow who could validate his own existence only by making others miserable and afraid. Also, he actually *liked* rock and roll, while most club owners Steve had known loathed it, preferring Yanni or Zanfir and his Pan Flute when they were alone in their cars. Deke was exactly the sort of guy that Steve, who had remembered to file a 1040 form exactly once in his life, really liked: a

ZERO PROBLEMS

kind of guy. His wife was also a good sort, easygoing and equipped with mild, sleepy eyes, a good sense of humor, beautiful breasts, and not, so far as Steve could tell, an unfaithful bone in her body. Best of all, Sandy was also a recovering bridge addict. Steve had had many deep conversations with her about the almost uncontrollable urge to overbid, especially in a money game.

In May of this year, Deke had purchased a very large club—a House of Blues kind of deal—in San Francisco. He and Sandy had left the East Coast three weeks ago. He had promised Steve a good job if Steve would pack up all their shit (albums, mostly, over two thousand of them, anachronisms like Hot Tuna and Quicksilver Messenger Service and Canned Heat) and drive it out in a rental truck. Steve's response:

NO PROBLEM, DEKE.

Hey, he hadn't been out to the West Coast in almost seven years, and he reckoned the change would do him good. Recharge those old Duracells.

It had taken him a little longer than he had expected to settle his Albany shit, get the truck, load the truck, and get rolling. There had been several phone calls from Deke, the last one sort of testy, and when Steve had mentioned this, Deke had said well, that was what three weeks of sleeping bags and making do with the same half a dozen tee-shirts did to a person—was he coming or not? I'm coming, I'm coming, Steve had replied. Cool it, big guy. And he had. Left three days ago, in fact. Everything groovy at first. Then, this afternoon, he had blown a hose or something, he had taken the Wentworth exit in search of the Great American Service Station, and then—whoa, dude—there had come a big bang from under the hood and all the dials on the dashboard started showing bad news. He hoped it was just a blown seal, but it had actually sounded more like a piston. In any case, the Ryder truck, which had been a beauty ever since he had left New York, had suddenly turned into a beast. Still,

NO PROBLEM;

just find Mr. Goodwrench and let him do his thing.

Steve had taken a wrong turn, though, away from the turnpike business area and into a much more suburban neighborhood, not the sort of place where Mr. Goodwrench was apt to hang out during working hours. He had really been babying the truck by then, steam coming out through the grille, oil-pressure dropping, temperature rising, an unpleasant fried smell coming in through the air vents . . . but really

NO PROBLEM, MAN.

Well . . . maybe a

VERY SMALL PROBLEM

for the Ryder people, that was true, but Steve had an idea they'd be able to bear up under the burden. Then—hey, beautiful, baby—a little neighborhood store with a blue pay-phone sign hung over the door . . . and the number to call if you had engine trouble was right up there on the driver's-side sun-visor.

ABSOLUTELY NO PROBLEM,

story of his life.

Only *now* there was a problem. One that made learning the soundboard at Club Smile look like a minor annoyance in comparison.

He was in a little house that smelled of pipe tobacco, he was in a living room with framed photos of animals—pretty special ones, according to the captions—on the walls, a living room where only the huge, shapeless chair in front of the TV looked really used, and he had just tied his bandanna around his leg where he had sustained a bullet-wound, shallow but a bona fide *bullet-wound* just the same, and people were yelling, scared and yelling, and the skinny woman in the sleeveless blouse was also wounded (nothing shallow about hers, either) and outside people were *dead,* and if all this wasn't a problem, then Steve guessed that "problem" was a concept without meaning.

His arm was grabbed above the wrist, and painfully. He wasn't just being grabbed, actually; he was being *pinched.* He looked down and saw the girl in the blue store duster, the one with the crazed hair. "Don't you freak on me," she said in a ragged voice. "That lady needs help or she's going to die, so *do not* freak on me."

"No problem, cookie," he said, and just hearing the words—any words—coming out of his mouth made him feel a little stronger.

"Don't call me cookie and I won't call you cake," she said in a prim little no-nonsense voice.

He burst out laughing. It sounded extremely weird in this room, but he didn't care. She didn't seem to, either. She was looking back at him with just the faintest touch of a smile at the corners of her mouth. "Okay," he said. "I won't call you cookie, and don't you call me cake, and neither of us'll freak, fair enough?"

"Yeah. What about your leg?"

"It's okay. Looks more like a floor-burn than a bullet-wound."

"Lucky you."

"Yeah. I might dump a little disinfectant on it if I get a chance, but compared to her—"

"Gary!" the object of comparison bawled. The arm, Steve saw, was now hardly attached to the rest of her body at all; it seemed to be hanging by a thin strap of flesh. Her husband, also skinny (but with a blooming suburban potbelly just beginning to take shape), did a kind of helpless, panicky dance around her. He reminded Steve of a native in an old jungle flick doing the Cool Jerk around a brooding stone idol.

"Gary!" she screamed again. Blood was running out

of her mangled shoulder in a steady stream, turning the left side of her pink top to a muddy maroon. Her paper-white face was drenched with sweat; her hair clung to the curve of her skull in clumps. *"Gary, quit acting like a dog looking for a place to piss and help me—"*

She collapsed back against the wall between the living room and the kitchenette, panting for breath. Steve expected her knees to buckle, but they didn't. Instead, she grasped her left wrist with her right hand and lifted her wounded arm carefully toward Steve and Cynthia. The blood-glistening twist of gristle that was still connecting it to the rest of her made a squelchy sound, like a wet dishrag when you wring it out, and Steve wanted to tell her not to do that, to stop fooling with herself before she tore the goddam thing off like a wing off a baked chicken.

Then Gary was doing the Cool Jerk in front of Steve, going up and down like a man on a pogo stick, patches of hectic red standing out on his pale face. Gimme a little bass with those eighty-eights, Steve thought.

"Help her!" Gary cried. "Help my wife! Bleeding to death!"

"I can't—" Steve began.

Gary reached out and seized the front of Steve's tee-shirt. *When there's no more room in hell,* this artifact said, *the dead will walk the earth.* He thrust his thin and feverish face up toward Steve's. His eyes glittered with gin and panic. "Are you with them? Are you one of them?"

"I don't—"

"Are you with the shooters? Tell me the truth!"

Angrier than he would have believed possible (anger was not, ordinarily, his thing at all), Steve knocked the man's hands away from his old and much-loved tee-shirt, then pushed him. Gary took a stagger-step backward, his eyes first widening, then narrowing again.

"Okay," he said. "Okay, yeah. You asked for it. You asked for it and now you're gonna get it." He started forward.

Cynthia got between them, glancing at Steve for a moment—probably to assure herself that he wasn't in attack-mode yet—and then glaring at Gary. "What the fuck's wrong with you?" she asked him.

Gary smiled tightly. "He's not from around here, is he?"

"Christ, neither am I! I'm from Bakersfield, California—does that make *me* one of them?"

"Gary!" It sounded like the yap of a dog that has run a long way on a dusty road and pretty much barked itself out. "Stop fucking around and help me! My arm . . ." She continued to hold it out, and what Steve thought of now—he didn't want to but couldn't help it—was Mucci's Fine Meats in Newton. Guy in a white shirt, white cap, and bloodstained apron, holding out a peeled joint of meat to his mother. *Serve it medium-rare with a little mint jelly on the side, Mrs. Ames, and your family will never ask for roast chicken again. I guarantee it.*

"Gary!"

The skinny guy with the gin on his breath took a step toward her, then looked back at Steve and

Cynthia. The tight, knowing smile was gone. Now he only looked sick. "I don't know what to do for her," he said.

"Gary, you diseased ratbrain," Marielle said in a low, hopeless voice. "You total dumbwit." Her face was growing ever whiter. She had gone, in fact, that fabled faded whiter shade of pale. There were brown patches beneath her eyes—they seemed to be unfurling like wings—and her left sneaker was now a solid red instead of white.

She's going to die if she doesn't get help right away, Steve thought. The idea made him feel both amazed and somehow stupid. *Professional* help was what he was thinking about, he supposed, *E.R.* guys in green suits who said things like "ten cc's of epi, stat." But there were no guys like that around, and apparently none coming. He could still hear no sirens, only the sound of thunder retreating slowly into the east.

On the wall to his left was a framed photograph of a small brown dog with eerily intelligent eyes. On the matting beneath the photo, carefully printed in block letters, was DAISY, PEMBROKE CORGI, AGE 9. COULD COUNT. SHOWED APPARENT ABILITY TO ADD SMALL NUMBERS. To the left of Daisy, its glass now splattered with the thin woman's blood, was a Collie that seemed to be grinning for the camera. The printed legend beneath this one read: CHARLOTTE, BORDER COLLIE, AGE 6. COULD SORT PHOTOS AND CULL OUT THOSE OF HUMANS KNOWN TO HER.

To the left of Charlotte was a photograph of a parrot which appeared to be smoking a Camel.

"None of this is happening," Steve said in a conversational—almost jovial—tone of voice. He didn't know if he was talking to Cynthia or to himself. "I think I'm in a hospital somewhere. I had a head-on in the truck out on the thruway, that's what I think. It's like *Alice in Wonderland,* only the Nine Inch Nails version."

Cynthia opened her mouth to reply and then the old guy—the one who had presumably observed Daisy the Pembroke Corgi adding six and two and coming up with eight,

ABSOLUTELY NO PROBLEM FOR DAISY—

came in carrying an old black bag. The cop (was his name actually Collie, Steve wondered, or was that just some weird fantasy engendered by the photographs on the walls of this room?) followed him, pulling his belt out of its loops. Last in line, drifting, looking dazed, came Peter What's-His-Face, husband of the woman who was lying dead out there.

"Help her!" Gary yelled, forgetting Steve and his conspiracy theories, at least for the time being. "Help her, Doc, she's bleedin like a stuck pig!"

"You know I'm not a real physician, don't you, Gary? Just an old horse-doctor is all I—"

"Don't you call me a pig," Marielle interrupted him. Her voice was almost too low to be heard, but her eyes, fixed on her husband, glowed with baleful life. She tried to straighten up, couldn't, and slipped lower against the wall instead. "Don't you . . . call me that."

The old horse-doctor turned to the cop, who was standing just inside the kitchen doorway, barechested with the belt now stretched between his fists. He looked like the bouncer in a leather-bar where Steve had once worked the board for a group called The Big Chrome Holes.

"I have to?" the barechested cop asked. He was pretty pale himself, but Steve thought he looked game, at least so far.

Billingsley nodded and put his bag down on the big easy-chair that sprawled in front of the television. He snapped it open and began rummaging through it. "And hurry. The more blood she loses, the worse her chances become." He looked up, a spool of suture in one gnarled old hand, a pair of bentnosed surgical scissors in the other. "This is no fun for me, either. The last time I saw a patient in anything like this situation, it was a pony that had been mistaken for a deer and shot in the foreleg. Get it as high on her shoulder as you can. Turn the buckle toward the breast and pull it *tight*."

"Where's Mary?" Peter asked. "Where's Mary? Where's Mary? *Where's Mary?*" Each time he asked the question his voice grew more plaintive. The fourth repetition was a little more than a falsetto squeak. Abruptly he clutched his face in his hands and turned away from all of them, leaning his forehead against the wall between BARON, a Labrador retriever that could spell its name with blocks, and DIRTYFACE, a morose-looking goat that was apparently able to play a number of rudimentary tunes on the harmonica. It occurred to Steve that if he ever heard a goat playing "The Yellow Rose of Texas" on a Hohner, he would probably fucking kill himself.

Marielle Soderson, meanwhile, was staring at Billingsley with the intensity of a vampire looking at a man with a shaving cut. "Hurts," she croaked. "Give me something for it."

"Yes," Billingsley said, "but first we tourniquet."

He nodded impatiently at the cop. The cop started forward. He had the tongue of his belt threaded through the buckle now, making a loop. He reached out gingerly to the skinny woman, whose blond hair had gone two shades darker with sweat. She reached out with her good arm and pushed him with surprising strength. The cop wasn't expecting it. He went back two steps, hit the arm of the old guy's sprawled-out easy-chair, and fell into it. He looked like a comic who's just taken a pratfall in a movie.

The skinny woman didn't give him a second glance. Her attention was focused on the old guy, and the old guy's black bag.

"Now!" she barked at him, and it really *did* sound as if she were barking. "Give me something for it *now,* you quacky old fuck, it's killing me!"

The cop struggled out of the chair and caught Steve's eye. Steve got the message, nodded, and began edging toward the woman named Marielle, drifting in from the right, flanking her. Be careful, he told himself, she's flipped out, apt to scratch or bite or any damn thing, so be careful.

Marielle thrust herself away from the wall, swayed, steadied, and advanced on the old guy. She was once more holding her arm out in front of her, as if it were Exhibit A in a trial. Billingsley backed up a step, looking nervously from the barechested cop to Steve.

"Give me some Demerol, you weasel!" she cried in her barking, exhausted voice. "You give it to me or I'll choke you until you bark like a bloodhound! I'll—"

The cop nodded to Steve again and sprang forward on the left. Steve moved with him and threw an arm around the woman's neck. He didn't want to choke her, but he was scared to go around her back, maybe grabbing her wounded arm by mistake and hurting it worse. "Hold still!" he shouted. He didn't mean to shout, he meant to just say it, but that wasn't how it came out. At the same moment the cop slipped the loop of his belt over her left hand and up her arm.

"Hold her, buddy!" the cop cried. "Hold her still!"

For a second or two Steve did, and then a drop of sweat, warm and stinging, ran into his eye, and he relaxed his choke-hold just as Collie Entragian ran the makeshift belt tourniquet tight. Marielle lurched to the right, her baleful falcon's gaze still fixed on the old guy, and her arm came off in the barechested cop's hands. Steve could see her wristwatch, an Indiglo with the second-hand stopped dead between the four and the five. The belt held on at her shoulder for a moment and then dropped to the floor, a loop with nothing in it. The counter-girl shrieked, her huge eyes fixed on the arm. The cop looked down at it with his mouth open.

"Get it on ice!" Gary bawled. "Get it on ice right away! Right aw—" Then, all at once, he seemed to really realize what had happened. What the cop was holding. He opened his mouth, twisted his head in a peculiar way, and unloaded on the photo of the cigarette-smoking parrot.

Marielle noticed none of it. She staggered toward the clearly terrified veterinarian, her remaining hand outstretched. "I want a shot and I want it *now*!" she croaked. "Do you hear me, you old woman? I want a fucking shuh-shuh—"

She collapsed onto her knees. Her head drooped, hung. Then, with an immense effort, she got her chin up again. For a moment her gimlet gaze met Steve's. "Who the fuck're you?" she asked in a clear, perfectly understandable voice, then slid forward on her face. The top of her head came to rest inches from the heels of Peter, the man who had lost his wife. Jackson, Steve thought suddenly. That's his last name, Jackson. Peter Jackson was still turned to the wall with his face clutched in his hands. If he takes a step backward, Steve thought, he'll trip over her.

"Fuck a duck," the cop said in a low, amazed voice. Then he looked down and realized he was still holding the woman's arm. He walked stiffly toward the kitchen with it held out in front of him. The sound of rain hissing down seemed very loud in Steve's ears.

"Come on," the old party said, rousing himself. "We're not done yet. Get that belt on her, son. Buckle in toward the breast. You game?"

"I guess," Steve said, but he was very relieved when Cynthia the counter-girl picked the belt up and then knelt beside the unconscious woman with it in her hands.

From "The Force Corridor," Episode 55 of MotoKops *2200, original teleplay by Allen Smithee:*

ACT 2

FADE IN ON:

INT. CRISIS CENTER, MOTOKOPS' HQ

The room is dominated, as always, by the huge Situscreen. Standing before it on a floatpad is COLONEL HENRY, *looking grave. Sitting at the horseshoe-shaped Crisis Desk are the rest of the MotoKops squad:* SNAKE HUNTER, BOUNTY, MAJOR PIKE, ROOTY, AND CASSIE.

On the Situscreen we see a SPACE VIEW. *In the distance is Earth, just a blue-green coin at this distance. It looks peaceful enough.*

SNAKE HUNTER *(with customary scorn)*

So what's the big deal? I don't see anything that looks very— What the—??!!

Suddenly the FORCE CORRIDOR *appears on the Situscreen, almost filling it, blotting out the stars on either side. It's like watching the arrival of Darth Vader's dreadnought at the beginning of the first Star Wars movie; in a word, awesome!*

The CORRIDOR *consists of two long metal plates with big square protrusions sticking out at intervals. The* CORRIDOR HUMS OMINOUSLY, *and* BLUE FIRE CRACKLES *from side to side between the square protrusions.*

CASSIE STYLES *gasps, looks at the Situ-screen with dismay.* COLONEL HENRY *pushes a button on his hand-control, and the screen goes into* FREEZE MODE. *We can still see Earth, but with the corridor on either side, it looks caught in a potentially lethal* WEB OF ELECTRICITY!

COLONEL HENRY (*to* SNAKE HUNTER)

That's the big deal! The Force Corridor, artifact of a long-vanished alien race! Destructive . . . and headed directly toward Earth!

CASSIE *(dismay)*

Oh, gosh!

COLONEL HENRY

Relax, Cassie—it's still over 150,000 light-years away. This is a composite shot.

MAJOR PIKE

Yeah, but how fast is it moving?

COLONEL HENRY

That's the problem. Let's just say that if we don't resolve this crisis in the next seventy-two hours, I think you can cancel your weekend plans.

ROOTY

Root-root-root-root!

SNAKE HUNTER

Shut up, Rooty.

(*to* COLONEL HENRY)

So what's our plan?

COLONEL HENRY *takes the floatpad further up, so he can use his highlighter to circle a couple of the protrusions on the inner sides of the corridor.*

COLONEL HENRY

Drone telemetry reports that the Force Corridor itself is over 200,000 miles long and 50,000 miles wide, a hallway of death in which nothing can live! But it may have a weakness! I think these square shapes are power-generators. If we could knock 'em out—

BOUNTY

Are we talkin' Power Wagon assault, boss?

We move in on COLONEL HENRY's *grim face.*

COLONEL HENRY

It's Earth's only chance.

INT. CRISIS DESK, WITH THE MOTOKOPS

SNAKE HUNTER

A deep-space Power Wagon assault? Could be a quick trip to that Boot Hill in the sky!

ROOTY

Root-root-root-root!

ALL

Shut up, Rooty!

INT. A HALLWAY IN THE CRISIS CENTER

COLONEL HENRY *and* CASSIE STYLES *are in the lead, the other MotoKops behind them.* ROOTY, *as usual, is bumbling along in the rear.*

COLONEL HENRY

You're worried, little one.

CASSIE

Of course I'm worried! Snake Hunter is right! The Power Wagons were never designed for the stresses of a deep-space assault!

COLONEL HENRY

But that's not all that's on your mind.

CASSIE

Sometimes I hate your telepathy, Hank.

COLONEL HENRY

Come on . . . give.

CASSIE

Something bothers me about those shapes inside the Force Corridor. What if they aren't power-generators?

COLONEL HENRY

What else could they be?

They have reached the slide-door to the Power Wagon Corral. COLONEL HENRY *slaps his hand into the palm-lock and the door slides up.*

CASSIE

I don't know, but . . .

INT. THE POWER WAGON CORRAL, FEATURING THE MOTOKOPS

CASSIE *gasps with shock, eyes widening!* COLONEL HENRY, *looking grim, puts his arm around her. The other squad-members gather round.*

ROOTY

Root-root-root-root!

SNAKE HUNTER

Yeah, Rooty, I couldn't agree more!

He stares bitterly at:

INT. THE POWER WAGON CORRAL, MOTOKOPS' POV

Floating in the middle of the parked Power Wagons, between SNAKE HUNTER'S *Tracker Arrow and the silver-sided Rooty-Toot, is a grim visitor: the Meatwagon,* HUMMING SOFTLY.

INT. RESUME MOTOKOPS SQUAD

COLONEL HENRY

MotoKops, prepare for battle!

SNAKE HUNTER (*his stun-pistol already out*)

Way ahead of you, boss.

The others draw.

INT. RESUME MEATWAGON

The Doom Turret SLIDES BACK, *revealing* NO FACE, *sinister as always in his black uniform. Sitting behind him at the controls, with her customary look of sexy hauteur, is* COUNTESS LILI. *The Hypno-Jewel around her neck* FLICKERS WILDLY *through the color spectrum.*

NO FACE

Floatpad, Countess. Now!

COUNTESS LILI

Yes, Excellent One.

The COUNTESS *pulls a lever. A floatpad appears.* NO FACE *steps onto it and is wafted down to the floor of the Corral. He is unarmed, and as* COLONEL HENRY *steps forward, he holsters his own stunner.*

COLONEL HENRY

Aren't you a little far from home, No Face?

NO FACE

Home is where the heart is, my dear Hank.

BOUNTY

This is no time for games.

NO FACE

As it happens, I couldn't agree more. The Force Corridor approaches. You, Colonel Henry, are planning a Power Wagon assault—

MAJOR PIKE

How do you know that?

NO FACE (*icy*)

Because it's what I'd do, you idiot!

(*to* COLONEL HENRY)

A Power Wagon assault is incredibly risky, but it may also be Earth's only chance. You'll need all the help you can get, and you have no vehicle at your command as powerful as the Meatwagon.

SNAKE HUNTER

That's a matter of opinion, you mutt. My Tracker Arrow—

COLONEL HENRY

Stow the gab!

(*to* NO FACE)

What are you offering?

NO FACE

A partnership until the crisis is past. Old quarrels put aside, at least temporarily. A joint attack on the Force Corridor.

He offers his black-gloved hand. COLONEL HENRY *starts to reciprocate, and then* MAJOR PIKE *steps forward. His almond-shaped eyes are wide, and his mouth-horn quivers with alarm.*

MAJOR PIKE

Don't do it, Hank! You can't trust him! It's a trick!

NO FACE

I understand how you feel, Major . . . we both do, do we not, Countess?

COUNTESS LILI

Yes, Excellent One.

NO FACE

But this time there are no tricks, no hidden cards.

COLONEL HENRY (*to* MAJOR PIKE)

And we have no choice.

NO FACE

Indeed we don't. Time is running out.

COLONEL HENRY *reaches out and takes* NO FACE's *hand.*

NO FACE

Partners?

COLONEL HENRY

For now.

ROOTY

Root-root-root-root!

WE FADE TO BLACK. ENDS ACT 2.

CHAPTER 6

1

Now speaking in the voice of Ben Cartwright, patriarch of the Ponderosa, Tak said: "Ma'am, it looks to me like you were planning on skedaddling."

"No . . ." It was her voice, but weak and distant, like a radio transmission coming in from the West Coast on a rainy night. "No, I was just going to the store. Because we're out of . . ." Out of *what*? What could they possibly be out of that this monster would care about, believe in? And, blessedly, something came to her. "Chocolate syrup! Hershey's!"

It came toward her from the den doorway, Seth Garin in MotoKops Underoos, only now she saw an amazing, horrid thing: the child's bare toes were dragging across the living-room carpet, but otherwise it was floating along like a boy-shaped balloon. It was Seth's body, poignantly grimy at the wrists and ankles, but there was no Seth in the eyes. None at all. Now it was just the thing that looked like it belonged in a swamp.

"Says she was just going to take a mosey down to the general store," said the voice of Ben Cartwright. Whatever else Tak might be, it was a hellishly good mimic. You had to give it that. "What do you think, Adam?"

"Think she's lying, Paw," said the voice of Pernell Roberts, the actor who had played Adam Cartwright. Roberts had lost his hair over the years, but he had gotten the best of the deal, anyway; the actors who had played his father and his brothers had all died in the years since *Bonanza* had galloped off into the sunset of reruns and cable TV.

Back to the voice of Ben as the thing drifted closer, close enough for her to be able to smell sour sweat and a sweet lingering ghost of No More Tears shampoo. "What do you think, Hoss? Speak up, boy."

"Lyin, Paw," Dan Blocker's voice said . . . and for a moment the almost-floating child actually *looked* like Blocker.

"Little Joe?"

"Lyin, Paw."

"Root-root-root-root!"

"Shut up, Rooty," said Snake Hunter's voice. It was as if some invisible ensemble of talented lunatics were putting on a show for her. When the thing in front of her spoke again, Snake Hunter was gone and Ben Cartwright was back, that stern Moses of the Sierra

Nevada. "We don't much abide liars on the Ponderosa, ma'am. Skedaddlers, either. Now what do you reckon we should do with you?"

Don't hurt me, she tried to say, but no words came out, not even a whisper of words. She tried to switch over to some internal circuit, visualizing the little red telephone, only with SETH stamped into the plastic of the handset now. It scared her to try and reach Seth directly, but she had never been in a jam like this. If it decided it wanted her dead . . .

She saw the phone in her mind, saw herself speaking into it, and what she had to say was painfully simple: Don't let it hurt me, Seth. You had power over it at the start, I know you did. Maybe not much, but a little. If you have any left—any power, any influence—please don't let it hurt me, please don't let it kill me. I'm miserable, but not miserable enough to want to die. Not yet.

She looked for a flicker of humanity in the floating thing's eyes, the slightest sign of Seth, and saw nothing.

Suddenly her left hand shot up and then slapped down, whacking her left cheek with a sound like a breaking stick of kindling. Heat flooded her skin; it was as if someone had turned a sunlamp on that side of her face. Her left eye began to water.

Now her right hand rose up in front of her eyes, like a Hindu swami's snake rising out of its basket. It hung in front of her for a moment, and then slowly folded itself into a fist.

No, she tried to say, please no, please, Seth, don't let it, but nothing came out this time, either, and the fist plummeted down, knuckles very white in the dim room, and then her nose seemed to explode upward in clouds of white dots like butterflies. They danced frantically in front of her eyes even as blood, warm and loose, began to run down over her lips and chin. She staggered backward.

"This woman is an affront to justice in the twenty-third century!" Colonel Henry said in his stern voice—a voice she found more hateful and self-righteous each time an episode of the fucking cartoon came on. "She must be shown the error of her ways."

Hoss: "That's right, Colonel! We got to show this bitch who's top hand!"

"Root-root-root-root!"

Cassie Styles: "I agree with Rooty! And a little sweetening up is just the way to start!"

She was walking again—being walked, rather. The living room flowed past her eyes like scenery running backward past the windows of a train. Her cheek throbbed. Her nose throbbed. She could taste blood on her teeth. Now she pictured a *MotoKops*-style phone, the kind where you could actually see the person you were talking to, pictured talking face-to-face with Seth on this phone. Please, Seth, it's your Aunt Audrey, do you recognize me even though my hair's a different color now? Tak made me dye it so it would look like Cassie's, and when I go out I have to wear a blue headband like Cassie does, but it's still me, still Aunt

Audrey, the one who took you in, the one who's been watching out for you, trying to, anyway, and now you have to watch out for me. Don't let it hurt me too badly, Seth, please don't let it.

The lights were off in the kitchen and it was a bowl of gloomy, swarming shadows. As she was propelled across the yellow linoleum (cheery when it was clean, but now dingy and jaundiced-looking), a thought occurred to her, one that was terrible with logic: Why *should* Seth help her? Even if he was receiving her message and even if he still could help, why should he? To escape Tak meant to abandon Seth to his fate, and that was just what she had been trying to do. If the boy was still there, he must know that as well as Tak.

A sob, as faint and distant as an invalid's breath, escaped her as the fingers of her bloodstained right hand felt for the light-switch by the stove, found it, and turned it.

"Sweeten her up, Paw!" Little Joe Cartwright yelped. "Sweeten her up, by Jasper!" The voice suddenly slid up, becoming the high-pitched laughter of Rooty the Robot. Audrey found herself wishing for insanity. It would be better than this, wouldn't it? It would have to be.

Instead she watched, a helpless passenger inside her own body, as Tak turned her, walked her over to the spice rack, and used her hand to open the cabinet above it. The other hand yanked out a yellow Tupperware container that hit the floor and sprayed macaroni across the linoleum in every direction. The flour went next, landing beside her foot and puffing up to coat her legs. The hand darted into the hole it had created and seized the plastic honey bear. The other hand grabbed the top, unscrewed it, tossed it aside. A moment later the bear was hanging upside down over her open, waiting mouth.

The hand wrapped around the bear's chubby stomach began to squeeze rhythmically, much as she had once squeezed the rubber bulb of the horn that had been mounted on her childhood bicycle. Blood from her ruptured nose slid down her throat. Then honey filled her mouth, thick and gagging-sweet.

"Swallow it!" Tak shouted, now in no one's voice but its own. "Swallow it, you bitch!"

She swallowed. One mouthful, then two, then three. On the third one her throat seemed to clench shut. She tried to breathe and couldn't. Her windpipe was blocked by a nightmare of sweet glue. She fell to her knees and began crawling across the kitchen floor, her dark-red hair hanging in her face, barking out great thick wads of blood-laced honey. It was up her nose as well, packing it and dripping from her nostrils.

For another few moments she still couldn't seem to breathe, and the white specks dancing in front of her eyes turned black. I'm going to drown, she thought. Drown in Sue Bee honey.

Then her windpipe opened up again, a little, anyway, enough, and she was gasping air into her lungs, pulling it down her slick, coated throat, weeping with terror and pain.

Tak dropped onto Seth Garin's scabby knees in front of her and began screaming into her face. "Don't you *ever* try to get away from me! Don't you *ever*! Don't you *ever*! Do you understand? Nod your head, you stupid cow, show me you understand!"

Its hands—the ones she couldn't see, the ones that were inside her head—seized her and all at once her head was swooping up and down, her forehead smacking the floor on each downstroke, and Tak was laughing. *Laughing.* She thought it would keep on pounding her head against the floor until she passed out and just sprawled here in the mess she had made.

Then, as suddenly as it had begun, it stopped. The hands were gone. The feel of its mind was gone, as well. She looked up cautiously, swiping at her nose with the side of her hand, still hitching for breath and letting it out in gasps that were half-retches. Her forehead throbbed. She could feel it swelling already.

The boy was looking at her. And she thought it *was* the boy. She wasn't completely sure, but—

"Seth?"

For a moment he only crouched there, not nodding, not shaking his head. Then he reached out with one dirty hand and wiped honey off her chin with fingers she could hardly feel.

"Seth, where did it go? Where's Tak?"

He struggled. She could see him struggling. With his fear, perhaps, but she wasn't sure he felt fear. Even if he did, it was more likely his own defective communications equipment he was working against right now. He made a gurgling noise, a sound like air in the bathroom pipes, and she thought that was probably all he'd be able to get out. Then, just as she was about to try for her feet, two choked words came from him.

"Gone. Building."

She looked at him, still breathing through a film of honey but not noticing it for the moment. She felt her heart begin to beat a little faster at the word *gone.* She should know better, especially after what had just happened, but—

"Is he in a building, honey? Gone to a building? Is that what you're saying? What building?"

"Building," Seth repeated. He struggled, his head shaking from side to side. Finally: *"Making."*

Building, yes. But the verb, not the noun. Tak was *building.* Tak was *making.* What was he making . . . besides trouble?

"He," Seth said. "He. He. *He—!*"

The boy struck down on his own thigh with a frustration she had never seen in him before. She picked up the fist he had hit himself with and soothed it back into a hand.

"No, Seth." Her diaphragm pulled in again, trying to retch—the honey was a heavy ball in her stomach—but she controlled it. "Don't, don't. Just relax. Tell me if you can. If you can't, it's okay." A lie, but if she wound him up any tighter than he was already, he would never be able to get it out. Worse, he might go away. Go away and leave the warm boy-vacancy that Tak inhabited so easily.

"He—!" Seth reached for her, touched her ears. Then he put the backs of his hands behind his own ears and pushed them forward. She saw that they were also dirty from his long hours in the sandbox—filthy—and her eyes stung with tears. But he was looking at her intently, and she nodded. Yes, she understood. When Seth really tried, he was quite good—as good as he had to be, anyway.

He listens to you, the boy was saying. Tak listens to you with my ears. And of course he did. *It* did. Tak the Magnificent, creature of a thousand voices, most of which came equipped with Western drawls, and one set of ears.

Tak had dropped down in front of her, but it was Seth that got up, just a skinny little boy in grimy underpants. He started for the door, then turned back. Audrey herself was still on her knees, trying to decide if she could reach out for the counter from where she was or if she should crawl a little closer first.

She cringed when she saw him coming back, thinking that Tak had returned, thinking she saw the hard shine of its intelligence in Seth's eyes. When he got closer, she saw that she had made a natural enough mistake. Seth was crying. She had never seen him cry before, not even when he came to her with scraped knees or a banged head. Until now she hadn't been entirely sure that he *could* cry.

He put his arms around her neck and dropped his forehead against hers. It hurt, but she didn't draw away. For a moment she had a blurred but very emphatic image of the red telephone, only grown to enormous size. Then it was gone, and she heard Seth's voice in her head. She'd thought on several occasions that she was hearing him, that he was trying to contact her telepathically. The sensation came most commonly as she was drifting off to sleep or just as she was waking up. It was always distant, like a voice calling through blankets of fog. Now, however, it was shockingly close. It was the voice of a child who sounded bright and not in the least defective.

I don't blame you for trying to run, the voice said. Audrey had a sense of hurry and furtiveness. It was like listening to a kid whisper some vital piece of classroom gossip to his seatmate while the teacher's back is briefly turned. *Get to the others, the ones across the street. You have to wait, but it won't be long. Because he's—*

No words, but another blurred image that filled her head completely, temporarily driving out all thought. It was Seth. He was dressed in jester's motley and a cap of bells. He was juggling. Not balls; dolls. Little china ones. Hummel figures. But until he dropped one and it shattered and she saw the broken face of Mary Jackson lying beside one of the jester's red-and-white curly-toed caliph's slippers, she did not realize that the dolls were her neighbors. She supposed she was responsible for at least some of that image—she had seen Kirstie Carver's Hummel figures (a tiresome hobby if ever there was one, in Audrey's opinion) a thousand times—but she understood that whatever she might have added didn't in the least change what Seth was trying to convey. Whatever craziness Tak was up to—his *building,* his *making*—it was keeping him very busy.

Not too busy to see me when I broke for the door a few minutes ago, she thought. Not too busy to stop me. Not too busy to punish me, either. Maybe next time it'll be salt going down my throat instead of honey.

Or drain-cleaner.

I'll tell you when, the child's voice returned. *Listen for me, Aunt Audrey. After the Power Wagons come again. Listen for me. It's important that you get away. Because—*

This time many images flickered past. Some came and went too fast for her to identify, but she got a few: an empty Chef Boyardee can lying in the trash, an old broken toilet lying on its side in the dump, a car up on blocks, no wheels, no glass. Things that were broken. Things that were used up.

The last thing she saw before he broke contact was the studio portrait of herself on the table in the front hall. The eyes of the portrait were gone, gouged out.

Seth released her and stood back, watching as she grasped the edge of the counter and struggled to her feet. Her belly, heavy and thick with the honey Tak had made her swallow, felt like a counterweight. Seth now looked as he usually did—distant and disconnected, with all the emotional gradient of a rock. Yet there were those clean streaks below his eyes. Yes, there were those.

"Ah-oh," he said in his toneless voice—soundings she and Herb had speculated might mean *Audrey, hello*—and then walked out of the kitchen. Back to the den, where the climactic shootout was still going on. And when it was done? Why, rewind to the FBI warning and start all over again, most likely.

But he talked to me, she thought. Out loud and inside my head. On his version of the PlaySkool phone. Only his version is so *big*.

She took the broom from its place in the pantry alcove and began to sweep up spilled flour and macaroni. In the den, Rory Calhoun yelled, "You ain't goin nowhere, you sowbelly Yankee!"

"It doesn't have to be this way, Jeb," Audrey murmured, sweeping.

"It doesn't have to be this way, Jeb," Ty Hardin—Deputy Laine in the movie—said, and then bad old Colonel Murdock shot him. His final act of villainy; in another thirty seconds he would be shot dead himself.

Audrey's diaphragm knotted again. Hard. She went to the sink, trailing the broom in one hand, and bent over. She gagged, but nothing came up. A moment later, the clench subsided. She turned on the cold-water tap, leaned over, drank directly from the faucet, then gingerly splashed a couple of handfuls on her throbbing forehead. It felt good. Wonderful.

She turned off the tap, went back to the pantry, and got the dustpan. Tak was building, Seth had said. Tak was making. But what? And as she dropped awkwardly to her knees by her pile of sweepings, the broom in one hand and the dustpan in the other, a more urgent question occurred to her: If she *did* get away, what would it do to her nephew? What would it do to Seth?

2

Belinda Josephson held the kitchen door for her husband, then straightened up and looked around. The overhead light wasn't on, but the room was still a little brighter than it had been. The storm was slackening, and she supposed that in another hour or two it would be hot and bright again.

She looked at the wall-clock over the kitchen table, and she felt a mild burst of unreality. 4:03? Was it possible so little time had gone by? She took a closer look and saw that the second-hand wasn't moving. She reached for the light-switch beside the door as Johnny crawled into the kitchen on his hands and knees and then stood up.

"Don't bother," Jim Reed said. He was sitting on the floor between the fridge and the stove with Ralphie Carver on his lap. Ralphie's thumb was in his mouth. His eyes were glazed and apathetic. Belinda had never liked him very much, didn't know anyone on the street who did (except for his mother and his dad, she supposed), but still her heart went out to him.

"Don't bother with what?" Johnny asked.

"The light-switch. Power's off."

She believed him but snapped the switch a couple of times anyway. Nothing.

There were a lot of people in this room—she made it eleven, counting herself—but the numb silence which had settled over them made it seem like less. Ellie Carver was still giving an occasional watery gasp, but her face was against her mother's breast, and Belinda thought she might actually be asleep. David Reed had his arm around Susi Geller. Sitting on the girl's other side, also with an arm around her (lucky girl, all that comfort, Belinda thought), was her mother. Cammie Reed, the twins' mother, was sitting against a door with a sign on it reading YE OLDE PANTRIE. Belinda didn't think Cammie was quite as out of it as some of the others; her eyes had a cool, thoughtful look.

"You said you heard screaming," Johnny said to Susi. "I don't hear any screaming."

"It's over," the girl said dully. "I think maybe it was Mrs. Soderson."

"Sure it was," Jim said. He shifted Ralphie on his lap, wincing a little as he did. "I recognized it. We've been listening to her scream at Gary for most of our lives. Haven't we, Dave?"

Dave Reed nodded. "I'd've murdered her by now. Honest."

"Ah, but you don't imbibe, my boy," Johnny said in his best W. C. Fields voice. He took the kitchen phone out of its cradle, listened, bopped the 0 button a couple of times, then hung it up again.

"Debbie's dead, isn't she?" Susi asked Belinda.

"Sh, baby, don't," Kim Geller said, sounding alarmed.

Susi took no notice. "She didn't go over next door at all. Did she? Don't lie about it, either."

Belinda thought about doing just that, but it didn't seem the right way to go on, somehow. In her experience, even well-intentioned lies usually made things worse. More crazy. Belinda thought things were crazy enough on Poplar Street already.

"Yes, honey," she said, marvelling at how southern she always sounded—to herself, anyway—when she had to give someone bad news. Perhaps it was part of the black experience that no one had yet gotten around to teaching in a college course. What made it particularly interesting in her case was that she had never been south of the Mason-Dixon line in her whole life. "Yes, honey, I'm afraid she is."

Susi put her hands over her face and began to sob. Dave Reed pulled her to him and Susi put her face against his shoulder. When Kim tried to pull her back, Susi stiffened her body and resisted.

Her mother gave David Reed a dirty look which the boy missed entirely. She turned her angry face to Belinda instead. "Why did you tell her that?"

"Girl's lying right out there on the stoop, and with all that red hair, she is kinda hard to miss."

"Hushnow," Brad told her. He took her by the wrist and drew her over to the sink. "Don't you upset her."

Oh dear, too late, Belinda thought, but prudently said nothing.

There was a screened window behind the sink. Looking through it to the right, she could see the stake fence separating the Carvers' plot from Old Doc's. She could also see the green roof of the Billingsley house. Above it, the clouds already appeared to be unravelling.

She turned and boosted herself, sitting sidesaddle on the edge of the sink. Then she leaned close to the screen, smelling its metal and all the wet summer straining through its mesh. The combined scents called up a momentary nostalgia for her childhood, a feeling that was both fine and fierce. It was strange, she thought, how it was almost always the smells of things that took you back the hardest.

"Halloo!" she called, cupping her hands around her mouth. Brad grabbed her shoulder, apparently wanting her to stop, and she shook him off emphatically. *"Halloo, Billingsley!"*

"Don't do that, Bee," Cammie Reed said. "It's not wise."

And what *would* be wise? Belinda thought. Just sitting on the kitchen floor and waiting for the cavalry to come?

"Hell, go on," Johnny said. "What harm can it do? If the people who did the shooting are still around, I imagine that where we are is hardly a big secret to them." An idea seemed to strike him at that, and he dropped on his hunkers in front of the late postman's wife. "Kirsten, did David have a gun? A hunting rifle, or maybe—"

"There's a pistol in his desk," she said. "Second drawer on the left of the kneehole. That drawer's locked, but the key's in the wide drawer at the top. It's on a piece of green yarn."

Johnny nodded. "And the desk? Where's that?"

"Oh. In his little office. Upstairs, the end of the hall."

She said all this while seeming to contemplate her own knees, then raised desperate, distracted eyes to look at him. "He's out in the rain, Johnny. So is Susi's friend. We shouldn't leave them out in the rain."

"It's stopping," Johnny said, and his face suggested he knew how inane that sounded. It seemed to satisfy Pie, though, at least temporarily, and Belinda supposed that was the important thing. Perhaps it was Johnny's tone. The words might be inane, but Belinda had never heard him sound so gentle. "Just take care of your kids, Kirstie, and don't concern yourself with the rest of it for the time being."

He got up and started for the swinging door, walking in a battlefield crouch.

"Mr. Marinville?" Jim Reed asked. "Can I come with you?" But when he attempted to set Ralphie aside, a panicked look came into the boy's eyes. His thumb came out of his mouth with an audible pop and he clung to Jim like a barnacle, muttering "No, Jim, no, Jim," under his breath in a way that made Belinda feel like shivering. She thought mad people probably talked that way when they were alone in their cells at night.

"Stay where you are, Jim," Johnny said. "Brad? What about you? Little trip to higher altitudes? Clear the old sinuses?"

"Sure." Brad looked at his wife with that expression of love and exasperation that is the sole property of people who have been married over ten years. "You really think it's okay for this woman of mine to be shooting off her mouth?"

"I repeat, what harm can it do?"

"Be careful," Belinda said. She smoothed a hand briefly across Brad's chest. "Keep your head down. Promise me."

"I promise to keep my head down."

She looked at Johnny. "Now you."

"Huh? Oh." He offered a charming grin, and Belinda had a sudden insight: that was the way Mr. John Edward Marinville always grinned when he made promises to women. "I promise."

They went out, dropping a little self-consciously to their knees as they passed through the swinging door and once more into the Carvers' front hall. Belinda leaned toward the screen again. Besides rain and wet grass, she could smell the old Hobart place burning. She realized she could hear it, too—a crackly, whooshing sound. The downpour would probably keep the fire from spreading, but where were the fire trucks, for Christ's sake? What did they pay their taxes for? *"Halloo, Billingsley's! Who's there?"*

After a moment, a man's voice (one she didn't recognize) called back. *"There are seven of us! The couple from up the block—"*

That had to be the Sodersons, Belinda thought.

—plus the cop, and the guy married to the dead woman. There's also Mr. Billingsley, and Cynthia, from the store!"

"Who are you?" Belinda called.

"Steve Ames! I'm from New York! I was having trouble with my truck, pulled off the Interstate, got lost! I stopped at the store down there to use the phone!"

"Poor guy," Dave Reed said. "Like winning the lottery in hell."

"What's going on?" the voice from the other side of the stake fence called. *"Do you know what's going on?"*

"No!" Belinda shouted back. She thought furiously. There must be more to say, other things to ask, but she couldn't think of anything at all.

"Have you looked up the street? Is it clear?" Ames called.

Belinda opened her mouth to reply, and then was distracted momentarily by the spider's web outside the screen. The window's overhang had protected it from the worst of the squall, but raindrops hung from the gossamer threads like tiny, quivering diamonds. The owner-operator was at the center of the web. Not moving. Maybe dead.

"Ma'am? I asked—"

"I don't know!" she called back. *"Johnny Marinville and my husband looked, but now they've gone upstairs to—"* But she didn't want to mention the gun. Stupid, maybe—rathole thinking—but it didn't change the way she felt. *"—to get a better look! What about you?"*

"It's been pretty busy here, ma'am! The woman from up the block—" A pause. *"Does your phone work?"*

"No!" Belinda called. *"No phone, no electric!"*

Another pause. Then, lower, barely audible over the diminishing hiss of the rain, she heard him say shit. Then there was another voice, one she knew but couldn't immediately place. *"Belinda, is that you?"*

"Yes!" she returned, and looked around at the others for help.

"It's Mr. Jackson," Jim Reed said, speaking around Ralphie's shoulder. The little boy had not quite managed to join his sister in the refuge of sleep, but Belinda didn't think it would be long; his thumb had already begun to sag between his lips.

"I've been to the front door!" Peter called. *"The street's deserted all the way down to the corner!* Completely *deserted! No gawkers or rubberneckers from Hyacinth or the next block of Poplar. Does that make any sense to you?"*

Belinda thought, frowning, then looked around. She saw only puzzled eyes and dropped heads. She turned back to the window. *"No!"*

Peter laughed. The sound chilled her the way that little Ralphie Carver's distraught muttering had chilled her. *"Join the club, Bee! Makes no sense to me, either!"*

"Who'd come on the block?" Kim Geller scoffed. "Who in their right minds? With guns going off and people screaming and everything?"

Belinda didn't know how to respond to that. It was logical, but it still didn't hold water . . . because people didn't behave logically when trouble broke out. They came and they gawked. Usually they did it at what they hoped was a safe distance, but they came.

"Are you sure there aren't people down below the corner?" she called.

This time the pause was so long she was about to repeat the question when a third voice spoke up. She had no trouble recognizing Old Doc. *"None of us sees anyone, but the rain has started a mist off the pavement! Until it clears, we can't tell for sure!"*

"But there are no sirens!" Peter again. *"Do you hear any coming from the north?"*

"No!" she returned. *"It must be the storm!"*

"I don't think so," Cammie Reed said. She spoke for herself, *to* herself, not the group; if YE OLDE PANTRIE hadn't been in close proximity to the sink, Belinda wouldn't have heard her. "Nope, I don't think so at all."

"I'm going out to get my wife!" Peter Jackson called. Other voices were immediately raised in protest against this idea. Belinda couldn't make out the words, but the emotional tone was unmistakable.

Suddenly the spider—the one she had assumed was dead—scuttered from the center of its web and, mounting one of the silk strands, scrambled up until it had disappeared under the eave. Not dead after all, Belinda thought. Only playing possum.

Then Kirsten Carver was leaning past her, bumping Belinda so hard with her shoulder that Belinda would have gone ass-deep into the sink if she hadn't managed to grab the corner of an overhead cabinet. Pie's face was parchment-pale, her eyes blazing with fear.

"Don't you go out there!" she screamed. *"They'll come back and kill you! They'll come back and kill us all!"*

No answer from the other house for several moments, and then Collie Entragian spoke up in a voice that sounded both apologetic and bemused: *"No good, ma'am! He's gone!"*

"You should have stopped him!" Kirsten screamed. Belinda put an arm around the woman's shoulders and was frightened by the steady high vibration she

felt. As if Kirsten was on the verge of exploding. *"What kind of policeman are you!"*

"He's *not*," Kim said. She spoke in a just-what-the-hell-did-you-expect tone. "He got kicked off the force. He was running a hot-car ring."

Susi raised her head. "I don't believe it."

"What do *you* know about it, a girl your age?" her mother asked.

Belinda was about to slide off the edge of the sink when she saw something on the back lawn that made her freeze. It was caught against one leg of the kids' swing set, and like the spiderweb, jeweled with hanging drops of rain.

"Cammie?"

"What?"

"Come here."

If anyone would know, Cammie would; she had a garden in her backyard, a jungle of potted plants inside her house, and a library's worth of books on growing things.

Cammie got up from her place by the pantry door, and came over. Susi and her mother joined her; so did Dave Reed.

"What?" Pie Carver asked, turning a wild gaze on Belinda. Pie's daughter had her arms wrapped around her mother's leg as if it were a treetrunk, and was still trying to hide her face against the hip of Pie's denim shorts. "What is it?"

Belinda ignored her and spoke to Cammie. "Look over there. By the swings. Do you see?"

Cammie started to say she didn't, then Belinda pointed and she did. Thunder mumbled to the east of them, and the breeze kicked up a brief gust. The spider-web outside the window shivered and shed tiny drop-lets of rain. The thing Belinda had seen got free of the swing set and rolled partway across the Carvers' back-yard, in the direction of the stake fence.

"That's impossible," Cammie said flatly. "Russian thistle doesn't grow in Ohio. Even if it did . . . this is summer. They *root* in summer."

"What's Russian thistle, Mom?" Dave asked. His arm was around Susi's waist. "I never heard of it."

"Tumbleweed," Cammie said in that same flat voice. "Russian thistle is tumbleweed."

3

Brad poked his head through Carver's office door just in time to see Johnny pull a green-and-white box of cartridges out of a desk drawer. In his other hand, the writer had David Carver's pistol. He had rolled the cylinder out to make sure the chambers were empty; they were, but he was still holding the gun awkwardly, with all of his fingers outside the trigger guard. To Brad he looked like one of those guys who sold dubious items on high-channel cable TV: *Folks, this little beauty will ventilate any nighttime intruder unwise enough to pick your house, yes, of course it will, but wait, there's more! It slices! It dices! And do you love scalloped potatoes but just never have time to make them at home?*

"Johnny."

He looked up, and for the first time Brad saw clearly how frightened the man was. It made him like Johnny better. He couldn't think of a reason why that should be, but it was.

"There's a fool out on Old Doc's lawn. Jackson, I guess."

"Shit. That's not very bright, is it?"

"No. Don't shoot yourself with that thing." Brad started out of the room, then turned back. "Are we crazy? Because it feels that way."

Johnny raised his hands in front of him, palms up, to indicate he didn't know.

4

Johnny looked into the chambers of the pistol one more time—as if a bullet might have grown in one of them while he wasn't looking—then snapped the cylinder back into place. He stuck the pistol in his belt and tucked the box of cartridges into his shirt pocket.

The front hall was a minefield of Ralphie Carver's boy-toys; the kid had apparently not yet been introduced by his doting parents to the concept of picking up after himself. Brad went into what had to be the little girl's bedroom. Johnny followed him. Brad pointed out the window.

Johnny looked down. It was Peter Jackson, all right. He was on Doc's lawn, kneeling beside his wife. He had gotten her into a sitting position again. One arm was around her back. He was working the other under her cocked knees. Her skirt was well up on her thighs, and Johnny thought again about her missing pants. Well, so what? So fucking what? Johnny could see the man's back shaking as sobs racked him.

Silver light ran across the top of his vision.

He looked up and saw what looked like an old Airstream trailer—or maybe a lunch-wagon—turning left onto Poplar from Hyacinth. Close behind it was the red van that had taken care of the dog and the paperboy, and behind that was the one with the dark blue metal-flake paint. He looked the other way, up toward Bear Street, and saw the van with the Mary Kay paint-job and the Valentine radar-dish, the yellow one that had first rear-ended Mary and then rode her off the street, and the black one with the turret.

Six of them. Six in two converging lines of three. He had seen American LAC vehicles in the same formation a long time ago, in Vietnam.

They were creating a fire-corridor.

For a moment he couldn't move. His hands seemed to hang at the ends of his arms like plugs of cement. You can't, he thought with a kind of sick, unbelieving fury. You can't come *back*, you bastards, you can't keep coming *back*.

Brad didn't see them; he was looking at the man on the lawn of the house next door, absorbed in Peter's effort to get up with his wife's dead weight in his arms. And Peter . . .

Johnny got his right hand moving. He wanted it to streak; it seemed to float instead. He got it around the handle of the gun and pulled it out of the waistband of his pants. Couldn't shoot it; no loads in the chambers. Couldn't load it, either, not in his current state. So he brought it down butt-first, shattering the glass of Ellen's bedroom window.

"Get inside!" he screamed at Peter, and his voice came out sounding low and strengthless to his own ears. Dear God, what nightmare was this, and how had they stumbled into it? *"Get inside! They're coming again! They're back! They're coming again!"*

Drawing found folded into an untitled notebook which apparently served as Audrey Wyler's journal. Although unsigned, it is almost certainly the work of Seth Garin. If one assumes that its placement in the Journal corresponds to the time it was done, then it was made in the summer of 1995, after the death of Herbert Wyler and the Hobart family's abrupt departure from Poplar Street.

CHAPTER 7

Poplar Street/4:44 P.M./July 15, 1996

They seem to come out of the mist rising off the street like materializing metal dinosaurs. Windows slide down; the porthole on the flank of the pink Dream Floater irises open again; the windshield of Bounty's blue Freedom van retracts into a smooth darkness from which three grayish shotgun barrels bristle.

Thunder rumbles and somewhere a bird cries harshly. There is a beat of silence, and then the shooting begins.

It's like the thunderstorm all over again, only worse, because this time it's personal. And the guns are louder than before; Collie Entragian, lying face-down in the doorway between Billingsley's kitchen and living room, is the first to notice this, but the others are not long in realizing it for themselves. Each shot is almost like a grenade blast, and each is followed by a low moaning sound, something caught between a buzz and a whistle.

Two shots from the red Tracker Arrow and the top of Collie Entragian's chimney is nothing but maroon dust in the wind and pebble-sized chunks of brick pattering down on his roof. A shot strikes the plastic spread over Cary Ripton, making it ripple like a parachute, and another tears off the rear wheel of his bike. Ahead of Tracker Arrow is the silver van, the one that looks like an old-fashioned lunch-wagon. Part of its roof rises at an angle, and a silver figure—it appears to be a robot in a Confederate infantryman's uniform—leans out. It mails three shotgun rounds special express into the burning Hobart house. Each report seems as loud as a dynamite blast.

Coming downhill from Bear Street, Dream Floater and the Justice Wagon pour fire into 251 and 249—the Josephson house and the Soderson house. The windows blow in. The doors blow open. A round that sounds like something thrown from a small anti-aircraft gun hits the back of Gary's old Saab. The back end crumples in, shards of red taillight glass fly, and there's a *whoomp!* as the gas-tank explodes, engulfing the little car in a ball of smoky orange flame. The bumper-stickers—I MAY BE SLOW BUT I'M AHEAD OF YOU on the right, MAFIA STAFF CAR on the left—shimmer in the heat like mirages. The south-moving trio of vans and the trio moving north meet, cross, and stop in front of the stake fences separating the Billingsley place from the Carver house above it and the Jackson house below it.

Audrey Wyler, who was eating a sandwich and drinking a can of lite beer in the kitchen when the shooting started, stands in the living room, staring out at the street with wide eyes, unaware that she's still holding half of a salami and lettuce on rye in one hand. The firing has merged into one continuous, ear-splitting World War III roar, but she is in no danger; all of it is currently being directed at the two houses across from her.

She sees Ralphie Carver's red wagon—Buster—rise into the air with one side blown into a twisted metal flower. It cartwheels over David Carver's soggy corpse, lands with its wheels up and spinning, and then another hit bends it almost double and sends it into the flowers to the left of the driveway. Another round blows the Carver screen door off its hinges and hammers it down the hall; two more from Bounty's Freedom van vaporize most of Pie's prized Hummel figures.

Holes open in the crushed back deck of Mary Jackson's Lumina, and then it too explodes, flames belching up and swallowing the car back to front. Bullets tear off two of Old Doc's shutters. A hole the size of a baseball appears in the mailbox mounted beside his door; the box drops to the welcome mat, smoking. Inside it, a Kmart circular and a letter from the Ohio Veterinary Society are blazing. Another ka-bam and the bungalow's door-knocker—a silver St. Bernard's head—disappears as conclusively as a coin in a magician's hand. Seeming oblivious of all this, Peter Jackson struggles to his feet with his dead wife in his arms. His round rimless glasses, the lenses spotted with water, glint in the strengthening light. His pale face is more than distracted; it is the face of a man whose entire bank of fuses has burned out. But he's standing there, Audrey sees, miraculously whole, miraculously—

Aunt Audrey!

Seth. Very faint, but definitely Seth.

Aunt Audrey, can you hear me?

Yes! Seth, what's happening?

Never mind! The voice sounds on the edge of panic. *You have the place you go, don't you? The safe place?*

Mohonk? Did he mean Mohonk? He must, she decided.

Yes, I—

Go there! the faint voice cries. *Go there* NOW! *Because—*

The voice doesn't finish, and doesn't have to. She has turned away from the furious shooting-gallery in the street, turned toward the den, where the movie—The Movie—is playing again. The volume has been cranked, somehow, far beyond what their Zenith should be able to produce. Seth's shadow bounces ecstatically up and down on the wall, elongated and somehow horrible; it reminds her of what scared her most as a child, the horned demon from the "Night on Bald Mountain" segment of *Fantasia*. It's as if Tak is twisting inside the child's body, warping it, stretching it, driving it ruthlessly beyond its ordinary limits and boundaries.

Nor is that all that's happening. She turns back to the window, stares out. At first she thinks it's her eyes, something wrong with her eyes—perhaps Tak has melted them somehow, or warped the lenses—but she holds her hands up in front of her and *they* look all right. No, it's Poplar Street that's wrong. It seems to be twisting out of perspective in some way she can't quite define, angles changing, corners bulging, colors blurring. It's as if reality is on the verge of liquefying, and she thinks she knows why: Tak's long period of preparation and quiet growth is over. The time of action has come. Tak is *making,* Tak is *building*. Seth told her to get out, at least for awhile, but where can *Seth* go?

Seth! she tries, concentrating as hard as she can. *Seth, come with me!*

I can't! Go, Aunt Audrey! Go now!

The agony in that voice is more than she can endure. She turns toward the arch again, the one which leads into the den, but sees a meadow slanting down to a rock wall instead. There are wild roses; she smells them and feels the sexy, delicate heat of spring now tending toward summer. And then Janice is beside her and Janice is asking her what her all-time favorite Simon and Garfunkel song is and soon they are deep in a discussion of "Homeward Bound" and "I Am a Rock," the one that goes "If I'd never loved, I never would have cried."

In the Carver kitchen, the refugees lie on the floor

with their hands laced over the backs of their heads and their faces pressed to the floor; around them the world seems to be tearing itself apart.

Glass shatters, furniture falls, something explodes. There are horrible punching sounds as bullets pound through the walls.

Suddenly Pie Carver can stand Ellie's clinging to her no more. She loves Ellen, of course she does, but it's Ralphie she wants now, and Ralphie she must have; smart, sassy Ralphie, who looks so much like his father. She pushes Ellen roughly away, ignoring the girl's cry of startled dismay, and bolts for the niche between the stove and the fridge, where Jim is hunched over the frantic, screaming Ralphie, holding one hand over the back of Ralphie's head like a cap.

"Mommmmeeee!" Ellen wails, and attempts to run after her. Cammie Reed pushes away from the pantry door, grabs the little girl around the waist, and drops her back to the floor just as something that sounds like a monster locust drones across the kitchen, strikes the kitchen faucet, and backflips it like a majorette's baton. Most of the spinning faucet tears through the screen and the spiderweb on the other side. Water spouts up from what's left, at first almost all the way to the ceiling.

"Give him to me!" Pie screams. *"Give me my son! Give me my s—"*

Another approaching drone, this one followed by a loud, unmusical clang as one of the copper pots hanging by the stove is hammered into a hulk of twisted fragments and flying shrapnel. And Pie is suddenly just screaming, no words now, just screaming. Her hands are clapped to her face. Blood pours through her fingers and down her neck. Threads of copper litter the front of her misbuttoned blouse. More copper is in her hair, and a large chunk quivers in the center of her forehead like the blade of a thrown knife.

"I can't see!" she shrieks, and drops her hands. Of course she can't; her eyes are gone. So is most of her face. Quills of copper bristle from her cheeks, her lips, her chin. *"Help me, I can't see! Help me, David! Where are you?"*

Johnny, lying face-down beside Brad in Ellen's room upstairs, can hear her screaming and understands that something terrible has happened. Bullets hemstitch the air above them. On the far wall is a picture of Eddie Vedder; as Johnny starts to wriggle toward the doorway to the hall, a huge bullet-hole appears in Eddie's chest. Another one hits the child-sized vanity mirror over Ellen's dresser and hammers it to sparkling fragments. Somewhere on the block, blending hellishly with the sounds of Pie Carver's screams from downstairs, comes the bray of a car alarm. And still the gunfire goes on.

As he crawls out into the toy-littered hall, he hears Brad beside him, panting harshly. This has been a hell of an aerobic day for a fellow with such a big stomach, Johnny thinks . . . but then that thought, the sound of the woman screaming downstairs, and the roar of the gunfire are all driven from his mind. For a moment he feels as if he has walked into a Mike Tyson right hand.

"It's the same guy," he whispers. "Oh Jesus-God, it's the same fucking one."

"Get down, fool!" Brad grabs his arm and yanks. Johnny collapses forward like a car slipping off a badly placed jack, not realizing he's been up on his hands and knees until he comes crashing back down again. Unseen bullets hunt the air over his head. The glass on a framed wedding picture at the head of the stairs shatters; the picture itself falls face-down on the carpet with a thump. A second later, the wooden ball atop the bannister's newel-post disintegrates, spewing a deadly bouquet of splinters. Brad ducks down, covering his face, but Johnny only stares at something on the hallway floor, oblivious of everything else.

"What's wrong with you?" Brad asks him. "You want to die?"

"It's him, Brad," Johnny repeats. He curls his fingers into his hair and gives a brief hard tug, as if to assure himself that all this is really happening. "The—" There's a vicious buzz, almost like a plucked guitar-string, over their heads, and the hall light-fixture explodes, showering glass down on them. "The guy that was driving the blue van," he finishes. "The other one shot her—the human—but this is the guy who was driving."

He reaches out and picks up one of Ralphie Carver's action figures from the hall floor, which is now littered with glass and splinters as well as toys. It's an alien with a bulging forehead, almond-shaped eyes that are dark and huge, and a mouth that isn't a mouth at all but a kind of fleshy horn. It's dressed in a greenish iridescent uniform. The head is bald except for a stiff blond strip of hair. To Johnny it looks like the comb on a Roman Centurion's helmet. Where's your hat? he thinks at the little figure as the bullets whine through the air above him, punching through the wallpaper, shattering the laths beneath. The figure looks a little like Spielberg's E.T. Where's your pinned-back cavalry hat, bub?

"What are you talking about?" Brad asks. He's lying full-length on his stomach. Now he takes the figure, which is perhaps seven inches tall, from Johnny and looks at it. There is a cut on one of Brad's plump cheeks. Falling glass from the light-fixture, Johnny assumes. Downstairs, the screaming woman falls silent. Brad looks at the alien, then stares at Johnny with eyes that are almost comically round. "You're full of shit," he says.

"No," Johnny says. "I'm not. With God as my witness I'm not. I never forget a face."

"What are you saying? That the people doing this are wearing masks so the survivors can't identify them later?"

The idea hasn't occurred to Johnny until this moment, but it's a pretty good one. "I suppose that must be it. But—"

"But what?"

"It didn't look like a mask. That's all. It didn't *look* like a mask."

Brad stares at him a moment longer, then tosses the

figure aside and begins wriggling toward the stair-well. Johnny picks it up, looks at it for a moment, then winces as another slug comes through the window at the end of the hall—the one facing the street—and drones directly over his head. He tucks the action figure into the pants pocket not holding the oversized slug and begins to wriggle after Brad.

On the lawn of Old Doc's house, Peter Jackson stands with his wife in his arms, woundless at the center of the firestorm. He sees the vans with their dark glass and futuristic contours, he sees the shotgun barrels, their muzzles belching fire, and between the silvery one and the red one he can see Gary Soderson's old shitbox Saab burning in the Soderson driveway. None of it makes much of an impression on him. He is thinking about how he just got home from work. That seems like a very big deal to him, for some reason. He thinks he will begin every account of this terrible afternoon (it has not occurred to him that he may not *survive* the terrible afternoon, at least not yet) by saying *I just got home from work*. This phrase already has become a kind of magical structure inside his head; a bridge back to the sane and orderly world which he assumed, only an hour ago, was his by right and would be for years and decades to come: *I just got home from work.*

He is also thinking of Mary's father, a professor at the Meermont College of Dentistry in Brooklyn. He has always been rather terrified of Henry Kaepner, of Henry Kaepner's somehow daunting integrity; in his heart Peter has always known that Henry Kaepner considers him unworthy of his daughter (and in his heart this is an opinion with which Peter Jackson has always concurred). And now Peter is standing in the firestorm with his feet in the wet grass, wondering how he'll ever be able to tell Mr. Kaepner that his father-in-law's worst unspoken fear has become reality: his unworthy son-in-law has gotten his only child killed.

It's not my fault, though, Peter thinks. Perhaps I can make him see that if I start by saying I just got home from w—

"Jackson."

The voice wipes out his worries, makes him sway on his feet, makes him feel like screaming. It is as if an alien mouth has opened inside his mind, tearing a hole in it. Mary slips in his arms, trying to slither out of his grip, and Peter hugs her tight against him again, ignoring the ache in his arms. At the same time he comes back to some vague appreciation of reality. Most of the vans are on the move again, but very slowly, still firing. The pink one and the yellow one are now pouring fire into the Reed and Geller residences, shattering birdbaths, blasting away faucet bibs, breaking basement windows, shredding flowers and bushes, slicing through raingutters that drop, slanting, to the lawns below.

One of them, however, is not moving. The black one. It is parked on the other side of the street, blocking most of the Wyler house from view. The turret has slid back, and now a shining figure, all bright gray and dead black, issues from it like a spook from the window of a haunted house. Except, Peter sees, the figure is standing on something. It looks like a floating pillow and seems to be humming.

Is it a man? He can't exactly tell. It appears to be wearing a Nazi uniform, all black, glossy fabric and silver rigging, but there is no human face above the wings of its collar; there is no face of any kind, in fact.

Just blackness.

"Jackson! Get over here, partner."

He tries to resist, to stand his ground, and when the voice comes again it isn't like a mouth but a fishhook, yanking inside his head, tearing his thoughts open. Now he knows what a hooked trout feels like.

"Get a move-on, pard!"

Peter walks across the rain-washed remains of a hopscotch grid on the sidewalk (Ellen Carver and her friend Mindy from a block over made it that very morning), then steps into the gutter. Rushing water fills one shoe, but he doesn't even feel it. In his mind he is now hearing a very strange thing, a kind of soundtrack. It's being played by a twanging guitar, sort of like an old Duane Eddy instrumental. A tune he knows but can't identify. It is the final maddening touch.

The bright figure on the floating pillow descends to street-level. As Peter draws closer, he expects to see the black cloth (perhaps nylon, perhaps silk) covering the man's face, giving him that spooky look of absence, but he *doesn't* see it, and as the plate-glass window of the E-Z Stop explodes down the street, he realizes an awful thing: he doesn't see it because it isn't there. The man from the black wagon really has no face.

"Oh God," he moans in a voice so low he can barely hear it himself. "Oh my God, please."

Two other figures are looking down from the turret of the black van. One is a bearded guy wearing the ruins of what looks like a Civil War uniform. The other is a woman with lank black hair and cruel, beautiful features. She's as pale as a comic-book vampire. Her uniform, like that of the faceless man, is black and silver, Gestapo-ish. Some sort of trumpery gem—it's as big as a pigeon's egg—hangs from a chain around her neck, flashing like a remnant of the psychedelic sixties.

She's a cartoon, Peter thinks. Some pubescent boy's first hesitant try at a sex-fantasy.

As he draws closer to the man with no face, he realizes an even more awful thing: he's not really there at all. Neither are the other two, and neither is the black van. He remembers a Saturday matinee—he couldn't have been more than six or seven years old—when he walked all the way down to the movie screen and stared up at it, realizing for the first time how cheesy the trick was. From twenty inches away the images were just gauze; the only reality was the bright reflective foundation of the screen, which was itself utterly blank, as featureless as a snowbank. It had to be, for the illusion to succeed. This is the same, and Peter feels the same sort of stupid surprise now that he felt then. I can see Herbie Wyler's house, he thinks. I can see it right through the van.

"*JACKSON!*"

But *that* is real, that voice, just as the bullet which took Mary's life was real. He screams through a grin of pain, jerking her body closer to his chest for a moment and then dropping her to the street in a tumble without even being aware of it. It is as if someone pressed the end of an electric bullhorn to one of his ears, turned the volume up all the way, and then bellowed his name into it. Blood bursts from his nose and begins to seep from the corners of his eyes.

"*THATAWAY, PARD!*" The black-and-silver figure, now insubstantial but still threatening, points at the Wyler house. The voice is the only reality, but it is all the reality Peter needs; it's like the blade of a chainsaw. He jerks his head back so hard his glasses fall askew on his face. "*WE GOT US SOME HOORAWIN TO DO! BEST GIT STARTED!*"

He doesn't walk toward Herbie and Audrey's house; he is *pulled* toward it, reeled in. As he walks through the black, faceless figure, a crazy image fills his mind for just a moment: spaghetti, the unnaturally red kind that comes in a can, and hamburger. All mixed together in a white bowl with Warner Bros. cartoon figures—Bugs, Elmer, Daffy—dancing around the rim. Just *thinking* about that kind of food usually nauseates him, but for the moment the image holds in his mind, he is desperately hungry; he lusts for those pallid strands of pasta and that unnatural red sauce. For that moment even the pain in his head ceases to exist.

He walks through the projected image of the black

van just as it starts to roll again, and then he's moving up the cement path to the house. His glasses finally give up their tenuous hold and fall off; he doesn't notice. He can still hear a few isolated gunshots, but they are distant, in another world. The twangy guitar is still playing in his head, and as the door to the Wyler house opens all by itself, the guitar is joined by horns and he places the tune. It's the theme to that old TV show, *Bonanza*.

I just got home from work, he thinks, stepping into a dark, fetid room that smells of sweat and old hamburger. I just got home from work, and the door slams shut behind him. I just got home from work, and he's crossing the living room, headed for the arch and the sound of the TV. "What are you wearing that uniform for?" someone asks. "War's been over near-bout three years, ain't you heard?"

I just got home from work, Peter thinks, as if that explained everything—his dead wife, the shooting, the man with no face, the rancid air of this little room—and then the thing sitting in front of the TV turns around to face him and Peter thinks nothing at all.

Out on the street, the vans which have composed the fire-corridor accelerate, the black one quickly catching up with Dream Floater and the Justice Wagon. The bearded man in the turret throws one final round. It hits the blue U.S. mailbox outside the E-Z Stop, putting a hole the size of a softball in it. Then the raiders turn left on Hyacinth and are gone. Rooty-Toot, Freedom, and Tracker Arrow leave on Bear

Street, disappearing into the mist which first blurs them and then swallows them.

In the Carver house, Ralphie and Ellen are shrieking at the sight of their mother, who has collapsed in the doorway leading to the hall. She isn't unconscious, however; her body snaps furiously from side to side as convulsions tear through her. It is as if her nervous system is being swept by hard squalls. Blood spatters from her shattered face in ropes, and she is making a complicated sound deep in her throat, a kind of singing growl.

"Mommy! Mommy!" Ralphie screams, and Jim Reed is losing his battle to keep the twisting, struggling boy from running to the woman dying in the kitchen doorway.

Johnny and Brad are coming down the stairs on their fannies—a riser at a time, like kids playing a game—but when Johnny gets to the bottom and understands what has happened, what is still happening, he gets to his feet and runs, first kicking aside the battered-in screen door, then crunching through the remains of Kirsten's beloved Hummels.

"No, get down!" Brad yells at him, but Johnny pays no attention. He's thinking only one thing, and that is to separate the dying woman from her kids as fast as he can. They don't need to see the rest of her suffering.

"Mommeeeee!" Ellen howls, trying to wriggle out from under Cammie. The girl's nose is bleeding. Her eyes are wild but hellishly aware. *"Mommmeeeeeee!"*

Unhearing, her days of caring about her children and her husband and her secret ambition to someday create beautiful Hummel figures of her own (most, she has thought, will probably look like her gorgeous son) all behind her, Kirsten Carver jitters mindlessly in the doorway, feet kicking, hands rising and falling, drumming briefly in her lap and then flying up again like startled birds. She growls and sings, growls and sings, sounds which are almost words.

"Get her out!" Cammie yells at Johnny. She stares at Pie with terror and pity. "Get her away from the kids, for Christ's sake!"

He bends, lifts, and then Belinda is there to help him. They carry Kirsten into her living room and set her on a couch that she agonized over for weeks and which is now bleeding stuffing from a gaping hole. Brad backs up before them to give them room, throwing nervous glances over his shoulder at the street, which appears once again to be deserted.

"Don't ask *me* to sew it," Pie says in an arch tone of voice, and then gives a horrible choked laugh.

"Kirsten," Belinda says, bending over her and taking one of her hands. "You're going to be all right. You're going to be fine."

"Don't ask *me* to sew it," the woman on the couch repeats. This time she sounds as if she is lecturing. The cushion under her head is growing dark, the bloodstain spreading visibly as the three of them stand looking down at her. To Johnny it looks like the kind of nimbus that Renaissance painters sometimes put around their Madonnas. And then the convulsions resume.

Belinda bends and seizes Kirsten's twisting shoulders. "Help me with her!" she chokes furiously at Johnny and her husband. She is weeping again. "Oh you stupids, I can't do it alone, *help* me with her!"

In the house next door, Tom Billingsley has gone on trying to save Marielle's life even at the height of the attack, working with the aplomb of a battlefield surgeon. Now she is sewn up, and the bleeding is down to a muddy seep through a triple fold of gauze, but when he looks up at Collie, Old Doc shakes his head. He is actually more upset by the cries from next door than by the operation he has just performed. He doesn't have much feeling about Marielle Soderson one way or the other, but he's almost positive the woman crying out over there is Kirstie Carver, and Kirstie he likes very much. "Boy oh boy," he says out loud. "I mean boy-howdy."

Collie looks toward Gary, wanting to make sure he's out of earshot, and spots him poking around in Doc's kitchenette, oblivious to the screaming and the weeping children next door, unaware that the operation on his wife is finished; he's opening and closing cupboards with the thoroughness of a dedicated alcoholic hunting for booze. His look into the fridge for beer or maybe some chilled vodka was an understandably short one; his wife's arm is there, on the second shelf. Collie put it in himself, sliding stuff around—salad dressing, pickles, the mayonnaise, some leftover sliced pork in Saran Wrap—until there was room for it. He doesn't think it will ever be reattached, not even in this age of miracles and wonders can such a thing be done, but he still couldn't bring himself to put it in Doc's pantry. Too warm. It would draw flies.

"Is she going to die?" Collie asks.

"I don't know," Billingsley says. He pauses, takes his own look at Gary, sighs, runs his hands through his Albert Einstein tangle of white hair. "Probably. Certainly, if she doesn't get to a hospital soon. She needs a lot of help. Most of all, a transfusion. And there's someone hurt next door, by the sound. Kirsten, I think. And maybe she's not the only one."

Collie nods.

"Mr. Entragian, what do you think is going on here?"

"I don't have the slightest idea."

Cynthia grabs a newspaper (it's the Columbus *Dispatch,* not the Wentworth *Shopper*) that has fallen to the living-room floor during the rumpus, rolls it up, and crawls slowly to the front door. She uses the newspaper to sweep broken glass—there is a surprising amount of it—out of her way as she goes.

Steve thinks of objecting, asking her if she maybe has a deathwish, then stows it. Sometimes he gets ideas about things. Pretty strong ones, as a matter of fact. Once, while peaceably reading palms on the boardwalk in Wildwood, he had an idea so strong that he quit the job that very night. It was an idea about a laughing seventeen-year-old girl with ovarian cancer. Malignant, advanced, maybe a month beyond any possible human remedy. Not the sort of idea you wanted to have about a pretty green-eyed high-school kid if your life's motto was

NO PROBLEM.

The idea he's having now is every bit as strong as that one but quite a bit more optimistic: the shooters are gone, at least for the time being. There's no way he can know that, but he feels certain of it, just the same.

Instead of calling Cynthia back, he joins her. The inside door has been blown open by several gunshots (it has also been so severely warped that Steve doubts it will ever close again), and the breeze coming through the shattered screen is heaven—sweet and cool on his sweaty face. The kids are still crying next door, but the screaming has stopped, at least for the time being, and that's a relief.

"Where is he?" Cynthia asks, sounding stunned. "Look, there's his wife"—she points to Mary's body, which is now lying in the street, close enough to the far side so that tendrils of her hair are wavering in the water rushing down the west gutter—"but where's *he*? Mr. Jackson?"

Steve points through the torn lower half of the screen. "In that house. Must be. See his glasses on the path?"

Cynthia squints, then nods.

"Who lives there?" Steve asks her.

"I don't know. I haven't been here anywhere near long enough to—"

"Mrs. Wyler and her nephew," Collie says from behind them. They turn and see him squatting on his hunkers, looking out between them. "The boy's autistic or dyslexic or catatonic . . . one of those damned icks, I can never keep them straight. Her husband died last year, so it's just the two of them. Jackson . . . must . . . must have . . ." He doesn't break off but runs down, the words getting smaller and smaller, finally diminishing into silence. When he speaks again, his voice is still low . . . and very thoughtful. "What the hell?"

"What?" Cynthia asks uneasily. "What?"

"Are you kidding me? You don't see?"

"See what? I see the woman, and I see her husband's gla . . ." Now it's her turn to run down.

Steve starts to ask what the deal is, then understands—sort of. He supposes he would have seen it earlier, even though he's a stranger to the street, if his attention hadn't been diverted by the body, the dropped spectacles, and his concern for Mrs. Soderson. He knows what he must do about that, and more than anything else he has been nerving himself up to do it.

Now, though, he simply looks across the street, letting his eyes move slowly from the E-Z Stop to the next building up, from that one to the one where the kids were playing Frisbee when he turned onto the street, and then on to the one directly opposite them, the one where Jackson must have gone to ground when the shooting got too hot.

There has been a change over there since the coming of the shooters in the vans.

Just how much he cannot tell, mostly because he is a stranger here, he *doesn't* know the street, partly because the smoke from the burning house and the mist still rising off the wet street give the houses over there a look which is almost spectral, like houses seen in a mirage . . . but there *has* been a change.

Siding has been replaced with logs on the Wyler house, and where there was a picture window there are now three more conventional—old-fashioned, one might almost say—multi-pane windows. The door has wooden supports hammered across its vertical boards in a Z-shape. The house next to it on the left . . .

"Tell me something," Collie says, looking at the same one. "Since when did the Reeds live in a log-fucking-cabin?"

"Since when did the Gellers live in an adobe *hacienda*?" Cynthia responds, looking at one farther down.

"You guys're kidding," Steve says. Then, weakly: "Aren't you?"

Neither of them replies. They look almost hypnotized.

"I'm not sure I'm really seeing it," Collie says at last. His voice is uncharacteristically hesitant. "It's . . ."

"Shimmery," the girl says.

He turns to her. "Yeah. Like when you look at something over the top of an incinerator, or—"

"Somebody help my wife!" Gary calls to them from the shadows of the living room. He has found a bottle of something—Steve can't see what—and is standing by the photo of Hester, a pigeon who liked to finger-paint. Not, Steve thinks, that pigeons exactly have fingers. Gary isn't steady on his feet and his words sound slurry. "Somebody help Mar'elle! Losser damn arm!"

"We need to get help for her," Collie says, nodding. "And—"

"—for the rest of us," Steve finishes. He's relieved, actually, to know that someone else realizes this, that maybe he won't have to go on his own. The boy next door has stopped crying, but Steve can still hear the girl, sobbing in big, watery hitches. Margrit the Maggot, he thinks. That's what her brother called her. Margrit the Maggot loves Ethan Hawke, he said.

Steve has a sudden urge, as strong as it is unaccustomed, to go next door and find that little girl. To kneel in front of her and take her in his arms and hug her and tell her she can love anyone she pleases. Ethan Hawke or Newt Gingrich or just anybody. He looks down the street instead. The E-Z Stop, so far as he can tell, hasn't changed; its style is still Late Century Convenience Store, sometimes known as Pastel Cinderblock, sometimes known as Still Life with Dumpster. Not beautiful, far from it, but a known quantity, and under the circumstances, that's a relief. The Ryder truck is still parked in front, the blue phone-sign is still hanging down from its hook, the Marlboro Man is still on the door, and . . .

. . . and the bike rack is gone.

Well, not *gone*, exactly; replaced.

By something that looks suspiciously like a hitching-rail in a Western movie.

With an effort, he drags first his eyes and then his mind back to the cop, who is saying Steve is right, they all need help. At the Carvers' as well as at Old Doc's, by the sound.

"There's a greenbelt behind the houses on this side of the street," Collie says. "There's a path that runs through it. Kids use it, mostly, but I'm partial to it myself. It forks behind the Jacksons' house. One arm runs down to Hyacinth. Comes out by the bus shelter halfway down the block. The other one goes east, over to Anderson Avenue. If Anderson's, pardon my French, fucked up—"

"Why should it be?" Cynthia asks. "There hasn't been any shooting from that direction."

He gives her a strange, patient look. "There hasn't been any *help* from that direction, either. And our street is fucked up in ways the shooting had nothing to do with, in case you haven't noticed."

"Oh," she says in a small voice.

"Anyway, if Anderson Avenue's as crazy as Poplar—I hope it isn't, but if it is—there's a viaduct that runs at least under the street, maybe farther. It could go all the way to Columbus Broad. There's got to be people there." He doesn't look as if he really believes it, though.

"I'll go with you," Steve says.

The cop looks surprised at the offer, then considering. "You sure that's a good idea?"

"Actually, yes. I think the bad guys're gone, at least for the time being."

"What makes you think that?"

Steve, who has absolutely no intention of bringing up his brief career as a boardwalk fortune-teller, says it's just a hunch. He sees Collie Entragian thinking it over, and knows the cop is going to agree even before he opens his mouth. Nothing psychic about it, either. Four people have been killed on Poplar Street this afternoon (not to mention Hannibal the Frisbee-stealing dog), more have been wounded, a house is burning flat without a single goddam fire-engine to attend it, there are crazy people running in the streets—homicidal maniacs—and the guy would have to be insane to want to go creeping alone through the woods between here and the next block.

"What about him?" Cynthia asks, jerking a thumb at Gary.

Collie grimaces. "Shape he's in, I wouldn't go to the movies with him, let alone into the woods with shit like this going down. But if you're serious, Mr. . . . Ames, is it?"

"Make it Steve. And I'm serious."

"Okay. Let's see if Old Doc's got a gun or two kicking around his basement. I bet he does."

They start back across the living room, bent low. Cynthia turns to follow them, then movement catches her eye. She turns back and her mouth drops open. Revulsion follows surprise, and she has to put a hand to her mouth to stifle the cry that wants to come out. She thinks of calling the men back, then doesn't. What would it change?

A buzzard—it *might* be a buzzard, although it looks like nothing she's ever seen in a book or a movie—has come cruising out of the billowing smoke from the Hobart house and landed in the street next to Mary Jackson. It's a huge unnatural awkwardness with an ugly, peeled head. It walks around the corpse, looking for all the world like a diner reconnoitering the buffet before actually grabbing a plate, and then it darts its head forward and pulls off most of the woman's nose.

Cynthia closes her eyes and tries to tell herself this is a dream, just a dream. It would be nice if she could believe it.

From Audrey Wyler's journal:

June 10, 1995

Scared tonight. So scared. It's been quiet lately—with Seth, I mean—but now all that's changed.

At first neither of us knew what was wrong—Herb as mystified as I was. We went out for ice cream at Milly's On The Square, part of our regular Saturday ritual if Seth is being "good" (which means if Seth is being Seth), and he was fine. Then, when we turned into the driveway, he started the sniffing thing he does sometimes—kind of raises his nose in the air and sniffs like a dog. I hate seeing him do that and so does Herb. The way farmers hate to hear tornado warnings on the radio, I suppose. I've read that the parents of epileptics learn to look for similar signs before seizures . . . obsessive head-scratching, swearing, even nose-picking. With Seth it's that sniffing thing. But it's not epileptic seizures. I only wish it was.

Herb asked him what was wrong as soon as he saw him doing it and got zilch, not even the usual vocalizing stuff he does. Same when I tried. No words; no gabble, even. Just more sniffing. And once he was in the house, that stalking thing—walking from place to place as if his legs won't bend. He went out back to the sandbox, he went upstairs to his room, he went downcellar, all in that ominous silence. Herb followed him for awhile, asking what was wrong, then gave up. While I was emptying the dishwasher, Herb came in waving a religious tract he found sticking out of the milkbox around at the side door & yelling "Hallelujah! Yes, Jesus!" He is a dear man, always trying to cheer me up, although I know he isn't doing all that well himself. His skin has gotten very pale, and I'm scared by all the weight he's lost, mostly since January or so. It must be at least 20 lbs and might be as much as 30, but whenever I ask him about it, he just laughs it off.

Anyway, the tract was typical Baptist bullshit. Had a picture on the front of a man in agony, with his tongue sticking out and sweat running down his face and his eyes rolled up. IMAGINE A MILLION YEARS WITHOUT ONE DRINK OF WATER! it says over the face. And under it, WELCOME TO HELL! I checked on the back and sure enough, Zion's Covenant Baptist Church. That bunch from Elder. "Look," Herb says, "it's my dad before he combs his hair in the morning."

I wanted to laugh—I know it makes him happy when he can make me laugh—but I just couldn't. I could feel Seth all around us, almost crackling on our skin. The way you can sometimes feel a storm building up, you know.

Just then he walked in—*stalked* in—with that horrible frown he gets on his face when something happens that doesn't fit into his general plan of life. Except it *isn't* him, it *isn't*. Seth is the sweetest, kindest, most accepting child I can imagine. But he has this other personality that we see more and more. The stiff-legged one. The one that sniffs the air like a dog.

Herb asked him what was wrong, what was on his mind, and then all at once he—Herb, I mean—reached up and grabbed his own lower lip. Pulled it out like a windowshade and started twisting it. Until it bled. And all the time his poor eyes were watering with pain and bugging out with fear and Seth was staring at him with that hateful frown he gets, the one that says "I'll do anything I please, you can't stop me." And maybe we can't, but I think that—sometimes, at least—Seth can.

"Stop making him do that!" I shouted at him. "You just stop it right now!"

When the other one, the *not*-Seth, gets really mad, his eyes seem to go from brown to black. He turned that look on me then, and all at once *my* hand came up and I slapped myself across the face. So hard my eye watered on that side.

"Make him stop, Seth," I said. "It's not fair. Whatever is wrong, we're not responsible for it. We don't even know what it is."

Nothing at first. Just more of the black look. My hand went up again, and then the hateful way he was looking at me changed a little. Not much, but enough. My hand went down and Seth turned and looked up into the open cabinet over the sink where we keep the glasses. My mother's are on the top shelf, nice Waterford crystal that I only take down for the holidays. They *were* up there, anyway. They burst when Seth looked at them, one after the other, like ducks in a shooting gallery. When they were gone, the eleven of them that were left, he looked at me with that mean, gloating smile he gets sometimes when you cross him and he hurts you for it. His eyes so black and somehow old in his child's face.

I started to cry. Couldn't help it. Called him

a bad boy & told him to go away. The smile slipped at that. He doesn't like to be told _anything_, but that least of all. I thought he might make me hurt myself again, but then Herb stepped in front of me and told him the same thing, to go away and calm down and then come back and maybe we could help him fix whatever was wrong.

Seth went off, and I could tell even before he got across the living room to the stairs that the other one was either gone or going. He wasn't walking in that horrible stiff way anymore. (Herb calls it "Seth's Rooty the Robot walk.") Then, later, we could hear him crying in his room.

Herb helped me clean up the glasses, me bawling like a fool the whole time. He didn't try to comfort me or jolly me outof it with any of his jokes, either. Sometimes he can be very wise. When it was done (neither of us got a single cut, sort of a miracle), he said the obvious, that Seth had lost something. I said no shit Sherlock, what was your first clue. Then felt bad and hugged him and said I was sorry, I didn't mean to be a bitch. Herb said he knew that, then turned over the stupid Baptist tract and wrote on the back of it "What are we going to do?"

I shook my head. Lots of times we don't even dare say stuff out loud for fear he's listening—the not-Seth, I mean. Herbie crumpled the tract & threw it in the trash, but that wasn't good enough for me. I took it out & tore it to shreds. But first I found myself looking at the sweaty, tortured face on the front of it. WELCOME TO HELL.

Is that Herb? Is it me? I want to say no, but sometimes it feels like hell. A lot of times, actually. Why else am I keeping this diary?

June 11, 1995

Seth sleeping. Exhausted, maybe. Herbie outside in the back yard, looking everywhere. Although I think Seth has already been looking. We know what's missing now, at least: his Dream Floater Power Wagon. He's got all the MotoKops shit—action figures, HQ Crisis Center, Cassie's Party Pad, Power Wagon Corral, two stun pistols, even "floatpad sheets" for his bed. But more than anything he loves the Power Wagons. They're battery-powered vans, quite large, VERY futuristic. Most have wings he can pop out by pushing a lever on the bottom, plus radar dishes that really turn on the roofs (the one on Cassie Styles's Dream Floater is shaped like a valentine, this after about thirty years' worth of talking about equal rights & female role-models for girls; I could just about puke), flashing lights, siren noises, space-blaster noises, etc., etc.

Anyway, Seth came back from California with all six that are currently on the market: the red one (Tracker Arrow), the yellow one (Justice Wagon), the blue one (Freedom), the black one (Meatwagon, belongs to the bad guy), the silver one (Rooty-Toot, & just think, someone gets paid to think this shit up), and the stupid pink one, driven by Cassie Styles, the love of our young nephew's life. His crush is actually sorta funny & sweet, but there's nothing funny about what's currently going on around here: Seth's "Dweem Fwoatah" is gone, and all this is a kind of tantrum.

Herbie shook me awake at six this morning, pulled me out of bed. His hand was cold as ice. I asked him what it was, what was wrong, and he wouldn't say. Just pulled me over to the window & asked me if I saw anything out there. I could tell what he meant was did I see what he was seeing.

I saw it, all right. It was Dream Floater, which looks sorta art deco, like something from the old Batman comic books. But it wasn't *Seth's* Dream Floater, not the toy. That's about two feet long & maybe a foot high. The one we were seeing was full-sized, probably twelve feet long and maybe seven feet high. The roof-hatch was part way up, & the heart-shaped radar dish was turning, just as it does on the show.

"Jesus Christ," I said. "Where did that come from?" All I could think was that it must have flown in on its stubby little retractable wings. It was like getting out of bed with one eye open and discovering a flying saucer has landed in your back yard. I couldn't get my breath. I felt like someone had punched me in the stomach!

At first when he told me it wasn't there I didn't understand what he meant, and then the sun came up a little more and I realized I could see the aspens behind our fence right through it. It really *wasn't* there. But at the same time it *was*.

"He's showing us what he couldn't tell us," Herb said.

I asked if Seth was awake & Herb said no, he'd been down the hall to check and Seth was fast asleep. That gave me a chill I can't describe. Because it meant we were standing there at our bedroom window in our pj's & looking out at our nephew's dream. It was there in the back yard like a big pink soap-bubble.

We stood there for about twenty minutes, watching it. I don't know if we expected Cassie Styles to come out or what, but nothing like that happened. The pink van just sat there with its roof-hatch partway up and its radar dish turning, and then it started to fade until it was just a shimmer. By the end you couldn't have told what it was, if you hadn't seen it when it was brighter. Then we heard Seth getting up and going down the hall. By the time the toilet flushed, it was gone.

At breakfast, Herb pulled his chair over next to Seth's, the way he does when he really wants to talk to him. In some ways I think Herb is braver than I ever could be. Especially since it's Herb that—

No, I won't put that down.

Anyway, Herbie puts his face close to Seth's—so that Seth has to look at him—& then talks in a low, kind voice. He tells Seth we know what's wrong, why he's so upset, but not to worry because Cassie's Power Wagon is sure to be in the house or in the back yard somewhere. We'll find it, he says. All during this Seth was fine. He kept eating his cereal & his face didn't change, but sometimes you just know it's him and that he's listening and understanding at least a little. Then Herb said, "And if we absolutely can't find it, we'll get you a new one," & everything went to hell.

Seth's cereal bowl went flipping across the room, spilling milk and cereal all over the kitchen floor. It hit the wall & broke. The drawer under the stove came open, and all the things I keep under there—frying pans, cookie-sheets, muffin-tins—came flying out. The sink faucets turned on. The dishwasher supposedly can't start with the door open, but it did & water went all over the floor. The vase I keep on the window-shelf over the sink flew all the way across the room & broke against the wall. Scariest of all was the toaster. It was on, I was making a couple of slices to have with my o.j., & all at once it glowed bright red inside the slots, as if it was a furnace instead of a little counter-gadget. The handle went up & the toast flew all the way up to the ceiling. It was black and smoking. Looked nuclear. It landed in the sink.

Seth got up and walked out of the room. His stalky walk. Herb and I just looked at each other for a second or two, & then he said, "That toast would probably taste okay with a little peanut butter on it." I just gaped at him at first but then I started laughing. That got him started. We laughed & laughed, with our heads down on the kitchen table. Trying to keep him from hearing, I guess, except that's stupid—Seth doesn't always have to hear to know. I'm not sure it's mind-reading he does, exactly, but it's <u>something</u>.

When I finally got control of myself enough to look up, Herb was getting the mop for under the dishwasher. He was still kind of chuckling and wiping at his eyes. Thank God for him. I went to get the dustpan and brush for the broken vase.

"I guess he's sort of committed to the old Dream Floater" is all Herb said. And why say any more? That pretty well covers it.

Now it's three in the afternoon and we have "been all over the geedee house," as my old school-friend Jan would say. Seth has tried to help, in his own peculiar way. It kinda broke my heart to see him turning up the sofa cushions, as if his missing van could've slipped under there like a quarter or a crust of pizza. Herb started out hopeful, saying it was too big & bright to miss, & I thought he was right. As a matter of fact I still think he's right, so how come we can't find it? From where I'm writing at the kitchen table I can see Herb down on his knees by the hedge at the back of the yard, poking along with the handle of a rake. I'd like to tell him to stop—it's the third time he's been along there—but I don't have the heart.

Noises upstairs. Seth's getting up from his nap, so I need to finish this. Put it out of sight. Try to put it out of mind, too. That should be okay, though. I think Seth has more success picking up what Herb is thinking than he does with me. No real reason, but the feeling is strong. And I've been careful not to tell Herb that I'm keeping a journal.

I know what anyone reading the journal would say: we're nuts. Nuts to keep him. Something is wrong with him, Badly wrong, and we don't know what it is. We know it's dangerous, though. So why do it? Why go on? I don't know, exactly. Because we love him? Because he's controlling us? No. Sometimes there _are_ things like that (Herb twisting his lip or me slapping myself), things like a powerful hypnosis, but not often. He's mostly just Seth, a child in the prison of his own mind. He's also the last little bit of my brother. But sure, beyond all that (and over it, and under it, and around it) is just loving. And every night when Herb and I lie down, I see in my husband's eyes what he must see in mine—that we made it thru another one, & if we made it thru today, we can make it thru tomorrow. At night it's easy to tell yourself that it's just another aspect of Seth's autism, really no big deal.

Footsteps overhead. He's going to the bathroom. When he finishes, he'll come downstairs, hoping we've found his missing toy. But which one will hear the bad news? Seth, who'll only look disappointed (and maybe cry a little)? Or the other one? The stalky one who throws things when he can't have what he wants?

I have thought about taking him back to the doctor, sure, of course, I'm sure Herb has, too . . . but not seriously. Not after the last time. We were both there & we both saw the way the other one, the _not_-Seth, hides. How Seth makes it _possible_ for it to hide: autism is one hell of a big shield.

But the real problem here is not autism, it doesn't matter what all the doctors in the world see or don't see. When i open my mind & set aside all i hope & all i wish, i know that. And when we tried to talk to the doctor, tried to tell him why we were really there, we couldn't. If anyone ever reads this, i wonder if you'll be able to understand how horrible that is, to have something that feels like a hand laid over the back of your mouth, a guard between your vocal cords and your tongue. WE COULDN'T FUCKING TALK.

i'm so afraid.

Afraid of the stalky one, yes, but afraid of other things, as well. Some i can't even express, and some i can express all too well. But for now, the thing i'm most afraid of is what might happen to us if we can't find Dream Floater. That stupid goddam pink van. Where can the damned thing be? If only we could find it—

CHAPTER 8

1

At the moment of Kirsten Carver's death, Johnny was thinking of his literary agent, Bill Harris, and Bill's reaction to Poplar Street: pure, unadulterated horror. Good agent that he was, he had managed to maintain a neutral, if slightly glazed, smile on the ride from the airport, but the smile began to slip when they entered the suburb of Wentworth (which a sign proclaimed to be OHIO'S "GOOD CHEER" COMMUNITY!), and it gave way entirely when his client, who had once been spoken of in the same breath with John Steinbeck, Sinclair Lewis, and (after *Delight*) Vladimir Nabokov, pulled into the driveway of the small and perfectly anonymous suburban house on the corner of Poplar and Bear. Bill had stared with a kind of dazed incomprehension at the lawn sprinkler, the aluminum screen door with the scrolled *M* in the center of it, and that avatar of suburban life, a grass-stained power-mower, standing in the driveway like a gasoline god waiting to be worshipped. From there Bill had turned his gaze upon a kid roller-blading down the far sidewalk with Walkman earphones on his head, a melting ice-cream cone from Milly's in his hand, and a happy brainless grin on his pimply face. Six years ago this had been, in the summer of 1990, and when Bill Harris, power agent, had looked back at Johnny again, the smile had been gone.

You can't be serious, Bill had said in a flat, disbelieving voice. Oh, Bill, but I think I am, Johnny had responded, and something in his tone seemed to get through to Bill, enough at least so that when he spoke again he'd sounded plaintive rather than disbelieving. But why? he asked. Dear Jesus, why *here*? I can sense my IQ dropping and I just fucking got here. I feel an almost irresistible urge to subscribe to *Reader's Digest* and listen to talk radio. So you tell me why. I think you owe me that. First the goddam puddy-tat detective, and now a neighborhood where fruit cocktail is probably considered a delicacy. Tell me what the deal is, okay? And Johnny had said okay, the deal is, it's all over.

No, of course not. *Belinda* had said that. Not Bill Harris but Belinda Josephson. Just now.

Johnny cleared his mind with an effort and looked around. He was sitting on the living-room floor, holding one of Kirsten's hands in both of his. The hand was cold and still. Belinda was leaning over Kirstie with a dishtowel in her hand and a square of white linen—it looked to Johnny like a for-best table napkin—folded over her shoulder like a waiter's towel. Belinda's eyes were tearless, but there was nevertheless an expression of love and sorrow on her face that moved Johnny's heart. She was wiping Kirsten's blood-masked face with the dishtowel, uncovering what remained of her features.

"Did you say—" Johnny began.

"You heard me." Belinda held the stained dishtowel out without looking, and Brad took it. She took the napkin off her shoulder, unfolded it, and spread it over Kirsten's face. "God have mercy on her soul."

"I second that," Johnny said. There was something hypnotic about the small red poppies blooming on the white linen napkin, three on one side of the draped shape that was Kirsten's nose, two on the other, maybe half a dozen above her brow. Johnny put his hand to his own brow and wiped away a palmful of sweat. "Jesus, I'm so sorry."

Belinda looked at him, then at her husband. "We're all sorry, I guess. The question is, what's next?"

Before either man could answer, Cammie Reed came into the room from the kitchen. Her face was pale but composed. "Mr. Marinville?"

He turned to her. "Johnny," he said.

She had to mull it over—another classic case of shock-slowed thinking—before understanding that he wanted her to call him by his first name. Then she got it and nodded. "Johnny, okay, sure. Did you find the pistol? And are there bullets to go with it?"

"Yes to both."

"Can I have them? My boys want to go for help. I've thought it over and have decided to give them my permission. If you'll let them take David's gun, that is."

"I don't have any objection to giving up the gun," Johnny said, not knowing if he was telling the complete truth about that or not, "but leaving shelter could be extremely dangerous, don't you think?"

She gave him a level look, no sign of impatience in her eyes or voice, but she fingered a spot of blood on her blouse as she spoke. A souvenir of Ellen Carver's nosebleed. "I'm aware of the danger, and if it were a question of using the street, I'd say no. But the boys know a path which runs through the greenbelt behind the houses on this side. They can use it to go over to Anderson Avenue. There's a deserted building over there that used to be a moving company's warehouse—"

"Veedon Brothers," Brad said, nodding.

"—and a waterpipe that runs from the lot behind it all the way over to Columbus Broad, where it empties into a stream. If nothing else, they can get to a working phone and report what's going on here."

"Cam, do either of your boys know how to use a gun?" Brad asked.

Again the level stare, one which did not quite come out and ask *Why do you insult my intelligence?* "They both took a safety course with their dad two years ago. The primary focus was on rifles and hunting safety, but handguns were covered, yes."

"If Jim and Dave know about this path, the shooters

who are doing this may, too," Johnny said. "Have you thought about that?"

"Yes." The impatience finally showing, but only a little. Johnny admired her control. "But these . . . lunatics . . . are strangers. They *have* to be. Have you ever seen any of those vans before today?"

I may have, at that, Johnny thought. I'm not sure where yet, but if I can just get a little time to think . . .

"No, but I believe—" Brad began.

"We moved here in 1982, when the boys were three," Cammie said. "They say there's a path that hardly anyone knows about or uses except for kids, and they say there's a pipe. I believe them."

Sure you do, Johnny thought, but that's secondary. So's the hope of their bringing back help. You just want them out of here, don't you? Of course you do, and I don't blame you.

"Johnny," she said, perhaps assuming his silence meant he was against the idea, "there were boys not much older than my sons fighting in Vietnam not so long ago."

"Some even younger," he said. "I was there. I saw them." He got up, pulled the pistol from the waistband of his slacks with one hand, pulled the box of cartridges out of his shirt pocket with the other. "I'll be glad to turn this over to your boys . . . but I'd like to go along with them."

Cammie glanced down at Johnny's belly—not as large as Brad's, but still considerable. She didn't ask him why he wanted to go, or what good he thought he could do. Her mind was, at least for the time being, colder than that. She said, "The boys play soccer in the fall and run track in the spring. Can you keep up with them?"

"Not in the mile or the four-forty, of course not," he replied. "On a path through the woods, and maybe through a viaduct? I think so."

"Are you kidding yourself, or what?" Belinda asked abruptly. It was Cammie she was talking to, not Johnny. "I mean, if there was still a working phone within earshot of Poplar Street, do you think we'd still be sitting here with dead people lying out front and a house burning to the ground?"

Cammie glanced at her, touched the blood-spot on her blouse again, then looked back at Johnny. Behind her, Ellie was peering around the corner into the living room. The girl's eyes were wide with shock and grief, her mouth and chin streaked with blood from her nose.

"If it's okay with the boys, it's okay with me," Cammie said, not addressing Belinda's question at all. Cammie Reed currently had no interest in speculation. Maybe later, but not now. Now there was only one thing that *did* interest her: rolling the dice while she judged the odds were still heavily in her favor. Rolling them and getting her sons out the back door.

"It will be," he said, and handed her the gun and the cartridges before heading back toward the kitchen. They were good boys, which was nice, and they were also boys who had been programmed to go along, in nine cases out of ten, with what their elders wanted. In this situation, that was even nicer. As Johnny walked, he touched the object he had stowed in his left front pants pocket. "But before we go, it's important that I talk to someone. Very important."

"Who?" Cammie asked.

Johnny picked Ellen Carver up. He hugged her, kissed one bloodstained cheek, and was glad when her arms went around his neck and she hugged him back fiercely. You couldn't buy a hug like that. "Ralphie Carver," he said, and carried Ralphie's sister back into the kitchen.

2

As it happened, Tom Billingsley *did* have a couple of guns kicking around, but first he found Collie a shirt. It wasn't much—an old Cleveland Browns tee with a rip under one arm—but it was an XL, and better than trying the path through the greenbelt naked from the waist up. Collie had used the route often enough to know there were blackberry bushes, plus assorted other prickers and brambles, out there.

"Thanks," he said, pulling the shirt on as Old Doc led them past the Ping-Pong table at the far end of his basement.

"Don't mention it," Billingsley said, reaching up and tugging the string that turned on the fluorescents. "Can't even remember where it came from. I've always been a Bengals fan, myself."

In the corner beyond the Ping-Pong table was a jumble of fishing equipment, a few orange hunting vests, and an unstrung bow. Old Doc squatted with a grimace, moved the vests, and uncovered a quilt that had been rolled and tied with twine. Inside it were four rifles, but two of them were in pieces. Billingsley held up the ones that were whole. "Should do," he said.

Collie took the .30-.06, which probably made a lot more sense for a woods patrol than his service pistol, anyway (and would raise fewer questions if he had to shoot someone). That left Ames with the other, smaller gun. A Mossberg. "It's only chambered for .22s," Doc said apologetically as he rummaged in a cabinet mounted next to the fusebox and laid out cartons of cartridges on the Ping-Pong table, "but it's a damned fine gun, just the same. Holds nine in a row for more go. What do you think?"

Ames offered a grin Collie couldn't help liking. "I think oy vey, such a deal," he said, taking the Mossy. Billingsley laughed at that—a cracked old man's chortle—and led them back upstairs.

Cynthia had put a pillow under Marielle's head, but she was still lying on the living-room floor (under the picture of Daisy, the mathematically inclined Corgi, actually). They hadn't dared move her; Billingsley was afraid his stitches might tear open again. She was still alive, which was good, and still unconscious, which might also be good, considering what had happened to her. But she was breathing in great, irregular gasps that did not sound good to Collie at all. It sounded like the kind of breathing that might stop any time.

Her husband, the charming Gary, was sitting in a

kitchen chair which he had turned around so he could at least look at his wife while he drank. Collie saw that the bottle he had found contained Mother DeLucca's Best Cooking Sherry, and felt his stomach turn over.

Gary saw him looking (or perhaps felt it), and looked over at Collie. His eyes were red and puffy. Sore-looking. Miserable. Collie hunted in his heart and found some sympathy for the man. Not much, though. "Losser damn arm," he told Collie in a furry, confiding voice. "Gaw hepper." Collie thought this over and translated it as Drunkish for either *Got to help her* or *God help her*.

"Yes," he said. "We're going to get her some help."

"Aw be here awreddy. Losser mahfuhn arm. Zin the mahfuhn *fritch*!"

"I know."

Cynthia joined them. "You used to be a vet, didn't you, Mr. Billingsley?"

Billingsley nodded.

"I thought so. Could you come here? Take a look at something out the front door?"

"Do you think that's safe?"

"For the time being, I think so. The thing that's out there . . . well, I'd rather you looked for yourself." She glanced at the other two men. *"Selves."*

She led Billingsley across the living room to the door looking out on Poplar Street. Collie glanced at Steve, who shrugged. Collie's assumption was that the girl wanted to show Billingsley how the houses across the street had changed, although what that had to do with Billingsley's being a vet he didn't know.

"Holy shit," he said to Steve as they reached the door. "They've gone back to normal! Or did we just imagine they'd changed in the first place?" It was the Geller house he kept staring at. Ten minutes ago, when he and the hippie and the counter-girl had been looking out this same door, he could have sworn that the Geller place had turned into an adobe—the sort of thing you saw in pictures of New Mexico and Arizona back when they were territories. Now it was clad in plain old Ohio aluminum siding again.

"We didn't imagine it and things haven't gone back to normal," Steve said. "At least, not all the way. Check that one."

Collie followed Steve's pointing finger and stared at the Reed house. The modern aluminized siding had returned, replacing the logs, and the roof was once more neat asphalt shingles instead of whatever it had been before (sod, he thought); the mid-sized satellite dish was back on top of the carport. But the house's foundation was rough wood planking instead of brick, and all the windows were tightly shuttered. There were loopholes in those shutters, too, as if the inhabitants of the house expected their day-to-day problems to include marauding Indians as well as Seventh-day Adventists and wandering insurance salesmen. Collie couldn't say for sure, but he didn't think the Reed house had even had shutters before this afternoon, let alone ones with rifleport loopholes.

"Sa-aaay." Billingsley sounded like a man who is finally getting the idea that all of this is a *Candid*

Camera stunt. "Are those *hitching-rails* in front of Audrey's? They are, aren't they? What is all this?"

"Never mind that," Cynthia said. She reached up, took the old man's face between her hands, and turned it like a camera on a tripod so he was looking at the corpse of Peter Jackson's wife.

"Oh my God," Collie said.

There was a large bird perched on the woman's bare thigh, its yellow talons buried in her skin. It had already snacked off most of her remaining face, and was now burrowing into the flesh under her chin. Collie had a brief, unwelcome memory of going after Kellie Eberhart in exactly the same place one night at the West Columbus Drive-In, her saying that if he gave her a hickey, her dad would probably shoot them both.

He didn't realize he had lifted the .30-.06 into firing position until Steve pushed the barrel back down with the palm of his hand. "No, man. I wouldn't. Better to keep quiet, maybe."

He was right, but . . . *God*. It wasn't just what it was doing, but what it *was*.

"Losser goddam arm!" Gary announced from the kitchen, as if afraid they might forget this if he allowed them to. Old Doc ignored him. He had crossed the living room looking like a man who expects to be shot dead in his tracks at any moment, but now he seemed to have forgotten all about killers, weird vans, and transforming houses.

"My good gosh, look at that!" he exclaimed in a tone that sounded very much like awe. "I ought to photograph it. Yes! Excuse me . . . I'll just get my camera . . ."

He began to turn away. Cynthia grabbed him by the shoulder. "The camera can wait, Mr. Billingsley."

He seemed to come back a little to their situation at that. "Yes . . . I suppose, but . . ."

The bird turned, as if hearing them, and seemed to stare at the vet's bungalow with its red-rimmed eyes. Its pink skull appeared black with stubble. Its beak was a simple yellow hook.

"Is that a buzzard?" Cynthia asked. "Or maybe a vulture?"

"Buzzard? *Vulture?*" Old Doc looked startled. "Good gosh, no. I've never seen a bird like that in my life."

"In Ohio, you mean," Collie said, knowing that *wasn't* what Billingsley meant, but wanting to hear it for himself.

"I mean *anywhere.*"

The hippie looked from the bird to Billingsley and then back to the bird again. "What is it, then? A new species?"

"New species my fanny! Excuse my French, young lady, but that's a fucking mutant!" Billingsley stared, rapt, as the bird opened its wings, flapping them in order to help it move a little farther up Mary's leg. "Look how big its body is, and how short its wings are in relation to it—damned thing makes an ostrich look like a miracle of aerodynamics! I don't think the wings are even the same *length*!"

"No," Collie said. "I don't think they are, either."

"How can it *fly*?" Doc demanded. "How can it possibly *fly*?"

"I don't know, but it does." Cynthia pointed down toward the thick billows which had now blotted out all vestiges of the world below Hyacinth Street. "It flew out of the smoke. I saw it."

"I'm sure you did, I didn't think someone pulled up in a . . . a Birdmobile and dropped it off, but how it can *possibly* fly is beyond all—" He broke off, peering at the thing. "Although I can understand how you might have thought it was a buzzard before the inevitable second thoughts set in." Collie thought Old Doc was mostly talking to himself by this point, but he listened intently just the same. "It does look a little like a buzzard. As a child might draw it, anyway."

"Huh?" Cynthia said.

"As a child might draw it," Billingsley repeated. "Perhaps one who got it all mixed up in his mind with a bald eagle."

3

The sight of Ralphie Carver hurt Johnny's heart. Put aside by Jim Reed, whose solicitude had been superseded by his excitement at the impending mission, Ralphie stood between the stove and the refrigerator with his thumb in his mouth and a big wet spot spreading on the front of his shorts. All his bratty bluster had departed. His eyes were huge and still and shiny. He looked to Johnny like drug addicts he had known.

Johnny stopped inside the kitchen door and put Ellie down. She didn't want to go, but at last he managed to pry her hands gently off his neck. Her eyes were also shocked, but held none of the merciful glaze Johnny could see in her brother's. He looked past her and saw Kim and Susi Geller sitting on the floor with their arms around each other. Probably suits Mom just fine, Johnny thought, remembering how the woman had seemed to struggle with young David Reed for possession of the girl. He had won then, but now David had bigger fish to fry; he was bound for Anderson Avenue and parts unknown. That didn't change the fact that there were two little kids here who had become orphans since lunch, however.

"Kim?" he asked. "Could you maybe help a little with—"

"No," she said. No more, no less. And calm. No defiance in her gaze, no hysteria in her tone . . . but no fellow feeling, either. She had an arm around her daughter, her daughter had an arm around her, cozy as can be, just a coupla white girls sittin around and waitin for the clouds to roll by. Understandable, maybe, but Johnny was furious with her, nevertheless; she was suddenly everyone he had ever known who looked bored when the conversation came around to AIDS, or homeless children, or the defoliation of the rain forests; she was everyone who had ever stepped over a homeless man or woman sleeping on the sidewalk without so much as a single glance down. As he had on occasion done himself. Johnny could picture himself grabbing her by the arms, hauling her to her feet, whirling her around, and planting a swift kick square in the middle of her narrow midwestern ass. Maybe that would wake her up. Even if it didn't, it would certainly make *him* feel a little better.

"No," he repeated, feeling his temples throb with stupid rage.

"No," she agreed, and gave him a wan little at-last-you-understand smile. Then she turned her head toward Susi and began to stroke the girl's hair.

"Come on, dear heart," Belinda said to Ellen, leaning down and opening her arms. "Come over here and spend some time with Bee." The girl came, silent, her face twisting in an awful cramp of grief that made the silence somehow even worse, and Belinda enfolded her.

The Reed twins watched this, but really didn't see. They were standing by the back door, looking bright-eyed and excited. Cammie approached them, stood in front of them, appraised them with an expression Johnny at first mistook for dourness. A moment more and he realized what it really was: terror so large it could only be partially concealed.

"All right," she said at last. Her voice was dry and businesslike. "Which one carries it?"

The boys looked at each other, and Johnny had a sense of communication between them—brief but complex, perhaps the sort of thing in which only twins could engage. Or perhaps, he thought, it's just that your brains have boiled, John. That was not actually so farfetched. They certainly *felt* boiled.

Jim held out his hand. For just a moment his mother's upper lip trembled. Then it firmed and she passed him David Carver's pistol. Dave took the shells and opened the box while his brother rolled the .45's cylinder and held the gun up to the light, checking to make sure the chambers were empty just as Johnny had done. We're careful because we understand the potential a gun has to maim and kill, Johnny thought, but it's more than that. On some level we know they're evil. Devilish. Even their biggest fans and partisans sense it.

Dave was holding out a palmful of shells to his brother. Jim took them one at a time, loading the gun.

"You act like your father was with you every minute," Cammie said as he did it. "If you think of doing something he wouldn't let you do if he was here, *don't*. Is that understood?"

"Yes, Mom." Jim snapped the pistol's cylinder closed and then held it at the end of his arm with his finger outside the trigger-guard and the muzzle pointing at the floor. He looked both embarrassed by his mother's orders—she sounded like the C.O. in an old Leon Uris novel, laying down the law for a couple of green privates—and wildly excited at the prospect of what lay ahead.

She turned her attention to the other twin. "David?"

"Yes, Mom?"

"If you see people—strangers—in the woods, come right back. That's the most important thing. Don't ask questions, don't respond to anything they might say, don't even approach them."

Jim began, "Mom, if they don't have guns—"

"Don't ask *questions,* don't *approach* them," she repeated. She didn't speak much louder, but there was something in her voice they both flinched back from a little. Something that finished the discussion.

"Suppose they see cops, Mrs. Reed?" Brad asked. "The police may have decided the greenbelt is their best approach to the street."

"Safest to stay away," Johnny said. "Any cops we run into are apt to be . . . well, nervous. Nervous cops have been known to hurt innocent people. They never mean to, but it's better to be safe. Avoid accidents."

"Are you coming with us, Mr. Marinville?" Jim asked.

"Yes."

Neither twin said anything, but Johnny liked the relief he saw in their eyes.

Cammie gave Johnny a forbidding look—*Are you done? May I get back to business?* it said—and then resumed her instructions. "Go to Anderson Avenue. If everything looks all right there . . ." She faltered a moment, as if realizing how unlikely that was, and then pushed on. ". . . ask to use someone's phone and call the police. But if Anderson Avenue's like it is here, or if things seem even the slightest bit . . . well . . ."

"Hinky," Johnny said. In Vietnam they'd had as many words for the feeling she was talking about as Indians had for variations in the weather, and it was funny how they all came back, turning on like neon signs in a dark room. Hinky. Weirded-out. Bent. Snafu'd. Dinky-dau. Yeah, doc, it's all coming back to me now. Pretty soon I'll be whipping a bandanna into a rope and tying it around my forehead to keep back the sweat, maybe leading the congregation in the Fish Cheer.

Cammie was still looking at her boys. Johnny hoped she'd hurry up. They were still looking back at her with respect (and a little fear), but most of what she had to say from this point on would go in one ear and out the other just the same.

"If you don't like what you see on Anderson Avenue, use that pipe you know about. Get over to Columbus Broad. Call the police. Tell them what's happened here. And don't you even *think* of coming back to Poplar Street!"

"But Mom—" Jim began.

She reached up and seized his lips, pinching them shut. Not painfully, but firmly. Johnny could easily imagine her doing the same thing when the twins were ten years younger, only bending down to do it.

"You save 'but Mom' for another time," she said. "This time you just *mind* Mom. Get to a safe place, call the police, then stay put until this craziness is over. Got it?"

They nodded. Cammie nodded back and let go of Jim's lips. Jim was smiling an embarrassed smile—ohboy, that's my ma—and blushing to the tips of his ears. He knew better than to remonstrate, however.

"And be careful," she finished. Something came in her eyes—an urge to kiss them, Johnny thought, or maybe just an urge to call the whole thing off while she still could. Then it was gone.

"Ready, Mr. Marinville?" Dave asked. He was looking enviously at the gun dangling at the end of his brother's arm. Johnny suspected they would not be too far down the path through the greenbelt before he asked to carry it awhile.

"Just a second," he said, and knelt down in front of Ralphie. Ralphie backed away until his little butt was flush against the wall, then looked at Johnny over his thumb. Down here at Ralphie's level, the smell of urine and fear was so strong it was jungly.

From his pocket Johnny took the figure he'd found in the upstairs hall—the alien with the big eyes, the horn of a mouth, and the stiff strip of yellow hair running up the center of his otherwise bald head. He held it in front of Ralphie's eyes. "Ralphie, what's this?"

For a moment he didn't think the boy was going to answer. Then, slowly, he reached out with the hand that wasn't anchored in his mouth and took it. For the first time since the shooting had begun, a spark of life showed in his face. "That's Major Pike," he said.

"Oh?"

"Yes. He's a Canopalean." He pronounced this word carefully, proudly. "That means he's a nailien. But a *good* nailien. Not like No Face." A pause. "Sometimes he drives Bounty's Power Wagon. Major Pike wasn't with them, was he?" Tears overspilled Ralphie's eyes, and Johnny suddenly remembered the story every kid used to know about the Black Sox baseball scandal in 1919. A weeping little boy had supposedly approached Shoeless Joe Jackson, begging the ballplayer to tell him that the fix hadn't been in—to say it wasn't so. And although Johnny *had* seen this freak—or someone wearing a mask to make him look like this freak—he immediately shook his head and gave Ralphie a comforting pat on the shoulder.

"Is Major Pike from a movie or a TV show?" Johnny asked, but he knew the answer already. It was coming together now, maybe should have come together a lot earlier. In the last few years he had taught a lot of classes in schools where grownups had to lean over seriously in order to drink from the water fountains, did a lot of readings in library rooms where the chairs were mostly three feet high. He listened to the run of their talk, but he didn't watch their shows or go to their movies. He knew instinctively that that sort of research would hinder his work rather than help it. So he didn't know everything, and still had plenty of questions, but he thought he was beginning to believe that this craziness *could* be understood.

"Ralphie?"

"From a TV show," Ralphie said around his thumb. He was still holding Major Pike up in front of his eyes, much as Johnny had done. "He's a MotoKop."

"And Dream Floater. What's that, Ralphie?"

"Mr. Marinville," Dave began, "we really ought to—"

"Give him a second, son," Brad said.

Johnny never took his eyes off Ralphie. "Dream Floater?"

"Cassie's Power Wagon," Ralphie said. "Cassie Styles. I think she's Colonel Henry's girlfriend. My friend Jason says she isn't because MotoKops don't have girlfriends, but I think she is. Why are the Power Wagons on Poplar Street, Mr. Marinville?"

"I don't know, Ralphie." Except he almost did.

"Why are they so *big*? And if they're good guys, why did they shoot my daddy and mommy?"

Ralphie dropped the Major Pike figure on the floor and kicked it all the way across the room. Then he put his hands over his face and began to sob. Cammie Reed started forward, but before she could get there, Ellen had wriggled free of Belinda. She went to Ralphie and put her arms around him. "Never mind," she said. "Never mind, Ralphie, I'll take care of you."

"Won't *that* be a treat," Ralphie said through his sobs, and Johnny clapped a hand over his mouth almost hard enough to make his lips bleed. It was the only way he could keep from bursting into mad, yodeling laughter.

If they're good guys, why did they shoot my daddy and mommy?

"Come on, boys," he said, standing up and turning to the Reed twins. "Let's go exploring."

4

On Poplar Street, the sun was starting to go down. It was too early for it to be going down, but it was, just the same. It glared above the horizon in the west like a baleful red eye, turning the puddles in the street and the driveways and on the stoops to fire. It turned the broken glass which littered the block into embers. It turned the eyes of the *faux*-buzzard into red pits as it lifted off from the body of Mary Jackson on its improbable wings and flew across the street to the Carver lawn. Here it alit, looking from David Carver's body to that of Susi Geller's friend. It seemed unsure upon which to start. So much to eat, so little time. At last it chose Ellen and Ralphie's father, approaching the dead man in a series of clumsy hops. One of its yellow claw-feet sported five talons, the other only two.

Across the street, in the Wyler house—in the smell of dirt, old hamburger, and tomato soup—the TV blared on. It was the first saloon scene of *The Regulators*.

"You're a right purty lady," Rory Calhoun was saying. That knowing leer in his voice, the one that said *Babydoll, I'm going to eat you like ice cream before this shitty little oat-opera is over, and both of us know it*. "Why don't you sit down n have a drink? Bring me some luck?"

"I don't drink with trash," Karen Steele responded coldly, and all of Rory Calhoun's men—the ones not currently hiding outside of town, that was—guffawed.

"Well ain't you a little spitfire?" Rory Calhoun said, relaxed, and his men guffawed some more.

"Want some Doritos, Pete?" Tak said. Now it spoke in the voice of Lucas McCain, who rode the cable-TV range in *The Rifleman*.

Peter Jackson, seated in the La-Z-Boy in front of the TV, didn't reply. He was grinning broadly. Moving shadows played across his face, occasionally making the grin look like a silent scream, but it was a grin, all right.

"He should have some, all right, Paw," Tak said, now in the almost-adolescent voice of Johnny Crawford, who had played Lucas's son. "They're the good ones. Cool Ranch. Come on, Mr. Jackson, over the teeth and over the gums, look out guts, 'cause here they come."

The boy held chips out in one grimy hand and waved them up and down in front of Peter Jackson's face. Peter took no notice. He stared at the TV, through the TV, with eyes that bulged out of his head like those of some exotic deep-dwelling fish that has undergone explosive decompression. And he grinned.

"Don't appear he's hongry, Paw."

"I think he is, son. Hongry as hell. You're hongry, ain't you, Pete? Just need a little help, that's all. *So take the damn chips!*"

There was a kind of humming in the room. A line of static appeared briefly on the TV, where Rory Calhoun was now trying to kiss Karen Steele. She slapped his face and knocked off his hat. That wiped away his leering, teasing grin. Folks—even womenfolks—didn't knock off Jeb Murdock's hat with impunity.

Peter slowly raised the chips. He bypassed his relentlessly grinning mouth and began poking them against his nose instead, crumbling them, catching some of the smaller pieces in his nostrils. His unnaturally bulging eyes never left the TV.

"Little too high, Mr. Jackson." Now it was the earnest voice of Hoss Cartwright. Hoss had been one of Seth's favorites before Tak came to stay inside him, and so now he was one of Tak's favorites, too. They rolled that way, like a wheel. "Let's try again, what do you say?"

The hand went down slowly and jerkily, like a freight elevator. This time the chips went into Peter's mouth, and he began to chew mechanically. Tak smiled at him with Seth's mouth. It hoped—in its strange way it did have emotions, although none of them were precisely human—that Peter was enjoying the Doritos, because they were going to be his last meal. It had sucked a great deal of life-force out of Peter, first replenishing the gaudy amounts of energy it had expended this afternoon, then taking in more. Getting ready for the next step.

Getting ready for the night.

Peter chewed and chewed, Dorito fragments spilling out of his grin and tumbling down the front of his tee-shirt, the one with happy old Mr. Smiley-Smile on the front. His eyeballs, bulging so far out of their sockets that they seemed to be lying on his cheeks, quivered with the motion of his jaw. The left one had split like a squeezed grape when Tak invaded his mind and stole most of it—the useful part—but he could still see a little out of the right one. Enough so he'd be able to do the next part mostly on his own. Once, that was, his motor was running again.

"Peter? I say, Peter, can you hear me, old boy?" Tak now spoke in the clipped British tones of Andrew

Case, Peter's department head. Like all of Tak's imitations, it was quite good. Not as good as its Western movie and TV show imitations (at which it had had much more practice), but still not bad.

And the voice of authority did wonders, it had found, even for the terminally brain-damaged. A vague flicker of life came into Peter's face. He turned and saw Andrew Case in a spiffy houndstooth jacket instead of Seth Garin in a pair of MotoKops Underoos decorated with reddish-orange blobs of Chef Boyardee sauce.

"I'll want you to go across the street now, old boy. Into the woods, eh? But you needn't toddle all the way to Grandmother's house. Just to the path. Do you know the path in the woods?"

Peter shook his head. His protruding eyeballs trembled above the stretched clown rictus of his lips.

"No matter, you'll find it. Hard to miss, old top. When you get to the fork, you can sit down with your . . . friend."

"My friend," Peter said. Not quite a question.

"Yes, that's right."

Peter had never actually met the man he would be joining at the fork in the path and never actually would, not really, but there was no sense in telling Peter these things. He didn't have mind enough left to understand them, for one thing. He was shortly going to be dead, for another. As dead as Herb Wyler. As dead as the man with the shopping cart, the one Peter would shortly be meeting in the woods.

"My friend," Peter said a second time. A little surer now.

"Yep." The British department head was gone; Tak returned to John Payne doing his Gary Cooper thing. "Best be crawling, pard."

"Down the path to the fork."

"Reckon so."

Peter rose to his feet like an old clockwork toy with rust in its gears. His eyeballs jiggled in the silver dreamlight from the TV.

"Best be crawling. And when I get to the fork, I can sit down with my friend."

"Yessir, that's the deal." Now it was the half-leering, half-laughing voice of Rory Calhoun. "He's quite the boy, your friend. You *could* say he got this whole thing started. Lit the fuse, anyway. You git on, now, pard. Happy trails to you, until we meet again."

Peter walked through the arch, not glancing with his one dying eye at Audrey, who was slumped over sideways in one of the living-room chairs with her eyes half-open. She appeared to be in a daze or perhaps even a state of coma. She was breathing slowly and regularly. Her legs, long and pretty (the first things about her to attract Herb back in the days when she had still been Audrey Garin), were stretched out before her, and Peter almost stumbled over them in his sleepwalk to the front door. When he opened the door and the red light of the declining day fell on his grin, it looked more like a scream than ever.

Halfway down the walk with that red light falling like strained blood through the rising pillar of smoke from the Hobart place, the Rory Calhoun voice filled his head, ripping at it like a razor blade: *Close the door behind you, partner, was you born in a barn?*

Peter made a drunken about-face, came back and did as he was told. The door was smooth and intact, the only one on the block not riddled with bullet-holes. He did another about-face (almost falling off the stoop in the process) and then set sail through the red light toward his own house, where he would walk up the driveway, past the breezeway, and into the back-yard. From there he would climb over the low wire fence and enter the greenbelt. Find the path. Find the fork. Find his friend. Sit down with his friend.

He stepped over the sprawled body of his wife, then paused as a wild cry rose in the hot, smoky air: *Wh-Wh-Whooo* . . . As far gone as he was, that cry brought a scatter of gooseflesh to his arms. What was a coyote doing in Ohio? In a suburb of Colum—

Best be crawling, pard. Git along, little dogie.

Pain, even more excruciating than before. He moaned through the frozen curve of his grin. Fresh blood oozed from his ruptured eye and trickled down his cheek.

He started forward again, and when the cry returned, this time joined by a second, a third, and finally a fourth—he didn't react. He thought only of the path, the fork, the friend. Tak made one final check of the man's mind (it did not take long, as there was not much mind left in Peter to check) and then withdrew.

Now there was only it and the woman. It supposed it knew why it had let her live, like the bird that is reputed to live in the very jaws of the crocodile, the bird safe from the croc's teeth because it cleans among them, but Tak would not save her much longer. In many ways the boy had been an inspired host—perhaps the *only* host in which it could have lived and grown so much—but there was this one ironic drawback: what Tak could conceive and desire, the boy's body could not carry out. It could dress the woman and dye her hair, it could strip her naked, it could make her pinch her own nipples and do all sorts of other puerile things if it desired. It did not desire. What it desired was to couple with her, and that it could not do. Under certain circumstances it felt that it might have been able to manage some sort of joining in spite of its host's immaturity . . . but Seth himself was still inside, and on the occasions it had really tried, Seth had prevented it. Tak could have challenged the boy and almost certainly prevailed, but it was perhaps wiser not to do so. It had not emerged from its black place under the Nevada dust, after all the millennia of imprisonment, to have sex with a woman who was much younger than Tak itself and much older than its host body.

And what *had* it come for?

Well . . . to have fun. And . . .

To *watch television*, a voice far back in its mind whispered. *To watch television, to eat SpaghettiOs, and to make. To build.*

"You want to try me, Sheriff?" Rory Calhoun asked, and Tak's eyes drifted back to the TV. Some of the others might be moving into the woods. It could have made sure of this one way or another if it had really desired, but it did not. Let them go into the woods if they wanted. They would not like what they found. And where could they go? Back, that was all. Back to the houses. In a very real sense, there *was* nowhere else. Meantime, it would save its energy. Just relax and watch the movie. Soon enough it would be time to bring on the night.

"Why don't we just stand down, think things over?" John Payne asked, and Seth and Tak came together again, as the Westerns—this one in particular—had always brought them together. Tak bent forward, eyes never leaving the screen, and picked up a bowl filled with a congealed mixture of Franco-American spaghetti and hamburger. It began to eat, eyes glued to the TV screen, oblivious of the chunks of meat that tumbled down its naked chest from time to time, coming to rest in its lap. Soon the final shootout would begin yet again—KA-POW and KA-BAM all the way home—and Tak let itself float into the story and the silvery black-and-white images, drinking in the atmosphere of violence, as ripe and electric as an impending thunderstorm.

As it watched, entranced, Seth Garin separated himself from Tak and moved away from it with the stealth of Jack creeping past the sleeping giant. He glanced at the TV and wasn't surprised to find that, whatever Tak might believe, he no longer liked *The Regulators* very much. Then he turned away, found one of the secret passages he had made for himself during Tak's reign, and disappeared quietly into it.

Deeper into his own mind he went, the passage taking him ever downward. He walked at first, then began to jog. He didn't understand much more of this world than he did the one outside, but now it was the only world he had.

From The Regulators, *screenplay by Craig Goodis and Quentin Woolrich:*

EXT. MAIN STREET DAY

SHERIFF STREETER *watches* DEPUTY LAINE *yank* CANDY *to his feet. Behind them, in the adobe which houses Lushan's Chinese Laundry, a number of Chinese workers watch from the doorway, where they are huddled.*

CANDY

What're you chinkies lookin' at?!

They don't recoil this time.

CHINESE LAUNDRYMAN

You! Clothes needee washee now, sure, sure!

The other CHINESE *laugh. Even* STREETER *smiles a little.* CANDY *looks dazed. Can't believe* STREETER *has beaten him in a fair fight, can't believe these "Chink-Chink-China Boys" are laughing at him, can't believe any of this is happening.*

STREETER

Best get on inside, boys.

The LAUNDRYMEN *go back inside, but look out the windows.*

STREETER (*to* LAINE)

Make sure he gets his hat, Josh. Wouldn't want him to have to go to jail without his hat.

Grinning, LAINE *picks up* CANDY'S *pinned-back Johnny Reb cavalry hat, which fell off* CANDY'S *head when* STREETER *knocked him over the hitching-rail. Now, grinning more broadly than ever,* DEPUTY LAINE *slams it down on the defeated thug's head. There is a puff of dust.*

LAINE

Come on, Cap'n. I done saved you the nicest tent in the bivouac. Wait'll you see it.

He shoves the dazed and defeated CANDY *toward the jail.* SHERIFF STREETER *is watching them go with a grin, and does not at first see the batwing doors of the Lady Day Saloon open as* MAJOR MURDOCK *pushes out onto the side-walk. For once,* MURDOCK'S *trademark grin is gone.*

SCENE CONTINUES

MURDOCK

You think puttin' Candy in jail's gonna solve your problems, Sheriff?

STREETER *turns toward him.* MURDOCK *pulls his mud-splattered cavalry duster back, freeing the butt of his Army-issue Colt.*

STREETER (*smiles*)

Could be I just arrested my first ghost. Where are the rest of your regulators holed up? Desatoya Canyon? Skate Rock? You ready to tell me yet?

MURDOCK

You're crazy as a snakebit varmit!

STREETER

That so? Well, we'll see. I'm guessing there won't be any ghosts riding tonight without Captain Candell to hand out the sheets.

Still smiling, STREETER *turns toward the jail again.*

SCENE CONTINUES

MURDOCK

Suppose I told you the regulators were a lot closer than Desatoya Mountain or Skate Rock? Suppose I told you they were right outside of town, just waitin' for the first gunshot? How would you like that, you damn Yankee?

STREETER

I think I'd like it just fine.

He looks up, raises his fingers to his mouth, and WHISTLES.

EXT. MAIN STREET ROOFTOPS, STREET POV

MEN *start appearing from behind every sign, chimney, and false front. Formerly terrified* TOWNSMEN, *now looking grim and carrying rifles. They're on the Chinese laundry, the Owl County Store, Worrell's Mercantile, even Craven's Undertaking Parlor. Among them we see* PREACHER YEOMAN *and* LAWYER BRADLEY. YEOMAN, *no longer concerned that the regulators are a supernatural visitation meant to punish the town for its sins, raises one hand to the* SHERIFF *in a salute.*

SCENE CONTINUES

RESUME MAIN STREET, WITH STREETER AND MURDOCK

STREETER *returns* YEOMAN'S *salute with a flick of his hand, then turns back to* MURDOCK, *who looks furious and confused. A dangerous combination!*

STREETER

Yep, bring 'em on, if that's your pleasure.

MURDOCK'S *face tightens. He drops his hand until it hovers just above the butt of his Colt. Neither of them sees* LAURA *push her way out of the saloon from behind* MURDOCK. *She's wearing one of her spangly outfits and carrying her* DERRINGER.

MURDOCK

You want to try me, Sheriff?

STREETER

Why don't we just stand down? Think this thing over?

But he knows it's too late, he's pushed MURDOCK *too far.* STREETER *drops his own hand to just above the butt of his gun.*

MURDOCK

Time for talking's done, Sheriff.

SCENE CONTINUES

STREETER

Wellnow, if that's the way you want it.

MURDOCK

You could have stood aside and nobody would have got hurt.

STREETER

That's not the way we do things around here. We—(*sees* LAURA)

STREETER

Laura, no!

While he's distracted, MURDOCK GOES FOR HIS GUN. LAURA *darts between the two men, pointing the* DERRINGER *at* MURDOCK. *She pulls the trigger, but there's only a* CLICK. MISFIRE! *A split second later,* MURDOCK *fires his cavalry Colt, and the bullet meant for* STREETER *hits* LAURA *instead. She* CRUMPLES.

EXT. ROOFTOPS

The TOWNSMEN *raise their guns to fire.*

RESUME MAIN STREET IN FRONT OF THE SALOON

MURDOCK *sees what's about to happen and dives back through the batwings*

SCENE CONTINUES

and into the relative safety of the Lady Day. STREETER *chases him with a couple of shots, then runs to laura and kneels beside her.*

RESUME ROOFTOPS

FLIP MORAN, *the hostler, lets go with a round. A couple of others follow suit, but only a couple, luckily.*

RESUME MAIN STREET IN FRONT OF THE SALOON

A BULLET WHINES *off one of the batwing doors, knocking a splinter out.*

STREETER

Don't shoot, he's gone!

RESUME ROOFTOPS

The men lower their guns. FLIP MORAN *looks confused and ashamed of himself.*

EXT. STREETER AND LAURA, CLOSE

The SHERIFF'S *hard shell is temporarily gone—smashed. He looks down at the* DYING DANCEHALL GIRL *and realizes he loves her!*

STREETER

Laura!

SCENE CONTINUES

LAURA (*coughing*)
Gun misfired . . . you always said . . . never trust a . . . a hideout gun . . .

She breaks down coughing.

STREETER
Don't talk. I'll send Joe Prudum for the doc—

LAURA (*coughing*)
Too . . . too late. Just hold me!

STREETER *does. She looks up at him* CURIOUSLY.

LAURA
Why, Sheriff! . . . are you crying?

EXT. REAR OF THE LADY DAY

MURDOCK *comes bursting out.* SERGEANT MATHIS *is still there, holding the horses.*

SARGE
What happened? I heard shootin'!

MURDOCK (*swings up on his horse*)

SCENE CONTINUES

Never mind. It's time to get
the boys.

SARGE

You mean--?!

Suddenly MURDOCK'S *insanity breaks free. His eyes* BLAZE. *His lips pull back in a snarl that looks almost like a grin. It is the grin of a cornered* ANIMAL!

MURDOCK

We're gonna wipe this town
off the map!

They wheel their horses away to join the rest of the regulators.

CHAPTER 9

1

There was no need for Steve and Collie to hop the fence at the far end of Doc's yard; there was a gate, although they had to tear out a fair amount of well-entrenched ivy before they could use it. They exchanged words only twice before reaching the path. The first time it was Steve who spoke. He looked around at the trees—scrubby, weedy-looking things, for the most part, now mysterious with the rustle of rainwater dripping off the leaves—and then asked: "Are these poplars?"

Collie, who had been working his way around a particularly vicious clump of thornbushes, looked back at him. "Say what?"

"I asked if these trees are poplars. Since Poplar Street is where we came from, I just wondered."

"Oh." Collie looked around doubtfully, swapping the .30-.06 from one hand to the other and then running an arm across his forehead. It was very hot in the greenbelt. "I don't know if they're poplars or pines or goddam eucalyptuses, to tell you the truth. Botany was never my thing. That one over there is a skinny-ass birch, and that's about all I know on the subject." With that, he started off again.

Five minutes later (Steve wondering by now if there really *was* a path back here, or only wishful thinking), Collie stopped. He looked back past Steve, his eyes so intense that Steve himself turned to see what he was looking at. He saw nothing but the tangled greenery through which they had already made their way. No sign of Old Doc's house; the Jacksons', either. He could see a tiny wedge of red that he thought might be the chimney atop the Carver house, but that was all. They almost could have been a hundred miles from the nearest human habitation. Thinking that—and realizing it was a true thought—gave Steve a chill.

"What?" he asked, thinking the cop would ask him why they couldn't hear any cars, not even some kid's glasspack-equipped low-rider, or a single bass-powered sound-system, or a motorcycle, or a horn, or a shout, or *anything*.

Instead, Collie said: "We're losing the light."

"We can't be. It's only—" Steve looked at his watch, but it had stopped. The battery had given out, probably; he'd never replaced it since his sister had given it to him for Christmas a couple of years ago. It was odd, though, that it should have stopped just past four o'clock, which had to be not long after the time he had first wheeled into this marvellous little neighborhood.

"Only what?"

"I can't say exactly, my watch has stopped, but just think about it. It *can't* be much more than five-thirty, five forty-five. Maybe even earlier. Don't they say you overestimate elapsed time when you're in a crisis situation?"

"I don't even know who 'they' are, never have," Collie said. "But look at the light. The *quality* of the light."

Steve did, and yes, the cop had a point. Steve didn't like to admit it, but he did. The light slanted through the tangle (and that was the proper word for it, not greenbelt) in hot red shafts. Red sun at night, sailor's delight, he thought, and suddenly, as if that was a trigger, it all tried to crash in on him, all the things that were wrong, and he couldn't stand it. He raised his hands and clapped them over his eyes, whacking himself a damned good one on the side of the head with the butt of the .22 he was carrying, feeling his bladder go loose, knowing he was close to watering his underwear and not caring. He staggered backward and—from a distance, it seemed—heard Collie Entragian asking if he was okay. With what felt like the greatest effort of his life, Steve said that he was and forced himself to lower his hands, to look into that delirious red light again.

"Let me ask you a very personal question," Steve said. He thought his voice did not sound even remotely like his own. "How scared are you?"

"Very." The big guy armed more sweat off his forehead. It was very hot in here, but in spite of the dripping, rustling leaves, the heat felt strangely dry to Steve, not in the least greenhouse-ish. The smells were that way, too. Not unpleasant, but dry. Egyptian, almost. "Don't lose hope, though. I see the path, I think."

It was indeed the path, they stepped onto it less than a minute after getting moving again, and Steve saw signs—comforting ones, under the circumstances—of the animals which had used this particular game-trail: a potato-chip bag, the wrapper from a pack of baseball cards, a couple of double-A batteries which had maybe been pried out of some kid's Walkman after they went dead, initials carved on a tree.

He saw something far less comforting on the other side of the track: a misshapen growth, prickly and virulent green, amid the sumac and scrub trees. Two more stood behind it, their lumpy arms sticking stiffly up like the arms of alien traffic cops.

"Holy shit, do you see those?" Steve asked.

Collie nodded. "They look like cactuses. Or cacti. Or whatever you say for more than one."

Yes, Steve thought, but only in the way that women painted by Picasso during his Cubist phase looked like real women. The simplicity of the cactuses and their lack of symmetry—like the bird with the mismatched wings—gave them a surreal aspect that hurt his head. It was like looking at something that wouldn't quite come into focus.

It does *look a little like a buzzard,* Old Doc had said. *As a child might draw it.*

Things were starting to group together in his mind. Not *fit* together, at least not yet, but forming themselves naturally into what they had been taught to call a set back in Algebra I. The vans, which looked like props from a kids' Saturday matinee. The bird. Now these violent green cactuses, like something you'd see in an energetic first-grader's picture.

Collie approached the one closest to the path and stuck out a tentative finger.

"Man, don't do that, you're nuts!" Steve said.

Collie ignored him. Reached the finger farther. Closer. And closer yet, until—

"*Ouch!* You mother!"

Steve jumped. Collie yanked his hand back and peered at it like a kid with an interesting new scrape. Then he turned to Steve and held it out. A bead of blood, small and dark and perfect, was forming on the pad of his index finger. "They're real enough to poke," he said. "This one is, anyway."

"Sure. And what if it poisons you? Like something from the Congo Basin, something like that?"

Collie shrugged as if to say too late now, pal, and started along the path. It was headed south at this point, toward Hyacinth. With the red-orange sunlight flooding through the trees from the right, it was at least impossible to become disoriented. They started down the hill. As they went, Steve saw more and more of the misshapen cacti in the woods to the east of the path. They were actually crowding out the trees in places. The underbrush was thinning, and for a very good reason: the topsoil was also thinning, being replaced by a grainy gray sandbed that looked like . . . like . . .

Sweat ran in Steve's eyes, stinging. He wiped it away. So hot, and the light so strong and red. He felt sick to his stomach.

"Look." Collie pointed. Twenty yards ahead, another clump of cacti guarded a fork in the path. Jutting out from them like the prow of a ship was an overturned shopping cart. In the dying light, the metal basket-rods looked as if they had been dipped in blood.

Collie jogged down to the fork. Steve hurried to keep up, not wanting to get separated from the other even by a few yards. As Collie reached the fork, howls rose in the strange air, sharp and yet somehow sickeningly sweet, like bad barbershop-quartet harmony: *Whoooo! Whoooo! Wh-Wh-Whooooo!* There was a pause and then they came again, more of them this time, mingling and yipping, bringing gooseflesh to every square inch of Steve's skin. My children of the night, he thought, and in his mind's eye saw Bela Lugosi, a spook in black and white, spreading his cloak. Maybe not such a great image, under the circumstances, but sometimes your mind went where it wanted.

"Christ!" Collie said, and Steve thought he meant those howls—coyotes howling somewhere to the east of them, where there were supposed to be houses and stores and five different kinds of McBurger restaurants—but the big cop wasn't looking that way. He was looking down. Steve followed his gaze and saw a man sitting beside the beached shopping cart. He was propped against a cactus, stuck to its spines like a grotesque human memo which had been left here for them to find.

Wh-Wh-Whoooo . . .

He reached out, not thinking about it, and found the cop's hand. Collie felt his touch and grabbed back. It was a hard grip, but Steve didn't mind.

"Oh shit, I've *seen* this guy," Collie said.

"How in Christ's name can you tell?" Steve asked.

"His clothes. His cart. He's been on the street two or three times since the start of the summer. If I saw him again, I was going to warn him off. Probably harmless, but—"

"But what?" Steve, who had been on the bum a time or two in his life, didn't know whether to be pissed or amused. "What'd you think he was going to do? Steal someone's favorite velvet Elvis painting? Try to hit that guy Soderson up for a drink?"

Collie shrugged.

The man pinned to the cactus was dressed in patched khaki pants and a tee-shirt even older, dirtier, and more ragged than the one Billingsley had found for Collie. His elderly sneakers were bound together with electrical tape. They were the clothes of a bum, and the possessions which had spilled out of the cart when it overturned suggested the same: an old pair of airtip dress shoes, a length of frayed rope, a Barbie doll, a blue jacket with BUCKEYE LANES printed on the back in gold thread, a bottle of wine, half full, stoppered with what looked like the finger of a lady's evening glove, and a boombox radio which had to be at least ten years old. Its plastic case had been mended with airplane glue. There were also at least a dozen plastic bags, each carefully rolled up and secured with twine.

A dead bum in the woods. But how in God's name had he died? His eyes had popped out of their sockets and hung on his cheeks from dried optic nerves. Both looked deflated, as if the force that had pushed them out had also split them. His nose had bled copiously over his lips and the salt-and-pepper stubble on his chin. The blood didn't obscure his mouth, though—Steve only wished it had. It was distended in a huge, loopy grin that seemed to have dragged the corners of the bum's mouth halfway to his grimy ears. Something—some force—had swatted him into the cactus-grove and killed him hard enough to shove his eyeballs clear out onto his face. Yet the same force had left him grinning.

Collie's hand was gripping harder than ever. Crushing his fingers.

"Can you let up?" Steve asked. "You're breaking my—"

He looked up the east-tending fork of the path, the one that was supposed to lead them out onto Anderson Avenue and help. It ran on for about ten yards and then opened like the mouth of a funnel into a nightmare desert world. That it bore no resemblance to Ohio made no impression on Steven Ames, for the simple reason that it bore no resemblance to any landscape he had ever seen in his life. Or glimpsed in his dreams.

Beyond the last few sane, green trees was a broad expanse of whitish hardpan running toward a troubled horizon of sawtooth mountain peaks. They had no shading or texture, no folds or outcrops or valleys. They were the dead black Crayola mountains of a child.

The path didn't disappear but widened out, became a kind of cartoon road. There was a half-buried wagon-wheel on the left. Beyond it was a stony ravine filled with shadows. On the right was a sign, black letters on bleached white board.

TO THE PONDEROSA

it said. The signpost was topped with a cow-skull as misshapen as the cacti. Beyond the sign, the road ran straight to the horizon in an artificially diminishing perspective that made Steve think of movie posters for *Close Encounters of the Third Kind*. There were already stars in the sky above the mountains, impossible stars that were much too big. They didn't seem to twinkle but to blink on and off like Christmas-tree lights. The howls rose again, this time not a trio or a quartet but a whole choir. Not from the foothills; there *were* no foothills. Just flat white desert, green blobs of cactus, the road, the ravine, and, in the distance, the sharktooth necklace of the mountains.

Collie whispered, "What in God's name is this?"

Before Steve could reply—*Some child's mind,* he would have said, given the chance—a low growl came from the ravine. To Steve it sounded almost like the idle of a powerful boat engine. Then two green eyes opened in the shadows and he took a step back, his mouth drying. He lifted the Mossberg, but his hands felt like blocks of wood and the gun looked puny, useless. The eyes (they floated like comic-strip eyes in a dark room) looked the size of goddam *footballs,* and he didn't think he wanted to see how big the animal that went with them might be. "Can we kill it?" he asked. "If it comes at us, do you think—"

"Look around you!" Collie interrupted. "Look what's happening!"

He did. The green world was retreating from them and the desert was advancing. The foliage under their feet first became pallid, as if something had sucked all the sap out of it, then disappeared as the dark, moist earth bleached and granulated. *Beads.* That was what he had been thinking a few moments ago, that the topsoil had been replaced by this weird round beadlike shit. To his right, one of the scrubby trees suddenly plumped out. This was accompanied by the sound you get when you stick your finger in your cheek and then pop it. The tree's whitish trunk turned green and grew spines. Its branches melted together, the color in the leaves seeming to spread and blur as they became cactus arms.

"You know, I think it might be time to beat a retreat here," Collie said.

Steve didn't bother to reply; he talked with his feet instead. A moment later and they were both running back along the path toward the place where they had stepped onto it. At first Steve thought only about not getting poked in the eye by a branch, running into a drift of brambles, or going past the discarded double-A batteries, which was where they'd want to turn dead west and head for Billingsley's gate. Then he heard the coughing growl again and everything else faded into insignificance. It was close. The green-eyed creature from the ravine was following them. Hell, *chasing* them. And gaining.

2

There was a gunshot, and Peter Jackson slowly turned his head toward it. He realized (so far as he was still capable of realizing anything) that he had been standing on the edge of his backyard and looking at (so far as he was still capable of looking at anything) the table on the patio. There was a stack of books and magazines on the table, most bristling with pink marker-slips. He had been working on a scholarly article called "James Dickey and the New Southern Reality," relishing the thought that it would stir a great deal of controversy in certain ivied bowers of academe. He might be invited to other colleges to be on panel discussions! Panel discussions to which he would travel with all expenses paid! (Within reason, of course.) How he had dreamed of that. Now it all seemed faraway and unimportant. Like the gunshot from the woods, and the scream that followed it, and the two shots which followed the scream. Even the snarling sounds—like a tiger that had escaped from the zoo and hidden in their greenbelt—seemed faraway and unimportant. All that mattered was . . . was . . .

"Finding my friend," he said. "Getting to the fork in the path and sitting down with my friend. Best . . . be crawling."

He crossed the patio on a diagonal, striking the edge of the table with his hip as he walked by. An issue of *Verse Georgia* and several of his research books fell off the stack and landed on the puddly pink brick. Peter ignored them. His fading sight was fixed on the greenbelt which ran behind the houses on the east side of Poplar Street. His almost lifelong interest in footnotes had deserted him.

3

When it happened, Jan wasn't exactly talking about Ray Soames; she was wondering why God had made a world where you couldn't help wanting to be kissed and touched by a man who often—hell, usually—had dirty ankles and washed his hair maybe four times a month. If it was a good month, that was. So she really was talking about Ray, just omitting the names.

And for the first time since she'd been coming here,

running here, Audrey felt a touch of impatience, the soft stroke of friend-weariness. She was finally losing patience with Jan's obsession, it seemed.

Audrey was standing at the entrance to the folly, looking down the meadow to the rock wall, listening to the hum of the bees and wondering what she was doing here, anyway. There were people who needed help, people she knew and, in most cases, liked. There was a part of her—quite persuasive it was, too—that was trying to make her believe that they didn't matter, that they were not only four hundred miles west of here but fourteen years in the future, except that was a lie, persuasive or not. *This* place was the illusion. *This* place was the lie.

But I need to be here, she thought. I really, really do.

Maybe, but Janice's love-hate relationship with Ray Soames suddenly bored her to tears. She felt like whirling on her heels and saying, *Well, why don't you quit whining and drop him? You're young, you're pretty, you've got a good body. I'm sure you can find someone with clean hair and breath to scratch the parts of you that itch the worst.*

Saying such an awful thing to Jan was apt to expel her from this place of safety as surely as Adam and Eve had been expelled from the Garden of Eden for eating the wrong apple, but that didn't change how she felt. And if she managed to keep her mouth shut about Jan's love-obsession, what would come next? Jan's hundred and fiftieth assertion that, while Paul might well be the cutest Beatle, John was the only one she would have seriously considered sleeping with?

As though the Beatles had never broken up; as though John had never died.

Then, before she could say or do anything, a new sound intruded in this quiet place where there was usually only the hum of bees, the rickety-rick of crickets in the grass, and the murmuring voices of the two young women. It was a jingling sound, light but somehow demanding, like the handbell of an old-timey schoolmistress, calling the children in from recess and back to their studies.

She turned, realizing that Jan's voice had ceased, and no wonder. Jan was gone. And on the splintery table, with its entwined initials stretching back almost to World War I, the Tak-phone was ringing.

For the first time in all her visits, the Tak-phone was ringing.

She walked toward it slowly—three little steps was all it took—and stared down at it, her heart beating hard. Part of her was screaming at her not to answer, that she knew now and had always known what that phone's ringing would mean: that Seth's demon had found her. But what else was there to do?

Run, a voice (perhaps it was the voice of her own demon) suggested coldly. Run out into this world, Audrey. Down the hill, scattering the butterflies before you, over the rock wall, and to the road on the other side. It goes to New Paltz, that road, and it doesn't matter if you have to walk all day to get there and finish up with blisters on both heels. It's a college town, and somewhere along Main Street there'll be a window with a sign in it—WAITRESS WANTED. You can work your way up from there. Go on. You're young, in your early twenties again, you're healthy, you're not bad-looking, and none of this nightmare has happened yet.

She couldn't do that . . . could she? None of this was *real,* after all. It was just a refuge in her mind.

Ring, ring, ring.

Light but demanding. Pick me up, it said. Pick me up, Audrey. Pick me up, podner. We got to ride on over to the Ponderosa, only this time you ain't never coming back.

Ring, ring, ring.

She bent down suddenly and planted a hand on either side of the little red phone. She felt the dry wood under her palms, she felt the shapes of carved initials under her fingertips and understood that if she took a splinter in this world, she would be bleeding when she arrived back in the other one. Because this *was* real, it *was,* and she knew who had created it. Seth had made this haven for her, she was suddenly sure of it. He'd woven it out of her best memories and sweetest dreams, had given her a place to go when madness threatened, and if the fantasy was getting a little threadbare, like a carpet starting to show strings where the foot-traffic was the heaviest, that wasn't his fault.

And she couldn't leave him to fend for himself. *Wouldn't.*

Audrey snatched up the handset of the phone. It was ridiculously small, child-sized, but she hardly noticed that. "Don't you hurt him!" she shouted.

"Don't you hurt him, you monster! If you have to hurt someone, hurt m—"

"Aunt Audrey!" It was Seth's voice, all right, but changed. There was no stuttering, no grasping for words, no lapses into gibberish, and although it was frightened, it did not seem to be in a panic. At least not yet. "Aunt Audrey, listen to me!"

"I *am*! Tell me!"

"Come back! You can get out of the house now! You can run! Tak's in the woods . . . but the Power Wagons will be coming back! You have to get out before they do!"

"What about you?"

"I'll be all right," the phone-voice said, and Audrey thought she heard a lie in it. Unsureness, at least. "You have to get to the others. But before you go . . ."

She listened to what he wanted her to do, and felt absurdly like laughing—why had she never thought of it herself? It was so simple! But . . .

"Can you hide it from Tak?" she asked.

"Yes. But you have to hurry!"

"What will we do? Even if I get to the others, what *can* we—"

"I can't explain now, there's no time. You have to trust me, Aunt Audrey! Come back now, and trust me! *Come back!* COME BACK!"

That last shriek was so loud that she tore the telephone away from her ear and took a step backward. There was an instant of perfect, vertiginous disorientation as she fell, and then she hit the floor with the side of her head. The blow was cushioned by the living-room carpet, but it sent a momentary flock of comets streaming across her vision anyway. She sat up, smelling old hamburger grease and the dank aroma of a house that hadn't had a comprehensive cleaning or top-to-bottom airing in a year or more. She looked first at the chair she had fallen out of, then at the telephone clutched in her right hand. She must have grabbed it off the table at the same moment she had grabbed the Tak-phone in the dream.

Except it had been no dream, no hallucination.

She brought the telephone to her ear (this one was black, and of a size that fit her face) and listened. Nothing, of course. There was electricity in this house if nowhere else on the block—Tak had to have its TV—but at some point it had killed the phone.

Audrey got up, looked at the arch leading into the den, and knew what she would see if she peeked in: Seth in a trance, Tak entirely gone. But not into the movie this time, or not precisely. She heard confused cries and what was almost certainly a gunshot from across the street, and a line from Genesis occurred to her, something about the spirit of God moving on the face of the waters. The spirit of Tak, she had an idea, was also in motion, busy with its own affairs, and if she tried to get away now she probably *would* make it. But if she got to the others and told them what she knew, and if they believed, what might they do in order to escape the glamor in which they had been ensnared? What might they do to Seth in order to escape Tak?

He told me to go, she thought. I better trust him. But first—

First there was the thing he had told her to do before she left. Such a simple thing . . . but it might solve a lot. Everything, if they were very lucky. Audrey hurried into the kitchen, ignoring the cries and babble of voices from across the street. Now that her mind was made up, she was all but overwhelmed by a need to hurry, to get this last chore done before Tak turned its attention back to her.

Or before it sent Colonel Henry and his friends again.

4

When things went wrong, they went wrong with spectacular suddenness. Johnny asked himself later how much of the blame was his—again and again he asked it—and never got any clear answer. Certainly his attention had lapsed, although that had been before the shit actually hit the fan.

He had followed along behind the Reed twins as they headed through the woods toward the path, and had allowed his mind to drift off because the boys were moving with agonized slowness, trying not to rustle a single bush or snap a single twig. None of them had the slightest idea that they were not alone in the greenbelt; by the time Johnny and the twins entered it, Collie and Steve were on the path and well ahead of them, moving quietly south.

Johnny's mind had gone back to Bill Harris's horrified survey of Poplar Street on the day of his visit back in 1990, Bill at first saying Johnny couldn't be serious, then, seeing he was, asking him what the deal was. And Johnny Marinville, who now chronicled the adventures of a cat who toted a fingerprint kit, had replied: *The deal is I don't want to die yet, and that means doing some personal editorial work. A second-draft Johnny Marinville, if you like. And I can do it. Because I have the desire, which is important, and because I have the tools, which is vital. You could say it's just another version of what I do. I'm rewriting my life. Re-sculpting my life.*

It was Terry, his first wife, who had provided him with what might really have been his last chance, although he hadn't said so to Bill. Bill didn't even know that, after almost fifteen years when their only communication had been through lawyers, Johnny and the former Theresa Marinville had commenced a cautious dialogue, sometimes by letter, mostly on the phone. That contact had increased since 1988, when Johnny had finally put the booze and drugs behind him—for good, he hoped. Yet there was still something wrong, and at some point in the spring of 1989 he had found himself telling his first ex-wife, whom he had once tried to stab with a butter-knife, that his sober life felt pointless and goalless. He could not, he said, imagine ever writing another novel. That fire seemed to be out, and he didn't miss waking up in the morning with it burning his brains . . . along with the inevitable hangover. That part seemed to be done. And he could accept that. The part he didn't think he could accept was how the old life of which his novels had been a part was still everywhere around him, whispering from the corners and murmuring from his old IBM every time he turned it on. I am what you were, the typewriter's hum said to him, and what you'll always be. It was never about self-image, or even ego, but only about what was printed in your genes from the very start. Run to the end of the earth and take a room in the last hotel and go to the end of the final corridor and when you open the door that's there, I'll be sitting on a table inside, humming my same old hum, the one you heard on so many shaky hungover mornings, and there'll be a can of Coors beside your book-notes and a gram of coke in the top drawer left, because in the end that's what you are and all you are. As some wise man or other once said, there is no gravity; the earth just sucks.

"You ought to dig out the kid's book," she had said, startling him out of this reverie.

"*What* kid's book? I never—"

"Don't you remember *Pat the Detective Kitty-Cat*?"

It took him a minute, but then he did. "Terry, that was just a little story I made up for your sister's rug-monkey one night when he wouldn't shut up and I thought she was going to have a nervous—"

"You liked it well enough to write it down, didn't you?"

"I don't remember," he had said, remembering.

"You *know* you did, and you've got it somewhere

because you never throw anything away. Anal bastard! I always suspected you of saving your goddam *boogers*. In a Sucrets box, maybe, like fishing lures."

"They'd probably make *good* fishing lures," he had said, not thinking about what he was saying but wondering instead where that little story—eight or nine handwritten pages—might be. The Marinville Collection at Fordham? Possible. The house in Connecticut he and Terry had once shared, the one she was living in, talking to him from, at that very moment? Quite possible. At the time of the conversation, that house had been less than ten miles away.

"You ought to find that story," she said. "It was good. You wrote it at a time when you were good in ways you didn't even know about." There was a pause. "You there?"

"Yeah."

"I always know when I'm telling you stuff you don't like," she said brightly, "because it's the only time you ever shut up. You get all broody."

"I do not get broody."

"Do so, do so." And then she had said what might have been the most important thing of all. Over twenty million dollars in royalties had been generated by her casual memory of the story he had once made up to get his rotten nephew to go to sleep, and gazillions of books chronicling Pat's silly adventures had been sold around the world, but the next thing out of her mouth had seemed more important than all the bucks and all the books. Had then, still did. He supposed she'd spoken in her perfectly ordinary tone of voice, but the words had struck into his heart like those of a prophetess standing in a Delphic grove.

"You need to double back," the woman who was now Terry Alvey had said.

"Huh?" he had asked when he'd caught his breath. He hadn't wanted her to understand how her words had rocked him. Didn't want her to know she still had that sort of power over him, even after all these years. "What does *that* mean?"

"To the time when you felt good. *Were* good. I remember that guy. He was all right. Not perfect, but all right."

"You can't go home again, Terr. You must have been sick the week they took up Thomas Wolfe in American Lit."

"Oh spare me. We've known each other too long for Debate Society games. You were born in Connecticut, raised in Connecticut, a success in Connecticut, and a drunken, narcotized bum in Connecticut. You don't need to go home, you need to *leave* home."

"That's not doubling back, that's what us A.A. guys call a geographic cure. And it doesn't work."

"You need to double back in your *head*," she replied—patient, as if speaking to a child. "And your body needs some new ground to walk on, I think. Besides, you're not drinking anymore. Or drugging, either." A slight pause. "Are you?"

"No," he said. "Well, the heroin."

"Ha-ha."

"Where would you suggest I go?"

"The place you'd think of last," she had replied without hesitation. "The unlikeliest place on earth. Akron or Afghanistan, makes no difference."

That call had made Terry rich, because he had shared his Kitty-Cat income with her, penny for penny. And that call had led him here. Not Akron but Wentworth, Ohio's Good Cheer Community. A place he had never been before. He had picked the area in the first place by shutting his eyes and sticking a pushpin into a wall-map of the United States, and Terry had turned out to be right, Bill Harris's horrified reaction notwithstanding. What he had originally regarded as a kind of sabbatical had—

Lost in his reverie, he walked straight into Jim Reed's back. The boys had stopped on the edge of the path. Jim had raised the gun and was pointing it south, his face pale and grim.

"What's—" Johnny began, and Dave Reed clapped a hand over his mouth before he could say any more.

5

There was a gunshot, then a scream. As if the scream had been a signal, Marielle Soderson opened her eyes, arched her back, uttered a long, guttural sound that might have been words, and then began to shiver all over. Her feet rattled on the floor.

"Doc!" Cynthia cried, running to Marielle. *"Doc!"*

Gary came first. He stumbled in the kitchen doorway and would have knee-dropped onto his wife's stomach if Cynthia hadn't pushed him backward. The smell of cooking sherry hung around him in a sweet cloud.

"Wass happen?" Gary asked. "Wass wrong my wi?"

Marielle whipped her head from side to side. It thumped against the wall. The picture of Daisy, the Corgi who could count and add, fell off and landed on her chest. Mercifully, the glass in the frame didn't break. Cynthia grabbed it and tossed it aside. As she did, she saw the gauze over the stump of the woman's arm had turned red. The stitches—some of them, at least—had broken.

"Doc!" she screamed.

He came hurrying across from the door, where he had been standing and staring out, almost hypnotized by the changes which were still taking place. There were snarling sounds from the greenbelt out back, more screams, more gunshots. At least two. Gary looked in that direction, blinking owlishly. "Wass happen?" he asked again.

Marielle stopped shivering. Her fingers moved, as if she was trying to snap them, and then that stopped, too. Her eyes stared up blankly at the ceiling. A single tear trickled from the corner of the left one. Doc took her wrist and felt for a pulse. He stared at Cynthia with a kind of desperate intensity as he did. "I guess if you want to go on working downstreet, you'll have to turn in that cashier's duster for a dancehall dress," he said. "The E-Z Stop's a saloon now. The Lady Day."

"Is she dead?" Cynthia asked.

"Yuh," Old Doc said, lowering Marielle's hand. "For whatever it's worth, I think she ran out of chances fifteen minutes ago. She needed a trauma unit, not an old veterinarian with shaky hands."

More screams. Shouts. Someone was crying out there, crying and shouting *you should have stopped him, you should have stopped him*. A sudden surety came to Cynthia: Steve, a guy she'd already come to like, was dead. The shooters were out there, and they'd killed him.

"Wass happen?" Gary asked for the third time. Neither the old man nor the girl answered him. Although he had been right there, kneeling in the kitchen doorway beside her when Billingsley pronounced his wife dead, Gary didn't seem to realize what had happened until Old Doc pulled the brown corduroy cover off his couch and spread it over her. Then, it got through to Gary, drunk or not. His face began to shiver. He groped under the couch cover, found his wife's hand, brought it out, kissed it. Then he held it against his cheek and began to cry.

6

When Jim Reed saw rapidly approaching shapes coming up the path toward him, his excitement vanished. Terror filled the space where it had been. For the first time it occurred to him that coming out here might not have been a very intelligent idea.

If you see strangers in the woods, come right back.

That was what his mom had said. But he couldn't even move. He was frozen. Then there was a horrible growling sound in the undergrowth, the sound of an animal, and he panicked. He did not see Collie Entragian and Steve Ames when they burst into view; he saw killers who had left their vans to infiltrate the woods. He didn't hear Johnny's muffled yell, or see Johnny struggling to free himself from Dave's clutching hands.

"Shoot, Jimmy!" Dave shrieked. His voice was a trembling, freaked-out falsetto. *"Shoot, Jeezum Crow, it's them!"*

Jim fired and the one on the left went down, clutching for the top of his head, which blew back in a red film of scalp and hair and bone. The rifle the man had been carrying tumbled to the side of the path. Blood poured through his fingers and sheeted down over his face.

"Get the other one!" Dave cried. *"Get him, Jimmy, get him before he gets us!"*

"No, don't shoot!" the other guy said, holding out his hands. There was a rifle in one of them. "Please, man, don't shoot me!"

He was going to, though, going to shoot him dead. Jim pointed the gun at him, hardly aware that he was yelling at the guy, calling him names: cocksucker, bastard, fuckwad. All he wanted to do was kill the guy and get back to his mother. Him and Dave both. Coming out here had been a terrible mistake.

7

Johnny rammed both elbows back into Dave Reed's stomach, which was trim and hard but unprepared. Dave let out a surprised *Ooof!* and Johnny tore out of his grasp. Before Jim could fire again, Johnny had seized his arm and twisted it savagely. The boy screamed in pain. His hand opened and David Carver's pistol thumped to the path.

"What are you doing?" Dave yelled. *"He'll kill us, are you crazy?"*

"Your brother just shot Collie Entragian from down the block, how's that for crazy?" Johnny said. Yes, that was what the boy had done, but whose fault was it? He was the adult here. He should have taken the gun as soon as they were safely away from Cammie Reed's fanatic eyes and dry orders. He could have done it; why hadn't he?

"No," Jim whispered, turning to him, shaking his head. "No!" But his eyes already knew; they were huge, and filling with tears.

"Why would *he* be out here?" Dave asked. "Why didn't he warn us, for God's—"

The growl, which had never really stopped, reasserted itself in the hot red air, quickly rising to a snarl. The man who was still on his feet—the guy from the rental truck—turned toward it, instinctively raising his hands. The rifle in them was a very small one, and the guy might be right to use it that way, shielding his neck with it rather than pointing it.

Then the creature which had chased them up the path sprang out of the woods. Johnny's ability to think consciously and coherently ceased when he saw it—all he could do was see. That clear sight—more curse than blessing—had never failed him before, nor did it now.

The thing was a nightmare with a tawny brown coat, crooked green eyes, and a mouthful of jagged orange teeth. Not a cat but a misbegotten feline freak. It leaped, splintering the upheld Mossberg rifle with its enormous claws and tearing it away from the clenched hands which had held it. Then, still snarling, it went for Steve's throat.

From Audrey Wyler's journal:

<u>June 12, 1995</u>

It happened again—the daydream thing. If that's what it is. 3rd or 4th time, but the first (I think) since I've been keeping this journal, & by far the most vivid. It always seems to happen when things around here aren't going well, & oh God are things around here ever not going well!

Herb got up with Seth this morning, ran through the shower with him (saves lots of time), and when they came down Seth was sulking & Herb had the start of a black eye. I didn't have to ask him about it. Seth made him punch himself, of course, the same way he made him twist his lip when we got back from the ice cream parlor and Seth discovered his damned Power Wagon was gone. I looked at Herb & he gave me a little head-shake, telling me to keep quiet. Which I did. I've discovered you can always find something to be grateful for, in this case that making Herb punch himself was <u>all</u> Seth did (although it's not really Seth who does the bad stuff but the other one, the Stalky Little Boy).

Seth likes to stand by the bathroom sink and watch Herb shave in the mornings. The SLB could have popped out and made him cut his throat with his own Bic disposable, I suppose. Frightens me to write such a thing, but sometimes it's better to have it out on the page. Like squeezing infected material out of a cut.

The Stalky Little Boy started in before I even had breakfast on the table—I always know when it's him instead of Seth because his eyes aren't dark brown but almost black. "Where my Dweem Fwoatah?" he asked.

"We haven't found Dream Floater yet," I said, "but I'm sure we will."

"I want my Dweem Fwoatah!" he screamed at the top of his lungs, and Herb kind of winced. I didn't. At least when he's screaming he's not throwing things. *"I want my fucking DWEEM FWOATAH!"*

"Don't you swear like that in front of your Aunt Audrey," Herb said, and I *was* afraid at the look the SLB threw at him then, very afraid, but Herb's look back never wavered. He is so brave. So simply, up-frontno-bullshit brave. And it was the SLB who finally looked down.

"I want my Dweem Fwoatah," he muttered

in the sulky voice I hate most of all. "I want my Dweem Fwoatah, you find it."

I made him French toast, usually his favorite, but he wouldn't eat. Just walked off (sorry, stalked off) to the den. Pretty soon I heard the VCR, then one of his MotoKops tapes started. He's got four or five, each with a dozen episodes on it. I have really gotten to hate those stupid cartoon voices, especially Cassie's. Sometimes I wish No Face would kill her and dump her decapitated body in a ditch somewhere. God help me, I wish I was joking but I'm not.

When they were cackling away in there (he always turns up the volume, which is sometimes good) I asked Herb how he was going to explain his black eye when he got to work. He put his voice up to the falsetto range & batted his eyes and said, "I'll just tell the boys I ran into a door, honey." Trying to make a joke of it. It didn't work.

The worst part of today hasn't been Seth throwing things like he did when Herb suggested we could buy a replacement Dream Floater. He didn't do that today. I almost wish he would. He simply goes from room to room, stalking, glaring, lower lip pooched out, still looking for the missing P.W. Sometimes he goes into the den to watch TV, but not even _Bonanza_ held him long today. I tried to get him to talk but he wouldn't. & the thing is . . . oh, I wish I could write better, express it so someone reading this (not that anyone ever will, I imagine) could understand. It's like he—the SLB—generates a kind of poison electricity when he's pissed. He seems to spin it right out of his body, like a spider spinning electric silk or thunderheads putting out lightning. It builds up and up until you feel like just running from room to room, screaming and beating your head against things. It's real, not just a feeling but a physical thing. It makes you sweat (& it's _stinky_ sweat, like when you have a high fever), & your muscles tremble, & your mouth gets dry. I'll write something in here I've never told Herb. Sometimes, when it gets like that, I go in the bathroom, lock the door, & masturbate like mad. It's the only thing that seems to take a little of the pressure off. The orgasms are so hard they're frightening. Like bombs going off!

I've felt all this before when the Stalky Little Boy inside Seth is pissed about something, but it's never gone on so long or revved up so high. By mid-afternoon it was like the whole house was full of natural gas, just waiting for a match to set it off. I was in the kitchen, walking aimlessly around, my head aching so badly that I could feel my eyeballs throbbing, & I kept wanting to grin. I don't know why, there's nothing funny about any of it, but the more my head ached and the more my eyes throbbed and the more I felt the atmosphere of the house pressing in on me, the more I wanted to grin. Christ!

I went to the sink & looked out the window into the back yard. Seth was sitting in the sandbox, playing with his other Power Wagons. Only if anyone but me had seen how he was playing, I'm sure he would have been in some sort of special installation by nightfall, some place where the government studies exceptional children.

The P.W.'s have pop-out wings, but they don't really fly, of course. Except sometimes Seth's do. He was sitting in the sand with his hands in his lap, and around and around his head they went, Tracker Arrow and Rooty-Toot and the Meat-wagon and the rest, dipping and diving under each other, swooping and doing rolls, coming in for touch-and-go's on a landing-strip Seth has made for them in the sandbox, sometimes doing formation flights down the yard to his swing, going under the seat like stunt pilots in a movie, then banking around and coming back. Kids' toys, all bright colors, flying missions in the back yard. I know I must sound like a raving madwoman, but I swear in the name of God that it's true. Sometimes he dive-bombs Hannibal, the neighbors' dog, with them & H. runs away with his tail between his legs. Herb has seen this, too.

Any other kid seeing the MotoKops' Power Wagons doing tricks like that would be laughing & clapping & cheering, but not the Stalky Little Boy. He just sits there in the sand with his lip shoved out & glares.

Seth watching the wagons and me watching him, feeling whatever is inside him coming out in waves, filling the air with a hum that's mostly in a person's head. I felt ready to come out of my skin, ready to flip out right there in front of the sink. & then, all at once, the daydream came. It is the most wonderful thing, and although I call it a daydream, that isn't how it feels; it feels real. In it I am reliving a weekend afternoon I spent at Mohonk Mountain House with my friend Jan. Back in 1982, this was, before either of us were married. We sat and talked for I don't know how long—her mostly about this goofy, greasy guy she was so crazy about back then, me about how i'd love to take three months off after graduation and see some of the country.

It's so beautiful there at Mohonk, so peaceful. We have a picnic lunch. The air is warm. Jan looks as gorgeous as I feel. I know it's not real, & that i've got all this mess to come back to, but for the time i'm there, none of that matters. Jan & I talk, I feel the sun on my face, I smell the flowers. It's wonderful. I don't know what it is or why it happens, but as an antidote to the SLB's rages, it beats rubbing off in the bathroom eight ways to Sunday. Does Seth have anything to do with it, I wonder?

I wish Herbie had a place to go, but I don't think he does. His silly jokes are as close as he can come, poor man. I wish I could tell him about my place, maybe even take him there, but it wouldn't be wise. I think the SLB can find things out from Herb that he can't from me. & Herb looks so tired. It's unfair to both of us that this should be happening, but it's horribly unfair to Herbie.

June 13, 1995

"Dweem Fwoatah" is back. Just now. I don't know whether to feel scared or relieved.

I mean of course I'm relieved, anyone would be, this place has been like a concentration camp since Saturday, but what happens next? How will the SLB react? Thank God he was napping when the doorbell rang, & thank God Herb's at work, because the SLB eavesdrops on Herb's mind sometimes, I know he does. I don't think he can do it to me unless I let him in, or unless I'm unprepared.

Boy. I just read this over and it's absolutely crazed. Let me take a deep breath and start from the beginning. I should have time. Seth hasn't slept well since Friday night, and if I'm lucky he might nap until 4:30. That gives me at least an hour.

Around 3:00, while I was vacuuming, there was a knock on the kitchen door. I opened it & there stood Mr. Hobart from down the street, and his son, who is a pudgy redhaired boy with thick glasses and pasty skin. Sort of repulsive-looking, if you want to know the truth. The kid had a Dream Floater van in his arms. There was no question it was Seth's. I didn't have to see the broken tail-light and the scratch up the driver's side to know that, but as a matter of fact I could see both. You could have knocked me over with a broom-straw. I tried to say something & couldn't, my throat was locked up. I don't know what would have come out if I <u>had</u> been able to talk!

It's hot today, mid 80s, but Wm. Hobart was dressed like a church deacon (which I'm sure he is) in a black suit & shoes. His kid was wearing the junior version of the same getup, & was snivelling. Had a pretty good bruise on one cheek, too. I'd bet my bank account his old man put it there.

It didn't matter that I couldn't talk, because Hobart had the whole thing scripted. "My son has something to say to you, Mrs. Wyler," he said, then looked down at the boy as if to say you're on, don't fuck it up. "Hugh?"

Snivelling harder than ever, Hugh said he'd given in to the Tempting Voice of Satan (I guess that's the TVS, just like the Stalky Little Boy is the SLB) & stolen Seth's toy. He talked real fast, crying harder & harder as he went along. The kid finished by saying, "You can go to the police and I will make a full confession. You can spank me, or my Dad will spank me." Listening to that part was like when you call the weather & the recording says, "For current conditions, press one. For the current forecast, press two. For road conditions, press three." I guess it was a blessing I was so stunned. If I hadn't been, I might've laughed, and there was nothing funny about the two of them, standing there so holy & ashamed. I was more scared of them—of the father, especially—than I am on most days of Seth.

Scared FOR them, too.

"I am very sorry," the kid says, still rapping it out as if it was on cue-cards in front of him. "I have asked my Dad for forgiveness, I have asked Lord Jesus for forgiveness, and now I am asking you for forgiveness."

I got my act together enough then to take the wagon from him—I was so wrought-up I almost dropped it on my toes—and told him that no spankings would be required.

"The boy also has to apologize to your son," Mr. Hobart said. He looks like Moses with a clean-shaven face and a good haircut, if you can imagine Moses in a double-vented three-piece from Sears. After the things that have been going on around here for the last few months, I have no problem imagining anything. That's part of my trouble. "If you'll just lead us to him, Mrs. Wyler—"

I'll be damned if the self-righteous SOB didn't start trying to push his way right in! I pushed him right back, I can tell you. (Almost dropped Dream Floater again in the process, too.) The last thing I wanted was that fat little thief standing in front of the Stalky Little Boy. What I wanted was for them to be out of my house, and quick. Before either their voices or their emotional vibes (and tho he wasn't crying, Hobart was at least as upset as his kid, maybe more) could wake him up.

"Seth's not my son, he's my nephew," I said, "and he's taking a nap right now."

"Very good," Hobart says, giving a stiff little nod. "We will come back later. Is tonight convenient? If not, I can bring Hugh back tomorrow afternoon. I can ill afford to take off a second afternoon—I work at the stamping mill in Ten Mile, you know—but God's business must always take precedence over man's."

His voice kept getting louder while he was talking, the way the voices of guys like him always seem to, it's like they can't tell you they've got to take a shit without turning it into a sermon. I started to feel really scared about Seth waking up. & all this time, I swear it's true, the kid's looking around like he wants to see if there's anything else worth hawking. I'd say the day is going to come when Hughie winds up on some shrinky-dink's couch, except that people like the Hobarts don't believe in shrinks, do they?

I herded them out the door & kept them going right down the walk, I mean I was on a roll. The kid, meanwhile, is asking "Do you forgive me? Do you forgive me?" over & over again, like a broken record. By the time I got them down to the sidewalk, I realized I was furious with both of them. Not just because of the hell we've been through but because they both acted like I was somehow responsible for the thieving little fart's immortal soul. Plus I kept remembering the way his eyes were going everywhere, seeing what we had in our house that he didn't have in his.

I'm pretty sure—almost positive, actually—that a lot of Seth's "strange powers" have a very short range, like the radio transmitters they used to have at the drive-ins, the ones that piped the movie sound directly into your car radio. So when I got them down to the street, I felt safe (relatively safe, anyway) to ask how Hugh Hobart had come to lift Seth's Power Wagon in the first place.

Père and fils exchanged a glance at that. It was a funny, uneasy glance, and I realized neither of them much minded the idea of a spanking or even a visit from the cops, but they didn't like the idea of talking about the actual theft itself. Not one little bit. No wonder the fundamentalists hate the Catholics so much. The idea of going to confession must make their balls shrivel.

Still, I had 'em in a corner, & finally it came out. William did most of the talking; by then the kid had decided he didn't like me. His eyes had gotten narrow, and they'd quit leaking, too.

Most of it I could've figured out myself. The Hobarts belong to the Zion's Covenant Baptist Church, and one of the things they do as good church members is to "spread the Gospel." This means leaving tracts like the one Herb found sticking out of our milkbox, the one about a million years in hell & not one drink of water. William and Hugh do this together, a father-and-son type of thing, I guess, a holy substitute for Little League or touch football. They stick mostly to houses that look temporarily empty, wanting "to spread the word & plant the seed, not engage in debate" (William Hobart's words), or they put their little love-notes under the windshields of cars on the street.

They must've hit our place right after we left for Milly's. Hugh ran up the driveway and stuck the tract under the milkbox, and of course he saw Dream Floater wherever Seth put it down. Later, after his father had declared him off-duty for the rest of the day but before we got back from the mall, Hugh wandered back up the street . . . & gave in to the ever-popular TVS (Tempting Voice of Satan). His mother found the P.W. yesterday, Monday, while Hugh was at school & she was cleaning in his room. Last night they had a "family conference" about it, then called their minister for his advice, had a little over-the-phone prayer, and now here they were.

Once the story was out, the kid started in on "Do you forgive me" again. The second time through, I said, "Quit saying that."

He looked like I'd slapped him and his father's face got all stiff. I didn't give a crap. I squatted down so I could look directly into Hugh's piggy little eyes. It wasn't all that easy to see them, either, because of the dandruff flakes and grease-smears on his glasses.

"Forgiveness is between you and your God," I said. "As for me, I'm going to keep quiet about what you did, and I'd advise the Hobarts to do the same." They will, I'm pretty sure. I only had to look at the bruise on Hugh's cheek, really, to know that. I don't know about the creep's mother, but what he did is absolutely killing his father.

Hugh backed a step away from me, and I could see in his face that this wasn't going the way it was supposed to, & he hated me for it. That's okay. I hate him a little, too. Not surprising, is it, after the weekend we put in because of his light fingers?

"We'll leave you now, Mrs. Wyler, if you're finished," Hobart said. "Hugh has got a lot of meditation to do. In his room. On his knees."

"But I'm not finished," I said. "Not quite." I didn't look at him. It was the boy I looked at. I think I was trying to look past the hate & shame & self-righteousness, to see if there was a real boy left inside anywhere. And did I see one? I truly don't know.

"Hugh," I said, "you know that people only

have to ask forgiveness if they do something wrong, don't you?"

He nodded cautiously . . . like he was testifying in a trial & thought one of the lawyers was laying a trap.

"So you know that stealing Seth's toy was wrong."

He nodded again, more reluctantly than ever. By then he was practically hiding behind his father's leg, as if he were three instead of eight or nine.

"Mrs. Wyler, I hardly think it's necessary to browbeat the boy," his old man said. Unbelievable prig! He's willing to let me turn the kid over my knee & whale on his ass like it was a snare drum, but when I want the kid to say out loud that he did wrong, all at once it's abuse. There's a lesson in this, but I'll be damned if I know what it is.

"I'm not browbeating him, but I want you to know that the last few days have been very difficult around here," I said. It was the adult I was answering but still the kid I was really talking to. "Seth loves his Power Wagons very much. So here is what I want, Hugh. I want you to tell me that what you did was wrong, and it was bad, and you're sorry. Then we'll be done."

Hugh glared at me, & if looks could kill, I wouldn't be writing in this book now. But was I scared? Please. When it comes to pissed-off kids, I live with the champ of champs.

"Mrs. Wyler, do you think that's really necessary?" Hobart asked.

"Yes, sir," I said. "More for your son than for me."

"Dad, do I have to?" he whines. He's still giving me the Death-Ray look from behind his smeary glasses.

"Go on and tell her what she wants to hear," Hobart said. "Bitter medicine is best swallowed in a single gulp." Then he patted the kid on the shoulder, as if to say yes, she's being mean, a real bitch, but we have to put up with it.

"It-was-wrong-it-was-bad-I'm-sorry," the kid says, like he's back on the cue-cards. Glaring at me the whole time—no more tears or snivelling. I looked up & saw the same stare coming from the father. The two of them never looked more alike than they did right then. People are amazing. They came up the street, scared but sort of exalted at the idea of getting crucified, just like their boss did. Instead I made the kid admit what he was, & it hurt, & they both hate me for it.

The important things, though, are these: 1.) D.F. is back, and 2.) the Hobarts won't talk about it. Sometimes shame is the only gag that works on people. I must think up a yarn to tell Seth, then tell the same one to Herb. The truth just isn't safe.

Feet upstairs, going down to the bathroom. He's up. Please God I hope I'm right about him not being able to see into my thoughts.

<u>Later</u>

Big sigh of relief. And maybe a self-administered pat on the back, as well. I think The Dream Floater Crisis is past, with no harm done (except for some broken dishes & my beautiful Waterford glasses, that is). Seth & Herb both sleeping. I intend to go up myself as soon as I've written a little in this book (keeping a journal under these circumstances may be dangerous, but God, it can be so soothing), then put it back on top of the kitchen cabinet where I keep it.

Seth getting up when he did, before I had much of a chance to think what I was going to tell him, turned out to be a blessing in disguise. When he came downstairs, still with his eyes mostly puffed shut, I just held D.F. out to him. What happened to his face—the way it opened up in surprise & delight, like a flower in the sun—was almost worth the whole damned horror show. I saw both of them in that glad look, Seth <u>and</u> the SLB. The SLB just glad to have his Power Wagon back. Seth, I think, glad for other reasons. Maybe I'm wrong, giving him too much credit, but I don't think so. I think Seth was glad because he knows the SLB will let up on us now. For a little while, anyway.

There was a time when I thought, good college girl that I am, that the SLB was just another aspect of Seth's personality—the amoral part Freudians call the id—but I'm no longer sure. I keep thinking about the trip the Garins took across the country just before Bill & June & the two older kids were killed. Then I think about how our father talked to us when we were teenagers, and going for our drivers' licenses, Bill first, then me. He told us there were three things we were never supposed to do: drive with our tire-pressure low, drive drunk, or pick up hitchhikers.

Could it be that Bill picked up a hitchhiker in the desert without even knowing it? That it's still riding around inside of Seth? Crazy idea, maybe, but I've noticed that this is when most of the crazy ideas come, late at night when the house is quiet & the others are asleep. And crazy does not always mean wrong.

Anyhow, with no time to lie fancy, I lied plain. I found it in the cellar, I said, when I went down to see if there were any more vacuum cleaner bags. We'd already poked around down there, of course, but I said it was way back under the stairs. Seth accepted it with no questions (I'm not sure he even cared, he was so happy to have "Dweem Fwoatah" back, but it was really the SLB I was talking to, anyway). Herb only had one question: how did the P.W. get down there in the first place? Seth never goes in the cellar, thinks it's spooky, and H. knows that. I said I didn't know, and—miracle of miracles—that seems to have closed the subject.

All night Seth sat in the den in his favorite chair, holding Dream Floater on his lap like a little girl might hold her favorite doll, watching the TV. Herb brought home a movie from The Video Clip. Just some old black-and-white thing from the Bargain Bin, but Seth really likes it. It's a Western (of course) from the late '50s. He's watched it twice already.

Rory Calhoun's in it. It's called The Regulators.

June 19, 1995

I think we're in trouble.

William Hobart over this morning, in a rage. Herb had left for work about twenty minutes before he showed up, thank God, and Seth was out back in the yard.

"I want to ask you a question, Mrs. Wyler," he said. "Did you or your husband have anything to do with what happened to my car last night? A simple yes or no will suffice. If you did, it would be best to say so now."

"I don't know what you're talking about," I said, and I must have sounded convincing, because he calmed down a little bit.

He led me down the front walk (I was happy to go, the farther away from Seth in the back yard, the better), & pointed down at his house. He drives one of those four-wheel things, an Explorer, maybe, something like that. It was standing on four flat tires, and all the windows had been broken. Including the windshield and the big one in back.

"Oh my God, I'm so sorry," I said. I was, too, although maybe not for the reasons he thought.

"I apologize for my accusation," he says, just as stiff as starch. "I suppose I thought . . the toy Hugh took . . . if you were still angry . . ." A vehicle for a vehicle, I think he meant, like an eye for an eye.

"I've put the whole thing behind me, Mr. Hobart," I said. "And I'm not what you'd call a vengeance-minded person under any circumstances."

"Vengeance is mine saith the Lord, I will repay," he says.

"Right!" I said. I don't know if it is or not, but by then I only wanted to get rid of him. He's creepy.

"It must have been vandals," he said.

"Drunkards. Surely no one on the street would do such a thing."

I hope it _was_ vandals. I hope it was. And how could it have been Seth—or the Stalky Little Boy, if you prefer—if I'm right about his powers having a short range? Unless his abilities are growing. His range widening.

I don't dare tell Herb about this.

<u>June 24, 1995</u>

When I came downstairs this morning to start breakfast, I saw the Reeds out on their walk, still in their robes. I went out. It's been hot, but it rained in the middle of the night—hard—& the air was cooler this morning, with that sweet wet smell it gets after summer rain.

Early Saturday morning, or the whole street would have turned out, I think. There was a police car parked in front of the Hobart house, where there was broken glass everywhere, in the driveway & on the lawn, twinkling in the sun. William and his wife (Irene) were standing on their front stoop in their pj's, talking to the cops. The little thief was standing on the stoop behind them, sucking his thumb. A little old for that, but it must have been a bad morning at chez Hobart. Every window in the house was out, it looked like, upstairs as well as down.

Cammie said it happened around quarter to six, she was just waking up & heard it. "Not as loud as you would've expected, all that glass, but loud enough so you could tell what it was," she said. "Weird, huh?"

"Very," I said. My voice sounded normal enough, but I didn't dare say any more in case it started to get shaky.

Cammie said she looked out almost as soon as she heard the noises, but the people who threw the rocks were gone already (if the police actually find any rocks, i'll eat them with spaghetti sauce). "Whoever it was, they must have moved very fast." She threw an elbow at Charlie. "The big lug here slept through the whole thing."

"First his car, now this," Charlie said. "Vandals, my butt. Someone's got it in for Will Hobart."

"Yes," I said. "Someone must."

Later

Found Seth's "wascally wabbit" slippers pushed way back under his bed. Just by accident. Was looking for a stray sock. Slippers wet, pink fur all matted, pieces of grass stuck to the bottoms. He was out in the night, then. Or early this morning. And I know where he went. Don't I?

Bad . . . but thank God his range isn't widening as I suspected it might be. That would be even worse.

June 26, 1995

Waited until Herb was at work—I didn't want him to go, he looked so pale and ill, but he said he had an important report to finish and a big presentation this afternoon—then went out back to talk to Seth.

He was sitting in the sandbox, playing quietly with his MotoKops guys, the HQ Crisis Center, and what Herb jokingly calls "the Ponderosa." This is a ranch-and-corral set-up that Herb saw at a yard-sale on his way home from work one day in March or April. He made a U-turn to go back & get it. It's not really the Ponderosa Ranch from Bonanza, of course, but the main house with its log sides does look a little like it. There is also a bunkhouse (part of the roof broken in but it's otherwise in good shape) and a number of plastic horses (a couple with only three legs) for the corral. Herb paid two bucks for it, & it's been one of Seth's favorite toys ever since. What's funny (& a little weird) is how quickly & effortlessly he incorporated the ranch into his MotoKops play-fantasies. I suppose all kids are that way, arbitrary boundaries don't interest 'em, especially when they're playing, but it's still a dizzy blending of genres to see Cassie or No Face riding a three-legged plastic nag around the old corral.

Not that I was thinking about any of that this morning, I can tell you. I was scared, heart pounding like a drum in my chest, but when he looked up at me, I felt a little better. It was Seth, not the other one. Every time I see Seth's pale, sweet little face, I love him more. It's crazy, maybe, but it's true. I want to protect him more, and I hate the other one more.

I asked him what was happening to the Hobarts—no sense kidding myself any longer that he's in the dark about what happened to Dream

Floater—& he didn't answer. Just sat looking at me. I asked him if he'd snuck out on Saturday morning and gone down there to break their windows. Still no answer. Then I asked him what he wanted, what had to happen before he would stop. I didn't think he was going to answer that, either. Then he said, very clearly for Seth: "They should move. They should move soon. I can't hold it back much longer."

"Hold what back?" I asked him, but he wouldn't say anything else, just went away to wherever it is he goes. Later on, while he was eating his lunch (the usual, Chef Boyardee & choco milk), I came upstairs & sat on the bed & thought. After my brother and his family were killed, the witnesses talked about a red van that maybe had a radar dish or some other form of telecommunications equipment on the roof. A mystery-van, the paper called it.

Tracker Arrow is red. And it has a dish on the roof.

I told myself I was completely crazy, and then I thought about the Dream Floater Herb & I saw in the back yard. It wasn't real, of course, but it was full-sized . . . and Seth was asleep when we saw it. Maybe not operating at full power.

Suppose the SLB gets tired of just breaking windows? Suppose he sends Tracker Arrow (or Dream Floater, the Justice Wagon, or Freedom) to do a little drive-by at the Hobarts'?

I can't hold it back much longer, Seth said.

June 27, 1995

Spent most of the day at Mohonk with Jan Goodlin. I know I shouldn't—it's as much a retreat as drugs or alcohol would be—but it's hard to resist. We talked about our folks, and embarrassing things that happened to us in high school, all the usual. Trivial and wonderful. Until the very end. I saw the little phone was gone, which means it's time to go back, & Jan said to me: "You know where he's getting the energy to work on the Hobarts, don't you, Aud?"

Sure I do: from Herb. He's stealing it like a vampire steals blood. And I think that Herb knows it, too.

June 28, 1995

Late this morning I was sitting at the kitchen table, making up a shopping list, when I heard the whoop-whoop-whoop of an ambulance siren. I went out front in time to see it pull up in front of the Hobarts' with its lights flashing. The EMTs got out & hurried inside. I went inside my own house—ran, actually—and looked out into the back yard from the kitchen. Seth was gone.

Power Wagons lined up in the sandbox, slant-parked the way he always puts them when he's done for awhile, the Ponderosa all neat with the plastic horses in their corral, the HQ Crisis Center down near the swing . . . but no Seth. If I told you I was surprised, I'd be lying.

By the time I got back to the front, people were standing out on their sidewalks all up and down the street, looking at the Hobart place. Dave and Jim Reed were in their driveway, and I asked them if they had seen Seth.

"There he is, Mrs. Wyler," Dave says, and points down to the store. Seth was standing by the bike rack, looking across the street, just like the rest of us. "He must have gone for a candybar."

"Yes," I reply, knowing that a.) Seth has no

money; b.) Seth can hardly talk to Herb and me, let alone to store-clerks he doesn't know; c.) Seth never leaves the back yard.

Seth doesn't, but sometimes the Stalky Little Boy does, it seems. To get into operating range, I think.

About five minutes later, the EMTs helped Irene Hobart out the door. Hugh, the son, was holding her hand & crying. I hated that kid, absolutely did, but I don't anymore. Now I only pity him & fear for him. There was blood all down the front of her dress. She was holding a compress on her nose, & one of the EMTs was pressing the top of her neck in the back. They got her into the ambulance—Hugh got in right behind her—& drove away.

She was back less than two hours later (by then Seth was safely tucked away in the den, watching old Westerns on cable). Kim Geller dropped by for coffee & told me she went down to see if she could do anything for Irene. She's the only one on the block who is what you could call friendly with the Hobarts. She said everything is under control, but that Irene had a scare. She has bad hypertension. Takes medication for it, but it's still barely controlled. She's had nosebleeds before, but never one as bad as this. She told Kim it went all at once, blood just spraying out of her nostrils, and it wouldn't stop even when she cold-packed it. Hugh got scared & called 911. The EMTs insisted on taking her to the hospital to see if she needed to have the inside of her nose cauterized, even tho the bleeding had mostly stopped by the time the ambulance got to the house.

I got Seth inside and started shaking him. Told him he had to stop. He only looked at me, his mouth trembling. I was the one who stopped, angry & ashamed of myself. I was shaking the wrong one.

I could see the other one, though. I swear I could. Hiding behind Seth's eyes and laughing at me. I think the most terrible thing of all is how the SLB knows to leave Hugh Hobart alone. To let him just watch.

June 29, 1995

Woke up this morning around 3 a.m. and the other half of the bed was empty. The bathroom, too. I went downstairs, scared. No one in the living room, den, or kitchen. I went out to the garage & found Herb sitting at his workbench, wearing nothing but the Jockeys he sleeps in, & crying. He put in hi-intensity lighting out there two years ago—metal-hooded lamps that look like the kinds you see in pool-parlors—& in their glow I could see how much weight he's lost. He looks horrible. Like he has anorexia nervosa. I took him in my arms & he wept like a baby. Kept saying he was tired, so tired all the time. I said something about taking him to see Dr. Evers first thing in the morning. He just laughed, said I knew what was wrong with him.

I do, of course.

July 1, 1995

Another ambulance at the Hobart house late this afternoon. As soon as I saw it I raced upstairs to check on Seth, who was supposedly napping. No Seth. Window open—second-floor window—& no Seth. When I went outside, I saw him across the street, holding old Tom Billingsley's hand. I ran across & grabbed him.

"No fear, he's all right, Aud," Tom said. "Just went wanderin' a little, didn't you, Sethie-boy?"

"Don't you ever cross the street on your own!" I told him. "Don't you *ever*!" Shook him again in spite of myself. Stupid; might as well shake a lump of wax.

This time when the EMTs came out, they were using their stretcher. Wm. Hobart was on it. "Seems like just lately if it wasn't for bad luck, those Hobarts wouldn't have any luck at all," Tom said.

This is supposed to be Mr. Hobart's vacation week, but he will be spending at least some of it in County General. He fell downstairs, broke his leg & hip. Kim told me later that he drinks, church deacon at Zion's Covenant or not. Maybe he *does* drink, but I don't think that's why he fell downstairs.

<u>July 3, 1995</u>

There's no Stalky Little Boy. Never was. There's a *thing* inside of Seth—not an id, not another manifestation of his personality, not a hitchhiker, but something like a tapeworm. It can think. And talk. It talked to me today—it calls itself Tak.

July 6, 1995

Someone shot the Hobarts' pet Angora cat last night. Apparently nothing left but blood & fur. Kim says Irene H. is hysterical, thinks everyone on the street is out to get them because they know the Hobarts are going to heaven & the rest of us are going to hell. "So they are making this hell on earth for us" is what she told Kim. She begged Kim to tell her who did it, said Hugh was devastated, wouldn't come out of his room, just lay there on his bed, crying & saying it was all his fault cause he was a sinner. When Kim said she didn't know and didn't think anyone on Poplar Street would shoot the Hobarts' cat, Mrs. Hobart said Kim was just like the rest & told her they weren't friends anymore. Kim very upset, but not as upset as I am.

What in God's name should I do? It hasn't hurt anyone too badly yet, but—

July 8, 1995

Oh God, thank you. A Mayflower van turned onto the street at just past nine this morning & stopped in front of the Hobarts'. They are moving out.

July 16, 1995

Oh you fucking little bastard you shit. Oh how could you. Oh you bastard if I could get at you. If you let Seth go & I could get at you. Oh God God God.

My fault? Yes. HOW MUCH my fault is the question. Dear Jesus how can I live without him. How go on with this. I didn't know there could be this much pain in the whole wide world & how much my fault HOW MUCH? You bastard Tak you bastard. i'm done writing in this book. What good did I ever think it could do anyway.

Oh Herb i'm so sorry, I love you, i'm sorry.

October 19, 1995

Got an answer to my letter today, ages after i'd given up expecting one. My respondent was a mining engineer named Allen Symes. He works at a place called the China Pit, in the town of Desperation, Nevada. Says he saw Bill and his family, but nothing happened, he just showed them the mine and they went on, nothing happened.

He's lying. i'll probably never know why, or what happened out there, but I know that much. He's lying.

God help me.

CHAPTER 10

1

It all happened fast, but Johnny's half-wonderful, half-terrible ability to see and sequence kept up.

Entragian, dying but too badly hurt to know it, was crawling toward one of the primitive cacti at the left side of the path, his head hanging so low it left a swath of blood on the ground-growth. His skull gleamed between hanging flaps of hair like a bleary pearl. He looked scalped.

In the middle of the path, a bizarre waltz was going on. The creature from the ravine—a sinister Picasso mountain lion with jutting orange teeth—was up on its hind legs, paws on Steve Ames's shoulders. If Steve had dropped his arms when the cat clawed the puny .22 away from him, he would have been dead already. He had crossed them over his chest instead, however, and now his elbows and forearms were against the cat's chest.

"Shoot it!" he screamed. *"For Christ's sake, shoot it!"*

Neither twin made a move for the dropped pistol. They were not identical twins, but their faces now wore identical expressions of anguish.

The mountain lion (it hurt Johnny's eyes just to look at it) uttered a womanish shrieking cry and darted its triangular head forward. Steve snapped his own head back and tried to throw the creature off to one side. It held on with its claws and the two of them tangoed drunkenly, the cat's claws digging deeper into Steve's shoulders, and now Johnny could see blood-blossoms spreading on his shirt where the claws—as wildly exaggerated as its teeth, only black instead of orange—were dug in. Its tail lashed madly back and forth.

They did another half-turn, and Steve's feet tangled in each other. For a moment he tottered on the edge of balance, still holding off the lunging mountain lion with his crossed arms. Beyond them, Entragian had reached the cactus. He butted the top of his bleeding and horribly distended head into its spines, then collapsed and rolled over on his side. To Johnny he looked like a machine that has finally run down. Coyotes wailed, still out of sight but closer now; the air was tangy with smoke from the burning house.

"Shoot this fucking thing!" Steve yelled. He had managed to catch his balance, but before long would be all out of backing-up room; he was at the edge of the path. One step into the thorny underbrush, two at most, and he would go over. Then the nightmare would rip his throat out. *"Shoot it, please, it's tearin me apart!"*

Johnny had never been so terrified in his life, but he nonetheless discovered that only the first step was actually hard; once the lock on his body was broken, the terror didn't seem to matter much. After all, the worst thing the creature could do to him was kill him, and dying would at least stop the feeling that an earthquake was going on inside his mind.

He scooped up Entragian's rifle—considerably larger than the one the cat had ripped out of the longhair's hands—saw the safety was on, and flicked it the other way with his thumb. Then he socked the .30–.06's muzzle against the side of the mountain lion's bulging head.

"Push!" he bellowed, and Steve pushed. The cat's head rocked up and away from his throat. Its bristle of teeth shone like poison coral. The sunset light was in its green eyes, making them look as if they were on fire. Johnny had time to wonder if Entragian had chambered a round—he was probably never going to write another Pat the Kitty-Cat book if Entragian hadn't—then turned his head slightly away and pulled the trigger. There was a satisfying whipcrack sound, a lick of fire from the barrel, and then Johnny could smell frying hair as well as burning house. The mountain lion fell sideways, its head mostly gone, the fur on the back of its neck smouldering. What was inside its lifted skull was not blood, bone, and tissue but fibrous pink stuff that reminded Johnny of the blown-in insulation he'd gotten for the second floor and attic of his new house the year after he'd moved in.

Steve tottered, waving his arms for balance. Marinville reached out a hand, but he was dazed and it was only a token effort. Steve went sprawling in the bushes at the side of the path, beside the mountain lion's twitching rear paws. Johnny bent down, grabbed his wrist, and hauled. Black spots flocked in front of his eyes, and for one awful second he thought he was going to pass out. Then Steve was on his feet and Johnny's vision was clearing again.

Wh-wh-whoooooo . . .

Johnny looked around nervously. He could still see nothing, but the sons of bitches sounded closer than ever.

2

Dave Reed kept thinking that pretty soon he would wake up. Never mind that he could smell the cop's blood and sweat as he knelt beside him, never mind the tortured sound of the cop's breathing (and his own), the cop's one dying eye, or the sight of his brain—his gray and wrinkled brain—pushing through a shattered window in his skull. It *had* to be a dream. Surely his brother could not have shot the guy from across the street, a crooked cop, yes, but also the guy who had once told Cary Ripton to try throwing a baseball with his fingers across the seams instead of lying along them . . . and who had then demonstrated by throwing a brain-busting rainbow change.

Smells like he shit his pants, Dave thought, and

suddenly felt like vomiting. He controlled it. He didn't want to vomit again, even in a dream.

The cop reached up and hooked his fingers into Dave's shirt.

"Hurt," he whispered hoarsely. *"Hurt."*

"Don't"—Dave swallowed, cleared his throat—"try to talk."

Behind him, incredibly, he could hear Johnny Marinville and the hippie guy talking about whether or not they should go on. They were insane, had to be. And Marinville . . . where had Marinville been? How could he have let this happen? He was a fucking *adult*!

With a shudder of effort, Collie Entragian got up on one elbow. His remaining eye stared at the boy with ferocious concentration. "Never," he whispered. *"Never—"*

"Sir . . . Mr. Entragian . . . you'd better just . . ."

Wh-wh-whoooooooo!

Close enough this time to make Dave Reed's skin feel as if it were freezing. He felt like ripping Johnny Marinville's face off for not stopping this before it had become irrevocable. Yet the cop's eye held him like a bug on a pin, and one of the cop's blood-streaked hands had knotted a handful of Dave's shirt into a loose fist. He could tear away from him, maybe, but . . .

But that was a lie. He *felt* like a bug on a pin.

"Never took drugs . . . sold them . . . any of it," Collie whispered. "Never took a dime. Framed. IA shooflies on the take . . . I found out."

"You—" Dave began.

"I found out! You understand . . . what I'm saying?" He held up the hand that wasn't knotted in Dave's shirt, opened it, appeared to examine it. "Hands . . . clean."

"Yeah, okay," Dave said. "But you better not try to talk. You got . . . well, a little crease, and—"

"Jim, no!" Marinville screamed from behind him. *"Don't!"*

Dave suddenly discovered he could pull away from the dying man quite easily.

3

"What do we do?" Johnny asked the longhair as, on the other side of the path, the dark-haired twin knelt by the man his brother had shot. Johnny could hear the faint sound of Entragian murmuring, as if he wanted to make a good confession before he died. Johnny had relearned a gruesome fact this afternoon: people died hard, by and large, and when they went out, they left without much dignity . . . and probably without realizing they were leaving at all.

"Do?" Steve asked. He stared at Johnny, almost comically amazed, and ran a hand through his hair, smearing red in with the gray. More blood was spreading on the shoulders of his shirt where the cat's claws had sunk in. "What do you mean, *do?"*

"Do we go on or do we go back?" Johnny asked. His voice was rough, urgent. "What's up ahead? What did you see?"

"Nothing," Steve said. "No, I take that back. It's worse than nothing. It—" His eyes shifted past Johnny and widened.

Johnny turned, thinking the hippie must have seen the coyotes, they had finally arrived, but it wasn't coyotes. *"Jim, no!"* he screamed. *"Don't!"* Knowing it was already too late, seeing it on young Jim Reed's pale face, where everything had been cancelled.

4

The boy stood there with the pistol pressed against the side of his head just long enough for Steve Ames to hope that maybe he wasn't going to do it, that he'd had a change of heart at the penultimate moment, that last little vestibule of maybe not before the endless hallway of too late, and then Jim pulled the trigger. His face contorted as if he had been struck with a gas-pain of moderate intensity. His skin seemed to pop sideways on his skull, the left cheek puffing out. Then his head blew apart, his ambitions to write great essays (not to mention those of getting into Susi Geller's pants) so much vapor in the strange sunset air, red goo that splattered across one of the insane cacti like spit. He staggered forward a step on buckling knees, the gun tumbling from his hand, then went down. Steve turned his thunderstruck face to Johnny's, thinking: I didn't see what I just saw. Rewind the tape, play it again, and you'll see, too. I didn't see what I just saw. Neither of us did. No, man. No.

Except he had. The kid, overcome with remorse and horror at what he had done to the guy from down the street, had just committed impulse suicide in front of him.

"You should have stopped him!" Dave Reed screamed, hurling himself at Johnny. *"You should have stopped him, why didn't you? Why didn't you stop him?"*

Steve tried to grab the kid on his way by, but the pain in his shoulders was excruciating. He could only watch helplessly as Dave Reed grabbed Johnny and bore him to the ground. They rolled over twice, from one side of the path to the other. Johnny wound up on top, at least for a moment. "David, listen to me—"

"No! No! You should have stopped him! You should have stopped him!"

The kid slapped Johnny first with his right hand, then his left. He was sobbing, tears streaming down his pale cheeks. Steve tried again to help and succeeded only in distracting Johnny, who had been trying to pin the boy's arms with his knees. Dave rocked up hard on one hip, throwing Johnny off the path to the left. Johnny put out a hand to break his fall and got a palmful of cactus spines instead. He roared in pain and surprise.

Steve got hold of Dave Reed's shoulder with his right hand—that arm was at least responding a little—but the boy shook him off easily, not even looking around, and then sprang onto Johnny Marinville's broad back, got his hands around his throat, and began to choke him. And, all around them in the swiftly darkening day, the coyotes howled—perfect round howls, the kind Steve had never heard when he was growing up, although he had been born and raised in Texas.

Howls like these you only heard in the movies.

5

Both men had wanted to come with her, but Cynthia wouldn't have it—one was old, the other drunk. The gate at the bottom of the lawn was still open. A moment after going through it, she was fighting her way through the underbrush toward the path. She saw several cacti before she got there (there were more of them now, and they were driving out the normal greenbelt vegetation), but didn't register them. She could hear the sounds of a struggle up ahead: harsh, strained breathing, a cry of pain, the thud of a landed blow. And coyotes. She didn't see them, but they sounded as if they were everywhere.

As she reached the path, a trim little blonde in jeans blew past her without so much as a glance. Cynthia knew who she was—Cammie Reed, the twins' mother. Following her and panting heavily was Brad Josephson. Rivulets of sweat were running down his cheeks; the late light made him look as if he were crying tears of blood.

Sun's going down, Cynthia thought as she turned onto the path and ran after the others. If we don't get out of here soon, we're apt to get lost. And wouldn't *that* be fun.

Then there was a scream from just ahead of her. No, not a scream but a *shriek.* Horror and grief mingled. The Reed woman. Cynthia heard Brad say "Oh no, oh fuck" just as she reached him.

For a moment Josephson's broad back obscured what was going on, and then he bent beside Cammie and Cynthia saw two bodies lying sprawled on either side of the path. In the thickening shadows she couldn't tell who they were—only that they had been male, and looked as if they had died unpleasantly—but she could see Steve standing to one side of the melee at the left of the path, and the sight of him made her feel glad. Almost at his feet was the carcass of a horribly misshapen animal with half its head blown away.

Cammie Reed was on her knees beside one of the corpses, not touching it but holding her shaking hands out over it, palms up, wailing. On her face was an expression of murderous agony. Cynthia saw the Eddie Bauer shorts and understood it was one of her sons.

But they had such perfect teeth, Cynthia thought stupidly. Must have cost her and her husband a fortune.

Brad worked at getting the other twin (Dave, Cynthia thought his name was, or maybe it was Doug) off Johnny Marinville. The big black man had gotten his arms under the teenager's arms, and had locked his large hands together behind Dave's neck, giving him full-nelson leverage. Still, the Reed boy did not come easily.

"Let me go!" he bawled. *"Let me go, you son of a bitch! He killed my brother! He killed Jimmy!"*

Mrs. Reed's keening stopped. She looked up and the still, questioning expression on her white face frightened Cynthia. "What?" she said, so low that she might have been speaking to herself. "*What* did you say?"

"He killed Jimmy!" Dave Reed bawled. His head was bent strenuously forward under the pressure Brad was exerting on his neck, but he still pointed unerringly at Johnny, who was getting to his feet. Blood trickled from one of the writer's nostrils.

"No," Johnny said heavily. The woman wasn't listening to him, Cynthia saw that clearly in her white and frozen face, but Marinville didn't. "I understand how you feel, David, but—"

The woman looked down. Cynthia looked down with her. They saw the .45 on the path at the same moment, and both of them went for it. Cynthia dropped to her knees and actually got her hand on it first, but it did her no good. Fingers as cold as marble and as strong as the talons of an eagle closed over her hand and plucked the pistol away.

"—it was all a terrible accident," Johnny was mumbling. He seemed to be speaking mostly to Dave. He looked ill, on the verge of fainting. "That's how you have to think of it. As—"

"Look out!" Steve cried, then: "Jesus Christ, lady, no! Don't!"

"You killed Jimmy?" the woman asked in a deadly-cold voice. "Why? Why would you do that?"

But she wasn't interested in the answer, it seemed. She lifted the .45, centering it on Johnny Marinville's forehead. There was no question in Cynthia's mind that she meant to kill him. *Would* have killed him, if not for the new arrival, who came between Cammie and her intended target just before she could squeeze the trigger.

6

Brad recognized the zombie in spite of its hitching, shambling walk and distorted face. He didn't know what kind of force had been responsible for changing the amiable college English teacher from down the block into the thing he was looking at now, and didn't want to know. Looking was bad enough. It was as if someone whose prodigious strength was only overmatched by his sadistic cruelty had gripped Peter Jackson's head between his hands and squeezed. The man's eyes bulged from their sockets; the left had actually burst and lay on his cheek. His grin was even worse, a grotesque ear-to-ear rictus that made Brad think of The Joker in the Batman comic books.

They all stopped moving; Coleridge's Ancient Mariner with his glittering, enchanted gaze might have entered their company. Brad felt his fingers, laced together at the nape of Dave's neck, loosen, but Dave made no immediate effort to pull away. The longhair in the bloodstained tee-shirt was partially blocking

Peter's way, and for a moment Brad thought there was going to be a collision. At the last second the hippie managed a single shaky backward step, making room. Peter turned his strangely distended head toward him. The fading light shone on his bulging eyeballs and grinning teeth.

"Find . . . my . . . friend," Peter said to the hippie. His voice was faint and queasy, as if he had been gassed enough to fuck him up but not quite enough to put him down. "Sit . . . down . . . with . . . my friend."

"Do it, man, knock yourself out," the hippie said in an unsteady voice, then hunched his shoulder in, away from the grinning man. The hippie had been wounded somehow and it obviously hurt him to do that, but he did it anyway. Brad didn't blame him. He wouldn't have wanted to be touched by that thing, either, even in passing.

It went on up the path, kicking the leg of the outstretched animal, and Brad saw a weird thing: the animal—it had been some sort of cat—was decaying with the speed of time-lapse photography, its pelt turning black and beginning to send up tendrils of nasty-smelling steam or smoke.

They remained frozen—the hippie with his bloody shoulders hunched; the counter-girl on one knee; Cammie standing in front of the girl and pointing the gun; Johnny with his hands up, as if he intended to try catching the bullet; Brad and Dave Reed caught in their wrestling pose—as Peter drifted south along the path, his back now to them. The evening was utterly still, poised on a diminishing shaft of daylight. Even the coyotes had gone still, at least for the moment.

Then Dave sensed the lack of strength in the hands holding his neck and tore out of Brad's grip. The boy showed no interest in Johnny, however. He charged at his mother instead.

"You too!" he screamed. *"You killed him, too!"*

She turned toward him, her face shocked and flabbergasted.

"Why did you send us out here, Ma? Why?"

He snatched the gun from her unresisting hand, held it up in front of his eyes for a moment, and then heaved it into the woods . . . except they *weren't* woods, not anymore. The changes had continued all around them even while they had been striving one with the other, and they were now standing in a bristling, alien forest of cacti. Even the smell of the burning house had changed; it now smelled like burning mesquite, or maybe sagebrush.

"Dave . . . Davey, I . . ."

She fell silent, only staring at him. He stared back, just as white, just as drawn. It occurred to Brad that not long ago the boy had been standing on his lawn, laughing and throwing a Frisbee. Dave's face began to contort. His mouth drew down and shuddered open. Gleaming strands of spit stretched between his lips. He began to wail. His mother put her arms around him and began to rock him. "No, it's all right," she said. Her own eyes were like smooth dark stones in a dry riverbed. "No, it's all right. No, honey, it's all right, Mom's here and it's all right."

Johnny stepped back onto the path. He looked briefly at the dead animal, which was now shimmering like something seen through a furnace-haze and oozing runnels of thick pink liquid. Then he looked at Cammie and her remaining son.

"Cammie," he said. "Mrs. Reed. I did not shoot Jim. I swear I didn't. What happened was—"

"Be still," she said, not looking at him. Dave was half a foot taller than his mother and had to outweigh her by seventy pounds, but she rocked him as easily now as she must have done when he was eight months old and colicky. "I don't want to hear what happened. I don't care what happened. Let's just go back. Do you want to go back, David?"

Weeping, not looking, he nodded against her shoulder.

She turned her terrible dry eyes toward Brad. "Bring my other boy. We're not leaving him out here with that thing." She looked briefly at the fuming, stinking carcass of the mountain lion, then back at Brad. "Bring him, do you understand?"

"Yes, ma'am," Brad said. "I absolutely do."

7

Tom Billingsley was standing at the kitchen door, peering out into the growing gloom toward his open back gate and trying to make sense of the sounds and voices he heard coming from beyond it. When a set of fingers tapped him on the shoulder, he almost had a heart attack.

Once he would have spun gracefully and cold-cocked the intruder with his fist or elbow before either of them knew what was happening, but the slim young man who had been capable of such speed and agility was long gone. He did strike out, but the red-headed woman in the blue shorts and sleeveless blouse had plenty of time to step back, and Tom's arthritis-bunched knuckles coldcocked nothing but thin air.

"Christ, woman!" he cried.

"I'm sorry." Audrey's face, normally pretty, was haggard. There was a hand-shaped bruise on her left cheek and her nose was swollen, the nostrils caked with dried blood. "I was going to say something, but I thought that might scare you even worse."

"What happened to you, Aud?"

"It doesn't matter. Where are the others?"

"Some in the woods, some next door. It—" A howl rose. The red light had faded from the air now, and all that remained was ashes of orange. "It doesn't sound too good for the ones that're out. A lot of screaming." He thought of something. "Where's Gary?"

She stood aside and pointed. Gary lay in the door-way between the kitchen and the living room. He had passed out while still holding his wife's hand. Now that the screaming and yelling from the greenbelt had stopped—at least temporarily—Old Doc could hear him snoring.

"That's Marielle under that coverlet?" Audrey asked.

Tom nodded.

"We have to get with the others, Tom. Before it starts again. Before they come back."

"Do you know what's happening here, Aud?"

"I don't think anyone knows exactly what's happening here, but I know some stuff, yes." She pressed the heels of her palms against her forehead and closed her eyes. To Tom she looked like a math student wrestling with some massive equation. Then she dropped her hands and looked at him again. "We better go next door. We should all be together."

He lifted his chin toward the snoring Gary. "What about him?"

"We couldn't carry him, couldn't lift him over David Carver's back fence even if we could. You'll be doing well to get over it yourself."

"I'll manage," he said, stung a little. "Don't you worry about me, Aud, I'll manage fine."

From the greenbelt there came a cry, another gunshot, and then an animal howling in agony. What seemed like a thousand coyotes howled in response.

"They shouldn't have gone out there," Audrey said. "I know why they did, but it was a bad idea."

Old Doc nodded. "I think they know that now," he said.

8

Peter reached the fork in the path and looked into the desert, bone-white in the glare of a rising moon, beyond it. Then he looked down and saw the man in the patched khaki pants pinned to the cactus.

"Hello . . . friend," he said. He moved the bum's

shopping cart so he could sit down beside him. As he settled against the cactus spines, feeling them slide into his back, he heard a cry and a gunshot and an agonized howl. All from far away. Not important. He put his hand on the dead bum's shoulder. Their grins were identical. "Hello . . . friend," the erstwhile James Dickey scholar said again.

He looked south. His remaining sight was almost gone, but there was enough left for him to see the perfectly round moon rising between the fangs of the black Crayola mountains. It was as silver as the back of an old-time pocket watch, and upon it was the smiling, one-eye-winked face of Mr. Moon from a child's book of Mother Goose rhymes.

Only this version of Mr. Moon appeared to be wearing a cowboy hat.

"Hello . . . friend," Peter said to it, and settled back further against the cactus. He did not feel the exaggerated spines that punctured his lungs, or the first trickles of blood that seeped out of his grinning mouth. He was with his friend. He was with his friend and now everything was all right, they were looking at Mr. Cowpoke Moon and everything was all right.

9

The light dropped out of the day with a speed that reminded Johnny of the tropics, and soon the spiny landscape around them was only a black blur. The path was clear, at least for the time being—a gray streak about two feet wide winding through the shadows—but if the moon hadn't come up, they would probably be in even deeper shit than they already were. He had watched the weather forecast that morning and knew the moon was new, not full, but that little contradiction didn't seem very important under the current circumstances.

They went up the path two by two, like animals mounting the gangplank to Noah's ark: Cammie and her surviving son, then he and Brad (with the corpse of Jim Reed swinging between them), then Cynthia and the hippie, whose name was Steve. The girl had picked up the .30–.06, and when the coyote—a nightmare even more misbegotten than the mountain lion had been—came out of a cactus grove to the east of the path, it was the girl who settled its account.

The moon was bringing out fantastic tangles of shadow everywhere, and for a moment Johnny thought the coyote was one of them. Then Brad yelled *"Hey, look OUT!"* and the girl fired almost at once. The recoil would have knocked her over like a bowling pin if the hippie hadn't grabbed her by the back of her pants.

The coyote yowled and flipped over backward, its mismatched legs spasming. There was enough moonlight for Johnny to see that its paws ended in appendages that looked horribly like human fingers, and that it wore a cartridge belt for a collar. Its mates raised their voices in howls of what might have been mourning or laughter.

The thing began to decay at once, paw-fingers

turning black, ribcage collapsing, eyes falling in like marbles. Steam began to rise from its fur, and the stench rose with it. A moment or two later, those thick pink streams began to ooze out of its liquefying corpse.

Johnny and Brad set Jim Reed's body gently down. Johnny reached for the .30–.06 and poked the barrel at the coyote. He blinked with surprise (*moderate* surprise; his capacity for any large emotional reaction seemed pretty well drained) as it slid past the darkening hide with no feeling of resistance at all.

"It's like prodding cigarette smoke," he said, handing the gun back to Cynthia. "I don't think it's here at all. I don't think *any* of it's here, not really."

Steve Ames stepped forward, took Johnny's hand, and guided it to the shoulder of his shirt. Johnny felt a line of ragged punctures made by the mountain lion's claws. Blood had soaked through the cotton enough for it to squelch under Johnny's fingers. "The thing that did this to me wasn't cigarette smoke," Steve said.

Johnny started to reply, then was distracted by a strange rattling sound. It reminded him of cocktail shakers in the be-bop bars of his youth. Back in the fifties, that had been, when you couldn't get smashed without a tie on if you were a member of the country club set. The sound was coming from Dave Reed, who was standing rigidly beside his mother. It was his teeth.

"Come on," Brad said. "Let's get the hell back under cover before something else comes. Vampire bats, maybe, or—"

"You want to stop right there," Cynthia said. "I'm warning you, big boy."

"Sorry," Brad said. Then, gently: "Get moving, Cammie, okay?"

"Don't you tell me to get moving!" she responded crossly. Her arm was around Dave's waist. She might as well have been hugging an iron bar, so far as Johnny could see. Except for the shivering, that was. And that weird thing with the teeth. "Can't you see he's scared to death?"

More howls drifted through the darkness. The stench of the coyote Cynthia had shot was rapidly becoming unbearable.

"Yes, Cammie, I can," Brad said. His voice was low and kind. Johnny thought the man could have made a fortune as a psychiatrist. "But you have to get moving. Else we'll have to go on and leave you here. We *have* to get inside. We *have* to get to shelter. You know that, don't you?"

"See that you bring my other boy," she said sharply. "You're not leaving him beside the path for the . . . you're just not leaving him beside the path. *Not!*"

"We'll bring him," Brad said in the same low, soothing voice. He bent and took hold of Jim Reed's legs again. "Won't we, John?"

"Yes," Johnny said, wondering what was going to be left of poor old Collie Entragian come morning . . . assuming there would be a morning. Collie didn't have a mother present to stand up for him.

Cammie watched them lift her son's corpse between them, then stood on tiptoe and whispered something into Dave's ear. It must have been the right thing, because the kid got moving again.

They had made only a few steps when there was a subdued rattle up ahead, the gritty crunch of a footstep on the new surface of the ground, then a muffled cry of exasperated pain. Dave Reed shrieked as piercingly as a starlet in a horror movie. This sound more than that of strangers in the woods made Johnny's balls pull up against his groin. From the corner of his eye he saw the hippie grab hold of the rifle barrel when Cynthia brought it up. Steve pushed it back down again, murmuring for her to hold on, just hold on.

"Don't shoot!" a voice called from the tangle of shadows up ahead and to their left. It was a voice Johnny recognized. "We're friends, so just take it easy. Okay?"

"Doc?" Johnny, who had come close to dropping his end of Jim Reed, now renewed his grip in spite of his aching arms and shoulders. Before the sounds from up ahead had begun, he'd been thinking of something from *Intruder in the Dust*. People got heavier just after they died, Faulkner had written. It was as if death was the only way stupid thief gravity knew how to celebrate its existence. "Doc, that you?"

"Yeah." Two shapes appeared in the dark and moved cautiously toward them. "I stuck hell out of myself on a goddam cactus. What are cactuses doing in Ohio?"

"Excellent question," Johnny said. "Who's that with you?"

"Audrey Wyler from across the street," a woman replied. "Can we get out of these woods, please?"

Johnny suddenly knew that he could not carry his end of Jim Reed's body all the way back to the Carver house, let alone help Brad boost it over the fence. He looked around. "Steve? Can you spell me on this for awhi—" He broke off, remembering Steve's dance with the Picasso mountain lion. "Shit, you can't, can you?"

"Oh, Chri . . . ist." Tom Billingsley's voice made one syllable into two, then cracked on the second one like a teenager's. "Which twin is that?"

"Jim," Johnny said. Then, as Tom stepped next to him: "You can't, Tom, you'll have a stroke, or something."

"I'll help," Audrey said, joining them. "Come on. Let's go."

10

Steve saw that the old veterinarian and the woman from across the street had come onto the path at the same place where he and Entragian had come onto it. There was a cow's skull half-buried in the ground where the discarded batteries had been and an old rusty horseshoe where the potato-chip bag had been, but the wrapper from the baseball cards was still there. Steve bent, picked it up, and held it so the moonlight would strike it. Upper Deck cards. Albert Belle with the bat coiled behind his head and a predatory look in his eye. Steve realized an odd thing: *this* felt like the anachronism, not the cacti or the cow's skull or even the freakish cat which had been hiding in the ravine. And us, he thought. We're the abnormalities now, maybe.

"What are you thinking about?" Cynthia asked.

"Nothing."

He let the wrapper drop from his fingers. Halfway to the ground it suddenly *spread*, filling out like a sail, turning from what might have been light green (it was hard to tell in the moonlight) to bright white. He gasped. Cynthia, who had turned to check the path behind them, wheeled back in a hurry. "What?"

"Did you see?"

"No. What?"

"This." He bent and picked it up. The baseball-card wrapper was now a sheet of rough paper. Staring out of it was a scruffy-bearded villain with hooded, half-bright eyes. WANTED, the poster blared. MURDER, BANK-ROBBERY, TRAIN-ROBBERY, THEFT OF RESERVATION FUNDS, MOLESTATION AND TERRORIZING, POISONING TOWN WELLS, CATTLE THEFT, HORSE THEFT, CLAIM-JUMPING. All that above the picture. Below it, in big black type, the villain's name: JEBEDIAH MURDOCK.

"Give me a break," Cynthia said softly.

"What do you mean?"

"That isn't a crook, it's some *actor*. I've seen him on TV."

Steve looked up and saw the others were pulling away. He took Cynthia by the hand and they hurried after them.

11

Tak dangled in the archway between the den and the living room with Seth's dirty toes barely touching the carpet. Its eyes were bright and feverish; it used the boy's lungs in quick, hard gasps. Seth's hair stood on end, not just on his head but all over his body. When any of this fine fuzz of body-hair brushed against the wall, it made a faint crackling noise. The muscles of the boy's body seemed not just to quiver but to *thrum.*

The death of the cop had ripped Tak out of its TV-daze, and it had snatched for the cop's essence quickly, instinctively, going all the way to the edge of its range . . . and then past, leaping for the prize like an outfielder stealing a home run that's already over the centerfield fence. And getting it! Energy had boomed into it like napalm, another barrier had fallen, and it had found itself closer than ever to Seth Garin's unique center. Not there yet—not quite—but now so close.

And its perceptions had also boomed. It saw the boy with the smoking pistol in his hand, understood what had happened, felt the boy's horror and guilt, sensed the potential. Without thinking—Tak didn't think, not really—it leaped into Jim Reed's mind. It could not control him physically at this range, but all the fail-safe equipment guarding the boy's emotional armory had temporarily shorted out, leaving that part of him wide open. Tak had only a second—two, at most—to get in and turn up all the dials, overloading the boy with feedback, but a second had been enough. The boy might even have done it, anyway. All Tak had done, after all, was to amplify emotions which had already been present.

The energy released by Jim Reed's suicide had lit Tak up like a flare and shot its borrowed nerves all the way into the red zone. Fresh energy—*young* energy—flooded in, replacing the enormous amounts it had expended thus far. And now it hung in the doorway, humming, totally loaded, ready to finish what it had started.

Food first. It was ravenous. Tak floated halfway across the living room, then stopped.

"Aunt Audrey?" it called in Seth's voice. A sweet voice, perhaps because it was so little used. "Aunt Audrey, are you here?"

No. It sensed she wasn't. Aunt Audrey was able—with Seth's help—to block off her mind sometimes, but never the steady pulse of that mind's existence; its *thereness.* That was gone, now, but only from the house. She could be with the others, probably was, but she had gone no farther. Because Poplar Street was surrounded by Nevada desert, now . . . except it wasn't exactly the *real* Nevada, more a Nevada of the mind, the one Tak had imagined into being. With Seth's help, of course. It couldn't have done *any* of this without Seth.

Tak moved toward the kitchen again. Aunt Audrey's leaving was probably for the best. It would make Seth easier to control, make it less likely that he'd become a distraction at a crucial moment. Not that the little feller could present much of a problem under any circumstances; he was powerful but in many crucial ways helpless. At first it had been an arm-wrestle between equally matched opponents . . . except they weren't equally matched, not really. In the long run, raw strength is never a match for craft, and Tak had had long millennia in which to hone its hooks and wiles. Now, little by little, it was gaining the upper hand, using Seth Garin's own extraordinary powers against him like a clever karate master matched against a strong but stupid opponent.

Seth? it asked as it drifted toward the refrigerator. *Seth, where are you, pard?*

For a moment it actually thought Seth might be gone . . . except that couldn't be. They were completely entwined now, partners in a relationship as saprophytic as that of Siamese twins fused at the spine. If Seth left this body, all the parasympathetic systems—heart, lungs, elimination, tissue-building, cerebral wave function—would cease. Tak could no more maintain them than an astronaut could maintain the thousands of complicated systems which first thrust him into space and then kept him there in a stable environment. Seth was the computer, and without him the computer operator would die. Yet suicide was not an option for Seth Garin. Tak could keep him from the act just as it had driven Jim Reed to it. And, it sensed, Seth did not *want* to commit suicide. Part of Seth, in fact, did not even want to be free of Tak, not really. Because Tak had changed everything. Tak had given him Power Wagons that weren't just toys; Tak had given him movies that were real; Tak had come out of the China Pit with a pair of seven-league cowboy boots just the right size for a lonely little buckaroo. Who would *want* such a magical friend to leave? Especially if you would once again be locked in the gulag of your own skull when your trusty trailmate was gone?

Seth? Tak asked again. *Where are you, y'old cayuse, you?*

And, far back in the network of caves and tunnels and boltholes the boy had constructed (the part of him that did *not* want Tak, the part that was horrified of the stranger now living in his head), Tak caught a glimmer, a faint pulse, that it recognized.

Thereness!

It was Seth, all right. Hiding. Confident that Tak couldn't see, hear, or smell him. Nor could it, exactly. But the pulse was present, a kind of sonar blip, and if it needed Seth, it could hunt him down and drag him out. Seth didn't know that, and if he was a good little trailhand, he would never have to find out.

Yessir, it thought, opening the fridge, I'm a regular one-man posse. But even posses got to eat. They get powerful hongry, posses do, chasin down them bank-thieves and cattle rustlers.

There was fresh chocolate milk on the top shelf. Tak took the tall white Tupperware pitcher out with Seth's grimy hands, set it on the counter, then inspected the contents of the meat drawer. There was hamburger, but it didn't know how to cook and there was certainly no information on the subject stored in Seth's memory-banks. Tak had no objection to raw meat—liked it, in fact—but on two or three occasions, eating hamburger that way had made Seth's body ill. At least Aunt Audrey said it was the raw meat which had made him sick, and Tak didn't *think* she was lying (although with Aunt Audrey, it could never be completely sure). The last go-round had been the worst—vomiting and shitting all night long. Tak had vacated the premises until it was over, just checking in every now and then to make sure there was no funny stuff going on. It hated Seth's eliminatory functions even when they were normal, and on that night they had been anything but.

So, no hamburger.

There was bologna, though, and a few Kraft cheese slices—the yellow ones that it particularly liked. It used Seth's hands to put the food on the counter and used the extraordinary mind it and Seth shared to float a plastic McDonald's glass across from the cabinet where they were kept. While it made itself a sandwich, slapping meat and cheese onto white bread slathered with mustard, the plastic pitcher rose and filled the McDonald's glass, upon which was a fading picture of Charles Barkley going one-on-one with the Tasmanian Devil.

Tak drank half the chocolate milk in four big gulps, belched, then emptied the glass. It poured a second glass with its mind while tearing into its sandwich, heedless of the mustard which dripped out and splattered on Seth's dirty feet. It swallowed, bit, smacked, swallowed, drank, belched. The roar in its gut began to subside. The thing about TV—especially when *The Regulators* or *MotoKops 2200* was on—was that Tak got interested, fell into its powerful dreams, and forgot to feed Seth's body. Then, all at once, both of them would be so ravenous it could hardly think, let alone act or plan.

It finished its second glass of chocolate milk, holding it over its mouth to catch the last few drops, then tossed the glass in the sink with the rest of the dirty dishes. "Ain't *nothin* beats chow around the campfire, Paw!" it cried in its best Little Joe Cartwright voice. Then it drifted back toward the kitchen door, a dirty boy-balloon with the remains of a sandwich in one hand.

Moonlight streamed through the living-room windows. Beyond them, Poplar Street was gone. It had been replaced by the Main Street of Desperation, Nevada, as it had been in 1858, two years after the few remaining gold miners had realized the troublesome blue clay they were scraping out of their claims was, in fact, raw silver . . . and the declining town had been revitalized by disappointed wildcat miners from the California goldfields. Different land, same old ambition: to grub a quick fortune out of the sleeping ground. Tak had known none of this and had certainly not picked it up in *The Regulators* (which was set in Colorado, not Nevada); it was information Seth had gotten from a man named Allen Symes shortly before he had met Tak. According to Symes, 1858 was the year the Rattlesnake Number One mine had caved in.

Across the street, where the Jackson and Billingsley

homes had been, were Lushan's Chinese Laundry and Worrell's Dry Goods. Where the Hobart house had been the Owl County General Store now stood, and although Tak could still smell smoke, the store wasn't showing so much as a single charred board.

Tak turned and saw one of the Power Wagons on the floor. It was poking out, almost shyly, from beside one end of the couch. Tak floated it into the air and brought it across the room. It stopped before Seth's dark-brown eyes, hanging in midair with its wheels slowly turning while Tak ate the rest of its sandwich. It was the Justice Wagon. Tak sometimes wished it was Little Joe Cartwright's Justice Wagon instead of Colonel Henry's. Then Sheriff Streeter from *The Regulators* could move to Virginia City and drive the blue Freedom van instead of riding a horse. Streeter and Jeb Murdock—who'd turn out to have been only wounded, not really dead—would become friends . . . friends with the Cartwrights, too . . . and then Lucas McCain and his son would move in from his spread in New Mexico . . . and . . . well . . .

"And I'd be Pa," it whispered. "Boss of the Ponderosa and the biggest man in the Nevada territory. Me."

Smiling, it sent the Justice Wagon around Seth Garin in two slow, beautiful circles. Then it swept the fantasies out of its head. They were lovely fantasies, though. Perhaps even attainable fantasies, if it could gain enough essence from the remaining people across the street—the stuff that came out of them when they died.

"It's getting to be time," it said. "Roundup time."

It closed its eyes, using the circuits of Seth's memory to visualize the Power Wagons . . . especially the Meatwagon, which would lead this assault. No Face driving, Countess Lili co-piloting, and Jeb Murdock in the gunner's turret. Because Murdock was the meanest.

Eyes closed, fresh power lighting up its mind like Fourth of July fireworks bursting in the summer sky, Tak began the job of powering up. It would take a little while, but now that things had gotten this far, it had time.

Soon enough, the regulators would come.

"Get ready, folks," Tak whispered. Seth's fists were clenched at the ends of its arms, clenched and shaking. "You just get ready, because we're gonna wipe this town off the map."

[Allen Symes worked for the Deep Earth Mining Corporation in the capacity of Geological Mining Engineer for twenty-six years, from 1969 to late 1995. Shortly before Christmas of 1995, he retired and moved to Clearwater, Florida, where he died of a heart attack on September 19th, 1996. The document which follows was found in his desk by his daughter. It was in a sealed envelope marked

CONCERNS STRANGE INCIDENT IN CHINA PIT AND READ AFTER MY DEATH, PLS.

This document is presented here exactly as it was found.—Ed.]

October 27th, 1995

To Whom It May Concern:

I am writing this for three reasons. First, I want to clarify something that happened fifteen months ago, in the summer of 1994. Second, I am hoping to ease my conscience, which had settled down some but has been considerably stirred up again ever since the Wyler woman wrote me from Ohio and I lied to her in my response. I don't know if a man can ease his conscience by writing things down in hopes they will be read later, but it's worth a try, I guess; and I may want to show this to someone—maybe even the Wyler woman—after I retire. Third, I can't get the way that little boy grinned out of my mind.

The way he _grinned_.

I lied to Mrs. Wyler to protect the company, and to protect my job, but most of all because I _could_ lie. July 24th, 1994 was a Sunday, the place was deserted, and I was the only one who saw them. I wouldn't have been there either, if I hadn't had paperwork to catch up on. Anyone who thinks being a mining engineer is all excitement and travel should see the tons of reports and forms I've had to plow through over the years!

Anyway, I was just finishing for the day when a Volvo station wagon pulled up out front and this whole family got out. I want to say here that I have never seen such excited people who weren't going to the circus in my whole life. They looked like the people on the TV ads who have just won the Publishers Clearing House Sweepstakes!

There were five of them: Dad (the Ohio woman's brother, he would have been), Mom, Big Brother, Big Sis, and Little Brother. L.B. looked to be four or so, although having read the Wyler woman's letter (which was sent in July of this year), I know now he was a little older, just small for his age.

Anyway, I saw them arrive from the

window by the desk where I had all my papers spread out. Clear as day, I saw them. They dithered around their car for a minute or two, pointing to the embankment south of town, just as excited as chickens in a rainstorm, and then the little guy dragged his Dad toward the office trailer.

All this occurred at Deep Earth's Nevada HQ, a double-wide trailer which is located about two miles off the main drag (Highway 50), on the outskirts of Desperation, a town known for its silver mining around the time of the Civil War. Our main mining operation these days is the China Pit, where we are leaching copper. Strip mining is what the "green people" call it, of course, although it's really not so bad as they like to make out.

Anyway, Little Brother pulled his Daddy right up the trailer steps, and I heard him say, "Knock, Daddy, there's someone home, I know there is." Dad looked surprised as heck at that, although I didn't know why, since my car was parked right out front, "big as Billy be damned." I soon found out it wasn't what the little tyke was saying but that he was saying anything at all!

Father looked around at the rest of his clan, and all of them said the same thing, knock on the door, knock on the door, go on and knock on the door! Excited as hell. Sort of funny and cute, too. I was curious, I'll freely admit it. I could see their license plate, and just couldn't figure what a family from Ohio was doing way the hell and gone out in Desperation on a Sunday afternoon. If Dad hadn't got up nerve enough to knock, I was going to go out myself and pass the time of day with him. "Curiosity killed the cat, but satisfaction brought him back," you know!

But he knocked, all right, and as soon as I opened the door, the little tyke went running in right past me! Right over to the wall he went, to the same bulletin board where Sally put up Mrs. Wyler's letter when it came in, marking it CAN ANYONE HELP THIS LADY in big red-ink letters.

The tyke tapped the aerial photographs of the China Pit we kept tacked on the bulletin board, one after the other. Maybe you had to be there to understand how strange it was, but take my word for it. It was like he'd been in the office a dozen times before.

"Here it is, Daddy!" he said, tapping his way around those pictures. "Here it is! Here it is! Here's the mine, the silver mine!"

"Well," I said, kind of laughing, "it's

copper, sonny, but I guess that's close enough."

Mr. Garin gave me a red-faced look and said, "I'm sorry, we don't mean to barge in." Then he barged in himself and grabbed his little boy up. I was some amused. Couldn't help but be.

He carried the tyke back out to the steps, where he must have thought they belonged. Being from Ohio, I don't guess he knew we take barging around pretty much for granted out in Nevada. The tyke didn't kick or have a tantrum, but his eyes never left those photos on the bulletin board. He looked as cute as a papoose, peeking over his Daddy's shoulder with his little bright eyes. The rest of the family clustered around down below, staring up. The bigger kids were near bursting with excitement, and Mom looked pretty much in the same emotions.

Father said they were from Toledo, then introduced himself, his wife, and the two big kids. "And this is Seth," he finished up. "Seth is a _special_ child."

"Why, I thought they were all special," I said, and stuck out my hand. "Put 'er there, Seth; I'm Allen Symes." He shook with me right smart. The rest of the family looked flabbergasted, his Dad in particular, although I couldn't see why. My own Dad taught me to shake hands when I was just three; it's not hard, like learning to juggle or floating aces up to the top of the deck. But things got clearer to me before long.

"Seth wants to know if he can see the mountain," Mr. Garin says, and pointed at the China Pit. The north face _does_ look a little like a mountain. "I think he actually means the mine—"

"Yes!" the tyke says. "The mine! Seth want to see the mine! Seth want to see the silver mine! Hoss! Little Joe! Adam! Hop Sing!"

I busted out laughing at that, it'd been so long since I'd heard those names, but the rest of 'em didn't. They just went on looking at that little boy like he was Jesus teaching the elders in the temple.

"Well," I says, "if you want to look at the Ponderosa Ranch, son, I believe you can, although it's a good way west of here. And there's mine-tours, too, some where they ride you right underground in a real ore gondola. The best is probably the Betty Carr, in Fallon. There's no tours of the China Pit, though. It's a working mine, and not as interesting as the old gold and silver shafts. Yonder wall that looks like a mountain to you is nothing but one side of a big hole in the ground."

"He won't follow much of what you're saying, Mr. Symes," his big brother said. "He's a good brother, but he's not very swift." And he tapped the side of his head.

The tyke _did_ get it, though, as was easy to see because he started to cry. Not all loud and spoiled, but soft, like a kid does when he's lost something he really likes. The rest of them looked all downcast when they heard it, like the family dog had died. The little girl even said something about how Seth never cried. Made me feel more curious than ever. I couldn't figure out what was going on with them, and it was giving me a hell of an itch. Now I wish I'd just let it go, but I didn't.

Mr. Garin asked if he could talk to me private for a minute or two, and I said sure. He handed off the tyke to his wife—the boy still crying in that soft way, big tears just rolling down his cheeks, and I'll be damned if Big Sister wasn't starting to dribble a little bit right along with him. Then Garin came inside the trailer and shut the door.

He told me a lot about little Seth Garin in a short time, but the most important thing was how much they all loved him. Not that Garin ever came out and said so in words (that I might not have trusted, anyway). It just _showed_. He said that Seth was autistic, hardly ever said a single word you could understand or showed much interest in "ordinary life," but that when he caught sight of the north wall of China Pit from the road, he started to gabble like crazy, pointing at it the whole time.

"At first we just humored him and kept on driving," Garin said. "Usually Seth's quiet, but he does go off on one of these babbling fits every now and then. June calls them his sermons. But then, when he saw we weren't turning around or even slowing down, he started to talk. Not just words but _sentences_. "Go back, _please_, Seth want to see mine, Seth want to see Hoss and Adam and Little Joe."

I know a little about autism; my best friend has a brother in Sierra Four, the state mental facility in Boulder City (outside of Vegas). I have been there with him on several occasions, have seen the autistic at first hand, and am not sure I would've believed what Garin was telling me if I hadn't seen some of it for myself. A lot of the folks in Sierra not only don't speak, they don't even move. The worst ones look dead, their eyes glazed, their chests hardly going up and down so you can see.

"He loves Western movies and TV shows," Mr. Garin said, "and all I can figure is that the pit-wall reminds him of something he must have seen on an episode of _Bonanza_."

I thought maybe he had even _seen_ it in an episode of _Bonanza_, although I don't recall telling Garin that. A lot of those old TV shows filmed scenic footage (what they call "second unit") out this way, and the China Pit has been in existence since '57, so it's possible.

"Anyway," he said, "this is a major breakthrough for Seth—except the word that really fits is _miracle_. Him talking like he is isn't all of it, either."

"Yes," I said, "he's really in the world for a change, isn't he?"

I was thinking of the people in Lacota Hall, where my friend's brother is. Those folks were _never_ in the world. Even when they were crying or laughing or making other noises, it was like they were phoning it in.

"Yes, he is," Garin says. "It's like a bank of lights went on inside him. I don't know what did it and I don't know how long it's going to last, but . . . is there any way at all you could take us up to the mining operation, Mr. Symes? I know you're not supposed to, and I bet your insurance company would have a fit if they found out, but it would mean so much to Seth. It would mean so much to _all_ of us. We're on kind of a tight budget, but I could give you forty dollars for your time."

"I wouldn't do it for four hundred," I said. "This kind of thing a man does for free or he doesn't do at all. Come on. We'll take one of the ATVs. Your older boy can drive it, if you don't have any objections. That's against company regs, too, but might as well be hung for a goat as a lamb, I guess."

Anyone who's reading this and maybe judging me for a fool (a _reckless_ fool, at that), I only wish you could have seen the way Bill Garin's face lit up. I'm sorry as hell for what happened to him and the others in California—which I only know about from his sister's letter—but believe me when I say that he was happy on that day, and I'm glad I had a chance to make him so.

We had ourselves quite an afternoon even before our "little scare." Garin did let his older boy, John, drive us out to the pit-wall, and was he excited? I almost think young Jack Garin would have voted me for God, if I'd been running for the job. They were a nice family, and devoted to the little boy. The whole tribe of them. I guess it was pretty amazing for him to just start up talking like he did, but how many people would change all their plans because of a thing like that, right on the spur of the moment, even so? These folks did, and without so much as a word of argument among them, so far as I could tell.

The tyke jabbered all the way out to the pit, a mile a minute. A lot was gibberish, but not all. He kept talking about the characters on <u>Bonanza</u>, and the Ponderosa, and outlaws, and the silver mines. Some cartoon show was on his mind, too. Motor Cops, I think it was. He showed me an action figure from the show, a lady with red hair and a blaster that he could take out of her holster and kind of stick in her hand. Also, he kept patting the ATV and calling it "the Justice Wagon." Then Jack'd kind of puff up behind the wheel (he must have been driving all of ten miles an hour) and say, "Yeah, and I'm Colonel Henry. Warning, Force Corridor dead ahead!" And they'd all laugh. Me too, because by then I was as swept up in the excitement of it as the rest of them.

I was excited enough so that one of the things he was saying didn't really hit home until later on. He kept talking about "the old mine." If I thought anything about that, I guess I thought it was something out of some _Bonanza_ show. It never crossed my mind to think he was talking about Rattlesnake Number One, because he couldn't know about it! Even the people in Desperation didn't know we'd uncovered it while blasting just the week before. Hell, that's why I had so much paperwork to "rassle" with on a Sunday afternoon, writing a report to the home office about what we'd uncovered and listing different ideas on how to handle it.

When the idea that Seth Garin was talking about Rattlesnake Number One _did_ occur to me, I remembered how he'd come running into the office trailer as if he'd been there a million times before. Right across to the photos on the bulletin board he went. That gave me a chill, but there was something else, something I saw after the Garin family had gone on its way to Carson, that gave me an even colder one. I'll get to it in a bit.

When we got to the foot of the embankment, I swapped seats with Jack and drove us up the equipment road, which is all nicely graveled and wider than some interstates. We crossed the top and went down the far side. They all oohed and aahed, and I guess it is a little more than just a hole in the ground. The pit is almost a thousand feet at its deepest, and cuts through layers of rock that go back all the way to the Paleozoic Era, three hundred and twenty-five million years ago. Some layers of the porphyry are very beautiful, being crammed with sparkly purple and green crystals we call "skarn garnets." From the top, the earth-moving equipment on the pit floor looks the size of toys. Mrs. Garin made a joke about how she didn't like heights and might have to throw up, but you know, it's not such a joke at that. Some people do throw up when they come over the edge and see the drop inside!

Then the little girl (sorry, can't remember her name, might have been Louise) pointed over across, down by the pit-floor, and said, "What's that hole with all the yellow tapes around it? It looks like a big black eye."

"That's our find of the year," I said. "Something so big it's still a dead secret. I'll tell you if you can keep it one awhile longer. You will, won't you? I might get in trouble with my company otherwise."

They promised, and I thought telling them was safe enough, them being through-travellers and all. Also, I thought the little boy would like to hear about it, him being so crazy about Bonanza and all. And, as I said, it never crossed my mind until later to think <u>he already knew about it</u>. Why would it, for God's sake?

"That's the old Rattlesnake Number One," I said. "At least, that's what we <u>think</u> it is. We uncovered it while we were blasting. The front part of the Rattlesnake caved in back in 1858."

Jack Garin wanted to know what was inside. I said we didn't know, no one had been in there on account of the MSHA regulations. Mrs. Garin (June) wanted to know if the company would be exploring it later, and I said maybe, if we could get the right permits. I didn't tell them any lies, but I <u>did</u> skirt the truth a bit. We'd gotten up the keep-out tapes like MSHA says to do, all right, but that didn't mean MSHA knew about our find. We uncovered it purely by accident—shot off a blast-pattern pretty much like any other and when the spill stopped rolling and the dust settled, there it was—but no one in the company was sure if it was the kind of accident we wanted to publicize.

There would have been some powerful interest if news of it got out, that's for sure. According to the stories, forty or fifty Chinese were sealed up inside when the mine caved in, and if so, they'd still be there, preserved like mummies in an Egyptian pyramid. The history buffs would've had a field day with just their clothing and mining gear, let alone the bodies themselves. Most of us on-site were pretty interested, too, but we couldn't do much exploring without wholehearted approval from the Deep Earth brass in Phoenix, and there wasn't anyone I worked with who thought we'd get it. Deep Earth is not a nonprofit organization, as I'm sure anyone reading this will understand, and mining, especially in this day and age, is a high-risk operation. China Pit had only been turning a profit since 1992 or so, and the people who work there never get up in the morning completely sure they'll still have a job when they get to the work-site. Much is dependent on the per-pound price of copper (leachbed mining is not cheap), but even more has to do with the environmental issues. Things are a little better lately, the current crop of pols has at least some sense, but there are still something like a dozen "injunctive suits" pending in the county or Federal courts, filed by people (mostly the "greens") who want to shut us down. There were a lot of people—including myself, I might as well say—who didn't think the top execs would want to add to those problems by shouting to the world that we'd found an old mine site, probably of great historical interest. As Yvonne Bateman, an engineer pal of mine, said just after the round of blast-field shots uncovered the hole, "It would be just like the tree-huggers to try and get the whole pit designated a historical landmark, either by the Feds or by the Nevada Historical Commission. It might be the way to stop us for good that they are always looking for." You can call that attitude paranoid if you want (plenty do), but when a fellow like me knows there are 90 or 100 men depending on the mine to keep their families fed, it changes your perspective and makes you cautious.

The daughter (Louise?) said it looked spooky to her, and I said it did to me, too. She asked if I'd go in it on a dare and I said no way. She asked if I was afraid of ghosts and I said no, of cave-ins. It's amazing that any of the shaft was still up. They drove it straight into hornfels and crystal rhyolite—leftovers from the volcanic event that emptied the Great Basin—and that's pretty shaky stuff even when you're not shooting off ANFO charges all over the place. I told her I wouldn't go in there even on a double dare unless and until it was shored up with concrete and steel every five feet.

Never knowing I'd be in there so deep I couldn't see the sun before the day was over!

I took them to the field office and got them hard-hats, then took them out and showed them all around—diggings, tailings, leachbeds, sorters, and heavy equipment. We had quite a field-trip for ourselves. Little Seth had pretty much quit talking then, but his eyes were as bright as the garnets we are always finding in the spoil-rock!

All right, I've come to the "little scare" that has caused me so many doubts and bad dreams (not to mention a bad case of conscience, no joke for a Mormon who takes the religion stuff pretty seriously). And it didn't seem so "little" to any of us at the time, and doesn't to me now, if I'm to tell the truth. I have been over it and over it in my mind, and while I was in Peru (which is where I was, looking at bauxite deposits, when Audrey Wyler's letter of inquiry came in to the Deep Earth post box in Desperation), I dreamed of it a dozen or more times. Because of the heat, maybe. It was <u>hot</u> inside the Rattlesnake Mine. I have been in a lot of shaft-mines in my time, and usually they are chilly or downright cold. I have read that some of the deep gold mines in S. Africa are warm, but I have never been in any of those. And this wasn't warm but hot. Humid, too, like in a greenhouse.

But I'm getting ahead of myself, and I don't want to do that. What I want is to tell it straight through, end to end, and thank God nothing like it will ever happen again. In early August, not two weeks after all this happened, the whole works collapsed. Maybe there was a little temblor deep down in the Devonian, or maybe the open air had a corrosive effect on the exposed support timbers. I'll never know for sure, but down it came, a million tons of shale and schist and limestone. When I think how close Mr. Garin and his little boy came to being under all that when it went (not to mention Mr. Allen Symes, Geologist Extraordinaire), I get the willies.

The older boy, Jack, wanted to see Mo, our biggest digger. She runs on treads and works the inner slopes, mostly digging out benches at fifty-foot intervals. There was a time in the early '70s when Mo was the biggest digger on Planet Earth, and most kids—the boys especially—are fascinated with her. Big boys too! Garin wanted to see her "close up" as much as young Jack did, and I assumed Seth would feel the same way. I was wrong about that, though.

I showed them the ladder that goes up

Mo's side to the operator's cab, which is almost 100 feet above the ground. Jack asked if they could go up and I said no, that was too dangerous, but they could take a stroll on the treads if they wanted. Doing that is quite an experience, each tread being as wide as a city street and each of the separate steel plates that make them up a yard across. Mr. Garin put Seth down, and they climbed up the ladder to Mo's treads. I climbed up behind them, hoping like mad nobody would fall. If they did, I was the one who'd most likely be on the hook in case of a lawsuit. June Garin stood back aways so she could take pictures of us standing up there with our arms around each other, laughing. We were clowning and mugging for the camera and having the time of our lives until the little girl called, "You come back, Seth! Right now! You shouldn't be way over there!"

I couldn't see him because up where I was on Mo's tread, all the rest of the digger was in the way, but I could see his mother just fine, and how scared she looked when she spotted him.

"Seth!" she yelled. _"You come back now!"_ She yelled it two or three times, then dropped her camera on the ground and just _ran_. That was all I needed to see, her dropping her expensive Nikon like a used cigarette pack. I was back down the ladder in about three jumps. Wonder I didn't fall off and break my neck. Even more of a wonder Garin or his older boy didn't, I suppose, but I never even thought about that at the time. Never thought about them at all, tell the truth.

The little boy was already climbing the slope to the opening of the old mine, which was only about twenty feet up from the pit floor. I saw that and knew his mother wasn't ever going to catch him before he got inside. Wasn't anyone going to catch him before he got inside, if that was what he meant to do. My heart wanted to sink into my boots, but I didn't let it. I got running as fast as I could, instead.

I overtook Mrs. Garin just as Seth reached the mine entrance. He stopped there for a second, and I hoped maybe he _wasn't_ going to go in. I thought there was a chance that if the dark didn't put him off, the smell of the place would—kind of an old campfire smell, like ashes and burned coffee and scraps of old meat all mixed together. Then he _did_ go in, and without so much as a look back at me yelling for him to quit it.

I told his Mom to stay clear, for God's sake, that I'd go in and bring him out. I told her to tell her son and husband the same thing, but of course Garin didn't listen. I don't think I would have, in his situation, either.

I climbed the slope and broke through the yellow tapes. The tyke was short enough so he'd been able to go right underneath. I could hear the faint roaring you almost always hear coming out of old mine-shafts. It sounds like the wind, or a far-off waterfall. I don't know what it really is, but I don't like it, never have. I don't know anyone who does. It's a ghostly sound.

That day, though, I heard another one I liked even less—a low, whispery squealing. I hadn't heard it any of the other times I'd been up to look into the shaft since it was uncovered, but I knew what it was right away—hornfels and rhyolite rubbing together. It's like the ground is talking. That sound always made the miners clear out in the olden days, because it meant the works could come down at any time. I guess the Chinamen who worked the Rattlesnake back in 1858 either didn't know what that sound meant or weren't allowed to heed it.

The footing slipped on me just after I broke through the tapes, and I went down on one knee. I saw something lying there on the ground when I did. It was his little plastic action figure, the redhead with the blaster. It must have fallen out of the boy's pocket just before he went into the shaft, and seeing it there laying in that broken-up rock-waste stuff we call gangue—seemed like the worst kind of sign, and gave me the creeps something fierce. I picked it up, stuck it in my pocket, and forgot all about it until later, when the excitement was over and I returned it to its proper owner. I described it to my young nephew and he said it's a Cassie Stiles (sp.?) figure, from the Motor Cops show the little tyke kept talking about.

I heard sliding rock and panting behind me; looked back and saw Garin coming up the slope. The other three were standing down below, huddled together. The little girl was crying.

"You go on back, now!" I said. "This shaft could come down any time! It's a hundred and thirty damn years old! More!"

"I don't care if it's a thousand years old," he said back, still coming. "That's my boy and I'm going in after him."

I wasn't about to stand there and argue with him; sometimes all you can do is get moving, keep moving, and hope that God will hold up the roof. And that's what we did.

I've been in some scary places during my

years as a mining engineer, but the ten minutes or so (it actually could have been more or less; I lost all sense of time) that we spent in the old Rattlesnake shaft was the scariest by far. The bore ran back and down at a pretty good angle, and we started to run out of daylight before we were more than twenty yards in. The smell of the place—cold ashes, old coffee, burned meat—got stronger in a hurry, and that was strange, too. Sometimes old mines have a "minerally" smell, but mostly that's all. The ground underfoot was fallen rubble, and we had to step pretty smart just to keep from stubbing our toes and going face-first. The supports and cross-beams were covered with Chinese characters, some carved in the wood, most just painted on in candlesmoke. Looking at something like that makes you realize that all the things you read about in your history books actually happened. Wasn't made up a bit.

Mr. Garin was yelling for the boy, telling him to come back, that it wasn't safe. I thought of telling him that just the sound of his voice might be enough to bring down the hangwall, the way people yelling can sometimes be enough to bring down avalanches up in the high country. I didn't, though. He wouldn't have been able to stop calling. All he could think of was the boy.

I keep a little fold-blade, a magnifying loop, and a Penlite on my key-ring. I got the Penlite unhooked and shone it out ahead of us. We went on down the shaft, with the loose hornfels muttering all around us, and that soft roaring sound in our ears, and that smell up our noses. I felt it getting warmer almost right away, and the warmer it got, the fresher that campfire smell got. Except by the end, it didn't smell like a campfire anymore. It smelled like something gone rotten. A carcass of some kind.

Then we came on the start of the bones. We—us with Deep Earth, I mean—had shone spotlights into the shaft, but they didn't show much. We'd gone back and forth a lot about whether or not there really *was* anything in there. Yvonne argued that there wasn't, that no one would have kept going down into a shaft-mine dug in ground like that, not even a bunch of bond-Chinamen. They said it was all just so much talk—legend-making, Yvonne called it—but once Garin and I were a couple of hundred yards in, my little Penlite was enough to show us that Yvonne was wrong.

There were bones littered everywhere on the shaft floor, cracked skulls and legs and hip-bones and pelvises. The ribcages were the worst, every one seeming to grin like the Cheshire cat in <u>Alice in Wonderland</u>. When we stepped on them they didn't even crunch, like you'd think such things would, just puffed up like powder. The smell was stronger than ever, and I could feel the sweat rolling down my face. It was like being in a boiler room instead of a mine. And the walls! They didn't just put on their names or initials down where we were; they wrote <u>all over</u> them with their candlesmoke. It was as if when the adit caved in and they found they were trapped in the shaft, they all decided to write their last wills and testaments on the support beams.

I grabbed Garin's shoulder and said, "We've gone too far. He was standing off to one side and we missed him in the dark."

"I don't think so," he said.

"Why not?" I asked.

"Because I still feel him up ahead," he said, then raised his voice. <u>"Seth! Please, honey! If you're down there, turn around and come to us!"</u>

What came back put the hackles up on my neck. Farther on down that shaft, with its floor of crumbled skarn and skulls and bones, we could hear singing. Not words, just the little boy's voice going "La-la-la" and "dum-deedle-dum." Not much of a tune, but enough so I could recognize the _Bonanza_ theme music.

Garin looked at me, his eyes all white and wide in the dark, and asked if I still thought we'd come past him. Wasn't anything I could say to that, and so we got moving again.

We started to see gear in amongst the bones—cups, picks with rusty heads and funny short handles, and little tin boxes with straps running through them that I recognized from the Miners' Museum in Ely. Keroseners, the miners called them. They wore them on their foreheads like phylacteries, with bandannas tucked in underneath to keep their skin from burning. And I started to see there were candlesmoke drawings on the walls as well as Chinese words. They were awful things—coyotes with heads like spiders, mountain lions with scorpions riding on their backs, bats with heads like babies. I've wondered since then if I really saw those things, or if the air was so bad that far down in the shaft that I hallucinated them. I didn't ask Garin later on if he saw any of those things. I don't know for sure if I just forgot or if maybe I didn't dare.

He stopped and bent down and picked something up. It was a little black cowboy boot that had been wedged between two rocks.

The tyke must have got it jammed and run right out of it. Mr. Garin held it up so I could see it in the light of my little flash, then stuck it in his shirt. We could still hear the la-las and dum-dee-dums, so we knew he was still up ahead. The sound seemed a little closer, but I wouldn't let myself hope. Underground you can never tell. Sound carries funny.

We went on and on, I don't know how far, but the ground kept sloping down, and the air kept getting hotter. There were less bones on the floor of the shaft but more fallen rock. I could have shone my light up to see what kind of shape the topshaft was in, but I didn't dare. I didn't even dare think about how deep we were by then. Had to have been at least a quarter of a mile from where the explosions cut into the shaft and opened it up. Probably more. And I'd started to feel pretty sure we'd never get out. The roof would just come down and that'd be it. It would be quick, at least, quicker than it had been for the Chinese miners who'd suffocated or died of thirst in the same shaft. I kept thinking of how I had five or six library books back at my house, and wondering who'd take them back, and if someone'd charge my little bit of an estate for the overdue fines. It's funny what goes through a person's head when he's in a tight corner.

Just before my light picked out the little boy, he changed his tune. I didn't recognize the new one, but his Dad told me after we got out that it was the Motor Cops theme song. I only mention it because for a moment or two there it sounded like *someone else* was singing the la-las and dum-dee-dums along with him, kind of harmonizing. I'm sure it was only that soft roaring sound I mentioned, but it gave me a hell of a bump, I can tell you. Garin heard it, too; I could see him a little bit in the light from my flash, and he looked almost as scared as I felt. The sweat was pouring down his face, and his shirt was stuck to his chest like with glue.

Then he points and says, "I think I see him! I do see him! There he is! Seth! Seth!" He went running for him, stumbling over the rubble and rocking like a drunk but somehow keeping his balance. All I could do was pray God he didn't fall into one of those old support baulks. It'd probably crumble to powder just like the bones we'd stepped on to get where we were, and that would be all she wrote.

Then *I* saw the kid, too—you couldn't very well mistake the jeans and the red shirt he was wearing. He was standing in front of the place where the shaft ended. You could tell it wasn't just another cave-in because it was a smooth rockface—what we call a "slide"—and not piled-up rubble. There was a crack running down the middle of it, and for a minute I thought the kid was trying to work his way into it. That scared me plenty, because he looked small enough to do it if he wanted to, and a couple of big guys like us would never have been able to follow him. He wasn't trying to do that, though. When I got a little closer, I saw that he was standing perfectly still. I must have been fooled by the shadows my little flashlight threw, that's all I can figure.

His Dad got to him first and pulled him into his arms. He had his face against the boy's chest, so he didn't see what I did, and I only saw it for a second. It wasn't just my eyes playing tricks on me that time. The boy was <u>grinning</u>, and it wasn't a nice grin, either. The corners of his mouth looked like they were pulled most of the way up to his ears, and I could see all his teeth. His face was so stretched that his eyes looked like they were bulging right out of his head. Then his father held him back so he could give him a kiss, and that grin went away. I was glad. While it was on his face, he didn't hardly look like the little boy I'd first met at all.

"What did you think you were doing?" his father asks him. He was shouting but it wasn't really much of a scold even so, because he gave the boy a kiss practically between every word. "Your mother is scared to _death_! Why did you do it? Why in God's name did you come in here?"

What he replied was the last real talking he did, and I remember it well. "Colonel Henry and Major Pike told me to," he said. "They told me I could see the Ponderosa. In there." He pointed at the crack running down the middle of the slide. "But I couldn't. Ponderosa all gone." Then he laid his head down on his father's shoulder and closed his eyes, like he was all tuckered out.

"Let's go back," I said. "I'll walk behind you and to your right, so I can shine the light on your footing. Don't linger, but don't run, either. And for Christ's sake try not to bump any of the jackstraws holding this place up."

Once we actually had the boy, that groaning in the ground seemed louder than ever. I fancied I could even hear the timbers creaking. I'm not usually an imaginative sort, but it sounded to me like they were trying to talk. Telling us to get out while we still could.

I couldn't resist shining my light into that crack once before we went, though. When I bent down I could feel air rushing out, so it wasn't just a crack in the slide; there was some sort of rift on the other side of it. Maybe a cave. The air coming out was as hot as air coming out of a furnace grate, and it stank something fierce. One whiff and I held my breath so I wouldn't vomit. It was the old-campfire smell, but a thousand times heavier. I've racked my brains trying to think of how something that deep underground could smell so bad, and keep coming up empty. Fresh air is the only thing that makes things stink like that, and that means some sort of vent, but Deep Earth has been burrowing in these parts ever since 1957, and if there had been a vent big enough to manufacture a stench like that, surely it would've been found and either plugged or followed to see where it went.

The crack looked like a zigzag S or a lightning-bolt, and there didn't seem like there was anything much in it <u>to</u> see, just a thickness of rock—at least two feet, maybe three. But I did get the sense of space opening out on the other side, and there was that hot air whooshing out, too. I thought I maybe saw a bunch of red specks like embers dancing in there, but that must have been my imagination, because when I blinked, they were gone.

I turned back to Garin and told him to move.

"In a second, just give me a second," he says. He'd taken the boy's little black cowboy boot out of his shirt and was sliding it on his foot. It was the tenderest thing. All you'd ever need to know about a father's love was in the way he did that. "Okay," he says when he had it right. "Let's go."

"Right," I says. "Just try to keep your footing."

We went as quick as we could, but it still seemed to take forever. In the dreams I mentioned, I always see the little circle of my Penlite sliding over skulls. There weren't that many that I saw when we were actually in there, and some of those had fallen apart, but in my dreams it seems like there are thousands, wall-to-wall skulls sticking up round like eggs in a carton, and they are all grinning just like the little one was grinning when his Dad picked him up, and in their eyesockets I see little red flecks dancing around, like embers rising from a wildfire.

It was a pretty awful walk, all in all.

I kept looking ahead for daylight, and for the longest time I didn't see it. Then, when I finally did (just a little tiny square I could have covered with the ball of my thumb at first), it seemed like the sound of the hornfels was louder than ever, and I made up my mind that the shaft was going to wait until we were almost out, then fall on us like a hand swatting flies. As if a hole in the ground could think! But when you're actually in a spot like that, your imagination is apt to go haywire. Sound carries funny; ideas do, too.

And I might as well say that I still have a few funny ideas about Rattlesnake Number One. I'm not going to say it was haunted, not even in a "backstage report" no one may ever read, but I'm not going to say it wasn't, either. After all, what place would be more likely to have ghosts than a mine full of dead men? But as to the other side of that slide of rock, if I actually did see something there—those dancing red lights—it wasn't ghosts.

The last hundred feet were the hardest. It took everything I had in me not to just shove past Mr. Garin and sprint for it, and I could see on his face that he felt the same way. But we didn't, probably because we both knew we'd scare the rest of the family even worse if we came busting out in a panic. We walked out like men instead, Garin with his boy in his arms, fast asleep.

That was our "little scare."

Mrs. Garin and both the two older kids were crying, and they all made of Seth, petting him and kissing him like they could hardly believe he was there. He woke up and smiled at them, but he didn't make any more words, just kind of "gobbled." Mr. Garin staggered off to the powder magazine, which is a little metal shed where we keep our blasting stuff, and sat down with his back against the side. He laced his hands together between his knees and then dropped his forehead into them. I knew just how he felt. His wife asked him if he was all right, and he said yes, he only needed to rest and catch his breath. I said I did, too. I asked Mrs. Garin if she'd take her kids back over to the ATV. I said maybe Jack would like to show his brother our Miss Mo. She kind of laughed like you do when nothing is funny and said, "I think we've had enough adventures for one day, Mr. Symes. I hope you won't take this the wrong way, but all I want to do is get out of here."

I said I understood, and I think she understood that I needed to have a little talk with her man before we picked up our marbles and called it a game. Not that I didn't need to collect myself some, too! My legs felt like rubber. I went over to the powder magazine and sat down beside Mr. Garin.

"If we report this, there's going to be a lot of trouble," I said. "For the company and also for me. I probably wouldn't end up fired, but I could."

"I'm not going to say a word," he said, raising his head out of his hands and looking me in the eye. And I don't think anyone will hold it against him if I add that he was crying. Any father would have cried, I think, after a scare like that. I was near tears myself, and I hadn't ever set eyes on the lot of them until that day. Every time I thought of the tender way Garin looked, slipping that tiny boot on his boy's foot, it raised a lump in my throat.

"I would appreciate that no end," I said.

"Nonsense," he said. "I don't know how to thank you. I don't even know how to start."

I was starting to feel a little embarrassed by then. "Come on, now," I said. "We did it together, and all's well that ends well."

I helped him to his feet, and we walked back toward the others. We were most of the way there when he put his hand on my arm and stopped me.

"You shouldn't let anybody go in there," he said. "Not even if the engineers say they can shore it up. There's something wrong in there."

"I know there is," I said. "I felt it." I thought of the grin on the boy's face—even now, all these months later, it makes me shiver to think of it—and almost told him that his boy had felt it, too. Then I decided not to. What good would it have done?

"If it were up to me," he said, "I'd toss a charge from your powder magazine in there and bring the whole thing down. It's a grave. Let the dead rest in it."

"Not a bad idea," I said, and God must have thought so, too, because He did it on His own not two weeks later. There was an explosion in there. And, so far as I know, no cause ever assigned.

Garin kind of laughed and shook his head and said, "Two hours on the road and I won't even be able to believe this happened."

I told him maybe that was just as well.

"But one thing I won't forget," he said, "is that Seth talked today. Not just words or phrases only his family could understand, either. He actually talked. You don't know how amazing that is, but we do." He waved at his family, who had got back into the ATV by then. "And if he can do it once, he can do it again." And maybe he has, I hope so. I'd like to know, too. I'm curious about that boy, and in more ways than one. When I gave him his little action figure woman, he smiled at me and kissed my cheek. A sweet kiss, too, though I seemed to catch a little whiff of the mine on his skin . . . that campfire smell, like ashes and meat and cold coffee.

We "bid a fond adieu" to the China Pit and I drove them back to the office trailer, where their car was. So far as I could see, no one took much notice of us, even though I drove right down Main Street. Desperation on a Sunday afternoon in the hot weather is like a ghost-town.

I remember standing there at the bottom of the trailer steps, waving as they drove off toward the awful thing Garin's sister said was waiting for them at the end of their trip—a senseless drive-by shooting. All of them waved back . . . except for Seth, that is. Whatever was in that mine, I think we were fortunate to get out . . . and for him to then be the only survivor of that shooting in San Jose! It's almost as if he's got what they call "a charmed life," isn't it?

As I said, I dreamed about it in Peru—mostly the skull-dream, and of shining my light into that crack—but days I didn't think of it much until I read Audrey Wyler's letter, the one that was tacked on the bulletin board when I came back from Peru. Sally lost the envelope, but said it just came addressed to "The Mining Company of Desperation." Reading it reinforced my belief that something happened out there when Seth was underhill (as we say in the business), something it might be wrong to lie about, but I did lie. How could I not, when I didn't even know what that something was?

Still, that grin.

That grin.

He was a nice little boy, and I am so glad he wasn't killed in the Rattlesnake (and he could have been; we all could have been) or with the rest of them in San Jose, but . . .

The grin didn't seem to belong to the boy at all. I wish I could say better, but that's as close as I can come.

I want to set down one more thing. You may remember me saying that Seth talked about "the old mine," but that I didn't connect that with the Rattlesnake shaft because hardly anyone in town knew about it, let alone through-travelers from Ohio. Well, I started thinking about what he'd said again while I was standing there, watching the dust from their car settle. That, and how he ran across the office trailer, right to the pictures of the China Pit on the bulletin board, like he'd been there a thousand times before. Like he *knew*. I had an idea then, and that cold feeling came with it. I went back inside to look at the pictures, knowing it was the only way I could lay that feeling to rest.

There were six in all, aerial photos the company had commissioned in the spring. I got the little magnifier off my keychain and ran it over them, one after another. My gut was rolling, telling me what I was going to see even before I saw it. The aerials were taken long before the blast-pattern that uncovered the Rattlesnake shaft, so there was no sign of it in them. *Except there was*. Remember me writing that he tapped his way around the pictures, saying "Here it is, here's what I want to see, here's the mine"? We thought he was talking about the *pit*-mine, because that's what the pictures were of. But with my magnifying loupe I could see the prints his fingers had left on the shiny surface of the photos. *Every one was on the south face*, where we uncovered the shaft. *That* was what he was telling us he wanted to see, not the pit-mine but the shaft-mine the pictures didn't even show. I know how crazy that must sound, but I have never doubted it. He knew it was there. To me, the marks of his finger on the photographs—not just one photo but all six—prove it. I know it wouldn't stand up in a court of law, but that doesn't change what I know. It's like something in that mine sensed him going past on the highway and called out to him. And of all my questions, there's maybe only one that really matters: Is Seth Garin all right? I would write Garin's sister and ask, have once or twice actually picked up a pen to do that, and then I remember that I lied, and a lie is hard for me to admit. Also, do I really want to prod a sleeping dog that might turn out to have big teeth? I don't think so, but . . .

There should be more to say, maybe, but there isn't. It all comes back to the grin.

I don't like the way he grinned.

This is my true statement of what happened; God, if only I knew what it was I saw!

Allen Symes

CHAPTER 11

1

Old Doc was the first one over the Carvers' back fence. He surprised them all (including himself) by going up easily, needing only a single boost in the butt from Johnny to get him started. He paused at the top for a second or two, setting his hands to his liking. To Brad Josephson he looked like a skinny monkey in the moonlight. He dropped. There was a soft grunt from the other side of the stakes.

"You all right, Doc?" Audrey asked.

"Yeah," Billingsley said. "Right as rain. Aren't I, Susi?"

"Sure," Susi Geller agreed nervously. Then, through the fence: "Mrs. Wyler, is that you? Where did *you* come from?"

"That doesn't matter right now. We need to—"

"What happened out there? Is everyone all right? My mom is having a cow. A *large* one."

Is everyone all right. That was a question Brad didn't want to answer. No one else did either, from the look.

"Mrs. Reed?" Johnny asked. "David next, then you?"

Cammie gave him her dry stare, then turned back to Dave. She murmured in his ear once more, stroking his hair as she did so. Dave listened with a troubled expression, then murmured back, just loud enough for Brad to hear, "I don't want to." She murmured again, more vehemently this time. Brad caught the words *your brother* near the end. This time Dave reached up, grabbed the top of the fence, and swung himself smoothly over to the other side. He did it, so far as Brad could see, with no expression save that look of faint unease on his face. Cammie went next, Audrey and Cynthia boosting. As she gained the top, Dave's hands rose to meet her. Cammie slipped into them, making no effort to keep hold of the fence for safety's sake. Brad had an idea that at this point she might have actually welcomed a fall. Maybe even a broken neck. *Why did you send us out here, Ma?* the kid had shouted, perhaps intuiting that his own eagerness to go—and Jim's—would never serve as a mitigating circumstance in her mind. Cammie would always blame herself, and he would probably always be willing to let her.

"Brad?" That was a voice he was glad to hear, although he rarely heard it sound so soft and worried. "You there, hon?"

"I'm here, Bee."

"You okay?"

"Fine. Listen, Bee, and don't lose your cool. Jim Reed is dead. So's Entragian from down the street."

There was a gasp, and then Susi Geller was screaming Jim's name over and over again. To Brad, who was emotionally as well as physically exhausted, those screams roused annoyance rather than pity . . . and the fear that they might draw something even less pleasant than the big cat or the coyote with the human fingers.

"Susi?" The alarmed voice of Kim Geller from the house. Then she was screaming, too, the sound seeming to cut the moonlit air like a sharp whirling blade: *"Soooooo-zeeeeee! Sooooo-zeeeeee!"*

"Shut up!" Johnny yelled. *"Jesus, Kim, SHUT UP!"*

For a wonder she did, but the girl went on and on, shrieking like a misbegotten fifth-act Juliet.

"Dear God," Audrey muttered. She put her palms over her ears and ran her fingers into her hair.

"Bee," Brad said through the fence, "shut that Chicken Little up. I don't care how."

"JIM!" Susi screamed. *"OHHHH GAWWWD, JIM! OH GAWWWD NO! OH—"*

There was a slap. The screams were cut off almost at once. Then:

"You can't hit my *daughter*! You can't hit my *daughter*, you bitch, I don't care what ideas you've gotten from . . . from affirmative action! You fat black *bitch*!"

"Oh fuck me til I cry," Cynthia said. She clutched her own double-dyed hair and squeezed her eyes shut like a kid who doesn't want to watch the final few minutes of a scary movie.

Brad kept his open and held his breath, waiting for Bee to go nuclear. Instead, Bee ignored the woman, calling softly through the fence: "Are you sending his body over, Bradley?" She sounded completely composed, for which Brad was completely thankful.

"Yeah. You and his mother and his brother catch hold of him when we do."

"We will." Still cool as a cucumber fresh out of the crock.

"Kim?" Brad called through the stakes of the fence. "Mrs. Geller? Why don't you go on in the house, ma'am?"

"Yes!" Kim said pleasantly. "I think that's a *good* idea. We'll just go in the house, won't we, Susi? Some cold water on our faces will make us feel better."

There were footfalls. The snuffling began to diminish, which was good. Then the coyotes began to howl again, which was bad. Brad looked over his shoulder and saw chips of moving silver light in the tangled darkness of the greenbelt. Eyes.

"We've got to hurry," Cynthia said.

"You don't know the half of it," Audrey said.

Brad thought: That's what I'm afraid of. He turned and took hold of Jim Reed's shoulders. He could smell, very faintly, the shampoo and aftershave the kid had used that morning. Probably he'd been thinking about the girls as he applied them. Johnny took a nervous look behind them—at those moving chips of light, Brad assumed—then moved down Jim's body until he had one arm around the dead boy's waist and the other supporting his butt. Audrey and Cynthia took his legs.

"Ready?" Johnny asked.

They nodded.

"On three, then. One . . . two . . . *three.*"

They raised the body like a quartet doing a team bench-lift. For one horrible moment Brad thought his back, having supported a shamefully large gut for the last ten years or so, was going to lock up on him. Then they had Jim's body up to the top of the fence. The dead boy's arms hung out to either side, the posture of a circus acrobat inviting applause at the climax of a fabulous stunt. His open palms were full of moonlight.

Beside Brad, Johnny sounded on the verge of cardiac arrest. Jim's head lolled limply backward on his neck. A drop of half-congealed blood fell and struck Brad's cheek. It made him think of mint jelly, for some mad reason, and his stomach clenched like a hand in a slick glove.

"Help us!" Cynthia gasped. "For Christ's sake, *someone—*"

Hands appeared, hovered above the blunt fence-stakes for a moment, then broke apart into fingers which grasped Jim's shirt and the waistband of his shorts. Just as Brad knew he couldn't hold the body another second (never until now had he really understood the concept of *dead weight*), it was pulled away from him. There was a meaty thud, and from a little distance away (the Carvers' back porch was Brad's guess), Susi Geller voiced another brief scream.

Johnny looked at him, and Brad was almost convinced the man was smiling. "Sounds like they dropped him," Johnny said in a low voice. He wiped an arm across his sweaty face, then lowered it. The smile—if it had been there in the first place—was gone.

"Whoops," Brad said.

"Yeah. Whoops-a-fuckin-daisy."

"Hey, Doc!" Cynthia cried in a low voice. "Catch! Don't worry, safety's on!" She lifted the .30–.06, stock first, standing on her toes in order to tip it over the fence.

"Got it," Billingsley said. Then, in a lower voice: "That woman and her idiot daughter finally went in the house."

Cynthia climbed the fence and swung easily over the top. Audrey needed a push and a hand on her hip for balance, and then she was over, as well. Steve went next, using Brad's and Johnny's interlaced hands as a stirrup and then sitting up top a moment, waiting for the pain in his clawed shoulders to subside a little. When it had, he swung over the fence to the Carvers' side and pushed off, jumping rather than trying to let himself down.

"I can't get over there," Johnny said. "No way. If there was a ladder in the garage—"

Wh-wh-whoooooo! . . . Wh-wh-whoooooooo!

From almost directly behind them. The two men jumped into each other's arms as unselfconsciously as small children. Brad turned his head and saw shapes closing in. Each was hulked up behind a pair of those glinting semi-circular moonchips.

"Cynthia!" Johnny shouted. "Shoot the gun!"

When her voice came back it sounded scared and uncertain. "You mean come back over the—"

"No! No! Just shoot it into the sky!"

She triggered the .30–.06 twice, the blasts whip-cracking the air. The bitter tang of gunsmoke seeped through the fence-stakes. The shapes coming toward them through the greenbelt paused. Didn't draw back, but at least paused.

"You still pooped, John?" Brad asked softly.

Johnny was looking back at the shapes in the shadows. There was a strange, shaky smile on his mouth. "Nah," he said. "Got my second wind. I . . . what do you think you're doing?"

"What's it look like?" Brad asked. He was down on his hands and knees at the base of the fence. "Hurry up, Daddy-O."

Johnny stepped onto his back. "Jesus," he said, "I feel like the President of South Africa."

Brad didn't seem to understand at first. When he did, he began giggling. His back hurt like hell. Johnny Marinville seemed to weigh at least five hundred pounds, the man's heels felt as if they were leaving divots in Brad's outraged spine, but the giggles poured out of him just the same; he couldn't help it. Here was a white American intellectual with a prep-school education of excruciating correctness—a writer who had once partied with the Panthers at Lenny Bernstein's pad—using a black man as a footstool. If it wasn't a liberal's idea of hell, Brad had never heard of one. He thought of moaning and crying, "Hurry up, massa, you killin dis po boy!" and his giggles became outright laughter. He was terrified of losing a section of his tender upturned ass to one of the slinkers back there in the woods, but he laughed anyway. I'll give him a chorus of "Old Black Joe," he thought, and howled like a coyote himself. Tears poured from his eyes. He pounded his fist on the ground.

"Brad, what's wrong?" Johnny whispered from above him.

"Never mind!" he said, still giggling. "Just get off my back! Holy shit, what you got on those shoes? Cleats?"

Then, blessedly, the weight was gone. There were grunting sounds as Johnny struggled to get his leg over the fence. Brad got up, rode through a scary moment when his back again seemed about to lock, then got one meaty shoulder planted under Johnny's ass. A moment later he could hear another grunt of effort and a muffled cry from Johnny as he came down.

Which left him, all alone and with no footstool.

Brad eyed the top of the fence and thought it looked about ninety feet high. Then he glanced behind him and saw the shapes on the move again, tightening around him in a collapsing crescent.

He seized two of the stakes, and as he did, something snarled behind him. Underbrush rattled. He looked back over his shoulder and saw a creature that looked more like a wild boar than a coyote . . . except what it really looked like was a badly made child's drawing, nothing more than a hurried scribble, really, that had somehow come to life. Its legs were all of different lengths and ended in blunt clubs unlike either paws or fingers. Its tail seemed to jut up from the middle of its back. Its eyes were blank silver circles. Its nose was a pig-pug. Only its teeth seemed really real, huge croggled things which spouted from either side of the beast's mouth.

Adrenaline hit Brad's nervous system like something shot from one of Old Doc's horse syringes. He forgot all about his back and yanked himself upward, tucking his knees between his chest and the fence when he heard the thing charge. It hit just below his feet, hard enough to shake the whole fence. Then Johnny had one of his wrists and Dave Reed had the other and Brad scrabbled to the top of the fence, leaving generous amounts of skin behind. He tried to get his left leg over the top and thumped the ankle on one of the blunt stakes instead. Then he was falling, tearing his shirt all the way down one side in his useless struggle to hold onto the top of the fence with his right hand. He let go in time to keep from breaking his arm, but when he landed (partly on top of Johnny, mostly on top of his admirably padded wife), he could feel blood trickling down from his armpit.

"Want to think about getting off me, handsome?" the admirably padded lady herself asked, sounding breathless. "I mean, if it wouldn't discommode you any?"

Brad crawled off them both, collapsed in a heap, then rolled over on his back. He looked up at alien stars, swollen things that blinked on and off like the Christmas lights they strung over small-town Main Streets every year on the day after Thanksgiving. What he was looking at were no more real stars than he was the King of Prussia . . . but they were up there, just the same. Yes they were, right over his head, and how bad was your situation when the sky itself was part of the damned conspiracy?

Brad closed his eyes so he wouldn't look at them anymore. In his mind's eye—the one that opened widest when the other two closed—he saw Cary Ripton tossing him his *Shopper*. Saw his own hand, the one not holding the hose, go up and catch it. *Good one, Mr. Josephson!* Cary called, honestly admiring. It came from far away, that voice, like something echoing down a canyon. Closer by, he heard howls from the greenbelt side of the fence (except now it was the desertbelt). These were followed by a series of hard thuds as the boar-coyotes threw themselves at it.

Christ.

"Brad," Johnny said. Low voice. Leaning over him, from the sound.

"What."

"You all right?"

"Fine as paint." Still not opening his eyes.

"Brad."

"What!"

"I had an idea. For a movie."

"You're a maniac, John." Eyes still shut. Things were better that way. "But I'll bite. What's it going to be called, this movie I can be in?"

"Black Men Can't Climb Fences," Johnny said, and began laughing wildly. It had an exhausted, half-crazy sound to it. "I'm gonna get Mario Fucking Van Peebles to direct. Larry Fishburne's gonna play you."

"Sure," Brad said, sitting up painfully. "I love Larry Fishburne. Very intense. Offer him a million up front. Who could resist?"

"Right, right," Johnny agreed, now laughing so hard he could barely talk . . . only tears were streaming down his face, and Brad didn't think they were tears of laughter. Not ten minutes ago, Cammie Reed had come within a hair of blowing his head off, and Brad doubted if Johnny had forgotten that. Brad doubted if Johnny forgot much of anything, in fact. It was probably a talent he would have traded, if given the opportunity.

Brad got on his feet, took Bee's hand, and helped her up. There were more thuds at the fence, more howls, then gnawing sounds, as if the hungry abortions over there were trying to eat their way through the stakes.

"So what do you think?" Johnny asked, letting Brad help him up as well. He staggered, found his balance, wiped his streaming eyes.

"I think that when the chips were down, I climbed just fine," Brad said. He slipped an arm around his wife, then looked at Johnny. "Come on, honky. You climbed to success over your first black man, you must be all tuckered out. Let's get in the house."

2

The thing which hopped unsteadily through the gate at the rear of Tom Billingsley's backyard was a child's version of the gila monster Jeb Murdock blows off a rock during his shooting contest with Candy about halfway through *The Regulators*. Its head, however, was that of an escapee from Jurassic Park.

It hopped up the back steps, slithered to the screen, and pushed at it with its snout. Nothing happened; the screen opened outward. The gila stretched its saurian head forward and began chomping at the bottom panel of the door with its teeth. Three bites was all it took, and then it was in Old Doc's kitchen.

Gary Soderson became distantly aware of a rotten breeze blowing into his face. He tried to wave it away, but it only grew stronger. He raised one hand, touched something that felt like an alligator shoe—a very large alligator shoe—and opened his eyes. What he saw leaning over him at kissing distance, staring at him with a curiosity which was almost human, was so grotesque that he could not even scream. The lizard-thing's eyes were bright orange.

Here it is, Gary thought, my first major attack of the dt's. Ahoy, mateys, A.A. dead ahead.

He closed his eyes. He tried to tell himself that he didn't smell swamp-breath or hear the toneless clickety-click of a tail dragging across kitchen linoleum. He held his dead wife's cold hand. He said, "Nothing there. Nothing there. Noth—"

Before he could finish the third repetition (and everyone knows the third time's the charm), the monster had plunged its teeth into his throat and torn it open.

3

Johnny saw small feet through the open pantry door and looked in. Ellie and Ralphie were lying in there on what looked like a futon, holding each other. They were fast asleep, gunshots from out back notwithstanding, but even in slumber they had not entirely escaped what was happening; their faces were white and strained, their breathing had a watery sound that made him think of stifled sobs, and Ralphie's feet twitched, as if he dreamed of running.

Johnny guessed that Ellen must have found the futon and brought it into the pantry for herself and her little brother to lie on; certainly Kim Geller hadn't done it. Kim and her daughter had resumed their former places by the wall, only now sitting in kitchen chairs instead of on the floor.

"Is Jim really dead?" Susi asked, looking at Johnny with wet, shiny eyes as Johnny came in behind Brad and Belinda. "I just can't believe it, we were playing Frisbee like we always do, and we were going out to the movies tonight—"

Johnny was completely out of patience with her. "Why don't you go out on the back porch and have a look for yourself?"

"Why are you being such a bastard?" Kim asked angrily. "My daughter may *never* get over serious trauma like this. She's had a *profound shock*!"

"She's not the only one," Johnny said. "And while we're at it—"

"Quit it, man, we don't need to get fighting," Steve Ames said.

Undoubtedly true, but Johnny no longer cared. He pointed a finger at Kim, who stared back at him along its length with hot, resentful eyes. "And while we're at it, the next time you call Belinda Josephson a black bitch, I'll knock your teeth down your throat."

"Oh gosh, don't you think *your* shit comes out smoking," Kim said, and rolled her eyes theatrically.

"Stop it, John," Belinda said, and took his arm. "Right now. We've got more important things to—"

"Fat black bitch," Kim Geller said. She didn't look at Belinda as she said it but at Johnny. Her eyes were still burning, but now she was smiling. He thought it was the most poisonous smile he had ever seen in his life. "Fat black *nigger* bitch." That said, she pointed her own finger at her mouth and visible teeth, like a woman trying to get *suicide* across in a game of charades. Her daughter was looking at her with a stunned expression. "Okay? Did you hear it? So come on. Knock my teeth down my throat. Let's see you try."

Johnny started forward, meaning to do just that. Brad grabbed one of his arms. Steve grabbed the other one.

"Get out of here, you idiot," Old Doc said. His voice was harsh and dry. It got through to Kim, somehow, and she gave him a startled, considering look. "Get out of here right now."

Kim rose from her chair, pulling Susi out of hers. For a moment it seemed they would go into the living room together, but then Susi pulled away. Kim reached for her, but Susi continued to back off.

"What do you think you're doing?" Kim asked. "We're going into the living room! We're going to get away from these—"

"Not me," Susi said, shaking her head quickly. "You, maybe. Not me. Uh-uh."

Kim stared at her, then looked back at Johnny. Her face was sick with a kind of hateful confusion.

"Get out of here, Kim," Johnny said. He could still see himself driving his fist into her mouth, but the madness was passing and his voice was almost steady. "You're not yourself."

"Susi? You get over here. We're going away from these hateful people."

Susi turned her back on her mother, trembling all over. Johnny supposed this did not change his opinion of the girl as a shallow, flighty creature . . . but she seemed a link or two up the food-chain from her mother, at least.

Slowly, like a rusty robot, Dave Reed raised his arms and put them around her. Cammie seemed about to object to this, then subsided.

"All right," Kim said. Her voice was clear and composed again, the voice of someone giving a speech in a dream. "When you want me, I'll be in the living room." Her eyes switched to Johnny, whom she seemed to have identified as the source of all her misery. "And you—"

"Stop it," Audrey said harshly. Startled, they all turned to look at her, except for Kim, who slipped off into the darkness of the living room. "We have no time for this *shit.* We might have a chance to get out of this—a small one—but if you fools stand around squabbling, all we're going to do is die."

"Who're you, ma'am?" Steve asked.

"Audrey Wyler." She was tall, her legs long and coltish and not unsexy below her blue shorts, but her face was pale and haggard. That face made Johnny think of the way the Carver kids looked as they lay sleeping in each other's arms, and suddenly he found himself trying to remember when he'd last seen Audrey, passed the time of day with her. He couldn't. It was as if she had dropped out of the casual, back-and-forth life of the street entirely.

Little bitty baby Smitty, he thought suddenly, *I seen you bite your mommy's titty.* Then he thought of the vans that had been on the floor of the Wyler den the afternoon he'd spent some time watching *Bonanza* with Seth. And once he had that, a kind of landslide started in his head. Outlaws that looked like movie stars. Major Pike, a good nailien gone bad. The Western scenery. That most of all. *He loves the old Westerns,* Audrey had said that day. She'd picked up a few of his toys as she spoke, doing it the way people do stuff when they're nervous. Bonanza *and* The Rifleman *are his favorites, but anything they'll bring back on the cable, he'll watch. If it has horses in it, that is.*

"It's your nephew, Audrey. Isn't it? It's Seth doing this."

"No." She raised a hand and wiped her eyes with it. "Not Seth. What's *inside* Seth."

4

"I'll tell you what I can, but there's not much time. The Power Wagons will be back before long."

"Who's inside them?" Old Doc asked. "Do you know, Aud?"

"Regulators. Outlaws. Sci-fi policemen. And this place where we are is partly the Old West as it exists on TV and partly a place called the Force Corridor, which only exists in a TV-cartoon version of the twenty-third century." She took a deep breath and ran her hands through her hair. "I don't know everything, but—"

"Take us through as much as you can," Johnny said.

She looked at her watch and made a sour face. "Stopped."

"Mine, too," Steve said. "Everybody's, I imagine."

"I think there's time," Audrey said. "Which is to say, I think it's too early for any . . . any *movement* just yet." She laughed suddenly, startling Johnny. Startling all of them, from the look. It wasn't the hysterical undertone so much as the genuine merriness on top. She saw their stares and brought herself under control. "Sorry—it's a kind of pun. No reason you should understand. Yet, anyway. We have to wait. If he brings the regulators back in the meantime, we'll have to just . . . endure them, I suppose."

"Are they getting stronger?" Cammie asked suddenly. "These regulators, are they getting more powerful?"

"Yes," Audrey said. "And if the thing doing this caught the energy from the people who died out there in the woods, the next run will be the worst yet. I pray that didn't happen, but I think it probably did."

She looked around at them, drew in a deep breath, and began.

5

"The thing inside Seth is named Tak."

"Is it a demon, Aud?" Old Doc asked. "Some kind of demon?"

"No. It has no . . . no religion, I suppose you'd say. Unless TV counts. It's more like a tumor, I think. One that's conscious and enjoys cruelty and violence. It's been inside him for almost two years now. I heard a story once about a Vermont woman who found a black widow spider in her sink. It apparently came into the house in an empty box her husband brought home from the supermarket where he worked. The box had been full of bananas from South America. The spider had gotten in with them when they were packed. That's pretty much how Tak got to Poplar Street, I think. Except we're talking about a black widow with a voice. It called Seth when he and his family were crossing the desert. Crossing *Nevada*. It sensed him, someone it could use, passing close by, and *called* him."

She looked down at her hands, which were knotted tightly together in her lap. Kim Geller was standing in the living-room doorway now, drawn back by Audrey's story. Audrey looked up again. She spoke to them all, but it was Johnny her eyes kept returning to.

"I think it was weak at first, but not too weak to understand that Seth's family posed a threat to it. I don't know how much they knew or suspected, but I do know that my last phone conversation with my brother was *very* strange. I think Bill could have told me a lot . . . if Tak had let him."

"It can do that?" Steve asked. "Impose control over people like that?"

She gestured at her swollen mouth. "My hand did this," she said, "but I wasn't running it."

"Christ," Cynthia said. She looked nervously at the knives hanging on their magnetized steel runners over the kitchen counter. "That's bad. *Very.*"

"It could be worse, though," Audrey said. "Tak can only physically control at short range."

"How short?" Cammie asked.

"Usually no more than twenty or thirty feet. Beyond that, its physical influence runs out in a hurry. *Usually.* Now, all bets are off. Because it's never been so loaded with energy."

"Let her tell her story," Johnny said. He could feel time almost as a tangible thing, slipping away from them. He didn't know if he was getting that from Audrey or if it was coming from inside himself, and he didn't care. Time was short. He had never felt an intuition so strongly in his whole life. Time was short.

"There's a boy still in there," she said, speaking slowly and with great emphasis. "A sweet, special child named Seth Garin. And the most despicable thing is that Tak has used what the child loves to do its killing. In the case of my brother and his family, it was Tracker Arrow, one of the MotoKops' Power Wagons. They were in California, at the end of the trip that took them through Nevada, when it happened. I don't know where Tak got enough energy to summon Tracker Arrow out of Seth's thoughts and dreams at that stage of its development. Seth is its basic power-supply, but Seth isn't enough. It needs more in order to really crank up."

"It's a vampire, isn't it?" Johnny said. "Only what it draws off is psychic energy instead of blood."

She nodded. "And the energy it uses is most abundantly available when someone is in pain. In the case of Bill and the rest of his family, maybe someone in the neighborhood died or was hurt. Or—"

"Or maybe there was someone it could hurt itself," Steve said. "A handy bum, for instance. Just some old wino pushing a shopping cart. Whoever it was, I bet he died with a smile on his face."

Audrey looked at him, her face sad and sickened. "You know."

"Not much, but what I know fits what you're saying," Steve told her. "There's a guy like that back there." He hooked a thumb in the general direction of the greenbelt. "Entragian recognized him. Said he'd been on the street two or three times before since the start of the summer. He got in your nephew's hooking range, didn't he? How?"

"I don't know," she said dully. "I must have been away."

"Where?" Cynthia asked. She'd had the idea that Mrs. Wyler was sort of a recluse.

"Never mind," Audrey said. "Just a place I go. You wouldn't understand. The point is, Tak killed my brother Bill and the rest of his family. And it used one of the Power Wagons to do it."

"Maybe he could only manage one lonely trombone then, but he's got the whole band playing now, doesn't he?" Johnny asked.

Audrey was looking away from them now, nibbling at lips that looked dry and sore. "Herb and I took him in, and in some ways—in many ways, actually—I was never sorry. We could never have children ourselves. He was a loving boy, a sweetheart of a boy—"

"Somebody probably loved Typhoid Mary, too," Cammie Reed said in a dry, rasping voice.

Audrey looked at her, still biting at her lips, then looked back at Johnny, appealing with her eyes for understanding. He didn't *want* to understand, not after all that had happened, especially not after seeing the terrible distortion in Jim Reed's face as the bullet slammed into his brain, but he thought maybe he did a little, anyway. Like it or not.

"The first six months or so were the best. Although even then we knew *something* was wrong, of course."

"Did you take him to the doctor?" Johnny asked.

"It wouldn't have done any good. Tak would have hidden. The tests would have shown nothing, I'm almost sure of it. And then . . . later . . . when we got home . . ."

Johnny studied her swollen mouth and said, "It would have punished you."

"Yes. Me and—" Her voice thickened, broke, resumed as little more than a whisper. "Me and Herb."

"Herb didn't kill himself, did he?" Tom asked. "This Tak-thing murdered him."

She nodded again. "Herb wanted us to get away from it. Tak sensed that. And it found it couldn't use Herb for . . . for something it wanted to do. To have sex . . . *experience* sex . . . with me. Herb wouldn't let it. That made Tak angry."

"My God," Brad said.

"It killed Herb and replenished itself. After that, Seth was its only hostage . . . but Seth was all it needed to keep me in line."

"Because you love him," Johnny said.

"Yes, that's right, because I love him." It wasn't defiance Johnny heard in her voice but a weird and awful shame. Cynthia handed her a paper towel, but Audrey only held it in her hand, as if she had no idea what to use it for. "So in a way, I suppose my love's responsible for all that's happened. It's terrible, but it's probably true." She turned her streaming eyes toward Cammie Reed, who sat on the floor with her arm around her remaining son. "I never believed it would come to this. You have to believe that. Even after it drove the Hobarts away and killed Herb, I had no idea of its powers. What its powers *could* be."

Cammie looked at her, saying nothing and giving nothing out of her stone of a face.

"Since Herb died, Seth and I have lived a quiet life," Audrey said. Johnny thought this was the first outright lie she had told them, although she had perhaps skirted the truth a time or two on her way to it. "Seth's eight, but school's not a problem. I fulfill certain home-education requirements and send in a form once a month to the Ohio Board of Education. It's a joke, really. Seth watches his movies and his TV shows over and over. That's his *real* education. He plays in the sandbox. He eats—hamburgers and Franco-American spaghetti, mostly—and drinks all the chocolate milk I'll make him. Mostly it *was* Seth." She looked at them pleadingly. "Mostly it *was.* Except . . . all that time . . . Tak was inside. Growing. Pushing its roots deeper and deeper. Invading him."

"And you didn't know any of this was going on?" Kim asked from the doorway. "Oh wait, I forgot. It killed your husband. But you just passed that off, didn't you? Probably as an acci—"

"You don't understand!" Audrey nearly screamed. "You don't know what it was to live with him, and with it inside him! It would be Seth, and then I might have a thought that I didn't shield well enough and I'd find myself running into a wall over and over again, as if I were a wind-up toy and the kid who owned me wanted to smash me apart. Or I'd punch myself in the face, or twist my . . . my skin . . ."

Now she used the paper towel, not to wipe her eyes but to blot perspiration from her forehead.

"It made me fall downstairs once," she said. "It was around Christmas, last year. All I did was tell him to stop shaking the packages under the tree. I thought it was Seth I was talking to, you see, that Tak was gone deep inside. Sleeping. Hibernating. Whatever it does. Then I saw his eyes were too dark, not Seth's eyes at all, but by then it was too late. I got out of my chair and walked up the stairs. I can't tell you what it's like, how horrible it is . . . like being a passenger in a car that's being driven by a maniac. I turned around at the top and then just . . . stepped off the landing. Like stepping off a diving board. I didn't break anything, because it cushioned the fall at the very last second. Or maybe it was Seth who did that. Either way, it was still a miracle I didn't break an arm or leg."

"Or your neck," Belinda said.

"Uh-huh, or my neck. All I'm trying to say was that, yes, I loved him—*him*—but I was terrified of *it*."

"Seth was the carrot and Tak was the stick," Johnny said.

"Right. And I had my place to go, too. When things got too crazy. Seth *did* help with that, I know he did. So the time just . . . passed. The way it does, maybe, for people who have cancer. You go on because there's no other choice. You get used to a certain level of pain and fear and you think that's where it's going to stop, where it *must* stop. I never knew it was planning *this*. You have to believe that. Most times I was able to shield my thoughts from it. It never occurred to me that Tak might have thoughts—*plans*—it was hiding from *me*. It waited . . . and then I suppose that bum showed up at the house while I was away . . . visiting with my friend, Jan . . . and then . . ."

She stopped, almost visibly catching hold of herself, settling herself down.

"This nightmare we're in is a combination of *The Regulators,* his favorite Western movie, and *MotoKops 2200,* his favorite cartoon show. One episode in particular, the one about the Force Corridor. I've seen it lots of times; Seth's got it on not just one but *three* of his compilation tapes. It's very, very scary for a cartoon show. Very *intense.* Seth was terrified of it—he wet the bed three nights in a row after seeing it for the first time—but he was also exhilarated by it. Mostly because of the way the show's continuing characters, both good and bad, band together in order to destroy the scary aliens hiding in the Force Corridor. These aliens are in cocoons Colonel Henry first mistakes for power-generators, and the part where they come bursting out and attack the MotoKops would scare just about anybody. Only I think that in this telling of 'The Force Corridor,' the cocoons are our *houses.* And *we . . .*"

"We're the scary aliens," Johnny said. He nodded. It all made horridly perfect sense. "And I suppose what appeals most to both parts of him—or it—is the idea of forced cooperation. Get along, or else. Kids like the concept because it absolves them of judging functions, which most of them aren't very good at to begin with."

Audrey was nodding, too. " Yes, that sounds right. Like how the characters from *The Regulators,* both good and bad, have always gotten along with the MotoKops in Seth's sandbox play-fantasies. In his fantasies, even Sheriff Streeter and Jeb Murdock get along, although they're deadly enemies in the movie."

"Is what's happening now still a play-fantasy to Seth?" Johnny asked. "What do you think, Aud?"

"I can't really tell," she said, "because it's hard to know where Tak leaves off and Seth begins . . . you have to kind of *feel* for that point. I mean, on some level he probably knows better, the way a kid knows better than to believe in Santa Claus once he gets to be eight or nine . . . but we hate to give up some of those make-believes, don't we? There's a—" She broke off for a moment. Her lower lip trembled, then firmed again. "There's a sweetness to the best of them, something that helps get us over the rough spots. Tak has allowed Seth to play out his fantasies on a wider screen than most of us get, that's all."

"Hell, he's getting to play them out in virtual reality," Steve said. "That's what you're describing—the ultimate virtual-reality game."

"There's another possibility," Audrey said. "Seth may not be able to stop Tak anymore, or even put a brake on it. Tak may have tied Seth up, gagged him, and thrown him in a closet."

"If Seth *could* stop Tak, would he?" Johnny asked. "What do you think? What do you *feel*?"

"I'm sure he would," Audrey said at once. "I'm sure that, somewhere inside, he's terrified. Like Mickey Mouse in *Fantasia*, when the brooms got out of control?"

"Let's say you're right. Let's say Tak is driving this thing that's happening to us all by himself now. *Why* is he driving it? What does he get out of it? What's the payback?"

"It," she said, her mouth drawing down in what Johnny thought was an entirely unconscious moue of disgust. "*It*, not he."

"All right, *it*. To Seth, Poplar Street is the Force Corridor, the houses are cocoons, and we're the evil aliens that live inside them. It's a shootout at the O.K. Corral, interstellar version. But what does *Tak* get out of it?"

"Something all its own," Audrey said, and Johnny suddenly thought of an old Beatles lyric: *What do you see when you turn out the light? I can't tell you, but I know it's mine.* "The fantasies were always strictly for Seth, I think—they're the way Tak taps into Seth's powers, which complement its own. Tak . . . I think Tak just likes what happens to us."

Silence in the room.

"Likes it," Belinda said at last. She spoke in a low, considering tone. "What do you mean, *likes* it?"

"When we hurt. We give something off when we hurt, something it . . . it licks up, like ice cream. And when we die, that's even better. It doesn't have to lick then. It can just gobble the stuff down whole."

"So we're dinner," Cynthia said. "That's what you're saying, right? To Seth we're a video game and to this Tak we're dinner."

"We're more," Audrey said. "Think what food is to us: the source of energy. Tak is *making*, that's what Seth told me. *Making* and *building*. I don't think the desert where Seth picked it up was its home; I think that was its prison. Its home is what it may ultimately try to re-create here."

"On the basis of what I've seen so far, I don't even want to visit its neighborhood, let alone live there," Steve said. "In fact—"

"Quit it," Cammie said. Her voice was harsh and impatient. "How do we kill him? You said there might be a way."

Audrey looked at her, shocked. "You're not killing *Seth,*" she said. "*No one* is killing *Seth.* You can get *that* thought right out of your mind. He's just a harmless little boy—"

Cammie leaped at her and grabbed her shoulders. It was done before Johnny could even think of moving. Her thumbs sank deeply into the tops of Audrey's breasts. "Tell it to Jimmy!" she shouted into Audrey's stunned face. "He's dead, my son is dead, so don't you go crying to me about how harmless your nephew is! Don't you *dare*! That thing is in him like a tapeworm in a horse's belly! *In him!* And if it won't come out—"

"But it will!" Audrey said. She began to regain control of herself, and her voice grew calm again. "It will."

Cammie relaxed her grip slowly, and her look was not trusting. "How? When?"

Before Audrey could reply, Kim said: "I hear a humming sound. Like electric motors." Her voice rose, trembling. "Oh God, they're coming back."

Now Johnny could hear it, too. It was the same electric humming he had heard before, only it was louder now. Somehow more vital. More threatening. He looked toward the cellar door and decided it was probably too late to try for the basement, especially with two sleeping children in the pantry.

"Down," he said. "Everyone down on the floor." He saw Cynthia take Steve's hand and point through the open pantry door with a finger which wasn't quite steady. Steve nodded and they went in to cover the children's bodies with their own.

The humming swelled.

"Pray," Belinda said suddenly. "Everybody pray."

Johnny was too frightened to pray.

From Audrey Wyler's journal:

February 7, 1996

Have noticed something interesting, what may be a key way of deciding which of them is in charge, at any given time, of the body they share. They both care a great deal for the Cassandra Styles action figure, but Tak's caring is almost completely sexual. It strokes her plastic breasts & rubs her plastic legs. Two days ago I saw it sitting on the stairs & licking the crotch of her blue shorts & sporting an erection (hard to miss, when all it wears most days are underpants). And, of course, the fact that it wants me to wear Cassie-type clothes and has gotten me to dye my hair Cassie Styles red (horrible shade, too) has not escaped me.

Seth, on the other hand . . . when it's Seth, sometimes he just hugs the figure of Cassie, or strokes its stiff red hair, or kisses its cheek. He is pretending it's his mother. I don't know how I know that, but I do.

Must stop now. Crying again.

CHAPTER 12

Main Street, Desperation / Regulator Time

As on their previous run, the vans appear like phantoms, only this time it's not mist from which they appear but blowing desert dust that shines like lamé in the glow of Old Mr. Cowpoke Moon.

Cassie's pink Dream Floater comes first, with Candy behind the wheel in his pinned-back cavalry hat and Cassie herself sitting beside him. On the roof, the Valentine-heart radar dish is turning briskly. Like a sign on a whorehouse roof, Johnny Marinville might have said had he seen it, but he does not; he is lying on the floor of the Carvers' kitchen next to Old Doc with his hands laced together over the top of his head and his eyes squeezed tightly shut; on his face is the expression of a man who expects Armageddon, and soon.

Dream Floater does not swing onto Desperation's

dusty Main Street from Hyacinth; Hyacinth is gone. Where it once ran there is now nothing but hardpan desert, almost featureless . . . as the sky overhead in this direction is almost completely starless. It's as if, when His eye turned south to the wastes beyond this tiny huddle of buildings, the Creator had lost most of His divine inspiration.

Dream Floater's stubby wings are extended, its wheels partially retracted; it cuts through the air about three feet above the wheel-ruts of the street. Its engine pulses steadily. As it passes the Lady Day on the corner, its firing port irises open. Laura DeMott from *The Regulators* leans out. In her delicate white hands is not her derringer but a shotgun. Just a double-barrelled shotgun, but when she fires it, the report is as loud as a detonating backpack missile. The report is followed by a short, high-pitched wail, and then the front of the saloon explodes. The batwing doors fly up, for a moment fluttering madly and looking like *real* wings. There's an instant of flicker across what remains of the saloon's front, almost like a heatwave, and for that one instant, anyone who had been looking would have seen the E-Z Stop behind the burning Lady Day like a ghost-building or a double exposure, the convenience store also half-demolished and also burning.

Behind Dream Floater comes Tracker Arrow, and behind Tracker Arrow comes Freedom. Freedom's polarized windshield slides down again. Major Pike, a good Canopalean gone bad, is currently behind the wheel of Bounty's van, but the Confederate uniform and pinned-back hat are gone (Candy has the hat on now; the regulators are always trading accessories and bits of uniform back and forth, it's part of the fun). The Major is wearing his iridescent MotoKops uniform again, and without a hat, his blond Mohawk 'do shows to good advantage. Sitting beside him in the nav-pit is the grizzled trapper type Johnny spotted earlier: Sergeant Mathis, Jeb Murdock's chief aide after the beating and capture of Captain Candell.

Collie Entragian's house has been replaced by the Two Sisters Millinery, where can be found The Finest in Ladies' Fashions. Sarge leans out, draws a bead on the storefront with his shotgun, and yanks the triggers. There is another shattering double crash, and again that long, wailing shriek, as of a bomb falling dead-center-true down the gravity-well toward its target.

"Make it stop!" Susi screams. *"Oh please someone MAKE IT STOP!"*

The top half of Two Sisters seems to lift off in a storm of boards and shingles and glass and nails. Again there is that flicker, almost as quick as a hummingbird's wing, and in it Entragian's house may be glimpsed, even Cary Ripton's bike and plastic-covered body may be glimpsed, shimmering like the mirages they have now become. Then the house is gone and it's the Two Sisters (where in *The Regulators* we first see Laura DeMott, saloon lass with a heart of gold, surreptitiously buying cloth for a church dress) again, with half its roof gone and all its windows blown in.

From the badlands (sagebrush and huge tumbled

boulders of cartoon roundness) north of Poplar Street, where Bear Street now isn't, the silver Rooty-Toot Power Wagon appears. Rooty is behind the wheel, his eyes flashing on and off like traffic lights; Little Joe Cartwright is in the seat next to him, devil-may-care grin on his face, a shotgun chrome-plated with futuristic swoops and doodads in his hands. Directly behind Rooty-Toot comes the Justice Wagon, and behind Justice there appears a humming electric nightmare. In the bonelight of the moon, the Meatwagon looks wrapped in black silk. No Face is in the steering-pit. Countess Lili is in the nav-pit, her sexy eyes gleaming in her ashy vampire-maiden's face. Jeb Murdock is above them, in the Doom Turret. In the prime shooting-station.

Because he is the meanest.

And so the final Power Wagon assault begins, with three vans swinging into the Force Corridor from the north and three more from the south. Hideously amplified shotgun blasts shake the air; the whistling passage of the shells thrown from the muzzles of those guns sounds like a flock of banshees. The Cattlemen's Hotel (formerly the Soderson house) is shivered backward on its foundations; the left side first slumps, then actually crumples, spitting off dry boards and wooden shingles. The house north of it—a wattle-and-daub construction Brad Josephson would never have recognized as his own lovingly maintained split-level—seems to explode outward in all directions, shooting jagged chunks of wood and slabs of dried mud into the air.

On the other side of the street, the false front of Worrell's Market & Mercantile (once Tom Billingsley's house; the corpses of the Sodersons lie in an aisle of big round bags, all labelled [illegible]) disintegrates under a series of rifle shots from the Justice Wagon—each arriving round as loud as a mortar shell. Colonel Henry is driving; poked out of the firing trap and doing the shooting is Chuck Connors, also known as the Rifleman. His son is right next to him, grinning from ear to ear. "Good shootin, Paw!" he exclaims as smoking boards from the false front ignite the decade's worth of trash and dust that has been hiding behind it. Soon the entire building will be on fire.

"Thanks, son," Lucas McCain says, and turns his missile-firing Winchester onto Lushan's Chinese Laundry. Lushan's, once the home of Peter and Mary Jackson, has been pretty well bashed about already by Rooty-Toot, but that doesn't deter the Rifleman. His son joins in, firing a pistol. It's a small one, but every round from it sounds like a bazooka shell, just the same.

At the end of the run, a haze of gunsmoke hangs over Main Street. Several of the houses on the west side of the street—the adobe *hacienda* where the Gellers once lived, the log cabin where the Reeds hung their assorted hats, the wattle-and-daub Brad and Belinda once called home—have been almost totally destroyed. The Cattlemen's is still standing—more or less—and so is the Two Sisters on the east side, but the Mercantile will soon join the Owl (formerly the Hobart place) as so much ash in the wind.

Only one house on the east side of the street remains as it was before the regulators came: the Carver place. There are bullet-holes in the siding and broken windows from the previous assault, but on this run it has been completely untouched.

Dream Floater, Tracker Arrow, and Freedom have reached the north end of what used to be Poplar Street's two-forty block. Rooty-Toot, Justice, and the Meatwagon have reached the south end. The firing slackens, then ceases entirely. The people in the Carver house can hear the crackle of fire from the other side of the fence—the Market & Mercantile they still think of as Old Doc's bungalow—but otherwise there is a deep quiet that lies like balm against their ringing ears. In it, the survivors cautiously raise their heads.

"Is it over, do you think?" Steve asks, in the tone of someone who doesn't want to come right out and say it wasn't as bad as he thought . . . but who is thinking it.

"We ought to—" Johnny begins.

"I hear it again!" Kim Geller cries from the living room. Her voice is high, shivering on the edge of hysteria, but the rest of them have no reason not to believe her; she is closest to the street, after all. "That awful humming! *Make it stop!*" She rushes through the door into the kitchen, her eyes bulging and crazed. *"Make it stop!"*

"Get down, Mom!" Susi calls, but she herself does not stir from beside Dave Reed, who is lying with one arm around her and his hand (the one his creepy mother can't see from where she is) against her breast.

Susi doesn't mind his hand a bit; would mind, in fact, if he took it away. Her terror and her almost maternal concern for the surviving twin have combined to make her really horny for the first time in her life. All she really wants right now is to be with David in a place where they can take their pants off without being noticed.

Kim ignores her daughter. She goes to Audrey, grabs her by her hair, yanks her head back. *"Make him stop it!"* she shouts into Audrey's pale face. *"He's your kin, you brought him here,* NOW MAKE HIM STOP!"

Belinda Josephson moves fast; she's up from where she's been lying, she's across the room, and she has Kim Geller's free arm twisted up behind her back almost before Brad can blink.

"Ow!" Kim screams, immediately letting go of Audrey's hair. *"Ow, let go! Let go, you black bi—"*

Belinda has taken all the tiresome racist shit she intends to for one day. She yanks Kim's arm up even further before she can finish. Susi's mom, who supports the Girl Scouts and never sends the Cancer Society lady away empty-handed, shrieks like a factory whistle at quitting time. Then Belinda turns her, hips her, and sends her flying back into the living room. Kim crashes into a wall. All around her more Hummel figures tumble to their doom.

"There," Belinda says in a businesslike voice. "She had that coming. I don't have to put up with that kind of—"

"Never mind," Johnny says. The humming is louder now, louder than it has ever been: a steady, cycling beat like the sound of a huge electric transformer. "Get down, Bee. Right now. Everybody. Steve, Cynthia? *Cover those children!*" Then he looks, almost apologetically, at Seth Garin's aunt. "*Can* you make him stop, Aud?"

She shakes her head. "It's *not* him. Not now. It's Tak." Before she puts her head back down, she sees Cammie Reed looking at her, and there is something in that dry glance that frightens her more than all of Kim Geller's shouting and hair-pulling. It's a *serious* look. No hysteria, only flat murder.

Who would Cammie murder, though? Her? Seth? Both? Audrey doesn't know. She only knows she cannot tell the others what she did before leaving, that simple thing that might solve so much—*if*. If the window of time she's hoping for opens; if she does the right thing when it does. She can't tell them there's hope, because if Tak is able to reach out and catch hold of their thoughts, all hopes will fail.

The thrumming grows louder. On Main Street, the Power Wagons are rolling again. Dream Floater, Tracker Arrow, and Freedom are closer to the Carver house and reach it first. They park in line, the red Tracker Arrow with Snake Hunter behind the wheel in the middle, blocking the driveway where the lord of the manor is lying dead (and looking much the worse for wear by this time). The other three—Rooty-Toot, Justice, and Meatwagon—come up from the south end of the street and lengthen the line of vehicles.

The Carver house (it is, perhaps ironically, a ranch-style home) is now entirely blocked off by Power Wagons. From the firing pit of Dream Floater, Laura DeMott trains her shotgun on the smashed picture window; from the firing pit of Tracker Arrow, Hoss Cartwright and a very young Clint Eastwood—he is Rowdy Yates of *Rawhide* in this incarnation, as a matter of fact—have also got the house covered. Jeb Murdock stands in the Doom Turret of the Meat-wagon with *two* shotguns, each sawed off four inches above the cocked triggers, the butts propped against the wishbones of his hips. He is grinning widely, his face that of Rory Calhoun in his prime.

Roof trapdoors bang open. Cowboys and aliens fill the remaining shooting-points.

"Gosh, Paw, looks like a damn turkey-shoot!" Mark McCain cries, and then utters a shrill laugh.

"Root-root-root!"

"SHUT UP, ROOTY!" they all chorus, and the laugh becomes general.

At the sound of that laughter, something inside of Kim Geller, something which has only been badly bent up to now, finally snaps. She gets to her feet in the living room and marches to the screen door beyond which Debbie Ross still lies. Kim's sneakers grit through the broken china shards of Pie Carver's prized Hummels. The sound of the cycling motors out front—that weird beat-beat-beat, like some sort of electric heart—is driving her insane. Still, it's easier to focus on that than it is to think about how that uppity nigger woman first almost broke her arm and then threw her into the other room as if she were a sack of laundry, or something.

The others are unaware she's left until they hear her voice, querulous and shrill: "You get out of here! You just stop it and get out of here *right now*! The police are already on their way, you know!"

At the sound of that voice, Susi forgets all about how nice it is to have Dave Reed touching her breast, and how she'd like to help him forget the death of his brother by taking him upstairs and balling him until his liver explodes. "Mummy!" she gasps, and starts to get up.

Dave hauls her back down, then clamps an arm around her waist to make completely sure she doesn't get up again. He has lost his brother, and he feels like that's enough for one day.

Come on, come on, come *on,* Audrey thinks . . . except she guesses it's actually a prayer. Her eyes are squeezed so tightly shut she can see exploding red dots behind the lids, and her hands are clamped into fists, the ragged remains of her nails digging into her palms. Come on, go to work the way you're supposed to, do your job, get started—

"Kick in," she whispers, unaware she's speaking out loud. Johnny, who has raised his head at the sound of Kim's voice, now looks at Audrey. "Kick in, can't you? For Christ's sake, *kick in!*"

"What are you talking about?" he asks, but she doesn't answer.

Outside, Kim moves down the walk toward the Power Wagons, which are parked at the curb. This is the only place along the former Poplar Street where there is any curb left.

"I'm giving you a chance," she says, her eyes drifting from one weirdo to the next. Some are dressed in ridiculous outer-space masks, and the one behind the wheel of the lunch-wagon thingy is actually wearing a whole-body robot costume. It makes him look like an oversized version of R2D2 in the Star Wars movies. Others look like refugees from a class in Western line-dancing. A few even seem familiar . . . but this is no time to be distracted by such foolish ideas.

"I'm giving you a chance," she repeats, coming to a stop just above the place where the Carvers' cement walk joins the remaining strip of Poplar Street side-walk. "Go while you still can. Otherwise—"

The slide door of the Freedom van opens, and Sheriff Streeter steps out. His star gleams a dull moonlit silver on the left flap of his vest. He looks up at Jeb Murdock—old enemy, new ally—in the Doom Turret of the Meatwagon.

"Well, Streeter?" Murdock says. "What do you think?"

"I think you should take the yappy bitch," Streeter says with a smile, and both of Murdock's sawed-offs explode with noise and white fire. At one moment Kim Geller is standing at the end of the Carvers' walk; at the next she's entirely gone. No; not quite gone. Her sneakers are still there, and her feet are still inside them.

A split-second later, something that could be a

bucket of dark, silty water but isn't hits the front of the Carver house. Then, with the sound of the twin shotgun blasts still rolling away, Streeter screams: *"Shoot! Shoot, goddammit! Wipe them off the map!"*

"Get down!" Johnny shouts again, knowing it will do no good; the house is going to disappear like a child's sand-castle before a tidal wave, and they are going to disappear with it.

The regulators begin firing, and it's like nothing Johnny ever heard in Vietnam. This, he thinks, is what it must have been like to be in the trenches at Ypres, or in Dresden thirty years or so later. The noise is incredible, a ground-zero concatenation of KA-POW and KA-BAM, and although he feels he should be immediately deafened (or perhaps killed outright by raw decibels alone), Johnny is still able to hear the sounds of the house being blown apart all around them: bursting boards, breaking windows, china figurines exploding like targets in a shooting gallery, the brittle spatter of thrown laths. Very faintly, he can also hear people screaming. The bitter tang of gunsmoke fills his nostrils. Something unseen but huge passes through the kitchen above them, screaming as it goes, and suddenly much of the kitchen's rear wall is just rubble fanned across the backyard and floating on the surface of the Kmart pool.

Yes, Johnny thinks. This is it, this is the end. And maybe that is just as well.

But then a strange thing begins to happen. The shooting doesn't stop, but it begins to *diminish,* as if someone is turning down the volume control. This isn't just true of the gunshots themselves, but of the screaming sound the shells make as they pass overhead. And it happens fast. Less than ten seconds after he first notices the diminution—and it might be more like five—the sounds are gone entirely. So is the queer, humming beat of the Power Wagons' engines.

They raise their heads and look around at each other. In the pantry, Cynthia sees that she and Steve are both as white as ghosts. She raises her arm and blows. Powder puffs up from her skin.

"Flour," she says.

Steve rakes through his long hair and holds an unsteady hand out to her. There's a cluster of shiny black things in the palm. "Flour's not so bad," he says. "I got olives."

She thinks she'll begin to laugh, but before she can, an amazing and totally unexpected thing happens.

Seth's Place / Seth's Time

Of all the passages he has dug for himself during the reign of Tak—Tak the Thief, Tak the Cruel, Tak the Despot—this is the longest. He has, in a way, re-created his own version of Rattlesnake Number One. The shaft goes deep into some black earth which he supposes is himself, then rises again toward the surface like a hope. At the end of it is a door of iron bands. He doesn't try to open it, but not for fear he will find it locked. Quite the opposite. This is a door he must not touch until he is completely ready; once through it, there will never be any coming back.

He prays it goes where he thinks it does.

Enough light comes through the cracks between the door's iron lengths to illuminate the place where he stands. There are pictures on the strange, fleshy walls; one a group portrait of his family with him sitting between his brother and sister, one a photo of him standing between Aunt Audrey and Uncle Herb on the lawn of this house. They are smiling. Seth, as always, is solemn, distant, not quite there. There is also a photograph of Allen Symes, standing beside (and dwarfed by) one of Miss Mo's treads. Mr. Symes is wearing his Deep Earth hardhat and grinning. No such photograph as this exists, but that doesn't matter. This is Seth's place, Seth's time, Seth's mind, and he decorates it as he likes. Not so long ago, there would have been pictures of the MotoKops and the characters from The Regulators *hung, not just here, but all along the length of the tunnel. No longer. They have lost their charm for him.*

I outgrew them, he thinks, and that is the truth of it. Autistic or not, only eight or not, he has gotten too old for shoot-em-up Westerns and Saturday-morning cartoons. He suddenly understands that this is almost certainly the bottom truth, and one Tak would never understand: he outgrew them. He has the Cassie Styles figure in his pocket (when he needs a pocket he just imagines one; it's handy) because he still loves her a little, but otherwise? No. The only question is whether or not he can escape them, sweet fantasies which might have been laced with poison all along.

And the time has come to find that out.

Beside the photo of Allen Symes, a little shelf juts out of the wall. Seth has seen and admired the shelves in the Carver hallway, each dedicated to its own Hummel figure, and this one was created with those in mind. Enough light seeps through the cracks in the door to see what's on it—not a Hummel shepherd or milkmaid but a red PlaySkool telephone.

He picks it up and spins out two-four-eight on the plastic phone's rotary dial. It's the Carvers' house number. In his ear the toy phone rings . . . rings . . . rings. But is it ringing on the other end? Does she hear it? Do any of them hear it?

"Come on," he whispers. He is entirely aware and alert; in this deep-inside place he's no more autistic than Steve Ames or Belinda Josephson or Johnny Marinville . . . is, in fact, something of a genius.

A frightened genius, right now.

"Come on . . . please, Aunt Audrey, please hear . . . please answer . . ."

Because time is short, and the time is now.

Main Street, Desperation / Regulator Time

The telephone in the Carver living room begins to ring, and as if this is some kind of signal aimed directly at his deepest and most delicate neural centers, Johnny Marinville's unique ability to see and sequence breaks down for the first time in his life. His perspective shivers like the shapes in a kaleidoscope when the tube is twirled, then falls apart in prisms and bright shards. If this is how the rest of the world sees and experiences during times of stress, he thinks, it's no wonder people make so many bad decisions when the heat is on. He doesn't like experiencing things this way. It's like having a high fever and seeing half a dozen people standing around your bed. You know that four of them are actually there . . . but *which* four? Susi Geller is crying and screaming her mother's name. The Carver kids are both awake again, of course; Ellen, her capacity to endure in relative stoicism finally gone, seems to be having a kind of emotional convulsion, screaming at the top of her lungs and pounding Steve's back as he tries to embrace and comfort her. And Ralphie wants to whale on his big sister! "Stop huggin Margrit!" he storms at Steve as Cynthia attempts to restrain him. "Stop huggin Margrit the Maggot! She shoulda give me *all* the candybar! She shoulda give me ALLLLL of it n none a this would happen!" Brad starts for the living room—to answer the phone, presumably—and Audrey grabs his arm. "No," she says, and then, with a kind of surreal politeness: "It's for me." And Susi is on her feet now, Susi is running down the hall toward the front door to see what's happened to her mother (a very unwise idea, in Johnny's humble opinion). Dave Reed tries to restrain her again and this time can't, so he follows her instead, calling her name. Johnny expects the boy's mother to restrain *him*, but Cammie lets him go while from out back coyotes that look like no coyotes which ever existed on God's earth lift their crooked snouts and sing mad love songs to the moon.

All of this at once, swirling like litter caught in a cyclone.

He's on his feet without even realizing it, following Brad and Belinda into the living room, which looks as if the Green Giant stomped through it in a snit. The kids are still shrieking from the pantry, and Susi is howling from the end of the entry hall. Welcome to the wonderful world of stereophonic hysteria, Johnny thinks.

Audrey, meanwhile, is looking for the phone, which is no longer on its little table beside the couch. The little table itself is no longer beside the couch, in fact; it's in a far corner, split in half. The phone lies beside it in a strew of broken glass. It's off the hook, the handset lying as far from the base as the cord will allow, but it's still ringing.

"Mind the glass, Aud," Johnny says sharply as she crosses to it.

Tom Billingsley goes to the jagged hole in the west wall where the picture window used to be, stepping over the smoking and exploded ruins of the TV in order to get there. "They're gone," he says. "The vans." He pauses, then adds: "Unfortunately, Poplar Street's gone, too. It looks like Deadwood, South Dakota, out there. Right around the time Jack McCall shot Wild Bill Hickok in the back."

Audrey picks up the telephone. Behind them, Ralphie Carver is now shrieking: *"I hate you, Margrit the Maggot! Make Mummy and Daddy come back or I'll hate you forever! I hate you, Margrit the Maggot!"* Beyond Audrey, Johnny can see Susi's struggles to get away from Dave Reed subsiding; he is hugging her out of horror and toward tears with a patience that, given the circumstances, Johnny can only admire.

"Hello?" Audrey says. She listens, her pale face

tense and solemn. "Yes," she says. "Yes, I will. Right away. I . . ." She listens some more, and this time her eyes lift to Johnny Marinville's face. "Yes, all right, just him. Seth? I love you."

She doesn't hang the telephone up, simply drops it. Why not? Johnny traces its connection-wire and sees that the concussion which tore apart the table and flung the phone into the corner has also pulled the jack out of the wall.

"Come on," Audrey says to him. "We're going across the street, Mr. Marinville. Just the two of us. Everyone else stays here."

"But—" Brad begins.

"No arguments, no time," she tells him. "We have to go right now. Johnny, are you ready?"

"Should I get the gun they brought from next door? It's in the kitchen."

"A gun wouldn't do any good. Come on."

She holds out her hand. Her face is set and sure . . . except for her eyes. They are terrified, pleading with him not to make her do this thing, whatever it is, on her own. Johnny takes the offered hand, his feet shuffling through rubble and broken glass. Her skin is cold, and her knuckles feel slightly swollen under his fingers. It's the hand the little monster made her hit herself with, he thinks.

They go out the living room's lower entrance and past the teenagers, who stand silently hugging each other. Johnny pushes open the screen door and lets Audrey precede him out and over the body of Debbie Ross. The front of the house, the stoop, and the dead girl's back are splattered with the remains of Kim Geller—streaks and daubs and lumps that look black in the light of the moon—but neither of them mentions this. Ahead, beyond the walk and the short section of curb where the Power Wagons no longer stand, is a broad and deeply rutted dirt street. A breath of breeze touches the side of Johnny's face—it carries a smoky smell with it, and a tumbleweed goes bouncing by, as if on a hidden spring. To Johnny it looks straight out of a Max Fleischer cartoon, but that doesn't surprise him. That is where they are, isn't it? In a kind of cartoon? Give me a lever and I'll move the world, Archimedes said; the thing across the street probably would have agreed. Of course, it was only a single block of Poplar Street it had wanted to move, and given the lever of Seth Garin's fantasies to pry with, it had accomplished that without much trouble.

Whatever may await them, there is a certain relief just in being out of the house and away from the noise.

The stoop of the Wyler house looks about the same, but that's all. The rest is now a long, low building made of logs. Hitching-posts are ranged along the front. Smoke puffs from the stone chimney in spite of the night's warmth. "Looks like a bunkhouse," he says.

Audrey nods. "The bunkhouse at the Ponderosa."

"Why did they go away, Audrey? Seth's regulators and future cops? What made them go away?"

"In at least one way, Tak's like the villain in a Grimms' fairy-tale," she says, leading him into the street. Dust puffs up from beneath their shoes. The wheelruts are dry and as hard as iron. "It has an Achilles' heel, something you'd never suspect if you hadn't lived with it as long as I have. It hates to be in Seth when Seth moves his bowels. I don't know if it's some weird kind of esthetic thing, or a psychological phobia, or maybe even a physical fact of its existence—the way we can't help flinching if someone makes like to punch us, for instance—and I don't care."

"How sure of this are you?" he asks. They have reached the other side of the broad Main Street now. Johnny looks both ways and sees no vans; just massed, rocky badlands to the right and emptiness—a kind of uncreation—to the left.

"Very," she says grimly. The cement walk leading up to 247 Poplar has become a flagstone path. Halfway up it, Johnny sees the broken-off rowel of some range-hand's spur glinting in the moonlight. "Seth has told me—I hear him in my head sometimes."

"Telepathy."

"Uh-huh, I guess. And when Seth talks on that level, he has no mental problems whatever. On that level he's so bright it's scary."

"But are you completely sure it was Seth talking to you? And even if it was, are you sure Tak was letting him tell the truth?"

She stops halfway to the bunkhouse door. She is still holding one of his hands; now she takes the other, turning him to face her.

"Listen, because there's only time for me to say this once and no time at all for you to ask questions. Sometimes when Seth talks to me, he lets Tak listen in . . .

because, I think, that way Tak believes it hears *all* our mental conversations. It doesn't, though." She sees him start to speak and squeezes his hands to shut him up. "And I *know* Tak leaves him when he moves his bowels. It doesn't just go deep, it comes *out* of him. I've seen it happen. It comes out of his eyes."

"Out of his eyes," Johnny whispers, fascinated and horrified and a little awed.

"I'm telling you because I want you to know it if you see it," she says. "Dancing red dots, like embers from a campfire. Okay?"

"Christ," Johnny mutters, then: "Okay."

"Seth loves chocolate milk," Audrey says, pulling him into motion again. "The kind you make with Hershey's syrup. And Tak loves what Seth loves . . . to a fault, I guess you could say."

"You put Ex-Lax in it, didn't you?" Johnny asks. "You put Ex-Lax in his chocolate milk." He almost feels like joining the coyotes in a good howl at the moon. Only he'd be howling with laughter. Life's more surrealistic possibilities never exhaust themselves, it seems; their one chance to survive this is a summer-camp stunt on a level with snipe hunts and short-sheeting the counsellor's bed.

"Seth told me what to do and I did it," she says. "Now come on. While he's still crapping his brains out. While there's still *time*. We've got to grab him and just run. Get him out of Tak's range before it can get back inside him. We can do it, too. Its range is short. We'll go down the hill. You carry him. And I'll bet that before we even get to where the store used to be, we're going to see one big fucking change in our environment. Just remember, the key is to be quick. Once we get started, no hesitation or pulling up allowed."

She reaches for the door and Johnny restrains her. She stares at him with a mixture of fear and fury.

"Did you hear me say we had to go *right now*?"

"Yes, but there's one question you *have* to answer, Aud."

They're being watched anxiously from across the street. Belinda Josephson breaks away from the little cluster doing the watching and goes back into the kitchen to see how Steve and Cynthia are making out with the little kids. Not bad, it appears. Ellen is sniffling but otherwise under control again, and Ralphie seems to have blown himself out, like a hurricane that moves inland. Belinda glances briefly around the empty kitchen, which is now open to the backyard, then turns to go back down the hall to the others. She takes a single step, then pauses. A narrow vertical crease—Bee's thought-line, her husband calls it—appears in the center of her forehead. It's not entirely dark down there by the screen door, there's moonlight . . . and these are her neighbors, of course. It's not very hard to tell them apart. Brad is easy to identify because he's her closest neighbor, so close she's been able to reach out and nudge him in the night for twenty-five years. Dave and Susi are easy because they're still hugging. Old Doc is easy because he's so thin. But Cammie isn't easy. Cammie isn't easy because Cammie isn't there. Not here in the kitchen, either. Has she gone upstairs or stepped outside through the hole in the kitchen wall? Maybe. And—

"You two!" she calls into the pantry, suddenly afraid.

"What?" Steve asks, sounding a bit impatient. In truth he feels a little impatient. They're finally getting the kids soothed down, and if this woman screws that up, he thinks he will brain her with the first pot or pan he can lay grip to.

"Mrs. Reed's gone," Bee says. "And she took that rifle with her. Was it empty? Come on, make me happy. Say it was empty."

"I don't think so," Steve says reluctantly.

"Shit-fire and save matches," Belinda says.

Cynthia is looking at her from around one of Ralphie's slumped shoulders, her eyes widening in alarm. "Have we got a problem here?" she asks.

"We might," Bee says.

Tak's Place / Tak's Time

In the den *where it has spent so many happy hours—at the breast of Seth Garin's captive imagination, one might say—Tak waits and listens. On the Zenith's screen, black-and-white cowboys dressed in ghostly gear ride across a desert landscape. Their passage is silent. Discorporeal now that it is out of Seth, Tak has muted the TV with the best remote control of all—its own mind.*

In the bathroom adjacent to the kitchen, it can hear the boy. The boy is making the low, piggy grunting sounds Tak has come to associate with its elimination function. For Tak, even the sounds are revolting, and the act itself, with its cramping and its sensations of sliding, helpless exit, is hideous. Even vomiting is better—it's quick, at least, up the throat and gone.

Now it knows what the woman did to him: drugged the milk with something to bring on not just a single act of elimination but shivering convulsions of it. How much did she give him? A huge wallop, from the way Seth felt just before Tak fled, and now it understands everything.

It flickers in a dark upper corner of the room—Tak the Cruel, Tak the Despot—like a little cluster of disembodied bicycle taillights that pulse and revolve around each other. It can't hear Aunt Audrey and Marinville even with the TV sound off, but it knows they're there, outside the front door. When they finally stop talking and come in, it will kill them—the man first, and simply to replenish the energy it has expended (being out of the boy's body is particularly depleting), Seth's aunt for what she has tried to do. It will feed on her as well, and she will die slowly, by her own hand.

The boy's punishment for trying to stand against Tak will be to watch it happen.

Yet Tak respects Seth; he has been a worthy opponent. (How could any vessel capable of containing Tak not be?) Since the wino came yesterday, Tak and the boy have been playing a nervy game of stud poker, just like Laura and Jeb Murdock in The Regulators. *Now everything is in the pot and all but the final hole cards are face-up on the table. When they are flipped, Tak knows it will win. Of course it will win. Its opponent is only a child, after all, no matter how brilliant the lower courses of his intellect may be, and in the end the child has believed just a little more than is healthy for him. It knew Seth had planned to drive it temporarily out of his body, and although the exact method was a surprise (a very unpleasant one), even that much knowledge is more than Seth knew it had. But there is something else, as well.*

Seth doesn't believe Tak can re-enter him while he is performing the disgusting act for which the little room adjacent to the kitchen has been set aside.

Seth is wrong. Tak can *re-enter. It will be unpleasant—painful, even—but it* can *re-enter. And how does it know that Seth hasn't seen this final card, as he has seen some of the others Tak has held, even in spite of its best efforts to hide them?*

Because he has called his beloved auntie back to the house to help him get away.

And when his beloved auntie finally stops hesitating out there on the stoop and comes in, she'll be . . . well . . .

Regulated.

Completely regulated.

The red lights in the shadows swirl faster, excited by the idea.

Main Street, Desperation / Regulator Time

"Did you hear me say we had to go *right now?"*

Johnny nods. Neither of them sees Cammie Reed cross the street from the adobe church that used to be Johnny Marinville's suburban retreat to the remains of the wattle-and-daub that used to be Brad and Belinda's house. She's got her head down and the .30–.06 in one hand.

"Yes, but there's still that one question I have, Aud."

"What?" she nearly screams. "For God's sake, *what*?"

"Can it jump to someone else? To you or me, for instance?"

A look of what might be relief appears briefly on her face. "No."

"How can you be sure? Did Seth tell you?"

He thinks for a moment she won't answer this, and not simply because she wants to get to the boy while he's still on the jakes. He at first mistakes her look for embarrassment, then sees it's deeper; not embarrassment but shame.

"Seth didn't tell me," she says. "I know because it tried to get into Herb. So it could . . . you know . . . have me."

"It wanted to make love to you," he says.

"Love?" she says, her voice barely under control "No. Oh, no. Tak understands nothing about love, cares nothing about love. It wanted to fuck me, that's all. When it discovered it couldn't use Herb to do that, it killed him." Tears are running down her face now. "It doesn't give up easily when it wants something, you know. What it did to him . . . well, imagine what would happen to one of little Ralphie Carver's shoes if you tried to get it on your big grown-up's foot. If you just kept jamming it and shoving it, harder and harder, oblivious of the pain, oblivious of what you were doing to it in your obsession to wear it, walk in it . . ."

"All right," he says. He looks down toward the bottom of the hill, almost expecting to see the vans coming back, but there is nothing. He looks up the street and sees more nothing; Cammie is standing out of sight in the shadow of the precariously leaning Cattlemen's Hotel. "I get the message."

"Then can we go in? Or do you even *intend* to go in? Have you lost your nerve?"

"No," he says, and sighs.

There's an old-fashioned iron thumb-latch on the bunkhouse door, but when he tries to grasp it, his thumb goes straight through. Below it, appearing like something floating up through dirty water, is a plain old suburban doorknob. When Johnny grasps it, a suburban door forms around it, first overlying the planks and iron bands, then replacing them. The knob turns and the door opens on a dark room that smells as stale as dirty laundry. The moonlight floods in, and what Johnny sees makes him think of stories he's read in the papers from time to time, the ones about elderly recluse millionaires who spend the last years of their lives in single rooms, stacking up books and magazines, collecting pets, shooting Demerol, eating meals out of cans.

"Quick, hurry," she says. "He'll be in the downstairs bathroom. It's off the kitchen."

She moves past him, taking his hand as she does, and leads him into the living room. There are no stacked books and magazines, but the sense of reclusion and insanity grows rather than lessens as they advance. The floor is tacky with spilled food and soda; there is an underlying sour smell of clabbered milk; the walls have been scribbled over with crayon drawings that are frightening in their primitive preoccupation with bloodshed and death. They remind him of a novel he read not so long ago, a book called *Blood Meridian*.

Movement flickers to his left. He turns that way, heart speeding up, adrenaline dumping into his bloodstream, but there are no gun-toting cowboys or sinister aliens, not even an attacking little kid with a knife. It's only a shimmer of reflected light. From the TV, he assumes, although there's no sound.

"No," she whispers, "don't go in there."

She leads him toward the doorway straight ahead. Light shines through it, printing a bright oblong onto the food-encrusted carpet. Electricity may not yet have been invented along the rest of what used to be Poplar Street, but there's still plenty here.

Now Johnny can hear grunting sounds, interspersed with mildly labored breathing. Sounds as human—and as instantly recognizable—as snoring, sneezing, wheezing, whistling. Someone going to the toilet. Doing number two, as they used to say when they were kids. A grade-school couplet comes to mind: *Mother gives me lemonade, around the corner fudge is made*. Whoa, Johnny thinks, that one's right up there with little bitty baby Smitty.

As they enter the kitchen and he looks around, it

occurs to Johnny that perhaps the good folk of Poplar Street deserve what's happening to them. She's been living like this for God knows how long and we never knew, he thinks. We're her neighbors, we all sent her flowers when her husband ate the end of his gun, most of us went to his funeral (Johnny himself had been in California, talking to a convention of children's librarians), but we never knew.

The counter jostles with jars, discarded packaging, empty glasses, and soft-drink cans. Many of the latter have become antfarms. He sees the Tupperware pitcher with the remains of the doctored chocolate milk in it, and the crust of Tak's bologna-and-cheese sandwich beside it. The sink is stacked with dirty dishes. Beside the dish drainer, a plastic bottle of detergent which might have been purchased when Herb Wyler was still alive lies overturned. Around its nozzle is a long-congealed puddle of green dishgoo. On the table are more stacks of dirty dishes, a squeeze-bottle of mustard, sprays of crumbs (there's a Van Halen cassette lying in one of these), an aerosol can of whipped cream, two bottles of catsup, one mostly empty and one mostly full, open pizza boxes littered with crusts, bread-wrappers, Twinkies wrappers, and a Doritos bag pulled down over an empty Pepsi bottle like a weird condom. There are also piles and piles of comic books. All those that Johnny can see are issues of Marvel's *MotoKops 2200* series. Spilled Sugar Pops are scattered across the cover of an issue which shows Cassie Styles and Snake Hunter standing hip-deep in a swamp and firing their stun-pistols at Countess Lili Marsh, who is attacking on what could be a jet-powered motorscooter. BAYOU BLAST! the title screams. In the far corner of the room is a heap of bulging plastic garbage bags, none secured with ties, most oozing ant-infested swill. All the cans seem to bear the smiling face of Chef Boyardee. The stove is covered with pots encrusted with the Chef's orange sauce. On top of the fridge, a bizarre crowning touch, is an old plastic statuette of Roy Rogers mounted on the faithful Trigger. Johnny knows without having to ask that it was a present to Seth from his uncle, something perhaps remembered from the days of Herb Wyler's own youth and patiently hunted out of a dust-covered attic carton.

Beyond the fridge is a half-open door, casting its own wedge of light out onto the filthy linoleum. The door's angle isn't too severe for Johnny to be able to read the sign on it:

EMPLOYEES MUST WASH HANDS
AFTER USING THE LAVATORY
(AND CUSTOMERS SHOULD)

"Seth!" Audrey stage-whispers, dropping Johnny's hand and rushing for the bathroom door. Johnny follows her.

From behind them, spots of dancing red light stream out of the den's arched doorway like meteor debris; they flash across the dark living room toward the kitchen. Even as they do, Cammie Reed steps through the door from outside. She has the gun in both hands now, and as she stands looking around the dim living room, she slips her right index finger inside the trigger-guard and nestles it against the trigger. She is hesitant, not sure where to go next. Her eye is drawn to the flicker of reflected TV-light from the den, her ear by the sound of people moving in the kitchen. The voice in her head, the one demanding revenge for Jimmy, has fallen silent, and she isn't sure which way to go. Her eye registers a brief strobe of red light, but her mind does nothing with the input; it is totally preoccupied with the question of how she should go on. Marinville and Wyler are in the kitchen, she's sure of that, but is the killer brat in there with them? She glances doubtfully toward the TV flicker again. No sound, but maybe autistic children watch it with the sound off.

She has to be *sure*, that's the thing. There are probably just a couple of rounds left in the .30–.06 . . . and they likely won't give her a chance to pull the trigger more than once or twice, anyway. She wishes the voice would speak up again, tell her what to do.

And then it does.

Across the street, on the cement path between the Carvers' front door and the sidewalk, Cynthia has seen Cammie go into the Wyler house. Her eyes widen. Before she can say anything, Steve nudges her sharply. She looks at him and sees he's got a finger to his lips. In his other hand he's got a knife from the Carvers' kitchen rack.

"Come on," he murmurs.

"You're not going to use that, are you?"

"I hope I don't have to," he says. "Are you coming?"

She nods and follows. As they step off the curb and into Tak's version of the Old West, a confusion of shrieks and shouts commences from inside the Wyler house. *Get out of him,* Cynthia hears, something like that, anyway, then more stuff she can't even begin to decipher. Most or all of it seems to be coming from the Wyler woman, although she hears a scream from Cammie Reed ("Put it down"? Is that what she's screaming?) and a hoarse cry that likely comes from Marinville. Then, two whipcracking rifle shots and a scream of either agony or extreme horror. Cynthia can't tell which, isn't sure she wants to know.

Nevertheless, by the time she and Steve reach the far side of Desperation's Main Street, both of them are running.

Seth's Place / Seth's Time

Now. It all comes down to now.

He turns away from the shelf with the PlaySkool phone on it. Built into the other side of the passage's wall is a small control panel, very similar to the ones built into the nav-pits of the Power Wagons. Jutting from it is a row of seven switches, each turned up to the position marked ON. *Above each switch, a small green telltale glows in the gloom. This panel wasn't here when Seth reached the end of the passage, only the pictures of his two families, the picture of Mr. Symes, and the telephone. But this is Seth's place, Seth's time, and it's like the pockets in his shorts: he can add pretty much whatever he wants to add, and whenever he wants to do it.*

Seth reaches toward the panel with a hand that trembles slightly. In the movies and on TV, the characters never seem afraid, and when Paw Cartwright has to act to save the Ponderosa, he always knows just what to do. Lucas McCain, Rowdy Yates, and Sheriff Streeter are never unsure of themselves. But Seth is. Plenty *unsure. The end of the game is now, and he's terrified of making an irrevocable mistake. For now he still knows what's going on upstairs (this is how he thinks of Tak's world now, as upstairs), but if he turns these switches—*

There's no time to reconsider, though. Audrey is in the bathroom. Audrey is rushing for the little boy sitting on the toilet with his underpants dangling from one grimy ankle, the little boy who is—for the time being, at least—just a wax dummy with lungs that breathe and a heart that beats, a human machine deserted by both its ghosts. She kneels before him and sweeps him into her arms. She begins to cover his face with kisses, unmindful of anything else—the room, the circumstances, Marinville standing behind her in the doorway.

And now Seth senses the red swarm that is Tak flashing across the kitchen like a stream of supernatural bees, and it has to be now, yes, has to be.

His hand reaches the panel and he begins snapping the switches down. The green telltales above them wink out; red telltales below them wink on. With each flicked switch, his knowledge of what's going on upstairs dims out more. He is not turning off the senses of the wax dummy his aunt is now covering with kisses, he's not sure he could do that if he wanted to, but he can block them off . . . and he is.

Finally there's nothing left but his mind. It will have to be enough. With his hand pressing down on the switches he has just turned so they cannot fly back up, Seth reaches out to Aunt Audrey, praying he can still find her in all this dark.

The Wyler House / Regulator Time

At the instant Audrey sweeps the boy off the toilet and into her arms, something blasts by Johnny Marinville, something which feels simultaneously as hot as a fever and as cold as frog-jelly. His head fills with a swirl of garish red light that makes him think of honkytonk neon and country music. When it clears, his ability to see everything and sequence even overlapping events has been restored. It's as if the thing that passed him administered some sort of electroshock. That, and a sickly flush across his thoughts that feels like slime.

As Audrey rises with Seth in her arms (the Underoos slip off his foot and he is entirely naked now), Johnny sees that swirl of avid light swing around the boy's head like a corona around the head of baby Jesus in an old painting. Then, like a swarm of termites, it settles, coating his cheeks, his ears, his sweaty hair. It crams into his open glazed eyes and lights his teeth scarlet.

"No!" Audrey shrieks. "Get *out* of him! *Get* OUT, *you bastard!"*

She leaps for the bathroom door with the boy in her arms. Seth's head seems to be burning. Johnny reaches out—for her? Seth? both? He doesn't know and it doesn't matter because she bursts past him into the filthy kitchen, shrieking and clawing at the dancing swarm of light around Seth's head. Her hand slides uselessly through the red stuff. As she and the boy pass him, Johnny's head is filled with a horrible machinelike buzzing sound. He screams, clapping his hands to his ears. It is only for a moment, as Audrey bolts by, but it is a moment which seems all but eternal, just the same. How can there be any boy left under that sound? he wonders. How in God's name can there be *anything* left under that sound?

"Let him GO*!"* she shrieks. *"Let him* GO*, cocksucker, let him* GO*!"*

Then the kitchen doorway is no longer empty. Cammie Reed is standing there with the .30–.06 in her hands.

Tak's Place / Tak's Time

When it reaches Seth *and finds all its usual ways in blocked, its rather indulgent respect for the boy's abilities breaks down for the first time since it sensed Seth's extraordinary mind passing by and called out to that mind with all of its strength. What replaces the indulgence first is realization; anger follows on in its wake.*

It has been wrong, it seems—Seth has known all along that Tak can re-enter, even during evacuation. Has known and has successfully hidden that knowledge, the way a clever gambler will hide an extra ace up his sleeve. In the end, though, not even that matters; it will get in anyway. There is no way the boy can keep it out. There will be no siege here; Seth Garin is his home now, and he will not be held out of his home.

As the woman carries Seth's body past the writer and into the kitchen, Tak assaults the boy's eyes, the ports of entry closest to that wonderful brain, and begins shoving at them like a burly cop shoving at a door being held by a weak man. It knows a moment of utterly uncharacteristic panic when at first nothing happens—it is like pushing against a brick wall. Then the bricks begin to soften and give way. Triumph flashes up in its cold mind.

Soon . . . another moment . . . two, at most . . .

Seth's Place / Seth's Time

Under his hand, *two of the switches are moving up. Even when he redoubles his efforts to hold them down, he can feel them straining under his hand like something alive. The telltales are still red, but not for much longer. Tak is right about one thing: however the two of them may stack up in the matter of wits, Seth is no longer a match for Tak's raw strength. Once, maybe. At the beginning. No more. Still, if he's right, that may not matter. If he is right, and if he is lucky.*

He glances toward the PlaySkool phone—what Aunt Audrey calls the Tak-phone—longingly for a moment, but of course he doesn't need a telephone, not really; it was always just a symbol, something concrete to help the telepathy flow more easily between them, as the switches and telltales are simply tools to help him concentrate his will. And telepathy isn't Seth's concern here, anyway. If telepathy were all the two of them could share, this would be futile.

Under his hand, the switches move stubbornly upward, driven by Tak's primitive force, Tak's primitive will. For a moment the red telltales beneath them flicker out and the green ones above them flicker on. Seth feels a terrible machinelike buzzing in his head, trying to overwhelm his thoughts; for a moment his inner vision is blurred by swirling crimson light in which embers flick and stutter.

Seth pushes the switches down with all his strength. The green lights go off. The red ones come back on. For the moment, anyway.

The time is now, there is only one down-card left in the game, and now Seth Garin turns it up.

The Wyler House / Johnny's Time

In a way it is like being caught in another barrage from the regulators, only this time what Johnny feels cutting past him are thoughts instead of bullets. But weren't they always thoughts, really?

The first one goes to Cammie Reed, standing in the kitchen doorway with the gun in her hands:

—Now! Do it now!

The second goes to Audrey Wyler, who recoils as if slapped and suddenly stops clawing at the spectral red miasma around Seth's head:

—Now, Aunt Audrey! The time is now!

And the last one, a terrible inhuman roar that fills Johnny's head and wipes out everything else:

==NO, YOU LITTLE BASTARD! NO, YOU CAN'T!

No, Johnny thinks, *he* can't. He never could. Then he raises his eyes to Cammie Reed's face. Her eyes bulge from their sockets; her lips are stretched in a dry and terrible smile.

But *she* can.

Tak's Place / Tak's Time

It has perhaps three seconds, *while the woman with the gun calls out, to realize it has been outplayed.* How *it has been outplayed. A few seconds of incredulity in which to wonder how that could happen after all the millennia it has spent trapped in the dark, thinking and planning. Then, even as it begins to realize that Seth isn't really inside the body it has been trying to re-enter, the woman in the doorway opens fire.*

The Wyler House / Johnny's Time

Cammie is no longer sure that she is acting of her own free will, but it doesn't matter; if her will was free, this is still what she would do. The Wyler woman is holding the monstrous brat curled naked in her arms like an oversized baby, its shanks painted with shit instead of blood and afterbirth. Holding it like a shield. Cammie could almost laugh at the idea.

"Put it down!" Cammie screams, but instead of putting Seth down, Audrey lifts him higher against her breast, as if in defiance. Still smiling her dry, vicious smile, her eyes appearing to start out of their sockets (Johnny will tell himself later that was an optical illusion, surely it was), Cammie centers the rifle on the child.

"No Cammie don't!" Johnny cries, and then she fires. The first shot takes eight-year-old Seth Garin, who is still shivering helplessly with bowel cramps, in the temple and blows the top of his head off, spattering his aunt's weirdly serene face with blood, hair, and bits of scalp. The slug drives all the way through his brain and exits the far side of his skull, where it enters Audrey's left breast. By then, however, it is too spent to do any further serious damage. It's the second shot that does that, catching her in the throat as she staggers back under the force of the first one. Her butt hits the overloaded kitchen table. Piled dishes fall off and shatter on the floor.

She turns to Johnny, the bloody child still in her

arms, and Johnny sees an astonishing thing: she looks happy. Cammie screams as Audrey goes down, perhaps in triumph, perhaps in horror at what she has done.

Audrey somehow keeps her grip on Seth even as she dies. And as she falls, the uneasy red thing rises from the remains of Seth's face like a caul. It swirls in the air above the filthy linoleum, bright scarlet bits orbiting each other like electrons.

Johnny and Cammie Reed face each other through this redness for he doesn't know how long—they are frozen, it seems—until someone screams: *"Oh shit! Oh* shit, *why'd you do that, you numb bitch?"*

Johnny sees Steve and Cynthia come forward through the darkened living room until they're standing just behind Cammie. Cynthia springs forward, grabs Cammie by the arm, and shakes her. *"Bitch! Stupid murdering* cunt, *what did you think, this would bring your kid back? Didn't you ever go to fucking* SCHOOL?"

Cammie seems not to hear. She is looking at the spinning red thing with wide, unblinking eyes, as if hypnotized . . . *and it is looking back at her*. Johnny doesn't know how he can know this, but he does. And suddenly it launches itself at her like a comet . . . or Snake Hunter's red Tracker Arrow on a Power Wagon assault.

He had asked Audrey if Tak could jump to someone else. She had said no, she was sure it couldn't, but what if she had been wrong? What if Tak had fooled her? If it had—

"Look out!" he shouts at Cynthia. *"Get back from her!"*

Little Miss Tu-Tone Hair only stares at him, uncomprehending, from over Cammie's shoulder. Steve doesn't look as if he understands, either, but he reacts to the unmistakable panic in Johnny's voice and yanks Cynthia back.

The swirling red specks divide in two. For a moment Tak's exterior form looks to Johnny like the sort of fork they used to toast marshmallows on back when they were teenagers, sitting around driftwood beach fires at Savin Rock. Only the tines of this fork plunge themselves directly into Cammie Reed's bulging eyes.

They glow a brilliant red, swell even further outward, then explode from their sockets. The grin on Cammie's face stretches so wide that her lips split open and begin to stream blood down her chin. The eyeless thing staggers forward, dropping the empty rifle and holding its hands out. They clutch blindly at the air. Johnny thinks he has never seen anything in his life so simultaneously weak and predatory.

"Tak," it proclaims in a guttural voice which is nothing like Cammie's. *"Tak ah wan! Tak ah lah! Mi him en tow!"* There is a pause. Then, in a grinding, inhuman voice Johnny knows he will hear in nightmares until the end of his life, the eyeless thing says: "I know you all. I'll *find* you all. I'll hunt you down. *Tak! Mi him, en tow!"*

Its skull begins to swell outward then; what remains of Cammie's head begins to look like a monster mushroom cap. Johnny hears a tearing sound like ripping paper and realizes it is the scant flesh over her skull pulling apart. The clotted sockets of her eyes stretch out long, turning into slits; the swelling skull pulls her nose up into a snout with long, lozenge-shaped nostrils.

So, Johnny thinks, Audrey was right. Only Seth was able to contain it. Seth or someone like Seth. Someone very special. Because—

As if to finish this thought in the most spectacular fashion imaginable, Cammie Reed's head explodes. Hot fragments, some still pulsing with life, pelt Johnny's face.

Screaming, revolted to the point of madness, Johnny wipes at the stuff, using his thumbs to try and clear his eyes. Faintly, the way you hear things when someone at the other end of the line temporarily puts the phone down, he can hear Steve and Cynthia, also screaming. Then blinding light fills up the room, as sudden and shocking as an unexpected slap. Johnny thinks at first it's an explosion of some sort—the end for all of them. But as his eyes (still burning and salty and full of Cammie's blood) begin to adjust, he sees it's not an explosion but daylight—the strong, hazy light of a summer afternoon. Thunder rumbles off in the east, a throaty sound with no real threat in it. The storm is over; it has lit up the Hobart place (that much he's sure of, because he can smell the smoke), then moved on to play hob with someone else's life. There's another sound, though, the one they waited for so eagerly and in vain earlier: the tangled wail of sirens. Police, fire engines, ambulances, maybe the fucking

National Guard, for all Johnny knows. Or cares. The sound of sirens doesn't interest him much at this point.

The storm is over.

Johnny thinks that regulator time is over, too.

He sits down heavily in one of the kitchen chairs and looks at the bodies of Audrey and Seth. They remind him of the senseless dead at Jonestown, in Guyana. Her arms are still around him, and his—poor thin wasted arms, unscratched from a single game of tag or follow-the-leader with other boys his own age—are around her neck.

Johnny wipes blood and bone and lumps of brain from his cheeks with his slick palms and begins to cry.

From Audrey Wyler's journal

<u>October 31, 1995</u>

Journal again. Never thought I'd resume, probably never will on a full-time basis, but it can be so comforting.

Seth came to me this morning & managed to ask, with a combination of words & grunts, if he could go out trick or treating, like the other kids in the neighborhood. There was no sign of Tak, and when he is just Seth, I find him all but impossible to refuse. It isn't hard for me to remember that Seth's not the one responsible for everything that's happened; it's quite easy, in fact. In a way, that's what makes it all so horrible. It seals off all my exits. I don't suppose anyone else could understand what I mean. I'm not sure I understand myself. But I feel it. Oh God, do I.

I told him okay, I'd take him trick or treating, it would be fun. I said I could probably put together a little cowboy outfit for him, if he'd like that, but if he wanted to go as a MotoKop, we'd have to go out to Payless and buy a store outfit.

He was shaking his head before I'd even finished, big back-and-forth shakes. He didn't want to go as a cowboy, and not as a MotoKop, either. There was something in the <u>violence</u> of his head-shaking that was close to horror. He might be getting tired of cowboys and police from the future, I think.

I wonder if the other one knows?

Anyway, I asked him what he did want to dress as, if not a cowboy or Snake Hunter or Major Pike. He waved one arm & jumped around the room. After a little bit of this pantomime, I realized he was pretending to be in a swordfight.

"A pirate?" I asked, & his whole face lit up in his sweet Seth Garin smile.

"Pi-ut!" he said, then tried harder and said it right "Pi-rate!"

So I found an old silk kerchief to tie over his head, and gave him a clip-on gold hoop to put in his ear, and unearthed an old pair of Herb's pj's for pantaloons. I used elastic bands on the bottoms & they belled out just right. With a mascara beard, an eyeliner scar, and an old toy sword (borrowed from Cammie Reed next door, a golden oldie from her twins' younger years), he looked quite fierce. And, when I took him out around four o'clock to "do" our block of Poplar Street and two blocks of Hyacinth, he looked no different than all the other goblins and witches and Barneys and pirates. When we got back he spread out all his candy on the living-room floor (he hasn't been in the den to watch TV all day, Tak must be sleeping deeply, I wish the bastard was dead but that's too much to hope for) & gloated over it as if it really were a pirate's treasure. Then he hugged me and kissed my neck. So happy.

Fuck you, Tak. Fuck you.

Fuck you and I hope you die.

March 16, 1996

The last week has been horror, complete horror, Tak in charge almost completely and goose-stepping. Dishes everywhere, glasses filmed with chocolate milk, the house a mess. Ants! Christ, ants in March! It looks like a house where lunatics live, and is that so wrong?

My nipples on fire from all the pinching it's

made me do. I know why, of course; it's angry because it can't do what it wants with its version of Cassandra Styles. I feed it, I buy the new MotoKops toys it wants (and the comic books, of course, which I must read to it because Seth doesn't have that skill for it to draw on), but for that other purpose I am useless.

As much of the week as I could, I spent with Jan.

Then, today, while I was trying to clean up a little (mostly I'm too exhausted and dispirited to even try), I broke my mother's favorite plate, the one with the Currier & Ives sledding scene on it. Tak had nothing to do with it; I picked it up off the mantel shelf in the dining room where I keep it displayed, wanting to give it a little dusting, & it simply slipped through my stupid fingers & broke on the floor. At first I thought my heart had broken with it. It wasn't the plate, of course, as much as I have always liked it. All at once it was like it was my life I was looking at instead of an old china plate smashed to shit on the dining-room floor. Cheap symbolism, Peter Jackson from across the street would probably say. Cheap & sentimental. Probably true, but when we are in pain we are rarely creative.

I got a plastic garbage bag from the kitchen & began picking up the pieces, sobbing all the while I did it. I didn't even hear the TV go off—Tak & Seth had been having a Motokops 2200 festival most of the day—but then a shadow fell over me and I looked up and there he was.

At first I thought it was Tak—Seth has been mostly gone this last week, or lying low—but then I saw the eyes. They both use the same set, you'd think they wouldn't change, couldn't, but they do. Seth's are lighter, and have a range of emotion Tak can never manage.

"I broke my mother's plate," I said. "It was all I had of her, and it slipped through my fingers."

It came on worse than ever then. I put my arms around my knees, put my face down on them, & just cried. Seth came closer, put his own arms around my neck, & hugged me. Something wonderful happened when he did. I can't explain it, exactly, but it was so good that it made visiting with Jan at Mohonk seem ordinary in comparison. Tak can make me feel bad—terrible, in fact, as if the whole world is nothing but a ball of mud squirming with worms just like me. Tak likes it when I feel bad. He licks those bad feelings right off my skin, like a kid with a candy cane. I know he does.

This was the opposite . . . and more. My tears stopped, & my feelings of sadness were replaced by such a sense of joy and . . . not ecstasy, exactly, but like that. Serenity & optimism all mixed together, as if everything couldn't help but turn out all right. As if everything was already all right, & I just couldn't see that in my ordinary state of mind. I was filled up, the way good food fills you up when you're hungry. I was renewed.

Seth did that. He did it when he hugged me. And he did it, I think (know), in exactly the same way Tak makes me feel the bad things and the sad things. Maroon is what I call it. When Tak wants to, it makes me feel maroon. But it can only do it because it has Seth's power to draw on. & I think that when Seth took away my sadness this afternoon, he was able to do it because he had Tak's power to draw on. And I don't think Tak knew he was doing that, or it would have made him stop.

Here's something that's never occurred to me until today: Seth may be stronger than Tak knows.

Much stronger.

CHAPTER 13

1

Johnny didn't know how long he sat in the kitchen chair, head down, body racked with sobs as strong as shivers, tears pouring out of his eyes, before he felt a soft hand on the back of his neck and looked up to see the girl from the market, the one with the schizo hair. Steve was no longer with her. Johnny looked through the living-room picture window—the angle was just right for him to be able to do that from where he was—and saw him standing on the dispirited grass of the Wyler lawn and looking down the street. Some of the sirens had died as the vehicles they belonged to reached the street and stopped; others were still whooping like Indians as they approached.

"You okay, Mr. Marinville?"

"Yeah." He tried to say more, but what came out instead of words was a hitching half-sob. He wiped snot off his nose with the back of his hand and then tried to smile. "Cynthia, isn't it?"

"Cynthia, yep."

"And I'm Johnny. Just Johnny."

"'Kay." She was looking down at the entwined bodies. Audrey's head was thrown back, her eyes closed, her face as still and serene as a deathmask. And the boy still looked like an infant in his fragile nakedness. One that had died in childbirth.

"Look at them," Cynthia said softly. "His arms around her neck like that. He must have loved her such a lot."

"He killed her," Johnny said flatly.

"That can't be!"

He sympathized with the shock on her face, but it didn't change what he knew. "It is, though. He called Cammie in on her."

"Called her in? What do you mean, called her in?"

He nodded as if she had offered agreement. "He did it the same way C.O.s in the bush used to call in artillery fire on enemy 'villes in Vietnam. He called her in on both of them, in fact. I heard him do it." He tapped his temple.

"You're saying Seth told Cammie to *kill* them?"

He nodded.

"The other one, maybe. You might have heard him . . . it—"

Johnny shook his head. "Nope. It was Seth, not Tak. I recognized his voice." He paused, looking down at the dead child, then looked back up at Cynthia. "Even in my head, he was a mouth-breather."

2

The houses had returned to what they really were, Steve saw, but that didn't mean they had returned to normal. They had clearly taken one hell of a pasting. The Hobart place was no longer burning, there was that much; the downpour had tamped the fire to a kind of sullen fume, like a volcano after the main eruption. The old veterinarian's bungalow was more fully involved, with flames leaping from the windows and black, charry patches spreading along the eaves and bubbling the paint. Between them, the house of Peter and Mary Jackson was a tumbled, shot-up ruin.

There were two fire engines on the street and more coming. Already hoses lay tangled on the lawns over there, looking like fat beige pythons. There were police-cars, too. Three were parked in front of Entragian's place, where the newsboy's body (and that of Hannibal, couldn't forget him) lay under plastic which was now puddled with water from the downpour. The cruisers' red lights swung and flashed. Two more cruisers were parked at the top of the street, blocking the Bear Street end off entirely.

That won't do any good if they come back, Steve thought. If the regulators come back, boys, they'll blow your little roadblock right over the nearest ice cap.

Except they wouldn't be back. That was what the sunlight meant, what the retreating thunder meant. It had all really happened—Steve only had to look at the burning houses and those that were all shot up to know that—but it had happened in some weird fistula of time that these cops would never know about, or want to know about. He looked down at his watch and wasn't surprised to see it was running again. 5:18, it said, and he guessed that was as close to the real time as his Timex was ever going to get.

He looked back down the street at the cops. Some of them had their guns out; some did not. Not one of them looked clear on how he or she was supposed to be behaving. Steve could understand that. They were looking at a shooting gallery, after all, and probably no one on the surrounding blocks had even heard any shots. Thunder, maybe, but shotguns that sounded like mortar shells? Nope.

They saw him on the lawn, and one of them beckoned. At the same time, two others were gesturing for him to go back into the Wyler house. They looked like a pretty mindfucked posse, all in all, and Steve didn't blame them. Something had gone on here, they could see that, but *what*?

You'll be awhile figuring it out, Steve thought, but you'll get something you can live with in the end. You guys always do. Whether it's a crashed flying saucer in Roswell, New Mexico, an empty ship in the middle of the Atlantic Ocean, or a suburban Ohio street turned into a fire-corridor, you always come up with something. You guys're never going to catch anyone, I'd bet my far-from-considerable life savings on that, and you won't believe a single goddam word any of us say (in fact, the less we say the easier it'll probably be for us), but in the end you'll find something that will allow you to re-holster your guns . . . and to sleep at night. And you know what I say to that?

NO PROBLEM,

that's what!

NO . . . FUCKING . . . PROBLEM!

One of the cops was now pointing a bullhorn at him. Steve wasn't crazy about that, but better a bullhorn than a gun, he supposed.

"ARE YOU A HOSTAGE?" Mr. Bullhorn boomed. "ARE YOU A HOSTAGE-TAKER?"

Steve grinned, cupped his hands around his mouth and called back, *"I'm a Libra! Friendly with strangers, loves good conversation!"*

A pause. Mr. Bullhorn conferred with several of his mates. There was a good deal of head-shaking, then he turned back to Steve and raised the bullhorn again. "WE DIDN'T GET THAT, WILL YOU REPEAT?"

Steve didn't. He'd spent most of his life in show-business—well, sort of—and he knew how easy it was to run a joke into the ground. More cops were arriving; whole convoys of black-and-whites with strobing red light-bars. More fire engines. Two ambulances. What looked like an armored assault vehicle. The cops were only letting the fire trucks through, at least for the time being, although thanks to the rain, neither blaze looked like much shakes to Steve.

Across from where he stood, Dave Reed and Susi Geller came out of the Carver house, arms around each other. They stepped carefully over the dead girl on the stoop and walked down to the sidewalk. Behind them came Brad and Belinda Josephson, shepherding the Carver children and shielding them from the sight of their father, still lying in his driveway and still as dead as ever. Behind them came Tom Billingsley. He had what looked like a linen tablecloth in his gnarled hands. This he shook out over the dead girl's corpse, taking no notice of the man down the block who was trying to hail him with the bullhorn.

"Where's my mom?" Dave called to Steve. His eyes looked simultaneously wild and exhausted. "Have you seen my mom?"

And Steve Ames, whose life's motto had been

NULLO IMPEDIMENTUM,

hadn't the slightest idea of what to say.

3

Johnny got into the living room, walking on tiptoe and stepping over as much of the mess Cammie had left as he could. Once past that obstacle, he started for the door with more speed and confidence. He had brought his tears under control, at least for the time being, and he supposed that was good. He didn't know why, but he supposed it was. He looked at the clock standing on the mantel. It said 5:21, and that felt about right.

Cynthia caught his arm. He turned to her, feeling a bit impatient. Through the picture window he could see the other Poplar Street survivors clustering in the middle of the street. So far they were ignoring the hails from the cops, who didn't seem to know if they should come up or hold their positions, and Johnny wanted to join his neighbors before they made up their minds one way or the other.

"Is it gone?" she asked. "Tak—that red thing whatever it was—is it gone?"

He looked back into the kitchen. It hurt him almost physically to do this, but he managed. There was plenty of red in there—the walls were painted with it, the ceiling too, for that matter—but no sign of the glowing, embery thing that had tried to find a safe harbor for itself in Cammie Reed's head after its primary host had been killed.

"Did it die when she did?" The girl was looking at him with pleading eyes. "Say it did, okay? Make me feel good and say it did."

"It must have," Johnny said. "If it hadn't, I imagine it would be trying one of us on for size right now."

She let out air in a gusty rush. "Yeah. That makes sense."

So it did, but Johnny didn't believe it. Not for a second. *I know you all,* it had said. *I'll find you all. I'll hunt you down.* Maybe it would. And maybe it would have a slightly more strenuous fight on its hands than it had bargained for, should it try. In any case, there was no sense in worrying about it now.

Tak ah wan! Tak ah lah! Mi him en tow!

"What is it?" Cynthia asked. "What's wrong?"

"What do you mean?"

"You're shivering."

Johnny smiled. "I guess a goose just walked over

my grave." He took her hand off his arm and folded his fingers through hers. "Come on. Let's go out and see how everyone's doing."

4

They were almost to the street and the others when Cynthia came to a stop. "Oh my God," she said in a soft, strengthless voice. "Oh my God, look."

Johnny turned. The storm had moved on, but there was one isolated thunderhead just west of them. It hung over downtown Columbus, connected to Ohio by a gauzy umbilicus of rain, and it made the shape of a gigantic cowboy galloping on a storm-colored stallion. The horse's grotesquely elongated snout pointed east, toward the Great Lakes; its tail stretched out long toward the prairies and deserts. The cowboy appeared to have his hat in one hand, perhaps waving it in a hooraw, and as Johnny watched, open-mouthed and transfixed, the man's head flickered with lightning.

"A ghost rider," Brad said. "Holy shit, a goddam ghost rider in the sky. Do you see it, Bee?"

Cynthia moaned through the hand she'd pressed to her mouth. Looked up at the cloud-shape, eyes bulging, head shaking from side to side in a useless gesture of negation. The others were looking now, as well—not the firemen and not the cops, who would break out of their indecision soon and come on up here to join the block party, but the Poplar Street folk who had survived the regulators.

Steve took Cynthia by her thin arms and drew her gently away from Johnny. "Stop it," he said. "It can't hurt us. It's just a cloud and it can't hurt us. It's going away already. See?"

It was true. The flank of the skyhorse was tearing open in some places, melting in others, letting the sun through in long, hazy rays. It was just a summer afternoon again, the very *rooftree* of summer, all watermelon and Kool-Aid and foul tips off the end of the bat.

Steve glanced down the street and saw a police car begin rolling, very slowly, up the hill toward them, running over the tangled firehoses as it came. He looked back at Johnny. "Yo."

"Yo what?"

"Did he commit suicide, that kid?"

"I don't know what else you'd call it," Johnny said, but he supposed he knew why the hippie had asked; it hadn't felt like suicide, somehow.

The police cruiser stopped. The man who got out was wearing a khaki uniform which came equipped with roughly one ton of gold braid. His eyes, a very sharp blue, were almost lost in a complex webwork of wrinkles. His gun, a big one, was in his hand. He looked like someone Johnny had seen before, and after a moment it came to him: the late Ben Johnson, who had played saintly ranchers (usually with beautiful daughters) and satanic outlaws with equal grace and ability.

"Someone want to tell me what in the name of Christ Jesus the Redeemer went on here?" he asked.

No one replied, and after a moment Johnny Marinville realized they were all looking at him. He stepped forward, read the little plaque pinned to the pocket of the man's crisp uniform blouse, and said: "Outlaws, Captain Richardson."

"I beg your pardon?"

"Outlaws. Regulators. Renegades from the wastes."

"My friend, if you see anything funny about this—"

"I don't, sir. No indeed. And it's going to get even further from funny when you look in there." Johnny pointed toward the Wyler house, and as he did suddenly thought of his guitar. It was like thinking about a glass of iced tea when you were hot and thirsty and tired. He thought of how nice it would be to sit on his porch step and strum and sing "The Ballad of Jesse James" in the key of D. That was the one that went, "Oh Jesse had a wife to mourn for his life, three children they were brave." He supposed his old Gibson might have a hole in it, his house looked pretty well trashed (looked as if it was no longer sitting exactly right on its foundations, for that matter), but on the other hand, it might be perfectly fine. Some of *them* had come through okay, after all.

Johnny started in that direction, already hearing the song as it would come from under his hand and out of his mouth: "Oh Robert Ford, Robert Ford, I wonder how you must feel? For you slept in Jesse's bed, and you ate of Jesse's bread, and you have laid Jesse James down in his grave."

"Hey!" the cop who looked like Ben Johnson called

truculently. "Just where in the hell do you think you're going?"

"To sing a song about the good guys and the bad guys," Johnny said. He put his head down and felt the hazy heat of the summer sun on his neck and kept walking.

Letter from Mrs. Patricia Allen to Katherine Anne Goodlowe, of Montpelier, Vermont:

Mohonk
Mountain House

A NATIONAL HISTORIC LANDMARK

June 19, 1986

Dear Kathi,

This is the most beautiful place in the whole world, I'm convinced of it. The honeymoon has been the sweetest nine days of my whole life, and the nights—! I was raised to believe that certain things you don't talk about, so just let me say that my fears of discovering, too late to do anything about it, that "saving it for marriage" was the worst mistake of my life, have proved unfounded. I feel like a kid living in a candy factory!

Enough of that, though; I didn't write to tell you about the new Mrs. Allen's sex-life (superb though it may be), or even about the beauty of the Catskills. I'm writing because Tom's downstairs for the nonce, shooting pool, and I know how much you love a "spooky story." Especially if there's an old hotel in it; you're the only person I know who's read not just one copy of The Shining to tatters, but two! If that was all, though, I probably would have just waited until Tom and I got back and then told you my tale face-to-face. But I might actually have some souvenirs of this particular "tale from beyond," and that has caused me to pick up my pen on this beautiful full-moon evening.

Lake Mohonk, New Paltz, New York 12561

Mohonk
Mountain House

A NATIONAL HISTORIC LANDMARK

The Mountain House was opened in 1869, so it certainly qualifies as an old hotel, and although I don't suppose it's much like Stephen King's Overlook, it has its share of odd nooks and spooky corridors. It has its share of ghost stories, too, but the one I'm writing you about is something of an oddity—not a single turn-of-the-century lady or 1929 Stock Market-crash suicide in it. These two ghosts—that's right, a pair, two for the price of one—have only been actively haunting for the last four years or so, as far as I have been able to find out, and I've been able to find out a fair amount. The staff is very helpful to visitors who want to do a little "ghost-hunting" on the side; adds to the ambience, I suppose!

Anyway, there are over a hundred little shelters spotted around the grounds, eccentric wooden huts which the guests sometimes call "follies" and the Mohonk brochures call "gazebos." You find these overlooking the choicest views. There's one located at the north end of an upland meadow about three miles from the Mountain House itself. On the map this meadow has no name (I actually checked the topographical plats in the office this morning), but the help has a name for it; they call it Mother and Son Meadow.

The ghosts of the eponymous mother and son were first spotted by guests in the summer of 1982. They are always seen around that

Lake Mohonk, New Paltz, New York 12561

Mohonk
Mountain House

A NATIONAL HISTORIC LANDMARK

particular gazebo, which is located at the top of a hill and looks down toward a rock wall which is pretty much buried in honeysuckle and wild roses. It isn't the most spectacular place on the resort, but I think it may prove to be my favorite when I think back on my honeymoon in later years. There's a serentiy there which certainly beggars my powers of description. Some of it's the scent of the flowers, and some is the sound of the bees, I suppose—a steady, sleepy drone. But never mind the bees and flowers and picturesque rock wall; if I know my Kath, it's the ghosts she'll be wanting. They aren't spooky ones at all, so don't get your hopes up on that score, but they are well-documented, at least. Adrian Givens, the concierge, told me they have been seen by perhaps three dozen guests since the sightings began, always in that same rough locale. And although none of the witnesses have known each other, making conspiracy or collusion seem unlikely, the descriptions are remarkably similar. The woman is described as being in her thirties, pretty, long legs, chestnut-brown hair. Her son (several witnesses have remarked on the physical resemblance between the two) is small and very slim, probably about six. Brown hair, like the woman. His face has been described as "intelligent," "lively," and even "beautiful." And although they've been seen by a variety of people over a

Lake Mohonk, New Paltz, New York 12561

course of years, they are always described as wearing the same clothes: white running shorts, sleeveless blouse, and lowtop sneakers for her; basketball shorts, a tank top, and cowboy boots for him. It's the cowboy boots that give me the most pause, Kath! How likely is it that all those people would put a kid in such an unlikely combination as shorts and cowboy boots, if they were just making it up? The defense rests.

Several people have theorized that they are real people, perhaps even a Mohonk employee and her child, because they've dropped a lot of empirical, lasting evidence for ghosts (who as a rule only leave a swirl of cold air or perhaps a little smear of ectoplasm behind, as I know you know). All sorts of little souvenirs have been found at that particular gazebo. You know the weirdest? Half-eaten plates of Chef Boyardee spaghetti! Yes! I know it sounds crazy, laughable, but stop and think a minute. Aside from hot dogs, is there anything in the world that kids love more than Chef's pasta?

There have been other things, as well—toys, a coloring book, a small silver makeup case that could well belong to a little boy's pretty mom but I admit it's those half-eaten bowls of kid-style spaghetti that get to me. Whoever heard of a spaghetti-eating

Mohonk
Mountain House

A NATIONAL HISTORIC LANDMARK

ghost? Or how 'bout this? In the fall of 1984, a group‸of hikers found a kid's plastic record-player in that gazebo, with a 45-rpm record on the spindle—Strawberry Fields Forever, by the Beatles. Fitting, eh?

My friend at the concierge's desk, Adrian, smiles and nods when you suggest it's a put-up job, that ghosts don't leave actual physical objects behind (or trample down the grass, or leave footprints in the gazebo). "Not ordinary ones, anyway," he says, "but maybe these aren't ordinary ghosts. For one thing, everyone who has seen them says they're solid. You can't look through them, like the ones in Ghostbusters. Maybe they're not ghosts, have you thought of that? They might be real people who are living on a slightly different plane than ours." I guess you don't have to be a guest at Mohonk to get a little astral; just working there seems to do the trick.

Adrian said that on at least three occasions a determined effort had been made to catch the mother and son by people who believed the whole thing was a hoax, and all three efforts had come to nothing (although once the searchers came back with another of those spaghetti-bowls). Also, he said—and I found this much more interesting—the apparitions had been showing up in and

Lake Mohonk, New Paltz, New York 12561

around that gazebo for four years. If they were real people, hoaxes or pranksters or both, how could the boy still be six or seven?

Okay, this is the point where, in a traditional ghost story, I would reveal that I myself had seen the ghosts or the Phantom Rickshaw. Except I didn't. I've still never seen a ghost in my whole life. But I can testify that there's something very special about that meadow, something hushed and—don't you dare laugh—almost holy. I didn't see ghosts, but there is definitely a feeling of presence there. I went without Tom, and will freely grant that probably made me more susceptible, but even so, I knew then and know now that I had come to a very extraordinary place. And there was a prickling along the back of my neck, a sensation—very clear and specific—of being watched.

Then, when I went into the gazebo itself to sit and rest up a little for the walk back, I found the items I'm enclosing. They are perfectly real, as you see, not a bit ghostly, and yet there is something very strange about them, don't you think?

The little woman-figure in the blue shorts is the more interesting of the two. It's obviosly what the kids call an "action figure," but I've been teaching kindergarten for three years now and thought I knew them all. I don't know this one, though. At first I thought it was Scarlet, from the G.I. Joe team, but this little lady's hair is a very different shade of red. Brighter. And usually kids treasure these things, will fight over them in the play-yard. This one was tossed into a corner, almost as if it had been thrown away. Save it for me, Kath, and I'll show it to my kindergartners next fall . . . but I'm betting right now that none of them will know her and all of them will want her! I think about what Adrian said, about how the ghosts in Mother and Son Meadow might live on a slightly different plane, maybe of the astral kind, maybe of the temporal kind, and sometimes (often, really) I think Miss Red might actually come from that plane! (Does the idea give you the shivers? It does me!)

Okay, okay, so a strong wind has come up outside and the lights are flickering. Put it down to that, if you want.

Then there's the picture. I found it under the little gazebo table. You're the art major, kiddo, tell me what you think. Is it some kind of gag—a hoax perpetrated by a local kid who enjoys teasing the guests? Or have I found a drawing made by a ghost? What a concept, huh?

Okay, girl, that's my creepy story for the night. I'm gonna stick the whole works in a little padded mailer from the gift-shop, then see if I can persuade Tom it's time to stop shooting bumper

A NATIONAL HISTORIC LANDMARK

pool in the game room and come to bed. Frankly, I'm not expecting it to be a problem.

I love being married, and I love this place, ghosts and all.

Still your fan,

Pat

PS: Please save the picture for me, okay? I want to keep it. Hoax or not, I think there's love in it. And a sense, almost, of coming home. P.

Lake Mohonk, New Paltz, New York 12561